Welcome to...

BannerFall

A storm of change has blown in from the South, ushering in the conquering army of the Saricon horde and their frightful war god Heln. Tall and powerful, their spirit and bodies born for war, the Saricon have swept all before them and now locked their cold blue gaze upon the lands of Dy'ain and the Kul-brite steel trade. For whosoever controls the precious metal of the Lords shall possess the power and wealth to reign supreme over all the lands of Corvell.

House Dormath, the rulers of Dy'ain, prepares for war. Their elite Legion, long-standing protectors of their land and Argonian faith, hoist shield and sword in defiance of the mighty invaders. But how can even the fearless Legion stop the Saricon where so many before them have fallen to their blades? Two religions, two separate ways of life, clash in an epic battle fueled by conquest and self-preservation as two young men, born of contrasting worlds and forged in violence and war, converge to become House Dormath's last hope.

Jason L McWhirter

Bannerfall

A Twiin Entertainment book

Books by Jason McWhirter

Cavalier Trilogy

The Cavalier, book one

The Rise of Malbeck, book two

Glimmer in the Shadow, book three

The Chronicles of Corvell
Steel Lord Series

BannerFall, book one
The Banner Lord, book two

Non-Fantasy

The Life of Ely

Published by Twiin Entertainment

www.twiinentertainment.com

Copyright © Jason L. McWhirter, 2014
Library of Congress
All rights reserved

Cover art by Luis Gama

All other art by Jason L. McWhirter

Without limiting the rights under copyright reserved above, no part of this publication may be reproduced, stored electronically, or transmitted, in any form, or by any means, without the prior written permission of the copyright owner.

AUTHOR'S NOTE

This is a work of fiction. Names, characters, places, and incidents are the product of the author's imagination or are used fictitiously, and any resemblance to actual persons, living or dead, business establishments, events, or locales is entirely coincidental.

Bannerfall

Dedication

    This book is dedicated to everyone who has helped me pursue my dreams. In summary, that would be my parents, my brother and sister, my wife, my teachers, my friends, and all my fans who share a love for reading and stories, and who have been my inspiration for creating tales of fiction. Thank you all very much.

    I would also like to thank the creative team behind one of my favorite old school martial arts films, Master Killer, for giving me some of the training ideas in this book.

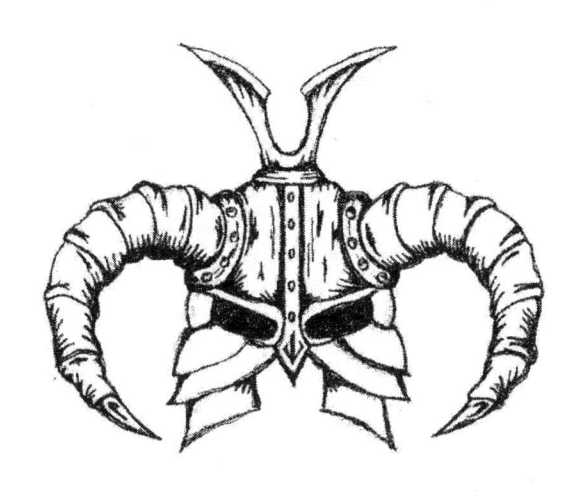

The Lands of Belorth and Corvell

BannerFall

The Chronicles of Corvell
Book One of the Steel Lord Series

Jason L McWhirter

Bannerfall

PROLOGUE

5090, 14th cyn after the Great Change

The cold night was dark, oppressive even, the blackness thick like oil. Clouds like coal covered the stars and even the intense glow of the moon could not penetrate them. It was a perfect night for shadows, the darkness welcoming them like a mother's open arms.

Thalon, veiled in the night, pushed more energy into his arms and hands, reinforcing his muscles and concentrating much of it in his claws as they penetrated the hard stone wall. The city of Eltus was like any other major city, the royal palace being located somewhere inside, protected by its own set of walls. As Thalon had moved through the shadowed alley ways, silently, like a dark fog in a starless night, his hood pulled low over his face, he had tasked energy from people that were still out walking the streets, filling his tarnum, his center, with aura energy. Now, as he climbed the steep palace wall, gliding effortlessly up the stone surface, he slowly released that energy into his extremities, his black claws strengthened by the energy he wove around them. Slowly his shadowed form worked its way up the wall. He wore black leggings and a black tunic under charcoal gray leather armor. And strapped to his back was a short sword, slightly curved, and sheathed in black leather.

Thalon was not just a skilled swordsman. He was also an Aura Mage. Thirty years ago he was on his way to being one of the top swordsmen in all of Layona. He had joined the king's army at the age of sixteen, and by his twenty first birthday there were few who could best him with the blade. But his military career, and nearly his life, had all come to a grinding halt when his secret had been exposed. His king had discovered he was an Aura Mage. His powers, known as the Way, surfaced late in life, when he was twenty, a handful of years later than adolescence when it typically manifested if one was so gifted. He was in battle, fighting for his king, when he was stabbed in the side by a marauding nomad whose armies often ventured into Layona for plunder. He thought himself dead, until he suddenly felt a wave of hot energy wash over him, and crying out he pushed the energy away, blasting the nearest nomads off their feet with an intense explosion of air. Not knowing it at the time, he had tasked energy from the warriors and sent it rushing back at them, the shockwave powerful enough to not go unnoticed. He had survived the wound, only to suffer more at the hands of the very person he had sworn to protect; his king's royal house. When they found out that he was an Aurit, one gifted in the Way, they had killed his father and mother, as well as his sister, and they had nearly killed him. But thanks to the help of several of the soldiers, he had escaped.

Thirty years of moving from town to town, hiding as an outlaw, sometimes begging and stealing, tasking energy from others, while trying to survive, had transformed him into something different, a being that no longer resembled his former self. Since he had never been taught about his power, he was forced to learn how to use it on his own, by trial and error. And much of it had been error. He hadn't been warned to avoid negative energy, and over the years he had used too much of it. The constant use of these negative energies had changed him, both physically and mentally. The mental changes were subtle, and so gradual that he didn't really realize he had intrinsically changed. To him, he had always been this way. But it wasn't true. He hadn't always been a killer. Circumstances had dictated his hand, forcing him to make difficult decisions, decisions that led him down paths that were slippery with his victims' blood. And how he hated the nobility, the people who changed his life, the aristocrats who tried to stamp out the Way in anyone other than the royal houses.

Thalon's physical transformation was not nearly as subtle. He had morphed into something quite different. The years of using negative energies had altered his body. His fingers had grown longer, and his nails had become claws, curved like those of a cat, and capable of rending flesh. His face had changed shape as well, becoming more elongated, with enlarged eyes, and iridescent lavender pupils that enabled him to see more clearly in the shadows. His skin had become pale, almost translucent, and his once thick and lustrous dark hair had completely fallen out, exposing his smooth bald head that resembled a large egg. But despite his age, he had also become faster and stronger, the continuous use of aura energy strengthening and enhancing his musculature.

In the years he had spent moving from town to town, city to city, he had occupied his time spying, killing, and adapting. And over the years he had met others like him. They sensed his power, and were attracted to it. They saw they were not alone; they needed something to give them hope. He had done that, uniting them as friends, but more importantly giving them purpose. They had become known as the Shadows. Their name was whispered in dark alleys, eventually gaining such an ominous reputation that few believed them to be real. A child's song was even created, the words whispered to scare little ones into being good.

The Shadows, black, pull you deep
The Shadows, thick, don't fall asleep
The Shadows, kill, don't you weep
The Shadows, real, creep, creep, creep

But they were real. And tonight King Kaleck and his family would know this truth.

Thalon pulled himself over the battlement and onto the narrow walkway. Hiding in the shadows, he concentrated on his tarnum, using the last of the remaining energy for his next spell, one that had proven useful time and time again. Manipulating the energy, he coated his body in it, weaving the magic into an outer shell identical to his surroundings. He had become invisible. Quietly, he raced along the top of the wall, heading for the stairs that would lead to the castle courtyard. From there, it was just a matter of time before he would be in the king's chambers.

On the roof, a small dark figure dropped down from the night, gliding silently to land softly on the clay tiles. Lyra released the energy of the fly spell, flipping her short compact bow from around her back and nocking an arrow. She had not perfected the fly spell and it still felt very strange, but she was better than Thalon, which was why he was entering the castle a different way. The spell created a spinning vortex of air on which she floated. Maneuverability was tricky, and it was pure luck that she landed as gracefully and silently as she had. Like Thalon, Lyra's petite form was clothed entirely in black. The hood of her cloak concealed her angular but feminine face, which was framed

Bannerfall

by short silver hair cut like a boy's. Besides the bow she held in her hand, she also carried two long knives strapped to each hip.

She reached out slowly, mentally searching for any auras. She sensed one several paces away to her right, and a second one underneath her. Silently she crept along the roofline and peered over the edge to the balcony below. She saw a woman standing on the balcony with her back to her looking over the railing to the palace grounds below. The woman wore a long translucent night robe and her cascading dark hair blew gently in the evening breeze. Her aura was calm, a soft orange. *Perhaps she couldn't sleep*, Lyra thought. Lyra tasked a small amount from her, storing it in her tarnum, which for her was located in the middle of her chest.

Lyra, like Thalon, was also an Aura Mage. She too was untrained, and like Thalon had fled, leaving her home in Gilia when her powers had surfaced. She was a courtesan, or had been. Both her parents had died of a plague when she was twelve, and she found herself alone and destitute, forced to beg and scrounge for food. One night she had attempted to grab a purse from the wrong person, a woman much quicker and stronger than she appeared. She was the mistress of one of Gilia's most popular houses of pleasure, and she was accustomed to dealing with poor young girls. Lyra was quickly conscripted to work for her. At first she cleaned, ran errands, and basically performed the most menial labor. But as she matured, her unique, rather exotic beauty began to attract the attention of many of the patrons. While some men favored voluptuous, curvy women, others were drawn to the more slender and petite body. And Lyra fell into that category. She was sinewy and strong, her body almost boy-like, but enhanced by the slight curve of her hips and her small firm breasts. Her large lustrous green eyes, high cheekbones, smooth olive skin, and silky black hair that fell to her waist further enhanced her unique beauty. And so, like others before her, she was forced to sell her body to the men of Gilia. But one night, after five years of working at the pleasure house, everything changed. When she was eighteen, her powers had surfaced, triggered by a patron who was known for his sadistic abuse. Before she knew what she was doing, she had tasked his aura energy, releasing it in a burst of flames that erupted from her fingers, completely melting the skin off the side of his face. She knew she had to run. She ran for nearly six years, until the night she had met Thalon. Now she had a purpose, and she, with Thalon's help, had learned to control her power. But like all untrained Aura Mages, she too had not gone unscathed by using her powers incorrectly. Tasking negative energies from others took its toll on her body. Her once lustrous black hair was now completely silver, and her ears had grown, elongating into sharp points at the top. But it was her striking lavender eyes, no longer green, that had been most affected by the use of negative energies and which drew the most unwanted attention.

    The woman at the railing turned around. It was her, Cassandra Kaleck, wife to Asdar Kaleck, heir to the Kingdom of Kael. Lyra had a clear shot, and there was no way her target could see her in the darkness above. Her only concern was if she had her towd, or aura site, turned on, although there would be no reason to do so at this time of night. Cassandra Kaleck was a powerful Aura Mage in her own right, and she was of noble blood, trained since her Way had materialized. If she indeed had her towd on than Lyra's aura would light up as clear as fire in the night.

    Lyra drew her bow back, aiming for her throat, an easy shot at this distance. She didn't want her to scream, and an arrow through the throat would silence any potential outcry. In a flash her arrow flew, slamming into Cassandra's throat and bursting out the back of her neck. The impact of the arrow snapped her head back and she rocked back on her heals. The torches flanking the door of her bedroom shed enough light on her face for Lyra to see her eyes roll back in shock, just before she stumbled to her knees. She opened her mouth as if to speak, but only a faint choking gurgle emerged as she fell to her side, her blood pooling around her.

    "Cassandra?" a concerned voice came from inside. It must be the other aura she detected, probably her second target.

    Lyra swore under her breath, and drew another arrow just as a shirtless man dressed only in loose white pants ran onto the balcony. As soon as he saw his wife, her blood covering the stones, he spun around and glanced up.

    His fiery eyes met hers and she swore again as she drew her arrow back and instantaneously released. The man was Asdar Kaleck, and he was a powerful Merger. He had clearly turned on his towd when he noticed that his wife had been shot with an arrow.

    Prince Kaleck had no weapon, but he was a trained Merger from a long noble line, and he instantly flooded his own aura energy into his

Bannerfall

muscles, spinning aside inhumanly fast as her arrow sparked across the stones, ricocheting harmlessly into the railing.

Lyra followed the path of her arrow, leaping to the balcony below. She landed hard, rolling forward to lessen the impact, dropping her bow and drawing both blades simultaneously. She came at him quickly, knives flashing left and right. Prince Kaleck spun and danced, expertly evading her blades, his right hand flashing out and striking the side of her face. The enhanced power of his attack was so strong it spun her body sideways so forcefully that she knew she was in trouble. Despite her skill, she would not be able to defeat a trained Merger of noble lineage in hand to hand combat. It didn't matter that he was weaponless. She needed a new plan. Lyra shook the pain away, drawing on the energy that she had taken from the princess before her death. She faced the advancing prince and pushed her blades forward, concentrating on the energy and molding it to her will. A wave of wind gushed forward, violently shoving the prince backwards until he hit the railing. He growled in a fury, both hands desperately gripping the railing to keep himself from being blown backwards into the night.

She had only enough energy left for one violent push, so as he hit the railing she threw one of her knives. Prince Kaleck saw the knife coming, but if he let go of the railing he would be blown backwards. Lyra saw the fear in his eyes as he recognized his predicament. He tried to let go with one hand to block the knife, but, despite his enhanced speed, he wasn't fast enough. The blade slammed into his throat as the last of the wind launched him off the balcony, disappearing into the darkness below.

I hope Thalon finishes quickly, Lyra thought, knowing that it wouldn't be long before one of the palace guards found the bodies. And she was vulnerable now, as she had no more energy to enact the fly spell to escape. The plan had been to kill them both in their sleep after she had tasked their auras, and then use that energy to fly away. She needed to find a guard, anyone from whom she could task energy, so she crept silently into the room for just that purpose.

Meanwhile, Thalon had made his way through the various halls without incident. The spell he was using didn't make him completely invisible; it simply altered his appearance by manipulating the light. It was almost like a reflective shield, the energy of the spell mirroring the surroundings. It worked nearly perfectly when one was standing still as the energy weave around the body could more easily match the surroundings. But, when moving it became less effective. If he moved too fast, it was possible for them to see a blur, or a glimmer of movement, so he moved slowly and deliberately, evading the guards and making his way closer to the king's chamber.

Getting to the anteroom that led to the king's personal chambers posed his first problem. The door was closed, and likely bolted at this time of night. Besides that, Thalon knew that there were at least a few guards stationed there, guarding the only entrance to the king's room. He had a simple plan, he just hoped it worked.

Reaching inside his tunic he produced a small bag containing a handful of metal balls. Then he knocked on the door. He heard footsteps and then someone fumbling with the door, which opened a few moments later.

A young guard looked right at him, but saw nothing, his invisible form pushed against the stone wall. Then he tossed the metal marbles down the hall. They landed about five paces in front of the guard and rolled across the stones, occasionally banging together.

"What is this!?" he gasped in surprise as he stepped through the door and into the hallway. Thalon slid silently through the open door into the anteroom as the guard stepped further into the hall, trying to figure out who had thrown the balls.

The anteroom was clearly a guardroom. Along the wall was a rack of weapons, several swords, four crossbows, bolts, four spears, and a few axes. Two other guards were sitting at a table playing some game of dice. The room was small; the size of a bedroom, and luckily for Thalon the other entrance was just a rounded arch leading into another hallway. Thalon ignored the guards as he tasked their energy, creeping silently by them through the opening and down the shadowed hallway until he came to a large oak door. It was locked, but Thalon didn't think that would pose a problem. He looked back, seeing shadows in the guard's room and hearing muffled voices as they tried to figure out what had happened. Just as he was about to remove his lock picks, a guard walked down the hallway carrying a lantern. It was the same guard that had opened the door, and obviously he was on alert, puzzled and concerned about the strange appearance of the metal balls. His first instinct was to look in on his king.

Thalon slowly moved away from the door, leaning back against the wall and hoping that the guard wouldn't sense him, see him, or maybe even smell him. He did task some energy form him, adding it to his tarnum. But the guard didn't even make it to the door, seeing that there was no one there, he turned around and rejoined his comrades.

Once the guard was gone, Thalon went to work on the lock. It took only a few moments before he heard the sound of the lock mechanism clicking open. He looked back one more time to see the guards still sitting at the table, surrounded by light from inside the room. The hallway was dark, and even if he hadn't been invisible it would be unlikely that they would be able to see him in the shadows. But if they heard the door open that would pose a problem. Reaching into another pocket inside his tunic he produced a small vial of oil and squirted a healthy amount on each hinge. Then slowly he opened the door. As the door silently inched open, Thalon slipped his body through, and emerged on the other side, quietly shutting the door behind him. Stealthily, he moved through the short hall, until he came to the large sleeping chamber of King Panrick Kaleck and his wife. Thalon quickly looked around, noticing there was a door to a balcony and an entrance into another room on his left, likely the washroom or dressing room, or both since there were no other doors or entryways. Cutting off the energy that rendered him invisible, his true self was revealed. Although he had enough energy to redo the spell, he thought it wise to keep it for his escape.

Slowly he glided to the bedside of the king, quietly removing his sword from its sheath. The sound of the blade being drawn from its scabbard made only the faintest sound, like a whisper in the wind that carried a message of death. They were both strong in the Way, and he had to make sure that he killed them quickly and silently. He would kill the king first, knowing that he was the most powerful. King Kaleck was on his stomach, his head turned towards his wife. Thalon angled the tip of his blade directly over the king's back, and without hesitation, plunged it downward with all his strength. The razor sharp blade parted flesh and bone, splitting his heart in two. The king's body went rigid and he involuntarily grunted, expelling a rush of air from his lungs. But he was already dead, and Thalon wasted no time. He quickly withdrew the blade and leaped over the king's prone body towards his wife who was now stirring as she sensed something amiss. By the time her sleepy eyes had opened, Thalon was already upon her, and she felt a sharp pain explode in her chest. Her eyes widened in shock as she coughed up

Bannerfall

blood. Thalon's blade had pierced her heart as well, and she was dead in an instant.

Thalon yanked the blade from her chest and ran quickly to the door that opened onto the balcony. As he opened it, he drew upon the reserves of energy that he had tasked from the guards, manipulating the magic and weaving it into a fly spell. He had not mastered this spell, which was why he had not used it to enter the palace. A crash landing would have been noisy and alerted the guards. But for his escape it would serve its purpose. All he needed to do was fly over the palace walls. If he could do that, then he would disappear into the night, never to be found. As he worked the energy into his spell, the air began to spin underneath him, lifting him into the night. He directed the air current to carry his body over the railing and into the safety of darkness.

***

Kahn Taruk rested his callused hands on the balcony rail, looking out on the city of Fara below. It was a magnificent view. The lights of the city, like a kaleidoscope of stars, sparkled in the night, and the sounds of the people in the streets drifted up to him as he stood on his perch. Kahn understood why the previous rulers had built the royal palace on the rocky slope that dominated the north side of the city. Not only was the location more secure, but the expansive balcony that had been constructed from the lord's own room allowed him to view his subjects below, just as Kahn Taruk was now doing. Kahn Taruk was a Tongra of Heln, the god of the Saricons. He was one of twelve Tongras whose job was to lead the Saricons in their conquest of foreign lands in order to bring Heln's word to the masses.

Kahn Taruk had been the leader of Fara for the last fifteen years. Lord Arathiam of Fara, subject to King Panrick Kaleck, had been ousted by Kahn's predecessor thirty years before. The previous Tongra had died in battle fifteen years ago providing the opportunity for Kahn Taruk to take his place. The other Tongras were busy ruling the vast lands conquered by the Saricon's and Kahn Taruk was voted by the council to take on the task of conquering Corvell once his predecessor had died in battle. Lord Arathiam, the previous ruler of Fara, and his family, had all been killed many years ago, but the King of Kael still held the capital city of Eltus, and despite the loss of one of his cities to the

Bannerfall

Saricons, his army was still strong. Kahn gripped the rail harder as he thought about King Kaleck. The king, who now must be in his sixties, had been a thorn in their side since they had invaded Kael. It had been nearly thirty years and their armies still had not found a weakness in the combined forces of King Kaleck and King Enden Dormath of Dy'ain. The two neighboring kingdoms had formed an alliance and thus far had prevented any further advances of the Saricon war machine. But he had a plan, a plan that he had set in motion many years ago.

Kahn turned from the railing and strode across the expansive balcony to a set of stairs that led to a lower balcony. Kahn was a large man, even for a Saricon. He stood half a head taller than the average Saricon, and most Saricons were at least a head taller than the inhabitants they had seen thus far on the continents of Belorth or Corvell. His blonde hair, bleached almost silver by the sun, reached to the middle of his muscled back. Two woven strands were pulled back over his ears and wound together into a single thick braid. Sharp features dominated his angular face and his blue eyes were like crystals held before an azure sea. He wore massive leather boots reinforced with steel, the heavy soles thudding across the stones as he made his way down the stairs. His clothing was of high quality and costly, but made to be functional; heavy gray trousers finely woven from the best quality wool and lined with combed cotton, along with a long sleeved soft leather jerkin under his hardened black leather armor that had been reinforced with plates of polished steel. The center of his cuirass was a steel plate polished to shine like silver, into which the red symbol of Heln, a horned helm, had been etched in graceful elegant lines. His heavy gray cloak fluttered behind him, and strapped to the center of his back, its blade fanning out behind his head, was a giant battle axe.

Only one door opened to the balcony on which he stood. It was the door to Lord Arathiam's former quarters, which was now his by default. But there was also a set of stairs on the right side of the balcony that led down to two doors which accessed a lower balcony. The nearest door led into a guards' room. The far other door opened into a large conference room, a room built to provide a meeting place for the lord and his military officers and dignitaries. The conference room also had another door opening into the interior hallway. And it was there that Kahn was heading.

Bannerfall

The balcony door was open and Kahn strode into the spacious room. Ten shields hung on the walls, each one crossed with different weapons. Some were swords and maces, while most were axes of Saricon designs. Originally the walls had been covered with large tapestries representing the weak gods of the Argonians, Argon and Felina. But those artifacts had been ripped down and burned when they had taken the city many years ago, along with every statue and symbol that had anything to do with the Argonian gods. Saricon shields had replaced the tapestries, each one marked with Heln's red symbol. Torches were lit along the walls and a handful of braziers lined the room, their flickering embers providing a bit of warmth to the room. In the center of the room was a large rectangular table with enough chairs to sit twenty two people. On this evening, however, there were only four.

"Tongra Taruk, it is very good to see you," one of the men said as he rose from his chair. The man was tall, like all Saricons, but still was forced to look up to Kahn Taruk. His long hair was also blonde, but where Kahn's face was smoothly shaven this man's face sprouted a bushy blonde beard that reached to the middle of his thick chest. He wore a cuirass embossed with Heln's symbol, and pieces of hardened leather covered in steel protected his muscular forearms and legs. Crossed on his back, with the handles facing up, were two short broad swords, their blades slightly curved at the tip. The man placed both fists together across his chest and bowed his head sharply in greeting.

"General Sigmar, I'm glad you could take time away from our forces. Please, have a seat," Kahn Taruk said.

Another man, clearly a Saricon, stood next to General Sigmar. He was slightly shorter than the general, but bulkier, more musclebound. The muscles of his large arms bulged from his brown leather tunic, and his blocky face was framed by dirty blonde hair. He too wore armor embossed with Heln's symbol and strapped to his back was a giant battle axe. "Greetings, Kahn Taruk," he said, tapping his fists together before his broad chest.

"And to you, Colonel Karnak," Kahn Taruk replied, motioning for him to sit next to the general.

One of the other men had also stood. He was obviously not a Saricon and was dwarfed by the other large warriors. But he knew protocol, and he too stood with feet together, his head slightly bowed, and brought his fists together in salute, "Tongra Taruk."

Kahn Taruk nodded, motioning for the man to sit. His name was Keltius and he was a sea captain from Argos. He was dark haired and swarthy, with a thin mustache above his lips and a pointy goatee, both black as night. His skin was heavily tanned, and weathered by the many years he had spent in the sun and on the open sea. He wore an expensive leather tunic over a loose flowing shirt made of costly silk cinched tight at his waist with a black leather belt. A long sword dangled from his side. Gray and black striped breeches tucked into knee high boots completed his functional but aristocratic wardrobe.

Kahn Taruk glanced at the fourth man who was, it seemed, ignoring conventional protocol by remaining in his seat. *This barbarian is pushing me*, Kahn thought. He was Askarian, a member of a small but powerful war-like tribe that controlled the lands north and east of the Callee Sea. The warrior was short and stocky, powerfully built, with long black hair pulled tightly back into a long tail that started at the top of his head, hanging all the way to his waist. He wore a leather shirt, breeches, and boots made from tulkick skin, a small four legged herbivore prevalent in the steppes. His chest was covered in a hardened leather cuirass, the center of which was made of a glossy sea turtle shell found along the coastal waters. At each hip he wore the traditional weapon of his tribe, a cab're, consisting of a long wooden handle from which extended a short thick blade that widened at the end. They were heavy but razor sharp, and in the hands of a skilled Askarian could be thrown like hand axes as well as used in hand to hand combat. Askarians were deadly fighters and most were skillful enough to fight with two cab'res at once.

As Kahn Taruk moved around the table, he glared at the barbarian, who still sat defiantly, either unaware of proper protocol, or he simply didn't care. *Probably the latter*, Kahn thought, knowing that the Askarians were not a people to abide by protocol or be cowed by rank. In the Askarian culture one's status was earned through Blood Rite, through combat, not through blood lines or family connections. Kahn had to admit that he respected the warrior's courage, but he had no doubt that if need be, he could show the obstinate barbarian that he had earned his own position through blood. In fact, part of him wanted to spin the axe off his shoulder and split his flat face in half for the obvious affront to his rank. But he refrained, and sat down at the table opposite the four men, a large map of Belorth and Corvell spread out before them. A collection of wooden markers sat atop the map; some were carved into ships while others were miniature statues of their god Heln, depicted as a bare chested, muscular man with long flowing hair and beard, his hands resting on a massive two handed sword. The carvings were quite beautiful and intricate. On the map, the Heln markers covered all of Belorth, stopping in the east at Torik, the land of the Askarians, which they had not yet conquered. The island nations of YaLara and Argos were also marked. But the only marker on Corvell was at Fara.

"How goes the fighting in the north?" Kahn Taruk addressed General Sigmar.

"We have gained some land, Tongra Taruk, but our enemy's forces have fought valiantly."

"How close are we to the Pelm River that blocks entrance into the lands of Dy'ain?"

"Two days ride. Tongra Taruk, it is now time to decide. Do we take our forces and try to take Eltus, or do we attack the garrison and break into the lands of Dy'ain?"

Kahn Taruk said nothing as he scrutinized the map. The city of Eltus, the capital of Kael, was located at the mouth of the narrow Dynel Strait leading into the Dark Sea. The only way to get a fleet of ships into the sea, and thus to Dy'ain, was to take the city of Eltus and control the strait.

"We will split our forces."

"But Tonga Taruk," General Sigmar responded, "we may not have enough men to take both the city and the garrison."

Kahn Taruk ignored him. "Most of our army will move east and attack Eltus. That will force the Kaelian army to withdraw to their capital city. Dy'ainian troops will not join them. They will have to stay at their garrison to protect their own borders. How many men does the garrison have, without the troops from Kael?"

"You plan to split their forces?" Keltius said, speaking in Drak, the language of the Saricons.

"That is part of the plan."

Sigmar looked at the map again. "We believe that the garrison has between four and five thousand troops."

Bannerfall

"How difficult would it be to take the garrison?"

"I do not know, but I think I could do it with five thousand men."

"Here is my plan. General Sigmar, you will take six thousand men and march towards the garrison, while Jorga will take the remaining forces and move towards Eltus from the east. I will be joining him and taking command of those forces as they near the city." Jorga was in charge of the main army while Sigmar and Karnack were in Fara. "Meanwhile," Kahn Taruk looked toward Keltius, "you will take my fleet of ships and block the southern opening of the Dynel Strait. From there you will be in position to attack the city from the sea."

"What of their navy?" Keltius asked. Everyone knew that there was no navy that could match the Kaelians. They had faster more maneuverable ships, and more of them, and there was no other people with more naval combat experience. Defeating the Kaelian navy would be no easy feat.

"I have a plan for that as well. Do not attack the city until you have orders to do so. By the time you arrive with my fleet, my plan will be in motion. If it works, which I am confident it will, there will be very few ships to meet you."

Keltius didn't look so confident. But he nodded his head in acquiescence.

Tongra Taruk turned his blue eyes on the Askarian nomad who thus far had said nothing, nor had he understood anything, since he himself did not speak Drak. "Obaty," he said in the nomad's own tongue, "are you ready to fulfill your end of the bargain?"

The Askarian looked up. "A man is nothing without his word."

"And you are sure that you can get an army of ten thousand men, led by Karnack here," he said, indicating the grim faced Saricon, "through the pass undetected?"

Obaty nodded his head. Then he looked at Karnack, his face void of emotion. "I will get you through the secret pass. But once we break through the mountains, you are on your own. First, I need half of my payment," he said flatly.

The Pyres Mountains blocked any northern movement from Torik to the Sil Desert. In fact, there was no way an army could move north, the tall jutting peaks, choked with freezing cold and snow, all but impassable. At least that is what everyone had always believed. Until they had met the Askarians, a people that had lived next to the mountains for a thousand years, and who once, long ago, had passed through the mountains, their descendants spreading out and claiming the lands south of the many tall peaks. They knew of a secret path through the mountains. It would take several months, and be very dangerous, but Obaty had convinced Kahn Taruk that it could be done. And Kahn Taruk had a plan for his army once they broke through the mountain pass. A plan, that in the end, would see Heln's flag waving high from the spires of Cythera, the capital city of Dy'ain.

But first things first, Kahn Taruk thought. None of this would come to fruition if they could not take the city of Eltus. "Keltius," Kahn said, now speaking in Newain, the most common language spoken throughout Corvell. He knew that even Obaty would now understand his words. "You will carry the troops by ship to the edge of the Pyres Mountains. You will drop Obaty and Karnack's troops there and then move north to your position off the coast of Eltus. Remember, do not engage until you receive word from me, which you will." Then he looked at the nomad. "As far as payment, you shall receive half when you get my army to the pass, and the other half once we are through, as we agreed."

Obaty grunted and leaned back in his chair.

"How will we take the city of Eltus?" Sigmar asked.

Kahn Taruk smiled for the first time. "I have sent in the Shadows."

Saricon Battle Plans

1. Split our forces and send the majority of our army to attack Eltus while six thousand attack Lyone, the border garrison into the land of Dy'ain.
2. Take the city of Eltus so we can control the Dynel Strait. Then send ten thousand troops through the secret pass in the Pyres Mountains.
3. After controlling Eltus and the Dynel Strait, send a fleet of men to the shores of Dy'ain while our second army secretly crosses the Sil Desert to enter the lands of Dy'ain from the north. All the while our third Saricon army takes Lyone and enters Dy'ain from the west, marching towards the city to meet up with the main Saricon army.
4. Both armies, in the dead of night, converge on Cythera and take the capital city of Dy'ain.

Chapter 1

*T*he Saricons arrived on the shores of the southern lands of Belorth, and with them came the winds of change. These strange foreigners arrived in 4880, the tenth cyn. Every fifty years a new cyn begins, and within two cyns the Saricons had conquered the kingdoms of Karak and Enoreth, and had then set their eyes on Vyalia and Ulstare, two cities ruled by the nomads of Anoroth, a people who worshiped nothing but their own strength, their steel, and their bloodlines. The advance of the Saricons was thus halted. So they moved north, towards new lands and new conquests, bringing with them new foods, new weapons, and a new faith. They were followers of Heln, an ancient and power hungry god. As an historian, I try to look at these events objectively and without bias, but the more I have learned about these Helnians, the more difficult that has become. To me their name conjures up mostly images of violence and domination, and I see nothing but large brutal warriors with pale skin and yellow hair, their weapons streaked with the blood of their victims. I see towns burning and I hear the screams of women and children, while the cold blue eyes of the Saricons focus only on their next conquest.

Before one cyn had passed the Helnians, as they came to be known, had reached their blood soaked hands into the island nations of YaLara and Argos, and even as far as the kingdoms of Kael, Gilia, and Layona. But again their bloody conquest was halted. For these kingdoms, though politically separate, had been unified by an intense zeal for their religion. They were all followers of their gods, Argon and Felina, and became known as Argonians.

It was in 4400, fourteen cyns ago, that a solitary cattle herder witnessed a vision of the two gods as they descended from the sky. The nameless herder spent three days in a trance as Argon and Felina communed with him. They spoke to him, delivering their message, providing guidance and rules for living, and demanding obedience. He spent the next five years writing down their teachings, sharing and preaching them to anyone who would listen. His intense zeal and fervor gradually won over the hearts of the people and the new belief system was embraced and strengthened within that time. The year that Argon and Felina descended from the heavens became known as The Year of the Great Change, and marked the beginning of the Argonian calendar. Eventually the writings and sermons of the lone herder were collected and preserved in the Argot, their holy book, which became the *foundation of Argonian belief. The herder never gave his name, believing it would be vain, and so he became known only as The One, and is revered by the Argonians almost as much as they revere Argon and Felina.*

And for the past fifty years these two belief systems, Helnian and Argonian clashed. The Saricons, foreign conquerors fought for power, control, and dominance, while the Argonians, a collection of different peoples used the one thing they shared in common, the strength of their faith, to unite them against this new enemy. But the Saricons were not only fierce in battle, they were smart, and experienced in the tactics of subterfuge and intrigue. They coveted the lands of Layona, Gilia, and Kael, but most of all they desired the lands of Dy'ain. For it was here that the precious metal, Kul-brite, could be found.

The Kingdom of Dy'ain, ruled by House Dormath, was the most powerful kingdom on the coast of the Alsace Sea. They traded in precious stones, but most of their wealth and power came from the many Kul-brite mines throughout the Devlin Mountains, the massive range of mountains whose tall peaks protected their western border. It was this rare metal that was used to forge the only weapons capable of holding the energy channeled by a Merger. The metal was so rare and costly, that wars were continually fought for its control. The Helnians desperately wanted to possess the mines, but House Dormath controlled them. But, true to their reputation, the Saricons had created an intricate plan of conquest. These newcomers, the followers of Heln, had crossed the Alsace Sea, and with them came the winds of change.

Journal entry 14
Kivalla Der'une, Historian, Keeper of the records in Cythera, capital of Dy'ain

---

5087, the 14th cyn after the Great Change

Brant Anwar lowered his head and lifted his left hand, dropping his shoulder and taking the powerful blow on the fleshy muscular part of his forearm. It hurt like hell but he growled through the pain, drawing forth a rush of aura energy into his right arm as he snapped his right fist forward, firing into the man's nose as if it were the point of a ballista bolt. One could hear the crunch of cartilage as his nose collapsed, splattering blood into the air.

Bannerfall

Brant leaped back as his opponent stumbled, his eyes rolling back into his head as he fell backwards, crashing onto the dirt floor with a heavy thud.

The crowd surrounding the combatants was silent for a moment as they stared at the fallen fighter, waiting to see if he would move. When it was obvious he wouldn't they erupted in a chorus of applause…while those who had bet on the wrong man swore in anger.

The fight had been tough one. Brant's opponent had come from a mining camp on the other side of the Devlin Mountains, and the local inhabitants had anticipated the fight with much excitement. Brant had gone undefeated since he had started fighting nearly six months ago. The other fighter, who Brant had learned was called Janrick, was strong and had a wicked right jab. But after several rounds, Brant had finally broken through his defenses. But he hadn't gone unscathed. His left eye was almost swollen shut, and he had numerous bruises on his heavily muscled, sweat drenched body. Despite his superficial injuries, Brant felt charged, the combination of adrenaline and aura energy filling him with vitality. He had won, again.

Jorna, Brant's father, walked up behind him. The man was an impressive figure himself, standing near six feet and covered in sinewy muscles. He was nearly fifty five years old, but a lifetime spent working the Kul-brite mines had a way of filtering out the weak. They didn't last very long, and Jorna had been working them his entire life, moving from one mining camp to another among the many that lay scattered throughout the Devlin Mountains. Long gray hair draped his craggy sun dried face which was covered in black and silver stubble. Bristly gray eyebrows rested on an overly pronounced brow, accentuating his dark, deep set eyes, dull and devoid of emotion. Jorna was not a man prone to smiles.

"I'll get the winnings. Meet me back at home," his father said brusquely.

Brant watched his father push his way through the crowd towards the winning table. *Thanks for the kind words, Father*, Brant thought to himself. But he smiled inwardly, laughing at himself for expecting anything more from his father. After all, he had never shown any tendency toward being a kind or loving father. Despite the money his fights had earned for them, he had yet to hear a word of praise, or see a sign of gratitude. Perhaps it was a result of a lifetime spent in the mines. For Brant himself had grown into a reserved, hard young man, prone to occasional fits of anger. He was quiet, almost taciturn, and had little use for mindless banter. The way he saw it most words seemed meaningless and empty, used mainly to deceive or to stroke someone's ego for personal gain. He hadn't learned much from his father, except how to fight, and to keep to oneself, to protect oneself from others, who, according to his father, were only out for themselves, despite the useless words they toss around to make you believe otherwise.

Several people from the crowd congratulated Brant on his win, smiling happily as they too had won some coin on the fight, and were already anticipating the wine and ale they would soon be drinking. There were others, however, that glared at him menacingly, their stares alone carrying the weight of a sword point piercing his flesh. They did not like losing their few, hard earned coins. Brant had no illusions that several of them would relish literally driving home that point. But Brant had a reputation. Despite his age, he was not someone to trifle with. He had just turned eighteen, but one would never know it. The young miner was even taller than his father, and more heavily built. He too had been working the Kul-brite mines since he was fourteen, and the constant swing of pick and hammer had built layers of dense muscle. Yet, in defiance of his bulk, he was incredibly quick and agile.

Overall he was a striking young man, handsome only in the roughest sort of way. His nose had been broken three times and was now slightly crooked and swollen on one side. Yet one could still see remnants of its once regal structure. His wide angular chin, covered in a soft growth of short black hair gave his face a look of strength and determination. Waves of black hair cascaded past his ears and down to the base of his neck. The hair on his crown was pulled back tightly and tied behind his head. It wouldn't do to have his sweaty hair fly into his eyes during a fight. And his eyes were his most striking feature. They were a luminous, almost iridescent green, the light green of spring's first leaves, but etched with thin tendrils of blue and gray. It was difficult for most people to notice his other features, so compelling was the intensity of his gaze.

Brant picked up his threadbare long shirt and put it on, the thin material clinging to his sweaty body. He moved through the dispersing crowd toward the tent entrance, pushing aside the heavy canvas that kept out the brisk mountain air. He paused momentarily, taking in a deep breath of fresh air, and looked about. It was dark, but fires were lit around the tent and several could be seen flickering down several alleys formed by the hundreds of heavy tents that made up the homes of the many miners that worked the camp. The simple structures were called bilts, owned by the king and rented to the miners, the money taken from their pay each week. The rent was high, leaving little left over for luxuries. But they were worked so hard that they rarely had time for luxuries anyway, the occasional fights providing their main source of entertainment. Sometimes the wardens, the king's men who worked, ran, and guarded the mines, would allow miners to come in from other nearby mines to fight the local talent, as they had done this night.

The bilts were of an ingenious design. The long poles were expertly cut so they interlocked in a way to hold up the heavy waterproof canvas. The open structure was strong, waterproof, and designed to be taken down and easily transported from one mine to another. The Devlin Mountains were peppered with Kul-brite mines, and if the production of one mine slowed, the small mining villages were loaded up and brought to a new location, always following the veins and deposits of this precious metal.

Brant flexed his hands, working out the soreness that was slowly creeping into his muscles. He sighed as he looked up at the mountain bathed in the soft blue light of the luminous moon. *Tomorrow would be a tough day* he thought. He knew he would be sore and bruised from the fight, but it mattered little; he would still be expected to work the mines with everyone else. But he had done it before, and he knew he could do it again. They worked seven days a week, and the hours were long, filled with crushing stone and moving rocks from deep within the mountain to the Separation Tents where specially trained wardens methodically chipped away rock to expose whatever Kul-brite steel they could find. The metal was extremely bright, mirror-like, and it was easy to spot in the small crushed rocks brought in by the miners. From there the wardens used precise tools and techniques unknown to the miners to separate the metal from the stone, an amount as small as the nail on one's smallest finger worth more than a miner's yearly wage. Other precious stones were also found in the process and sorted; everything from gold to diamonds and rubies. Needless to say the Separation Tents were guarded more heavily than the king himself.

The wardens were elite fighting men, taken from the best soldiers that House Dormath, the ruling family of Dy'ain, could find throughout their kingdom. Each warrior was trained further, in both combat and various skills associated with the mining of Kul-brite steel.

Bannerfall

Wardens were skilled and extremely tough, but even they were no match for the Dygon Guards, warriors with the Way that exhibited sufficient strength and aptitude while at the warden training camps to move to the Advanced Warden School. There they were forged into the strongest, most skillful, tough, and intelligent fighters in all of the lands of Corvell. These warriors were typically sons of the various lords throughout Dy'ain, all eager for the honor of becoming a Dygon Guard, warriors who sole job was to protect the Kul-brite caravans as they transported the rare metal to the various smithies throughout Dy'ain. It was very rare, but occasionally brigands or Shulg nomads, tribes living throughout the steppes bordering the Devlin Mountains, worked up the courage to attack the caravans. The draw of a king's ransom in Kul-brite steel had a way of interfering with good judgment. Having the temerity to attack one Dygon warrior, let alone fifty, was as good as slitting your own throat. Theft at the mines was also virtually nonexistent. All miners were checked entering the mines and leaving the mines, and anyone caught with Kul-brite metal would be sentenced to death.

A dozen or so men remained in the mess tent where the fight had occurred as Brant left to go home, but no one said a word to him, or to each other for that matter, as they headed to their own bilts. Most of the miners were already thinking of bed, knowing that they would be up soon with pick in hand and the wardens yelling at them to work harder. Several wardens patrolled the alleys, dressed in silver armor, their red capes fluttering behind them as they watched the workers with dark hooded eyes. They carried long spears and from their leather belts hung long curved swords and daggers.

Brant made his way down the left alley to their bilt, the last one on the right. The wooden door was unlocked; after all they had nothing a thief would want. The open interior was sparse and simple. Two cots, covered in thick wool blankets, sat on opposite ends of the square room. At the base of each bed was a wooden trunk filled with their few possessions. A wide metal brazier containing burning red embers sat in the middle of the room, the smoke from the coals drifting lazily to the small opening at the top of the bilt, which was designed in such a way to let smoke out but protect the brazier from the outside elements. The room smelt of sweat and smoke, an aroma you might expect from two men who spent their days working in dark and dingy mineshafts. A small wooden table and two chairs completed the furnishings, all property of the king. Leaning against the far wall was a collection of picks and hammers, tools of the trade.

On the table was a clay jug filled with cool water. Brant sat down at the table, sighed tiredly, and took a long pull from the pitcher, nearly draining the contents in several deep gulps. The cold fresh liquid quenched his thirst and drove away the dryness in his mouth brought on by the fight. He leaned back, looking up at the canvas ceiling, sighing wearily.

The loud clang of the door as it slammed shut snapped him from his reverie. His father strode into the room and tossed him a small bag of coins which jingled as they hit the table. "There you go, boy."

Brant looked at the bag as his father warmed his hands over the coals. "How much did we get?"

"Why don't you look in the bag and not bother me with useless questions?"

Brant did. There were two gold dracks, three silver shikes, and five copper tiggs. It was a decent haul, but he had expected more. "I thought there would be more."

Jorna grunted, ignoring the comment. Brant had no doubt that his father had taken most of the coin.

"How much did you take?" Brant asked, his frustration evident in his voice. Brant had had a suspicion that his father had been pocketing most of the coin ever since he started fighting. His father had begun teaching him how to fight from the time he had taken his first steps. The physical and mental abuse of these lessons had, over time, solidified a strained, and less than caring, relationship. And once he had started fighting for money, they seldom talked or saw one another. They typically worked in different shafts, and his father spent most of his nights spending his new coin on cheap norg, a powerful alcohol made from the fynel root found in the steppes.

Jorna, who had been warming his hands over the hot embers of the brazier, stopped and turned his menacing eyes on his son. "What did you say, boy?"

"You heard me."

Jorna was a big man, but he could move as quickly as an angry bear if he had to. In a blink he lunged toward Brant and hit him in the face with the knuckle side of his left hand, the powerful blow knocking his son's head back and tipping the chair over, as Brant fell, his head hitting the ground hard. "You got what you deserve, boy! And be thankful for it!" he yelled as he straddled his son's prone body.

Brant growled angrily, pushing his father off and struggling to his feet. Jorna had once been a powerful and successful fighter in his own right, and despite his age Brant knew that if they fought now, that one, or both, would get seriously hurt. He was already tired from the fight, and he had no desire to get into a scuffle with his father. He wiped the blood from his lip, and glared at him with undisguised hatred. Then he spit blood on the ground at his father's feet, took one long stride that brought him to the table where he grabbed his bag of coins and stormed through the wooden door, slamming it behind him.

The morning came quickly, much too quickly, the mining bell ringing loudly throughout the camp. It was time to get up, grab breakfast at the mess tent, and head into the mines. Brant sat up slowly, his aching body reminding him of the previous night's fight. He looked over at his father who was sprawled out on his cot, presumably still drunk. After he had left that night, he had walked around the camp, hoping to loosen up his aching muscles, calm himself, and give his father enough time to get drunk and pass out. The cool night air had done him some good and by the time he returned to their bilt his father was either asleep, or passed out, either one preferable to another violent confrontation.

Brant stood, threw on his wool coat, and walked over to the table to get a drink of water and lace up his leather work boots. His father had still not roused himself even after the loud ringing of the morning work bell. After drinking a large cup of water he walked over to his father, gently shaking him.

"Father, wake up. You're going to be late."

There was no reaction, not even a moan.

"Morlock's balls, wake up father. Do you want to be fined again?" This time Brant shook him harder. Still nothing.

Brant reached under his father and rolled his heavy body over on the cot, nearly upturning the bed in the process. Seeing his father's face, he stepped back in shock. Jorna's eyes were wide open, vacant and lifeless, his chest unmoving. Brant quickly went to him, putting his hand on his chest and his ear near his mouth, listening intently for any breath, for any sign of life. But there was none. His father was dead.

Brant ran immediately to the head warden's tent. He didn't know what to do, but he figured the Warden General would. Brant had never formally met Warden General Kane, although he had seen him on several occasions throughout the camp. When he told the guards what had happened they had led him into the large tent, where one of the wardens accompanied him and ordered him to take a seat before a large and ornately carved wooden desk. The room was spacious compared to his own small quarters, and he knew that beyond the inner tent flap was probably a larger room that acted as the Warden General's personal quarters.

The warden, who Brant recognized as a new guard that went by the name of Warden Tyan, walked over to the inner tent flap. "You are Brant, right?" The warden asked as he covered the distance in a few strides. He probably knew him from the fights. Generally the wardens did not participate in the fights, but it was not uncommon for a few to bet on the outcomes.

"Yes."

"Last name?"

"Anwar, Brant Anwar."

The warden was young, maybe twenty five, with jet black hair cut short and a small tuft of hair left below his lip. "Warden General, I'm sorry to interrupt you but we seem to have an incident," the young warden spoke through the flap.

"What is it?" an annoyed voice came from the next room.

"Sir, a miner is here reporting the death of his father. His name is Brant Anwar."

"I'll be right out."

Warden Tyan moved away from the flap and stood guard next to Brant, his hand casually resting on the hilt of his sword and his wary eyes staring down at him. Brant looked away, his own mind trying to deal with what had happened. Brant didn't know what he was feeling. He wasn't sad, but that was to be expected. Was it fear? Fear of what would happen to him now that his father was dead? He didn't think so. Anxious maybe, or was it a feeling of emptiness? He shared no love for his father, but nonetheless Jorna *was* his father. Now that he was gone, he felt an empty hole somewhere inside him. That was it.

The tent flap flung open and a tall man in warden's armor quickly entered, stopping momentarily to gaze down at the boy. The Warden General was a full hand taller than Brant, but not nearly as muscular. He was lean, with weathered skin browned by the sun. A sparse crop of silver gray hair crowned the top of his head which was losing its battle with baldness. The short hair above his ears was silver as well, but streaked with black, as if a painter had used a dry brush lightly covered with black paint to add some contrast to the grayness. His eyes were bright blue, like lightening, and they looked at Brant now.

"You're the fighter. Right, boy?" the Warden General asked.

Brant cleared his throat. "Yes."

Warden General Kane sat down at his chair behind the desk, his piercing eyes showing no emotion. "Address me as Warden General."

Brant didn't like his pompous tone. His immediate instinct was to jump across the desk and grab the man by the throat. It was the reaction he too often had that too quickly surfaced when someone challenged him, physically or verbally. Perhaps it was from the years of abuse from his father. Taking orders for so long from a man he despised left him with little patience to take it from others. Whatever the reason, it was a part of his personality that had gotten him into some trouble at the camps. But it was not prudent to confront the wardens and he had learned early on, in those situations, to curb his violent emotions. "I'm sorry…Warden General."

"So what happened?"

"I woke up this morning and found my father dead."

"How did he die?"

"I'm not sure. He drank last night. Maybe his heart gave out."

"How old was your father? Jorna was his name, right?"

"Yes, Warden General, his name was Jorna. I believe he was fifty five."

The Warden General sat back in his chair, seemingly mulling something over in his head. "That's a long time to have worked in the mines. I'm surprised he lasted that long."

"My father was a tough man." Brant was not boasting for his father. He was simply stating a fact.

"It is said that you are as well."

They heard a small commotion outside the tent, then the outer flap opened and a warrior entered, striding quickly over to stand next to Brant's chair. A smile finally broke through the Warden General's stern demeanor as he recognized the newcomer. Brant noticed his armor and his heartbeat quickened. It was a Dygon Guard. The warrior looked down at Brant with black eyes, his stern face emotionless. But when he

Bannerfall

looked back at the Warden General, he met the man with a smile, and a raised hand. They shook hands briefly, greeting one another warmly as if Brant did not exist.

"Kulvar Rand, it is good to see you. I expected you a few days from now. You must have made good time," the Warden General said. "Can I get you some refreshments?"

At the mention of the man's name, Brant blanched, unsure of what he should do and feeling completely out of his element. Kulvar Rand was a name everyone knew. The man was a legend. Dygon Guards were the most skilled and elite warriors in all of Dy'ain, and Kulvar Rand was their leader, thought to be the best swordsman in the realm. His hair was shaved short, close to the scalp, the typical style for Dygon Guards, and his black travel worn cape was covered in dust. He wore silver armor, like a warden's, but what made his different was the center of the breast plate. The center of his cuirass was black, and etched into the black metal was the silver symbol of House Dormath, two swords crossed over a mountain. The work was beautifully done, with silver inlays so intricately done they reproduced in meticulous detail the designs of the sword hilts and showed every nook and cranny of Bone Mountain, the tallest peak in the Devlin Mountain Range. It must have cost a fortune. Brant glanced at the sword and dagger at his hip. The hilt of the sword was unadorned and wrapped in black leather. He had heard tales of Kulvar Rand's prowess with his Kul-brite sword. Everyone had. And now, here he was seeing it, that very sword no more than an arm's reach away. He marveled that it was really Kul-brite forged, not fully coming to terms with the value of such a thing so close to him.

"Some water would be nice. And yes, we made good time."

The Warden General motioned for Warden Tyan to bring some water. "Please, have a seat."

"Thank you but I need to make camp with my men. I just wanted to let you know that we had arrived. Besides, you seem busy at the moment." Kulvar glanced down at Brant, his face unreadable.

"It's nothing. The boy's father died last night. We were just discussing what to do about it."

"I see." Kulvar turned to face Brant. "What's your name?"

"Ummm…"

"Stand up," the Warden General ordered.

Brant faced the Warden General, his eyes narrowing in anger. The Warden General was just about to say something else when Brant glanced up at Kulvar Rand, sensing his dark eyes on him. The Dygon Guard's eyes bore into him, but he looked slightly amused, the corners of his mouth subtly arched. Brant stood up, the chair sliding out behind him. "I'm sorry, Master Rand, I am just a miner and not aware of protocol." Brant was not one for apologies, but the aura of this man seemed to demand it.

"Son, do not fret. I'm no king. Besides, your father has died and I believe that allows you some latitude. Now, what is your name?"

"Brant, sir. Brant Anwar."

Kulvar stood a bit shorter than Brant, but his charismatic presence made him seem larger. His dark eyes looked him over. "You look strong. How long have you been working in the mines?"

"Since I came of age. My mother died giving birth to me and my father was forced to work the mines so we wouldn't starve." Any children brought to the mines had to begin working when they turned fourteen. If they couldn't handle the work they would be turned out on their own. Working the mines was not something to which one aspired. It was often a last resort for those who had no other options due to unfortunate circumstances or need. The job alone was difficult enough to weed out most men. That, combined with the long hours and low pay, were enough to discourage everyone but the most desperate or destitute. It was a profession that few entered willingly. Nearly everything the miners possessed was owned by the king, and once their rent and the cost of food was taken from their pay, there was little left, a few coins to bet on a fight or to squander on cheap norg.

"He's a fighter with quite a reputation. If I recall, you have not lost a match since you started competing," the Warden General added, addressing Brant personally. The other warden handed Kulvar a cup of water he had poured from a jug on the side table.

"That's true," Brant replied.

"Really?" Kulvar asked. "That is quite an accomplishment for one so young." Brant, not sure how to reply, said nothing. Kulvar seemed to notice his discomfort. "Please, sit, boy," he said, not unkindly. "So, what are your plans now?" he asked as Brant sat down. "Will you stay and continue to work the mines, or will you go out on your own?"

Brant looked at Warden General Kane. "Do I have a choice?"

"How old are you?" the Warden General asked.

"Eighteen."

"Then yes, you have a choice."

"Well, I think..."

"...but," the Warden General interrupted. "Your father has a debt to pay if I recall." The Warden General stood up from his chair and went to a chest of drawers in the corner of the room. Opening one, he started thumbing through some papers, finally producing the one he sought. Returning to his seat he perused the document quickly.

"What does my father's debt have to do with me?"

"You are responsible for it," Kulvar Rand answered for the Warden General. "It is the law."

Now Brant was angry. It made no sense. Why would someone else have to pay for another's mistakes? "My father was a drunk and a fool. I will not pay for his mistakes."

Kulvar raised his eyes in amusement and looked at the Warden General, whose face showed no sign of mirth.

"You *will* pay for them," the Warden General said sternly.

Brant seethed. But what could he do? Even in death his father found a way to hurt him. "How much does he owe?"

"Well, over the years he has accumulated a debt of thirty gold dracks."

"What!? How can I pay off such a debt!?" Brant had collected six gold dracks, five silver shikes, and maybe ten copper tiggs from his fights, which didn't even come close to what he now apparently owed. Besides, if he used his money to pay it, then he would have none left over to pay for his rent, food, or anything else if he wished to leave.

"You'll have to keep working until you do," the Warden General said matter-of-factly.

"But my father had some coin," Brant said hastily, trying to figure a way out of this predicament. If his father had taken most of the coin from the fights he had won, then perhaps there was enough stored away to pay this debt. But he knew that was doubtful. He knew full well that his father had spent nearly all of his money on drink and the cheap whores that moved through the mining camps.

As if on cue another warden entered the tent and set a small bag of coin on the Warden General's desk. He grabbed it and dumped out the contents. A handful of coins jingled across the wooden top. It looked to be about the equivalent of fifteen gold dracks.

"What's this?" Brant asked.

"The money we found in your bilt."

"You have no right!" Brant stormed as he jumped up from his chair.

Warden Tyan reached for his blade, but before his hand even touched the hilt, Kulvar Rand's Kul-brite blade rang from his scabbard and rested lightly on Brant's throat, stopping him instantly.

"Calm yourself, boy," Kulvar admonished, his voice eerily devoid of emotion. "Sit back down."

Brant looked down at the blade resting on his neck. The shiny surface was so bright that it nearly blinded him, and despite the light touch of the master swordsman, he could feel the metal cut through his skin, releasing a small trickle of blood that dripped down his neck. He wasn't sure if he was imagining it, but he thought he caught a flicker of green light that quickly danced across the silver blade.

Brant sat down, trying to quell his anger as Kulvar sheathed his sword in one smooth motion.

Finally the Warden General spoke. "We have every right. Everything you have is ours, owned by the king."

"But not the coin," Brant pleaded. "That is all I have." Brant thought that his father would have had more, and he suspected that the warden had taken some before bringing the contents back to the Warden General.

"You owe a debt, so yes, even the coin is ours."

"What am I to do?"

"The only thing you can do," the Warden General said. "Work until it's paid off."

Brant ground his teeth in frustration, rubbing his eyes and trying to come up with another solution. He did not want to remain in the mines. He didn't know what he would do, but he knew he didn't want to end up like his father and work the mines his entire life, dying with nothing to show for a lifetime of work.

"I do not want to spend my life working the mines," Brant whispered softly.

"I may have a solution," Kulvar announced.

Brant looked up at him. "Anything, sir. I will do anything."

Kulvar smiled. "How about another fight?"

Brant looked at him quizzically, trying to figure out if he was serious. Then he looked at the Warden General who was equally surprised. "But I owe nearly fifteen gold dracks. How can one fight pay for that?"

"I will cover your debt if you fight one of the wardens," Kulvar said. "And if you win, I will give you five gold dracks for the road if you still wish to leave."

"But why would you do this?" Brant asked, confused.

"For sport and curiosity. And my men will enjoy it. Fifteen gold dracks is nothing to me, well worth a good fight. What do you say?"

"Fight a warden? That's insane," Brant said, mostly to himself. Wardens were highly trained fighters, and with the exception of the Dygon Guard and the king's Sentinels, wardens were the most deadly fighting men in Dy'ain.

"But is it worth fifteen gold dracks?" Kulvar asked softly.

Brant thought about it. Even if he lost, which he likely would, his debt would be paid. But what then? He would have no money left to live on. He would have to leave coinless, or stay and work the mines until he had saved enough to leave. But if he won, his debt would be paid and he would have some coin for the road. Five dracks would not get him far, but it would at least be a start. If he didn't fight, he would be forced to work for a long while before he could pay off that debt, and then he would be right back to where he started. He felt like he was trapped in a corner; neither decision a good one, though one would at least give him a chance to leave the mines sooner rather than later.

Brant looked up at Kulvar. "I will fight."

Brant stood shirtless before his opponent. The man he was fighting was a warden that he had only seen on few occasions. His name was Bargos. Brant had never spoken with him and he had observed that he was not prone to idle chatter. And he looked every bit the soldier. He was older than Brant, maybe early thirties, and his body reflected a lifetime of fighting. Numerous scars covered his forearms with a particularly wicked one running down the side of his cheek. He was half a head shorter than Brant, but his arms, which were covered with thick well defined muscles, a result of years of swinging a sword and lifting a shield, more than made up for his lesser stature. He had long light brown hair, rare for this part of the world, and his eyes were a blue gray, piercing and hawk-like.

Kulvar Rand stood between them. "Both fighters ready?" Nodding their heads in acknowledgement, both fighters shifted back and forth on the balls of their feet. "Remember, the fight is over when one man is knocked unconscious or submits." Neither said anything in response; they both knew the rule. And they knew that was the only rule, that in fact there were no rules.

The crowd was the largest that Brant had ever seen. It looked as if the entire camp was out, as well as the wardens that were not guarding the stores of Kul-brite. In fact, they had to move the fight outside in order to accommodate the crowd. Fifteen large braziers formed a circle approximately thirty paces in diameter, their fires casting an orange glow across the clearing as the sun disappeared behind Bone Peak, the tallest peak in the Devlin Range.

"You may begin," Kulvar announced, stepping back to the edge of the perimeter.

The two combatants slowly circled each other. Brant had to admit that he was nervous. Wardens were skilled, highly trained fighters, and this man certainly looked the part. He had no idea how much of their training included hand to hand fighting, but he figured he was about to find out.

Brant felt his aura energy surrounding him, and he gently eased it into his powerful arms, enhancing them with strength and speed. He had no idea how this power had come to be. He had started to feel it when he had reached adolescence, a gentle tingling of energy surrounding his body. Being sheltered his entire life in the camps, he had never heard of the Way, nor witnessed the power himself. All he knew, over years of experimenting, was that he could channel the energy into his arms and legs to give him extra strength, speed, and endurance. The first day he realized this was when he was sixteen and swinging a pick deep in a mine shaft. He was exhausted and could hardly move his arms. Then, seemingly out of nowhere, he felt a new energy hovering around his body. It was his aura, although at the time he knew not what it was. He was somehow able to direct it into his extremities and gradually the pick began to get lighter, as if it were a feather. The sensation had felt awkward at first, like a warm light cloth fluttering around his torso. But as he swung the pick the energy around him seemed eager to push into his legs and arms, and he let it, releasing the damn and filling his muscles in his legs and arms with new energy. The metal head came down again and again, shattering stone in a shower of sparks. He had reveled in this new power, his body stronger than it had ever been. But he learned something else that day. His body could only provide so much aura energy at a time, and once gone, he deflated like a wine skin in a bar. He had barely made it back to his bilt that evening. Since then, he had learned to control the amount of energy he expelled, dispersing it in small amounts and sudden quick movements. He found that when he ate and rested, his aura strength returned. Exhausting it all quickly would leave him so weak that he could barely walk, but if he used small amounts in quick doses, it would last much longer and allow his body time to replenish the energy, how that happened he was unsure.

Brant lifted his hands to protect his face and moved in, jabbing with his left hand, trying to get a feel for his opponent. Bargos danced around lightly, exuding confidence as he dodged the jab, returning it with his own impossibly quick strike. Brant lifted his arm to deflect it, but at the last moment realized it was a ruse. Coming in fast and low, Bargos crouched and shot forward, wrapping his strong arms around Brant's thighs and lifting up with his powerful legs. The warden carried him forward before slamming him down on his back. It felt like a bull had hit him.

The crowd screamed as Brant grunted, the air rushing from his lungs, the impact slamming his head onto the ground. Seeing stars, Brant wrapped his arms around the warden's waist, sent a rush of aura energy into them and leaned back, tossing the warden through the air with intense strength. Bargos landed five paces away but quickly regained his footing, seemingly unaffected by the throw, but a bit more wary as he looked at Brant with a mixture of surprise and curiosity. Brant was still feeling a bit dazed and his movements were neither confident nor spry. But he stood up as quickly as he could, breathing deeply as he tried to refill his lungs. His head was pounding and his back felt bruised, but he had been through worse.

Bargos closed the distance quickly, fists flashing out incredibly fast. They traded blows and blocks, neither gaining much of an advantage. After a quick exchange of punches and blocks, Bargos changed tactics and kicked out with his right leg. Brant didn't expect it. Most fighters relied solely on their fists, and Brant had relatively little experience fighting someone who also used their feet as weapons. As the warden's foot shot quickly forward, the ball of his foot connected solidly with Brant's chin, snapping his head back violently. Luckily his mouth was closed. The blow was so hard he could have broken some teeth or even bitten off his tongue. He staggered, nearly falling over, and without really thinking, instinctively channeled some aura energy into his head, trying to clear away the blackness threatening to overwhelm him. He had never used the energy that way; he had never had to. But he knew that if he didn't regain his senses he would find himself on the ground in mere moments.

And he was right. Bargos followed the kick with a series of lightning fast jabs, but somehow the aura energy had helped Brant shake off the dizziness and lift up his hands, blocking the blows sufficiently to prevent any major damage. Bargos was caught a bit by surprise; he had thought Brant was done. And, as a result, he was not suspecting Brant's next move. Sending some aura energy into his right leg, Brant kicked out in a sideways arc, hoping to connect solidly with the side of the warden's left leg. His right foot slammed into the side of Bargos's knee, flipping his leg out from under him with such power that it flung his body into the air. He came down hard, landing on his side. The warden screamed in pain, stunned, as Brant pounced on him, straddling him with his powerful legs and bringing both fists down on his head again and again.

Bargos, despite his damaged knee, had enough sense to raise his arms to block the blows from striking his face. He had never felt such strength in one so young; each fist enhanced by aura energy, smashing into his forearms as he tried to protect his face. Bargos roared with fury, reached up with his strong arms and latched onto Brant's neck, pulling him in to close the distance and take away his advantage by disabling Brant's ability to use his fists. Then he did something that Brant had never seen before. He pulled Brant toward him and lifted his good leg up and around Brant's neck, simultaneously gripping Brant's right wrist and spinning him to the side. Before Brant could realize what happened he was face down in the dirt, his head wrapped in Bargos's strong legs, while his arm was held, tightly twisted in Bargos's powerful grip. The warden screamed in anger and with the intensity of his effort as he arched his back, exerting extreme pressure on Brant's elbow and shoulder.

Now it was Brant's turn to scream. He felt his arm flex under the strain, but he could do nothing. He tried to pulse aura energy into his arm, but he could not concentrate enough through the pain. His arm was going to break, he had no doubt.

"Do you submit?!" Bargos growled through clenched teeth.

Bannerfall

Brant held on for a few more moments, but he knew almost immediately that Bargos was going to break his arm, ending the fight. "Yes!" he yelled. "I submit!"

The intense pain vanished as Bargos released his hold and scooted away. The crowd yelled and cheered, clearly excited and pleased with the fight. The warden slowly stood on his one good leg while Brant got to his knees, his right arm hanging limply at his side. Bargos reached down with his hand, smiling for the first time. "You're a tough kid."

Brant said nothing, but gripped his hand as the warden helped him to his feet, the crowd still howling in excitement. "I've never seen a move like that," Brant stammered through deep breaths, slowly moving his right arm to make sure it wasn't seriously injured.

"I should think not," was all Bargos said before limping away into the crowd.

Kulvar Rand strode toward Brant. "How is your arm?"

"I'm not sure. It doesn't seem to be broken. But it sure feels like it."

"I imagine so. You did well."

"It doesn't feel like it," Brant murmured, smiling wanly.

"You fought a warden. It shouldn't have lasted that long. We need to talk."

"What about?"

"You will find out soon enough. The Dygon Guard is camped just outside the camp. Meet me there shortly."

Brant nodded. "I'll be there," he said, apprehensive but curious.

Brant found their camp easily enough and several perimeter guards, recognizing him from the fight, escorted him to Kulvar Rand's tent. When he entered Kulvar was at a small desk going through some papers. He looked up when Brant entered and motioned for him to sit in a chair opposite him.

"Care for a drink?"

Brant was still sore and thirsty from the fight. "Yes, sir."

Kulvar poured some yellow juice from a pitcher at his table. "It is amayis juice, have you had it before?"

Brant had not, although he had heard of it. It was a fruit that came from the southern reaches of Belorth. They did not receive any luxuries in the camp, nor did they have the coin to purchase any even if they did. "I have not."

"It is tart but refreshing, with just a hint of sweetness. I think you will enjoy it."

Brant took a sip and smiled. Kulvar was right. It was delicious. His mouth puckered slightly at first and then the acidic taste melted away and was replaced by a honey-like sweetness. It was absolutely delicious and Brant took another long quaff. "It's amazing."

Kulvar smiled. "Let us get to business." Brant sat up straighter, sensing the serious change in the warrior's demeanor. "Young man, you did something today that could get you into some serious trouble."

Brant narrowed his eyes and set the cup back down on the table. *He did something? How can he say that*, Brant thought? His father had just died and he had been forced to pay off his debt by fighting a trained warden. Why would *he* be in trouble? His anger began to rise. "What do you mean?" he said guardedly.

Kulvar blinked and turned on his towd, or aura sight, noticing clearly that Brant's aura had instantly changed from a calm yellow to a wavy red. Kulvar was a Merger, a born Aurit like his father before him, and he had been trained how to use and control it. His father, the lord of House Rand, a powerful family from Tanwen, had steered Kulvar into warden training at a young age, and by the time he had turned twenty three he had already made it through the advanced warden training and had become a Dygon Guard. You didn't have to have the Way to be a warden, but you needed it to become a Dygon Guard. And Kulvar was the best, not just with the blade, but there was no Merger he had yet met that could match him in strength. "Calm yourself, young man, you are not in any trouble...at least not from me."

Brant relaxed a bit, but only slightly. "I don't understand."

Kulvar leaned forward and looked into Brant's penetrating gaze, his own black eyes equally intense. "Brant, you are a Merger. Do you know what that is?"

Brant sat back in his chair. He had heard the word before, but only in idle gossip from other miners, and he wasn't exactly sure what it meant. "I've heard the word. But I do not really know its meaning."

"It means you are an Aurit. You were born with the ability to control your aura, to harness it to give you more strength. These abilities are very rare outside the noble families, and in fact illegal in many kingdoms throughout Corvell and Belorth. In Gilia or Layona,

Bannerfall

you would be hunted down and killed. So I'm trying to warn you. Use this power sparingly, and be careful when you do."

Brant's mind was spinning. So that was what it was called. He was a Merger, and the power he was accessing was his aura. "What is an aura and how did you know I had this ability?"

"For one, I could tell when you fought Bargos. That throw was powerful, and your punches stunned even the mighty Bargos. And that kick to your chin should have knocked you out, yet you were able to shake it off. I suspect that even he knows there is something special about you. On top of that, I am able to perceive your aura when I so choose. It is not so difficult to recognize the use of the Way in one's aura." Kulvar took a sip of his amayis juice. "As far as your aura, well that is difficult to explain. Every person has an aura, an energy field around their bodies. Some think it is part of our soul, others think it is given to us by Argon and Felina, while still others believe it is simply left over energy from the source that keeps us alive and moving. I do not know. But there are only a relative few who possess the Way, the ability to control this aura, and that gift has been carefully guarded within the noble families of Corvell and even Belorth. Some can channel their aura energy into their muscles, giving them enhanced strength and speed and some can even send this energy into their weapons. These people are like you and I. They are Mergers."

"You are a Merger?"

"I am. All Dygon Guards must be Mergers, which is why we are all from noble houses. You see, this power is carefully guarded, kept within the royal lineages through hundreds of years of marriage and breeding among the noble families. That is why we are not allowed to marry outside the noble families. But there are occasions when noble men and women break these laws, sometimes producing a common bastard who has the Way. And, as I said, any common boy or girl exhibiting these powers is usually hunted down and killed. In some kingdoms, like Dy'ain, they are not, at least as long as House Dormath has been in charge. Previous ruling houses had not all shared their sentiments, but, even with House Dormath ruling Dy'ain, their powers are still seen as a threat and such individuals are often shunned, banned, or even persecuted. Let's just say that it would not be in your best interest if others found out about your ability. You may be banished from the kingdom, or even worse, imprisoned."

"But I've done nothing wrong."

Bannerfall

Kulvar smiled dismissively. "It matters not. You're power is a threat to the ruling houses."

"So why are you telling me this?"

"I like you. You have courage. And just because I'm of noble blood does not mean I agree with everything the aristocracy believes. I personally believe that if Argon and Felina saw fit to gift you with such power, that it must be for a reason. Who am I to deny the desires of the gods?"

Brant was not a religious man. It was hard for him to believe in gods that seemed to allow so many injustices in the world. The camps were not really a place where the topic of religion was discussed, but he did know that most people in Corvell would consider themselves Argonians, though some still worshipped the old gods. Clearly Kulvar Rand was Argonian.

"You said that Mergers can channel their aura into their weapons. How is this done?"

"Very carefully," Kulvar said with a smile. "It takes some time to learn how to do this without destroying the blade. But once mastered the one who possesses such a skill can become a formidable warrior. Have you ever wondered why Kul-brite metal is so costly?"

"I thought it was because it was so rare, and of course strong."

"Partly so, but the real value of the metal comes from its properties. It is the only metal able to withstand the power of aura energy. But even Kul-brite has its limitations. A really powerful Merger may produce enough energy to burn even a Kul-brite blade. One must learn to control that kind of power. If I were to channel my energy into a regular sword, the metal would heat up and break very quickly. Or if the Merger was particularly powerful he could produce enough energy to completely incinerate the blade. But Kul-brite steel can withstand the intense power, especially if the Merger can control it, making the weapon itself even more powerful. Lords and kings all across the lands will pay exorbitant amounts for a Kul-brite blade or armor."

Brant's eyes widened in surprise. "Armor? I can't imagine how expensive that would be," he muttered to himself. Of course he had seen small amounts of Kul-brite metal, and he knew the value of just those small nuggets, making it almost incomprehensible to imagine a full suit of armor made from it.

"Only a king could afford such a thing," Kulvar agreed. "How long have you been using this power?"

Bannerfall

"I guess since I was sixteen."

"Have you started having hallucinations yet?"

Brant frowned. "Hallucinations? You mean seeing things?"

"Yes, but more like tracers...like a colorful flickering of lights surrounding people."

Brant shook his head. "Nothing like that."

"That may come soon. Once you begin to really unlock the power, you will start to see the auras of people around you. The ability to see the auras of others is known as the towd, which is how I knew you were a Merger, since I have that ability. You must learn to control this or it will overwhelm you. Imagine seeing dancing colors around every person surrounding you. It can be disorientating unless you learn to shut off your towd."

"But how do I learn to do this?"

"I cannot teach you this during a casual conversation. It is something you will have to learn to do on your own. All I can tell you is that you need to find something on which to concentrate, a focal point to distract you, and once you can train your mind to focus on that, then you can turn your towd on and off at will. This requires some mental training and practice." Kulvar Rand paused for a moment, giving Brant some time to let everything sink in. "Now, I'm afraid I do not have the time to teach you more about Aurit abilities. I have a shipment moving out tomorrow and preparations to complete," Kulvar said as he grabbed a small bag on the table and tossed it to Brant. "In the bag is some coin." Brant was just about to ask him about it when Kulvar waved him off. "Do not fret. You fought hard and will need it to survive. It is nothing to me but may be everything to you." Brant was thankful, knowing that it was not part of the deal. Kulvar Rand had only promised to pay his debt. There was to be no extra coin unless he had won the fight, which he had not. "Remember what I said, be careful and use your power sparingly and only when there is desperate need. I wish you luck, young man."

Brant picked up the bag of coins as he rose to his feet. "I appreciate your help," he said, offering his hand, "thank you."

Kulvar shook it. "If I may give you a suggestion I would recommend you stay away from the big cities. Go to the small towns near Kreb or Tanwen, try to find work as a laborer. Many farmers will be planting soon and you may find work with them."

Bannerfall

Brant nodded. "Thanks again." Then he turned and walked out the tent, his mind a whirlwind of thoughts. He was apprehensive and excited at the same time. What would he do? Where would he go? He had no idea, but that in itself was exciting. For once his day would not be planned for him. For once he would not be wielding a pick or hammer from dawn until dusk. The road before him was unknown, but he smiled, welcoming the uncertainty, as he walked back to the mining camp, eager to grab his few belongings and start his new life.

Chapter 2

The Way; not much is known about the origin of these mysterious powers. Some say the first known accounts of the Way came soon after the Great Change, but I have seen written accounts of similar powers going back five cyns before that. Argonians believe the power was gifted to them by Argon and Felina, but I tend to believe the origins of the Way are not that simple. It seems to me that this ability may be something innate that has evolved over time, which also leads me to think that the Way is not a god given power. I know it is sacrilege to speak of such things, but as an historian I must look at the picture through an unbiased lens, putting the pieces together until the puzzle is solved.

It is now known that the Helnians have a similar power. They call it The Fury, and when their warriors utilize the power in combat, they become frenzied combatants with great strength and speed. We do not know much about The Fury, but the Saricons believe it was given to them by Heln, just as the Argonians believe that the Way was a blessing from Argon and Felina. My educated mind of course says that they both cannot be right; therefore the source of these powers must lie elsewhere.

We do know some things about the Way. We know that those who are gifted with this ability will fit into one of four different categories, either an Aura Mage, a Merger, a Channeler, or a Sapper. The unique skills of each category vary, depending on the inner strength of the person possessing them. Thus, the Way will be stronger in some than in others. We know that there has never been any accounts of a female Merger, although we have little idea why. I have spent countless evenings reading, researching, and writing about this topic, but I'm afraid I have answered very few questions about the true origins of the Way. I'm convinced, however, that with time, we will learn more about the intricacies of the Way. I may not be the one who finds the answers, but hopefully my work will be a part of the process.

Journal entry 21
Kivalla Der'une, Historian, Keeper of the records in Cythera, capital of Dy'ain

Bannerfall

5088, the 14th cyn after the Great Change

    Prince Jarak Dormath was moving slowly through the throngs of people in Market Square, his towd turned on, concentrating on those closest to him as he passed, looking for intricacies within their auras. He was *tasking*, slowly pulling small amounts of energy from each person, and storing it in his *tarnum*, a place Jarak had created in his abdomen. One's tarnum was not really a place, it was simply a focal point, in which to briefly store the energy before it would be released in the form of a spell. Some Aura Mages created their tarnums in their chests, or even their heads, but always it was considered their center, a place to concentrate on the energy they were about to release.

    Nearly eighteen, Jarak was still a young, inexperienced Aura Mage, but being the heir to House Dormath meant that his Aurit powers were strong. His training had started when the Way had emerged at the age of fourteen. He remembered how difficult tasking had been nearly four years ago, but now he was able to concentrate on just the people nearby, shutting out the others and preventing himself from being overwhelmed by all the other auras around him. The first time he had tried to task, he had eventually collapsed in exhaustion, overwhelmed by the hundreds of auras assaulting him at once. His towd had shut down automatically, a built in fail safe to prevent him from passing out, or causing other permanent bodily damage. After that first attempt he ended up with a headache that lasted for days.

    "Watch out for the burning aura on your left," Serix said from behind. Serix Rilonan was one of two brothers of House Rilonan, an influential noble house from Kreb. He was a powerful Aura Mage who had been given the job of training Jarak, a job he had begun four years earlier and would continue until Jarak turned twenty one.

    Serix was dressed in the clothing of a common trader, allowing him to blend in with the people that frequented Market Square. He was of average height, though quite thin. His hair, too, was a nondescript pale brown, long and straight and pulled back behind his ears and held in place by the typical wide brimmed hat of a farmer. His thin face was dark, tanned by the sun. Brown eyes, a straight nose, and thin lips complemented his unassuming face.

    Jarak too was wearing clothes typical of a trader; gray wool trousers, a heavy wool coat, and a worn and tattered farmer's hat similar to the one Serix wore. Their goal today was to practice tasking, and that would be almost impossible if anyone recognized either of them. Prince Dormath, however, was far from unassuming. His hair was a rich darker brown, long, thick, and wavy, and despite his relative youth he had already managed a decent growth of stubble. Jarak's features were handsome, with a prominent narrow nose and a strong chin and jawline. His large hazel eyes and long thick eyelashes would make any princess jealous. And even his plain clothing could not completely disguise his strong, athletic frame.

Jarak quickly glanced to his left, and saw the fiery red aura on a young man striding quickly by him. His aura was dancing brightly, and near the man's skin it was turning a dark red, nearly black. The man was obviously angry, or perhaps consumed by negative thoughts, and Jarak did not want to inadvertently take any of his aura. It was always dangerous for an Aura Mage to use negative energies, as the negative influences of those energies, over time, could cause physical and mental changes in the mage, or result in sickness, even death. That was why, under conditions where negative energies were abundant, like combat, an Aura Mage almost always needed to be working with a Channeler, someone with the ability to take in and filter the energy of other's auras. Channelers were similar to an Aura Mage, but they did not have the ability to convert the energy into spells. All they can do is take in the aura energy, filter it, converting it into a clean source of power, and store it briefly for an Aura Mage to use. If there were no mage available to harness the power, the Channeler would have to dissipate the energy into the ground, or risk being consumed by it. A powerful Channeler and Aura Mage working together were a deadly combination. Jarak circumvented the burning aura, blocking its energy and continued tasking from others whose auras were clean.

"How does your tarnum feel?" Serix asked as he moved next to Jarak.

"Good, but nearly full."

"Shut off your towd and concentrate on the energy in your tarnum. Keep it stored until we make it back to the palace," Serix ordered.

"All the way back?" Jarak asked, a bit worried.

"Yes. You can do it. Focus and push in with your own aura. Keep the energy in place until we make it back."

Morlock's balls, Jarak though. "I will do my best," Jarak said, not really confident that he could perform the task.

Bannerfall

Sensing his concern Serix tried to reassure him. "You can do it. Trust me."

Jarak was already anxiously focusing on the task, and his tarnum was beginning to build up heat. The walk back to the palace was five city blocks, and that was a long time to keep a large amount of energy stored in one's tarnum. Aura energy, like all energy wants to be used. And now it felt as if it were expanding inside him, ready to burst out and be released. The longer he held it, the more painful it became. But, as they moved their way through the streets, he worked on his concentration, focusing on his own aura, and using it to form a wall around his tarnum like he had been taught, and keeping the energy there. After several blocks, the tall towers of the inner palace rose above the buildings surrounding them, beckoning him on as his tarnum continued to burn in his gut.

"Almost there," Serix reassured him, knowing from experience how uncomfortable Jarak was feeling.

A couple more blocks brought them to the palace's north entrance. The portcullis was down, blocking the entrance. The inner castle was protected by a thirty foot wall, and the barbican protecting the gate and portcullis was sturdy and strong, constructed of massive blocks of gray granite.

Two Sentinels, the elite palace guards, stood before the portcullis in full armor, carrying long spears with swords at their hips, their gold capes wrapped around their shoulders. More Sentinels walked the walls, peering out from the battlements at the large bustling city below. The palace, built hundreds of years ago when the city was ruled by House Banrothus, was positioned on top of a hill directly in the middle of the vast city. Cythera was the largest city in all of Dy'ain, and perhaps even Corvell. The Kul-brite mines brought incredible amounts of wealth to the city, and to House Dormath.

Serix and Jarak took off their hats and the two Sentinels recognized them immediately. One guard yelled to a Sentinel on the barbican. "Open the portcullis! The prince has returned!"

Jarak and Serix moved inside quickly as the gate reversed direction, once again sealing the inner palace from the city. The courtyard was mostly empty, although a handful of Sentinels and servants went about their daily chores. Inside the walls was a magnificent palace. The palace was U shaped, the open end facing the main gate they had just entered. The royal residence consisted of three stories and contained over fifty rooms. Immaculate gardens, manicured lawns, and a copse of fruit trees filled the inner courtyard between the two wings of the palace. A straight stone path directed visitors to a series of wide steps which led to a large covered entryway. Colossal white stone columns flanking two huge oak doors marked the entrance; the entire expanse of the massive double door was a carved depiction of the symbol of House Dormath, two swords crossed over a mountain peak. Other stone paths branched from the main one, meandering through the gardens and trees, forming an intricate pattern of walkways from which one could enjoy the spectacular botanical views of exotic plants and flowers that had been collected from kingdoms near and far. On either side of the palace were storerooms, an armory, a smithy, stables, and the barracks for the two hundred Sentinels that guarded the king and his family at all times,

"Okay," Serix announced as he walked up behind the prince. "I want you to create a fire chain where you release the flames in six bursts, the first one reaching five paces and continuing one pace further for each consecutive burst. Imagine an enemy at the end of each burst, and each time the fire chain reaches its target, create an intense explosion. You ready?"

Prince Jarak nodded his head and planted his feet wide. He could have just released the energy harmlessly, leaching it into the ground through his feet. But he knew that Serix would not allow that, that he would want him to practice some sort of offensive spell. His tarnum was burning and he desperately wanted to release the energy stored there, but he had to control it in order to do as Serix instructed. Gritting his teeth, he closed his eyes briefly and concentrated on his tarnum, visualizing the fire chain as he slowly moved his arms in a graceful circular pattern. Instantly fire burst from his hands, and as his arms moved the fire pushed out, forming rope-like appendages of intense white hot fire. The ropes seemed to dance around him like fire whips, then, after concentrating on the task, he pushed out with his right hand, the fire rope lashing out fifteen paces and exploding in a shower of flames. He followed suit with his left arm, sending another fiery chain forward, exploding another pace further from the last. In less than twenty heartbeats he had successfully launched six bursts of fire, each one moving further away and ending in a brief explosion; the last burst, however, was less than stellar as he had run out of energy.

Bannerfall

Once he had released all the energy, his hands dropped like lead and he took a long deep breath as his body adjusted to the loss of power. Serix walked over to him and placed his hand on his shoulder.

"Good, Jarak, but where did you err?"

Jarak thought for a moment. He was happy with his performance, but he was pretty sure he knew the answer. "At the end, I did not have enough energy for a proper explosion. I used too much at the beginning."

"That's correct. You were so eager to release the energy that you used too much at the start. It would not do to have incinerated five of your enemies only to leave one at the end to finish you off. Learn to adjust the release of power. Do not be so eager to get rid of the very thing that may save your life." Serix patted him on the shoulder. "That was well done though. I know it was painful for you to contain that much energy."

"Perhaps less painful than a sword blade," Jarak added, clearly realizing the importance of the lesson.

Serix smiled. "That is true. That is enough for the day. You are excused."

Prince Jarak bowed his head slightly. "Thank you, Master Serix."

The prince was more than happy to be finished with his lesson. Although he enjoyed his time with Serix, he was getting tired of all the classes and training required of him. He smiled as he made his way through the palace grounds towards his quarters. It was nearly dark and he had plans for the night. He knew he should study as he had a history exam tomorrow, but he didn't care. Tonight he was going to have some fun.

Later that evening, Prince Jarak crept quickly and quietly down the long hallway, being careful not to alert the palace guards. It would not do to be caught roaming the halls when he should be in his chambers. The young Prince of Dy'ain and heir to House Dormath was not yet eighteen, and therefore had to abide by his father's rules, one of which was to remain inside the palace after the sun had set. Prince Jarak, however, chafed at such restrictions, and in this, his eighteenth year, had developed the habit of sneaking out at night to visit the local taverns and brothels. And though he tried to disguise himself, more often than not he was recognized for who he was, which caused significant embarrassment for House Dormath, and unpleasant consequences for Jarak. The combination of a little freedom and a little ale often led to some poor decisions. If he were fortunate enough to not be recognized he would often be drawn into a barroom brawl. More often, however, he would find himself spending exorbitant amounts of his father's gold in the city's most exclusive brothels. His behavior was not very princely, and his father had repeatedly scolded and threatened him, until finally he had assigned two of his personal guards to follow him around like his shadow. But after three months of good behavior, his father had called off his babysitters, and Jarak had waited all of one night before taking advantage of his new freedom.

With eager anticipation he was on the prowl again, but this time he wanted some company, a partner in crime. So he was heading two floors below, to the room of his tutor, and for the last ten years, his close friend as well. He had been bored out of his mind the last few months, occupying his days with his mandatory classes, which to him seemed endless and pointless. Why would he ever need to know how many bags of grain would be needed to feed a thousand men, or how long the grain would last before it spoiled? After all, he would soon be king, and he would have someone else more knowledgeable on the subject make those decisions for him. But he did enjoy the riding and weapons training, which were his only escapes from the countless classes that his station seemed to require of him. He was an excellent rider, and his lithe but muscular frame made him a decent swordsman. Still, the sword drills and daily rides were not enough to satisfy the prince's restless spirit. Even his Aurit lessons with Serix did little to calm him. Despite the energy and concentration needed to master the complicated skills of an Aura Mage, the lessons, though mentally and physically taxing, did little to tire the exuberant youth. And so, he would typically blow off some steam in one of the local taverns, or in the arms of a buxom lady at the Black Cat. But after he had been caught several times those evening escapes from his daily drudgery disappeared like a noble's coin in the Stye, the poorest and most dangerous section of Cythera, the capital city of Dy'ain.

To get to Rath's room he couldn't go through the halls as he was sure to run into guards who were stationed all over the castle, especially at anterooms that acted as hubs for the many halls that connected the two wings and three levels of the castle. The layout was purposeful as there was no way any intruder could gain access to the wings and upper levels without passing through the anterooms, all of which were guard bases for the Sentinels, House Dormath's elite guards.

But the prince had another idea. He was running barefoot so his boots wouldn't be heard on the dark smooth stone that covered the corridor's floors. He quietly slid to a stop outside a guest room that he knew to be empty.

The polished stone used throughout the castle was extremely rare, with veins of gold and silver running throughout it. It was worth more than the total wealth of most kingdoms, testament to the wealth of House Dormath. There was no other location in all of Corvell, or even Belorth for that matter, that controlled Kul-brite mines as productive as the mines that existed in the Devlin Mountains. And whoever controlled Kul-brite steel controlled nearly everything else. The rare metal was used to forge Kul-brite blades, blades capable of containing the aura energy produced by a Merger, like his father and grandfather before him. Experienced and powerful Mergers could even cause their swords to flare and burn with this fiery energy, or in rare cases, even propel flames from their blade for short distances. But Jarak was not a Merger like his father; he was an Aura Mage. He had started his training at a young age and was already becoming quite proficient in his inherent skill. Aura Mages could pull the aura energies from people around them and manipulate the energy into various forms. Skilled mages could harness this energy, creating both offensive and defensive spells.

Jarak was unarmed except for his short sword, a weapon given to him by his father when he had turned sixteen. Most Aura Mages were not always particularly skilled with a blade since most of their time was spent learning the mental intricacies of working with aura energy. But Jarak was taught by Serix Rilonan who was a talented sword wielder in his own right. He had always directed Jarak to learn another skill and to not rely on his innate abilities in combat. The young prince enjoyed swordplay and had found that it was a great way to relieve the mental stress associated with learning the craft of a mage. He also carried his Mage Stone, given to him by Serix when he had turned sixteen. These rare red gemstones were capable of storing aura energy. Serix was believed to be the most powerful Aura Mage in Dy'ain and had created the stone for him. It was capable of storing enough energy for at least one offensive or defensive spell. Serix had commissioned an artisan to set the stone into a beautifully handcrafted silver belt buckle, the same buckle worn on the belt now holding his short sword. Along with his blade, the young prince wore simple breeches, a faded gray tunic, and a coarse wool over-shirt, hoping that he would blend in well with the common folk.

With his boots slung over his shoulder, he quietly shuffled into the vacant guestroom and quickly shut the door. The spacious room was beautifully furnished, befitting a royal guest, but Jarak paid little attention to the rich accoutrements as he quickly, but silently, made his way towards the balcony and out to the carved stone railing. He reached into his tunic and pulled out a long rope, quickly tying one end around the sturdy stone railing and tossing the other over the edge. He had previously tied knots at regular intervals into the rope, allowing him to scurry down the rope like a skulking rat. Jarak used his legs to gently rock back and forth, causing the rope to sway until he was swinging over the balcony of Rath's room. His bare feet gripped the stone railing and pulled him over onto the balcony, leaving the rope in place so he could return the way he had come. The glass door into Rath's room was not locked and Jarak entered like a mist, his bare feet making not a sound.

"Rath," Jarak whispered as he quickly tip toed over to the young man sleeping soundly in the bed against the wall. Rath was born into the noble family of a minor lord who owned land along the northern sections of the Pelm River west of the Devlin Mountains. He had exhibited a precocious intelligence at an early age, and when he turned eight his father had sent him to Cythera for schooling, where he quickly advanced through the most difficult classes. It was not long before he caught the attention of the school's headmaster. So, when House Dormath came and requested a tutor for the young prince, Rath's name had been at the top of the list. King Enden Dormath was looking for a smart young man, a little older than Jarak, someone capable enough to provide a sound education for his son, but young enough to be able to relate well with the prince. Rath was two years older than Jarak, and appeared in all other ways to be a perfect match. Although Rath was older, he did not look it. Where Jarak was tall and his body was quickly maturing into that of a young man, Rath was slight of build, with the softer look of a young boy. But despite their physical differences, they had developed a strong friendship over the years. "Rath," Jarak whispered again, as he sat down on the bed, gently shaking his body to wake him.

"What," Rath moaned sleepily, rolling over and slowly opening his eyes. "Jarak…what are you doing here?" He sat up slowly and rubbed his tired eyes. "Your father is going to kill you."

"He won't punish us because he will never find out," Jarak said with a mischievous smile.

This time Rath scooted up in bed and shook his head vehemently. "Oh no, *we* aren't doing anything. Besides, you have an exam tomorrow. I am not getting suckered into another nighttime adventure," Rath said adamantly. Rath had chestnut brown hair that was cut short and close above his ears. His large round eyes, almost coal black, contrasted sharply with his smooth olive skin. His features were sharp, but delicate, almost feminine, which contributed to his boyish appearance.

"Rath, I am your prince and I am ordering you to come with me. Father cannot get mad at you if you don't have a choice," Jarak said as he stood up. "Now hurry up and get dressed. I have some coin that is burning a hole in my pocket."

Rath shook his head defiantly. "Yes, I do have a choice. Last time we got caught Master Fallon threatened to kick me out of school." Rath took various classes at the school working around his schedule as the prince's tutor. He had less than a year to go before he graduated. "I will not take another chance like that. Besides, your father, the *king*, has more authority than you."

Jarak turned toward Rath and smiled, putting his hands on his hips confidently. "Rath, you know as well as I do that Master Fallon could never kick you out of that school if I wished you to stay, and besides, we will not get caught this time. I promise I will be good. Now get up. That's an order."

Rath was obstinate, and he crossed his arms and looked away, avoiding the young prince's gaze.

"Besides…I know you want to come with me anyway. I have coin enough for both of us. And guess who will be at the Black Cat tonight?" Jarak teased with an upraised eyebrow. Rath didn't move his head, but his eyes betrayed his resolve and they pivoted with interest in Jarak's direction. "That lovely redhead, Tayna, and I know how much you like her." Jarak was not really sure if she would be working tonight, but he hoped that the information, even if false, would be enough to persuade Rath to join him.

Rath slowly turned and faced Jarak, and once he saw Jarak's toothy grin and determined gaze, his stoic defiance melted, revealing the eager youth that he was. "Okay, but we can't stay out for long and you have to promise to keep your audacious behavior under control."

"My what?"

Exasperated, Rath threw up his hands in frustration and got out of bed. "Just be good...do you understand *that*!?"

"Do not worry, my friend. I will be on my best behavior."

Rath was quietly moving about putting on his clothes. "That's what I'm afraid of... your *best* behavior often leaves something to be desired."

Jarak stood up straight and crossed his arms firmly. "Not tonight. You have my word."

Rath was now sitting on the edge of the bed pulling on his heavy leather boots. He was clever enough to choose clothing similar to Jaraks, knowing full well that where they were going they needed to blend in. Finally he stood and grabbed a heavy long sleeved wool shirt. "Okay, lead the way."

Jarak smiled and ran out to the balcony.

Getting out of the palace was a bit trickier than getting to Rath's room. But this was not the first time they had accomplished it, and luckily for them Jarak's route had not yet been discovered. The palace grounds had numerous trees, and one in particular had grown quite large, with one of its branches reaching out and hanging over the eastern wall. It was impossible for someone on the outside to take advantage of this, but from the inside one could easily climb the tree from the inside and move out onto the thick branch, and drop to the wall several paces below. Jarak had stashed a rope in the tree's branches, and after making sure there were no guards nearby, he tied it to one of the many iron rungs embedded into the outside of the castle wall every five feet. The rungs were used to attach ladders to when the walls needed to be repaired or cleaned. They were placed just on the outside of the battlements, which enabled the boys to easily step onto the raised battlement, and climb down the knotted rope. Even Rath, who was not overly strong, had no problem descending the rope. The only possible problem would be that a guard might spot the rope. But it was unlikely as they seldom patrolled the wall from the outside.

Bannerfall

They made their way through the city, heading towards the Black Cat, a brothel located a block from the Stye, which was definitely a place they did not want to venture at this time of night.

It wasn't all that late and the city was just coming alive. During the day, Cythera bustled with activity as people worked and traded their wares. Thousands of merchants, farmers, and craftsmen, swarmed into the city to sell their goods at Market Square. During the lull when the merchants left, people prepared their suppers and settled in for the night. However, as evening deepened, a whole new group of people emerged, and not all of them were out for fun and entertainment. So they stuck to the well-traveled routes, meandering through busy streets, and looking into the empty shops as they made their way to their destination.

As Rath passed a bakery, the delightful aroma of sweet bread slowed his steps. "Hey, Jarak, let's get a few sweet rolls for the walk."

Jarak had also caught a whiff of the pleasant aroma and didn't need much convincing. "Good idea," he said as he opened the door and entered the establishment. The place was small, with room for a few empty tables arranged before a small counter covered with freshly baked rolls, meat pies, and sweets. There was a door that went to the back where Jarak guessed the kitchen and baking oven were located. At the counter, laying out some steaming sweet rolls, was a young girl about their age. Her flour covered baker's apron failed to fully conceal the subtle curves of her body. Wisps of auburn hair had escaped the confines of her baking hat, and clung to her glistening face. She had clearly just been back by the oven, and perspiration gave her smooth olive skin a warm glow, which was further complemented by her bright hazel eyes and full lips.

"What can I do for you this evening?" she asked, setting the now empty tray down on a counter behind her.

Rath was eyeing the warm rolls, but Jarak paid them no heed, as he continued to gaze at the young woman behind the counter. "I'd like two of your freshly baked sweet breads," Rath replied as he dug into his coin purse. "How much?"

"A tigg each," she said, taking a pre-cut piece of paper and placing two steaming rolls on it. She gave Rath the rolls as he handed her the two coins. "And for you?" she asked, glancing at Jarak.

"Your name please," he said with a confident smile.

"That will be...," she paused, clearly confused by what he said. "What?"

"I'd like your name, Miss."

Rath rolled his eyes, bit into one of the rolls, and stepped out of Jarak's way.

The baker shyly hesitated then said, "My name is Landria."

"It is very nice to meet you. Landria is a very beautiful name. I am Jarak."

Landria smiled, blushing slightly. "Can I get you something to eat, Jarak?"

"Of course. What here was made by you?"

"My mother makes most of it. But I did bake these sugar sticks," she said as she pointed to four pastries, each one looking like a mini braid, coated with caramelized sugar and dusted with some sort of reddish brown powder.

"They look fabulous. What is that sprinkled on top of them?"

"Nutmeg."

"I will take all four of them," Jarak announced.

Landria smiled, taking the pastries and wrapping them in brown paper. "That will be four tiggs please."

Jarak reached into his coin purse and withdrew two silver shikes, handing the coins to her.

"That is too much, sir," she said, handing the coins back to him as Jarak took the pastries with his other hand.

He knew it was too much. One silver shike was equivalent to five copper tiggs, and he had just given her more than double the amount that he owed. He put his hand up, refusing to accept the coins. "Keep them. It is a small price to pay for a glimpse of beauty."

She smiled, pausing, unsure of how to react to such a bold comment. "Thank you, sir, but my mo..."

"It was a pleasure to meet you," Jarak said, smiling flirtatiously. Then he stepped back, bowing slightly, and added, "Until we meet again, Landria." Then he turned and left, Rath close on his heels.

As they shut the door behind them, Rath stepped over to Jarak. "A small price to pay for a glimpse of beauty?" he mimicked.

"Watch and learn, my good friend. She will be thinking of me for days. Now, let us have some real fun."

Bannerfall

They walked another block when Jarak suddenly stopped, forcing Rath to follow suit and look back at him, his mouth full of sweet bread. "What is it?" Rath mumbled.

Jarak ignored him and walked down a side street, the darkness of the shadowed alley swallowing him completely.

Rath moved quickly to see what he was doing. When he neared him he noticed that he was squatting next to a young boy who was huddled in a door jam, his bony arms wrapped tightly around his body. Rath smelt the urchin before he even saw him. He must have been around eight. His hair was greasy, the tousled brown locks tangled like a rat's nest. The boy's face and bear arms were smudged with dirt and he was clearly hungry, cold, and scared.

"What is your name?" Jarak asked as he knelt before the boy. The boy said nothing, his large eyes wide with fright. "Don't worry, I won't hurt you. Here, do you want some food?" Jarak held out one of the sugar sticks. Clearly starving, the boy reached out quickly and took the food, shoving it into his mouth and swallowing it in several great gulps. "Now, what is your name?"

"Korben," the boy responded shyly.

"Where are your parents?"

"My papa died."

Jarak figured that his mother was not around for whatever reason. "Do you have anywhere to go?"

"Jarak," Rath said. "There are many kids like this in the Stye. We can't help them all."

Again, Jarak ignored him. "Korben, my name is Jarak and I'm going to give you something. Then I am going to give you a quest. Do you know what a quest is?"

Korben shook his head no.

"It's like an adventure…do you know what that is?" This time Korben nodded his head. "Good. I'm going to give you this ring," he said as he took off his gold ring.

"Jarak, you can't give him your signet ring," Rath quickly added. His signet ring bore the symbol of House Dormath and represented great power and wealth. The gold and jewel value of the ring alone was quite large, but the real value came from the fact that whoever held it had the full backing of House Dormath.

This time Jarak did acknowledge him, turning to face Rath with a steely gaze. "I can, and I will." Then he turned back to Korben. "Now, this ring is very valuable but you can't sell it. I want you to go to the temple at the end of Main Street and ask for a man named Toth. Give him this ring and tell him that Prince Jarak has ordered that you be housed, bathed, and fed. He will take care of you. Do you understand?"

Korben nodded his head quickly, looking at the gold ring with open amazement. "I understand."

"Good. Now repeat back to me your quest."

"I am to take your ring and go to the temple at the end of Main Street. Once there I need to find a man named Toth and give him your ring."

"And?" Jarak coaxed.

"And tell him that you ordered him to take care of me," Korben answered quickly.

"Very good. Now, you must do what I say. If you sell this ring I will know and you will be in a lot of trouble. Do you believe me?"

Korben nodded his head vigorously.

"Good." Jarak handed the young boy the ring and stood up. "Now be off with you and make haste."

Korben smiled for the first time, jumped up and ran out of the alley.

"Do you think he will sell the ring?" Rath asked.

"No. He wouldn't even know where to sell it. I think he will do as instructed."

"That was very kind of you."

Jarak winked at him. "Don't tell anyone. They might think I've grown soft."

"And what is wrong with that?" Rath asked as they moved back out to the street.

"Women, my friend, are not attracted to soft men."

Rath shook his head. "Are all your actions rooted in the desire to swoon women?"

"Why of course, I should think that would be obvious by now."

They continued their casual banter, eating most of their remaining treats in the process. It wasn't long before they were standing at the entrance to the Black Cat. The entrance was located down a side alley lit with four torches attached to brackets on the narrow walls facing the door. The thick oak door was painted a deep red, and standing before it was a large man in black leather, with a gray wool cloak draping his broad shoulders, and a long sword dangling from his hip. His unusually large head was shaved clean, revealing two prominent scars, one that went from his left eye to the top of his skull, while the second one crossed perpendicularly over the first, where it ended at his right ear. He would have looked formidable enough without the scars, but with them he looked downright frightening. Which was probably the point, Jarak assumed.

"Banrigar, it is good to see you," Jarak announced.

The big man smiled, shaking his head in disbelief. He knew the prince should not be there. "My Prince, what can I do for you?" The gossip was that Banrigar was a brawler from Hagstead, a large coastal town in the Kingdom of Karak far south and west of Dy'ain. The word was that he was a killer, and Jarak had to admit that he looked the part. But he had always been civil to Jarak, perhaps because he was the prince, or maybe the rumors were untrue. Either way, Jarak had to admit that he liked the man.

This time it was Jarak's turn to smile. "I think you know the answer to that question."

"If the king finds out I let you in," Banrigar said nervously, "there will be no end to my punishment."

"Perhaps this will help," Jarak said as he held out two gold dracks. Jarak knew that that was more coin than Banrigar would make in a week, and he topped off the deal with another incentive. "And you can have my last two pastries."

They had played this game before, and Banrigar's knowing smile suggested he was not yet done bartering. "What of your friend? Rath, right?"

"Yes, sir," Rath said, looking to Jarak, knowing full well that the negotiations were not quite done.

Jarak reached into his coin purse, withdrew a silver shike and handed it to the guard. "I think a silver shall cover my friend."

Banrigar took the coin and stepped aside, opening the heavy oak door. "Have fun, gentlemen. And Jarak, please stay out of trouble. If the king knows you are here I'm afraid we will all feel his wrath."

"Yes, Mother," Jarak scoffed as they entered the building.

The Black Cat was a typical establishment that offered various forms of entertainment. One could consume exotic drinks created from the many different fruits that grew in the various regions of Corvell. One could also taste the exotic flesh of these lands as well. Not literally

Bannerfall

of course, but there were in fact many beautiful women from all over Corvell, and even a few from Belorth, that if one were so inclined, and had the coin, could enjoy a delightful evening with any one of them.

The Black Cat was a fairly upscale establishment, and the interior suggested that the patrons who ventured here were either accustomed to a rather extravagant lifestyle, or they had simply saved enough coin to make the night a special occasion. A large bar occupied the middle of the spacious main room, while the perimeter was filled with many intimate booths and tables, giving the occupants a sense of privacy. Four huge columns, at each corner of the bar, rose all the way to the top of the towering ceiling. Stairs to the left of the bar led to a second story where private rooms could be found if one possessed sufficient coin to afford them.

Jarak and Rath stood just inside the entrance, grinning like children in a sweet shop. "I'll never tire of this place," Jarak whispered, turning to his friend. "Let's get a drink."

There were probably thirty or so people sitting at various tables, lounging at the bar, or just having a good time as they stood or wandered about. About half as many of the occupants were women, wearing only a little more than their wide inviting smiles. They moved gracefully about the room, talking with customers and bartering for their coin. Two musicians sat on a raised platform at one end of the room playing a slow seductive melody, the hypnotic notes drifting lazily throughout the bar. One, a heavy set man, played a black flute like instrument called a tolbin, while the other, a dark haired middle aged woman, gently strummed a small harp. Serving girls dressed in red, low cut tops, and flowing short black skirts, moved about with practiced precision, making sure that all their clients were satisfied and happy.

Jarak and Rath approached the bar, smiling as the beautiful and exotic bartender, a slim raven haired young woman, approached them. "Good evening, what can I..." She stopped mid-sentence as she recognized Jarak.

"Good evening, Eva, it is good to see you again," Jarak said. "May we have a bottle of Gilian Red?"

"My prince, what are you doing here?"

"Why is everyone asking me this? I should think the answer is obvious," Jarak said with mock petulance. He leaned against the bar and scanned the occupants of the chairs nearby. Two men, wearing clothing covered with the dust of travel, sat next to him, drinking a pitcher of ale. Jarak noticed them look over at the mention of *my prince*. "And please, Eva, do not announce my identity for all to hear."

Eva reached below the bar, producing a bottle of the rare and costly wine. "I'm sorry, Pri...I mean Jarak. But you are not supposed to be here." She leaned closer, and they could smell her musky flora scent, and whispered. "The king was very clear about that."

"Let me handle him," Jarak said. "Besides, no blame can come to you. You are simply following the orders of your prince."

She sighed, popped the cork and poured them two glasses of the rare wine. Eva was older than them both, nearly thirty, but her creamy unblemished skin made her look younger. Her shoulder length hair was jet black, which contrasted nicely with her smooth ivory skin and luminous crimson lips, painted with some sort of dark rouge. Her eyes were also surrounded in shadow, a smoky blend of gray and black liner expertly blended and applied, which further accentuated her dark and exotic eyes.

Jarak and Rath grabbed their glasses, along with the dusty bottle of wine. "Is Tayna working tonight?" Jarak asked.

Rath narrowed his eyes at Jarak. "I thought you said she was working tonight."

Jarak drained half of his glass, shrugging his shoulders in mock innocence. "I may have embellished the truth a little."

"She is working," Eva confirmed.

"There you go, she *is* here tonight. So there is nothing to get upset about," Jarak said, relieved to be able to cool Rath's rising anger. "We are going to find a booth. Can you send her over, along with another lady of your choice?"

"My choice? I am the bartender, not the Madame, and I do not know your particular tastes in women."

Jarak looked Eva up and down, smiling wickedly. "Well, find me someone like you, or we could make it easier and *you* could join me."

Eva blushed. "That is not my job, but I will see what I can do."

"Thank you, Eva. It is a pleasure to see you again." Jarak smiled contentedly and turned to find a booth where he and Rath could begin to enjoy the evening.

"Do you always flirt with women?" Rath asked, taking a sip of his wine. "Wow, I forgot how lovely this wine is."

"Just the beautiful ones."

Bannerfall

They found a nearby booth, the soft cushions covered in ruby red velvet thick and soft to the touch. Three candles flickered in the center of their table, casting a soft light that was reflected back into their booth by the tall backs of the seats which enclosed it. They sat down with their wine, gazing out at the motley collection of patrons milling about the establishment.

"You see, this isn't so bad," Jarak said, as he drained the remaining wine from his goblet.

"Not yet, but the night is just beginning."

"You have little faith, my good friend."

"Faith has nothing to do with it. I know you, Jarak. You will drink more, you will get more boisterous, and before you know it we will be in some kind of trouble." Rath gave his friend a serious look. "You know I'm right."

Jarak pursed his lips, nodding his head in affirmation. "Okay, I will admit that what you say has occurred during previous outings. But not tonight. I will keep my drinking under control. I just want to relax with some good wine and enjoy the company of some beautiful women. Is that so much to ask for?"

"For a prince? Yes, it is."

Jarak frowned. "What do you mean?"

"Jarak, you are a prince, and the heir to the most wealthy and powerful kingdom in all of Corvell. With that kind of power comes certain responsibilities. You cannot just decide to go out and mingle with the common folk and frolic with bar maids. You are putting the kingdom at risk every time you sneak out like this. Do you realize what could happen?"

"Nothing could happen. You said it yourself. I am the heir to the most powerful throne in Corvell. Who would be stupid enough to challenge me in anyway? I am just as safe here as I am inside the palace."

Rath shook his head. "I disagree. Come on Jarak, you've studied history. At least that is what I thought you have been doing under my tutelage. There are countless examples of assassinations, usurpers taking over the thrones of established kingdoms, as well as mass murders and genocides, events that seemed unlikely or impossible until they actually happened."

"You sound like my father," Jarak said as he poured himself another goblet of the delectable liquid.

Bannerfall

"Your father is wise. You should listen to him."

"What do we have here?" The voice was seductive, interrupting their conversation with a casual hint of desire.

Two beautiful women stood before them. The one who spoke was tall, with cascading red hair, creamy white skin, and dazzling green eyes. Her smile was wide, accentuated by brilliant red lips. But it was her dimples that really added to her appeal; they added warmth to her beauty. She wore a semi-sheer white gown that flowed around her body as she moved, clinging to just the right places. The other woman was in stark contrast to the redhead. She was a little shorter, and more buxom, her ample breasts accentuated by a tightly cinched black corset. Her long legs were covered, just above her knees, by a short, black dress that flitted around her as she shifted nervously before them. Her long black hair was pulled back tight with a jeweled clasp, fully revealing her smooth tanned skin and her exotic features. Full seductive lips glistened as she smiled, and her rich brown almond eyes twinkled with a mixture of excitement and nervousness. She clearly knew who Jarak was, and genuinely seemed excited to be meeting him.

"Tayna, it is so good to see you," Jarak said, rising and reaching for her hand, kissing it softly before turning to the new girl. "And you are?"

"Sofia, my Prince," she said softly, smiling invitingly.

Jarak moved to her, allowing Rath to say hello to Tayna. "Please, Sofia, you may call me Jarak. Please have a seat."

Rath held both of Tayna's hands in his. "I was hoping you'd be working tonight," he said, a bit awkwardly.

"You were?" she smiled, flattered that he seemed so shy. She found it rather charming.

"Yes, will you please sit with us?"

"Of course."

They all sat down at the booth, Sofia next to Jarak while Tayna sat on Rath's right. "What would you like to drink?" Jarak asked them both.

"Whatever you are drinking, my Prince," Sofia said, her voice soft and sensual.

"Gillian Red?"

"That sounds wonderful," Sofia said, smiling with anticipation. She had not yet had the good fortune to sample such high quality wine.

"My favorite," Tayna added.

Bannerfall

As if on cue, a serving girl approached the table, bowing deeply. "Can I bring you anything, my Prince?" Eva, the bartender, must have told her who he was. The serving girls at the Black Cat knew their job well. When any of the working ladies sat with customers, it was standard policy for the gentlemen to buy them drink, and food if they so desired, all part of the price for their company and services. The waitress was short, and pretty in a youthful way. She appeared to be no older than Jarak.

"What is your name?"

"Savi, my Prince."

"Savi, please do not refer to me by my title. I do not wish to be recognized at the moment. Now, we would love another bottle of Gillian Red. No, make that two bottles, and please bring us two orders of steamed crab. And don't forget that amazing spiced butter with it. That is my favorite."

"Yes, my Pri...sir," she said, catching herself and moving away quickly.

The next couple hours went by quickly as they laughed and chatted, savoring the lovely wine and other exotic foods that had been expertly prepared for them. But secrets are difficult to keep in such an establishment, and word had spread quickly that the prince was in attendance, and they couldn't help but notice more than a few stares and wandering eyes look their way.

Jarak was thoroughly enjoying Sofia's company. He had learned that both her parents had died of the black fever when it swept through Cythera fifteen years ago. She had been raised at the orphanage until she turned eighteen. She had quickly caught the attention of Angel, the Madame and owner of the Black Cat, who knew that girls from the orphanage, having no family to support or protect them, were ripe for the picking. Jarak knew that Angel was definitely not her real name, nor did her name reflect her character. He had a strong suspicion that she was anything but an angel. He had only met her twice, but both times had left him unnerved, although he could not identify why. Perhaps it was the mystery and rumors surrounding her. No one really seemed to know much about her origins. Or maybe it was simply the power that she wielded. She owned several establishments throughout Cythera, making her one of the wealthiest individuals outside the noble families.

Bannerfall

Rath, with the aid of wine, had finally overcome his nervousness and Tayna seemed to genuinely enjoy his intelligent conversation. Her background was nothing like Sofia's. She had grown up in the household of one of Cythera's lesser nobles, and had been well educated. Because of her intelligence and sophistication she had become a popular choice for the elite gentlemen who visited the Black Cat. Despite her family upbringing, Tayna had rebelled against an overly protective father, and guided more by the impetuousness of youth than by rationality, she gradually ended up selling her wares to rich men just like him. And there was no going back. Her family had disowned her.

Jarak was in mid-sentence when two men approached their table. He recognized them immediately as the two men that had overheard his conversation with Eva at the bar. They both carried short swords and daggers, and wore the clothes of a merchant, although dusty and worn from travel. One man looked to be in his forties, with a short brown beard and hair the same color that fell to his shoulders. His face, only a shade or two lighter than his hair, had obviously been baked by countless hours in the sun. The other man was younger, in his mid-twenties, with a short growth of dark hair on his chin and his curly hair cut above the ears of his plump round face. His eyes, darting back and forth around the room, revealed his nervousness.

"May we have a word with you, Prince Jarak?" the older man asked.

Jarak frowned at the interruption. "No offense, gentlemen, but I'm trying to have a relaxing evening with these beautiful women. I'm sure you understand."

"I'm sure your father would understand as well," the older man said.

The conversation halted as Jarak gave the man a wary look. "Excuse me?" Instantly he began to task, taking in a small amount of energy from Rath, Tayna, and Sofia. Their auras were clean and relaxed, and he borrowed just enough to perform a quick spell if necessary. Serix had drilled into him, that when the possibility of danger appeared, to always task immediately, checking for any positive auras. And he did it instinctively, almost without realizing it.

The younger man shifted his feet uneasily. "We are simple traders, sir, wondering if you could spare some coin," the older man continued.

Jarak knew what was happening. They were attempting to blackmail him, to request coin in return for not telling the king that he had been seen at the Black Cat. It was a courageous move, but nonetheless the audacity of it made Jarak angry.

"Let me get this straight," Jarak replied, "You are extorting a few coins from the Prince of Dy'ain in return for your silence about my presence here?"

The older man cleared his throat nervously. "Well, I like to think of it as a charity. A few coins to you mean nothing, but to us it means food for the table."

Jarak looked around. "But you can find the time and money to visit this establishment, and to drink expensive ale from Eltus instead of putting food on your table?"

The younger man's eyes darted nervously to his companion, who merely shrugged at the comment. "All men need to relax somehow; you yourself just suggested that to be true."

"You wear well-tailored merchant's clothes, and finely crafted swords, so either you are lying about your meager livelihood, or you are thieves. Which is it?" This time Jarak rose from the booth and stood facing the men, who were now speechless as they shifted away, their confidence ebbing. Jarak looked them both up and down. "What are your names?"

"Carthos, sir," the younger one blurted out.

The older man glared at his partner, his frustration clearly evident. It seemed pretty obvious that he did not want to give his name. "My name is, Kallick, Prince Dormath."

"You are either very brave or very stupid." Jarak produced two silver shikes from his coin purse and handed them to Kallick. "Buy yourselves a few rounds on me." Then he stepped a bit close and raised his right hand, producing a flickering ball of blue fire. Immediately the two men jumped back, just as Jarak extinguished the fire that he had brought forth. "Do not press me for more coin, and if one word of this reaches my father, I will find you. Do you understand?"

They nodded their heads and quickly stepped away without another word. Jarak sat back down. "Now, where were we?"

Sofia snuggled up next to him. "That was amazing." All citizens knew that the royal lineages possessed the Way, but few had ever witnessed it. Even though Jarak had conjured the flames for no more than a blink, his move had created quite a stir. "Do you want to go upstairs?" Sophia whispered in his ear as she ran her fingers lightly down his thigh.

"As a matter of fact I do." Just then Jarak was distracted by a commotion at the door. He stood up again, then cringed as three Sentinels approached him. The bar's patrons moved away from them as if they were the plague. No one wanted any sort of confrontation with the king's guard.

The man leading the trio was quite large, but he moved deceptively quick, his long muscular legs bringing him before the prince in an instant. His stoic eyes bore into each of them briefly before returning to the prince. "I knew I would find you here, my Prince."

"Tul'gon, it is so good to see you," Prince Jarak said with mock civility.

Tul'gon, the captain of the Sentinels, was a grim faced warrior with dark shoulder length hair and a short, meticulously trimmed, black beard. All three wore the armor of a Sentinel, forged from bronze, with the symbol of House Dormath etched into their cuirass. Their gold capes, made from a blend of the finest cotton and wool, were pinned across their chests with a bronze clip, in the center of which was a beautifully polished black stone. Each one carried a spear and wore a sword at their hip.

Tul'gon smiled, but it looked more like a grimace on his stern face. "We found the rope. King Enden wants you back immediately." Then he turned his stern eyes to Rath. "You are required to join him as well."

"He had nothing to do with this. I made him come with me," Jarak said.

"I'm sorry, my Prince. He was very clear about that."

Rath sighed and removed himself from the booth. Tayna and Sofia were now standing behind them.

"Let's just get this over with," Rath said, turning to say goodbye to Tayna. "I'm sorry, Tayna, but we have to go. I had a pleasant, albeit brief, evening with you."

She smiled and bowed her head slightly. "As did I, Rath," she whispered softly.

Jarak held both of Sophia's hands in his, raised one and kissed it gently. "You are a lovely creature. Thank you for an enjoyable evening."

"The pleasure was mine, my Prince."

Bannerfall

"And please, ladies, accept this token of our appreciation for your time," he said, placing two gold dracks in her hand. He smiled one last time, turned, and followed the Sentinels out of the bar.

King Enden slammed his fist on the table, shaking the wine goblet and pitcher, the sound echoing in the chamber. They were in the anteroom to the king and queen's private chambers. "I have had enough of this behavior, Jarak!" he thundered. "You are the Prince of Dy'ain and you can't just frolic in a local bar at your will!"

"But Father, we were just drinking wine and talking. I swear…"

"It matters not!" the king interrupted. "You put yourself at risk, you put your position at risk, but more importantly you put your kingdom at risk. And not for the first time. Do you not understand that everything we have, everything we do, we do for our people!?"

"I do not see how sharing a few glasses of wine with a beautiful woman can put the kingdom in danger."

King Enden sighed in frustration, turning his back on his son. His long dark hair reached his shoulders, and despite the fact that he was nearly fifty five years old, he stood tall, his broad shoulders and strong back evident beneath the night robe he wore. "Our people must feel confident in their prince. In their future king," King Enden continued, his voice softer, his anger seemingly spent. "You are more to them than just a man. You are a symbol. You represent everything that makes Dy'ain strong and respected, and if you fail to exhibit those qualities, they will lose respect for you. You cannot lead without respect." The king turned around to face them both. "Jarak, I am sending you away to the home of your uncle. You will go to Lyone on the Pell River and serve my brother. Maybe there you will learn what it means to be a leader."

Rath glanced at Jarak who stood speechless, a look of surprise and disbelief on his face. Lyone was the western garrison located on the Pell River, near Kael. It protected the kingdom's western border, and over the last fifty years has been a war zone. The Saricons took the city of Fara nearly thirty years ago, and since then have been fighting the last remaining cities still under control of House Kaleck, the ruling family of Kael. Lyone was perhaps the most dangerous place to be in all of Dy'ain as it protected the border between Kael and Dy'ain. House Dormath signed a treaty over twenty years ago wherein they vowed to help stop the Saricon war machine, sending troops from the garrison into Kaelian lands to help them fight against the common enemy, one who eventually wanted to control Dy'ain and the Kul-brite steel mines. So far the combined forces of House Kaleck and Dormath have kept them at bay; but the conflict between the Saricons and Kaelians has kept the region unstable for years. And eventually, if the combined armies of Kael and Dy'ain are defeated, then the invading Saricon armies would spill over the Pell River and into Dy'ain.

"But Father," Jarak stammered. "I...it is dangerous there."

"It is. You will leave in two days. Serix will go with you to continue your training." The king saw Jarak's eyes dart to Rath. "And no, Rath will not be joining you." King Enden addressed Rath for the first time. "Son, I know you were dragged into this so you will not be punished. You will remain here and continue your studies. In time, if you show the talent that Master Fallon speaks of, then I may call on you to serve House Dormath again. But for now, complete your studies and stay out of trouble. You may go."

"But, my King, I was partly to blame for this outing. I knew it was wrong and yet I succumbed to Jarak's urging."

"Which is why I am not punishing you."

Rath was shaking his head. "I am the prince's tutor, and I willingly joined Jarak when I knew in my gut I should not. I should be punished as well. Let me go with Prince Jarak as punishment so I may continue his education."

"I appreciate your dedication and honesty, young man, but the type of training that Jarak will endure will not involve books and paper. You will not be needed there and you would only be a distraction to him. My decision is final. You may go."

Rath gave Jarak a mournful and defeated look. He was worried for his friend. But there was nothing he could do, so he turned and walked out through the anteroom's solid oak door.

"Father, please give me another chance," Jarak pleaded.

The king sighed wearily. "I'm sorry son, but you've had enough chances. I've been too easy on you, and I've sheltered you far too long. You need to learn what it means to be a king. Now I must get some sleep. I suggest you do the same." He walked around the desk and placed his calloused hand on his son's shoulder, then sighed, and left him to his own thoughts.

Bannerfall

    The next day King Enden Dormath woke early, his restless sleep plagued by the knowledge that he was sending his son into certain danger. Quietly slipping out of bed, he dressed silently as the first rays of the morning sun crept through the large draped window that occupied most of the western wall. He needed to think, and the best place for that was at his private temple.

    He made his way through the silent halls until he came to the large double doors on the far end of the grand entrance to the palace. The palace was U shaped, and the impressive temple was built on the bottom of the U, extending beyond the palace and connected to it only by the doors attached to the grand entrance. The double doors were twice the height of a man, and the two together were just as wide. Expertly carved into the doors was Argon's symbol, a circle with four intersecting lines, each ending in a point just beyond the circle. The points represented all four directions, symbolically representing Argon's all-encompassing power. The two doors split the carving in two, and it was so expertly done that you had to look close to see the doors seem. The lines were filigree's of a darker wood, elegant and decorative, and no matter how many times he had passed through these doors, their exquisite craftsmanship never failed to impress him.

    He pushed open the doors and walked inside to the spacious room. The high ceilings made the room seem even larger. Rows of benches faced a giant wooden statue of Argon, with his wife, Felina standing behind him, her long arms wrapped around him in a loving embrace. Argon wore a loose flowing robe, draped gracefully around his body and leaving his strong muscular arms exposed. Every fold of the fabric, every detail of his musculature, and every wavy strand of hair was meticulously carved, adding to its life-like appearance. The entire sculpture was three times taller than the king, and both figures had been carved from the trunk of a giant oak tree. His father's father before him had built the temple and commissioned the piece. It was the most impressive carving he had ever seen. If he didn't know better he would swear that every time he looked at the statue it seemed to move, as if the giant figures were standing in a gentle breeze, causing the gossamer fabric of their robes and the long strands of their hair to subtly move in the air. Placed before the impressive statue was an altar carved from a slab of white marble that had been polished to a smooth sheen. Argon's symbol had been carved into the front of the stone that faced the benches, and inside the circle the symbol of House Dormath, a mountain with crossed swords before it, had also been included. Square windows occupied the upper reaches of the tall walls, flooding the spacious room with light. During religious festivals or other events the temple could accommodate up to two hundred people.

King Enden walked toward the statue, his footsteps on the white stone pavers echoing in the empty chamber. Just as he sat before the altar, a door to his left opened and a tall man wearing the dark gray robes of a prelate stepped inside. The man looked over and when he saw the king, a smile quickly replaced his startled expression.

"Forgive me, my King, I did not expect you at such an early hour."

"Worry not, Prelate Tyrick, I could not sleep and needed to do some thinking. Do you mind sitting for a while? I could use some council."

"Of course, I was just coming in early to prepare for today's service." Prelate Tyrick was in his sixties, but he moved with the grace of one much younger. His graying black hair was shaved short to the scalp. Dark bushy eyebrows contrasted sharply with his fair skin which, despite his age, shone with vibrancy typical of one much younger. High cheekbones and an angular jawline made him the most handsome prelate in Cythera. Prelates were at the top of the Argonian religious hierarchy. The clergy was organized into three rankings. There were ten First Rank prelates scattered throughout Dy'ain, Kael, Gilia, and Layona. They formed the Grand Council which governed all Argonian temples throughout Corvell. Below them were Second Rank prelates who managed the larger temples of the more populous cities throughout the lands, followed by Third Rank prelates whose job was to run the smaller temples that were more common in small towns and rural villages. Prelate Tyrick, having the honor of running the king's private temple, was a prelate of First Rank. All prelates came from noble families, and as such inherently possessed the Way. Tyrick was a Sapper, having the ability to draw in spells and diffuse them, making them harmless. He had never used his abilities in combat, which was fine by him as he would rather spend his days studying the words of the Argot. Tyrick sat down next to King Enden, his intelligent blue eyes looking deep into him. "What is on your mind?"

"I am sending the prince to Lyone tomorrow," he whispered, looking up at the large statue of Argon and Felina before him.

Tyrick paused, waiting to see if he would continue. But he didn't, so he spoke up. "And you are wondering if it was a wise decision?"

The king looked at him, his eyes pleading. "Lyone is dangerous, and he is untried…I," he paused, his hands balling into fists as he looked away again. "I do not know if the lessons he will learn there are worth the risks."

"You mean the risk of him dying."

"Yes."

"I am reminded of something mentioned by The One in the Argot. He said, 'Man is nothing without risk, as it is risk that makes a man. The absence of risk is bones, white and bare, stripped of life, unmoving beneath the heavens.'"

King Enden put his forehead in his hands, rubbed his eyes and sighed in frustration. "Poetic words but they help me little. I understand the need to take chances, but he is my son."

"That is where you are wrong."

King Enden stopped rubbing his face and lifted his head, his dark eyes narrowing as he looked at the prelate. "What do you mean?"

"I meant no offense, my King. But first and foremost he is *our* prince, the next king of Dy'ain. His relation to you as your son is an emotional connection and nothing more. You need to let go of those emotions before you can decide if your choice was a good one."

"How do I do that?"

"Ask yourself this question…is Prince Jarak ready to rule?"

"He is not," King Enden replied instantly.

"Can he learn to rule here at Cythera?"

King Enden thought for a moment. "He cannot, which is why I sent him away."

"I see. And what can he learn at Lyone?"

"To lead men, to earn respect, to fight…to be a king."

"Well then, you have answered your own question. If you just want a son, then keep him here. If you want a king, then send him away. It is not an easy thing for a father, but you are not just a father, you are a king. Is there anything else I can do for you? If not, I have some work to attend to."

King Enden was shaking his head, but his mind was elsewhere, processing the simple logic. "No, no, you may go. Thank you, Tyrick, as usual your council is wise."

Bannerfall

Prelate Tyrick stood and bowed. "I am at your service." Then he turned away, stepped up onto the raised dais, and slipped through a door hidden behind a large stone column.

King Enden Dormath looked up at the statue of Argon and Felina. "I don't ask much of you, but today I ask that you protect my son. Please, keep him safe so that he may spread your word." Then he closed his eyes, whispering the words of the protection prayer that he had been taught so long ago. "The light of Argon warms us, The tears of Felina nurture us, The power of them both watches over us, Wherever we are, they protect us, and where they are, all is well."

Chapter 3

At first we didn't know much about the Saricons. They were a foreign people, arriving on the shores of Karak in the largest ships that anyone had ever seen. Their skin was very pale compared to the people of Belorth or Corvell, although a similar skin tone can be found if you travel far north to the lands of Palatone. Their hair, too, was light, occasionally almost white, their eyes shades of blue and green. They had large imposing frames, and were easily a head taller than the peoples of Belorth and Corvell. Their women were nearly as tall as the men, and strong, often fighting alongside their men. And although it is not unheard of for women to become warriors in Corvell, it certainly isn't common. But these strange newcomers held few distinctions between the sexes, and some women even became military leaders, leading armies into battle.

But it didn't take more than a few cyns before we began to learn more. They were a marauding people who lived for war, their angry god Heln the catalyst for conquest. They lived to conquer, to plunder, to gain wealth, and to spread their religion. After taking most of the lands of Belorth, they had set their eyes on Corvell, their main goal to control the Kul-brite trade.

Saricon leadership consists of a ruling council of Tongras, or warrior priests. There are twelve Tongras, each having earned his or her position through intelligence, commitment, and strength. We know that these Tongras attained their positions by attending some sort of school where they underwent specialized training. Young Saricon children that show promise are recruited and hand-picked to attend this school. Over the next fifteen years they are indoctrinated into their religion and forged into warriors, with only the very best reaching the pinnacle of leadership, to become a Tongra.

A Tongra presides over any land they conquer, reporting back to the Great Council. The Council would become smaller as more territories are conquered and the Tongras remain to rule them. We know that a Tongra sits on each of the thrones in Karak, Enoreth, Argos, YaLara, and the city of Fara, from where we have learned they are trying to take the lands of Kael, their main target, Dy'ain and the Kul-brite trade. We can only assume that a few Tongras remained at home, wherever that home may be, leaving at least a handful to lead their armies as they

Bannerfall

conquer Belorth and Corvell. This is the extent of the knowledge we have so far about the Saricons, but I fear we will learn more than we desire soon enough.

Journal entry 23
Kivalla Der'une, Historian, Keeper of the records in Cythera, capital of Dy'ain

---

5087, the 14th cyn after the Great Change

Brant had been walking all day, his wool bag filled with his few personal belongings slung over his shoulder. He had been told by the wardens that a small village could be reached within the day if one pushed himself, which was exactly what Brant had done. He was tired, but he had certainly experienced worse fatigue than what he was now feeling. The mines and the fighting had made him extremely strong and fit, but he had to admit that his feet were a bit sore. His threadbare socks did little to protect them from his hardened leather boots, and they simply were not accustomed to walking long distances.

Luckily, just as dusk was beginning to fade into night, he spotted the glowing lights of the small village just up ahead. Brant sighed gratefully, eager for some warm food and rest for his weary feet. He had plenty of water in his water skin, but the only food he had was a small hunk of cheese and stale bread that he was able to purchase for a tigg prior to his departure. He had eaten hardly anything since his morning meal, and his meager provisions were gone by mid-day.

As he approached the village he observed that it was no more than a small collection of buildings flanking the main road. Kulvar Rand had told him that the village was called Bygon, named after the creek that flowed through the middle of it. The headwaters of the creek started at the Devlin Mountains, the tall, sharp peaks jutting into the sky, now silhouetted by the setting sun. From where he stood it was a picturesque view, white snowcapped peaks highlighted in pinks and blues, rising in the distance behind the village. Kulvar had also informed him that the outlying lands surrounding the village supported many small farms and grazing land for sheep and cattle herders, the small creek providing water for irrigation and their animals. The steppes of Dy'ain emerged from the rolling hills east of the Devlin Mountains, continuing across the kingdom before dissipating into the forested region along the coast. The treeless grasslands provided a vast and fertile landscape for farming and grazing, and since they were far from any major metropolis, the land was cheap, with minimal taxes. A hard working individual could make a living for himself in these parts, and Brant was hoping that he might find someone willing to offer him some work.

    The road leading into the village was only barely illuminated by the faint lights from the buildings that lined it. But the building he was interested in was well marked with burning torches, positioned so one could read the sign in the front of it. At this time of the evening there would only be a few shops open, and the one he was looking for was called the Axe Room, the local inn and eatery. The sign was built of weathered wood, and attached to it by metal brackets was an old rusty battle axe, and underneath the axe was the word 'room'. He had found the Axe Room.

    As he neared the heavy oak door he heard the faint sounds of music and laughter. He smiled in anticipation, eager to start his adventure. As he pushed the door open a wave of warm air enveloped him, soothing his cold and windblown face. The small room was simple and cozy, warmed by a large open fire in the middle, the smoke rising up through a gap in the roof, and protected by a raised roof above that. The square fire pit was built of large rough stones, and an assortment of tables and chairs filled the space around it. At the back was a small serving bar, behind which were stored large barrels of ale and wine, each one labeled with a wooden placard. Oil lanterns adorned and illuminated each table, while more hung from metal brackets along the walls and beams that formed the stick built frame of the room.

    Brant looked about, noticing maybe ten people sitting in various locations, talking, drinking and eating, a few of them stopping momentarily to look at the newcomer. To his right was a young woman playing a harp, the soft melodious notes filling the small space with a sense of tranquility. He maneuvered his way through the tables and approached the bar. Behind the counter stood a gray haired man, his back to Brant, filling a clay jug from a barrel labeled 'Ander's Red'. A young serving girl stood at the bar, her tray resting on the counter and filled with a large plate of smoked meats and cheeses.

    She glanced over at Brant as he sat on one of the empty stools, and the first thing he noticed was her large green almond shaped eyes. Her straight hair, black as night, was cut just above her shoulders and framed her round sun tanned face. Her face was wide and flat, not terribly attractive, but her astonishing eyes and wide smile made up for those features. Simple clothes adorned her stocky frame, a long brown skirt of coarse wool, and a long sleeved muslin blouse, gathered loosely at her wrists, all of which was covered by a dirty apron stained with food and drink.

She gave Brant a wide smile. "Welcome traveler, what can I do for ya?"

Hungry and parched, Brant answered quickly, "Some reasonably priced food and drink. And would you know of anyone who needs any extra help? I'm looking for work."

She looked him up and down, seemingly appraising him. "Well, I can help with the food and drink, but Anders here will have to help with the latter."

As if on cue, the gray haired bartender turned around and set the large jug of ale on her tray. "Go on with your task, Kaylin, I will help the newcomer," he said, not unkindly.

Kaylin flashed her smile one more time before departing, bringing her tray to a table near the fire. Anders was short and stocky, with a build similar to Kaylin's. His skin, too, was browned by the sun, though more weathered than Kaylin's, with fine lines etched around his eyes and mouth. His silver gray hair hung to the base of his neck. Brant had heard of the Schulg, a nomadic warrior tribe living deep in the steppes, and he wondered if perhaps Anders and Kaylin had some Schulg blood in them. They certainly were not Dy'ainian and they looked similar to Schulg descriptions he had heard from his father.

"We have a warm mutton pie or, if you prefer, a platter of dried meats, cheeses, and fresh bread and butter. I brew all the ale here myself, but we also have wine or water," Anders said matter-of-factly, his demeanor brisk and businesslike, the complete opposite of the smiling serving girl.

"How much for the meat pie? And I'll just have water," Brant replied, the warm food sounded wonderful.

"Two tiggs."

"That's reasonable. I'll have a serving of that."

"Very good," Anders said, departing through the door behind him.

Brant eyed the barrels behind the bar and sure enough each one had a placard revealing the name of the brew. One was labeled Boar

Bannerfall

Piss, and another Kaylin's Delight. A third was named Felina's Tears. Brant figured they must be Argonians, as were most of the people in Dy'ain. In fact, if there were any who still followed the old gods they were well advised to keep it secret, for they were often persecuted, beaten or even killed. Brant had not been brought up to believe in any one faith, but his father had always advised him that if anyone asked, to just say he was Argonian. It wasn't that Brant didn't necessarily believe in Argon or Felina, it was just that he had not been raised in a religious environment. He did not know much about the beliefs or doctrines of any of the religions; therefore he had no basis on which to build a foundation of faith.

Anders moved through the door and set a tray down in front of him containing a steaming meat pie, and a large cup of water. Then he turned around without a word and filled up a clay mug from the barrel labeled 'Boar Piss'. Brant dug into the food with relish, looking up momentarily as Anders set the mug down next to him.

"I didn't…"

"It's on the house. Let me know what you think," Ander's said. Brant gave the man a guarded look, not quite knowing how to respond. "Thank you would be the proper response," he added solemnly.

Brant was not accustomed to people giving him anything so he was immediately wary. "Thank you."

Anders grunted acknowledgment and began to wipe clean a tray of mugs. "So you're looking for work?"

"I am."

"Where you coming from?"

"The mines," Brant mumbled through a mouthful of mutton. The pie was warm and delicious, with a rich and savory meat filling wrapped in a flaky thick pastry. He reached over and took a long drink of the ale. He wasn't sure what to expect with a name like 'Boar Piss', and though he had never had the occasion to sample boar piss, he was certain that this did not taste like it. The ale was floral, with a smooth nutty flavor. There was just enough bitterness, countered with something sweet, maybe honey or something fruity. It was delicious. Brant took another swallow, paused, and looked at Anders appreciatively, a smile beginning to form on his face. Anders continued wiping down the mugs, seemingly unconcerned, but he was looking straight at Brant, patiently waiting for a response. The barkeep smiled back, showing his first sign of emotion.

Bannerfall

"Good isn't it?"

"It's the best ale I've ever had." Brant wasn't lying. Although he hadn't sampled many ales, this was the best he had tasted.

"I know someone, a man named Kaan with a farm half a day's walk north. His wife died recently and he may need help. He's raising two kids and trying to run a farm. I don't know what he can offer you, but if anyone around town needs help, it's him."

"I'll go see him tomorrow. How much for a room tonight and breakfast in the morning?" Brant asked.

"I can give you a room and breakfast for a silver. If you'd like I can have a bath drawn for an extra tigg."

Brant thought about it. The price was fair, and the bath, although a luxury, sounded amazing, and a tigg was not a huge expense. "That sounds fair. And I'll take you up on the bath."

Ander's nodded. "Enjoy the food and ale. I'll let you know when the bath is ready." The barkeep left again through the door, leaving Brant to enjoy his meal.

Brant departed first thing in the morning after a warm meal of smoked ham, eggs, and a large biscuit lathered in creamed butter and honey. He had never felt so content. His belly was full of delicious food, and the long hot bath had cleaned his body and soothed his mind. And hopefully he would have work soon enough.

Anders had been correct in his estimation. Brant reached the small farm in less than half a day following a rough cart trail along Bygon Creek. It was a nice spot to build a home. The farm sat in a clearing in the center of a copse of trees, one of the few Brant had seen along the road that paralleled the creek. The walls of the small square farmhouse were built of stone, forming a square base on which logs rested on the top connected together at the peak of the thatched roof. Trees were relatively scarce on the steppe, and most of the structures in this region were built of stone. Some settlers, however, chose to live in bilts, making it easy to pick up and leave if necessary. The stone farmhouse had several shuttered windows and one main door, the wood planks connected by black iron bands. The structure looked strong, built for protection and practicality, not luxury. Brant also saw a large barn made of wood and surrounded by a fence, which at the time seemed to house several cows and pigs. The owner must have traveled far, harvesting the few trees that grew along the creek to get enough wood to build the barn.

The path led away from the creek to the edge of the property, where Brant stopped, not wanting to startle anyone. He looked around but didn't see anyone. "Hello! Is anyone home?!" he shouted.

A few moments later the door opened slowly and a young dark haired girl peeked out. She looked to be about thirteen, and her face and apron were covered with white dust. She must be baking he thought.

"Stay inside, Jana," a voice came from Brant's right, from the barn. Brant looked and saw a man approach, holding a crossbow aimed at his chest. "Who are you?"

Brant's heart began to pound as he quickly tried to assess the situation, wondering if he could reach the man before he fired the weapon. But his initial defensive reaction dissipated quickly as the logical part of his mind realized the man was just protecting his family and home from a possible intruder. "My name is Brant," he said, lifting his hands harmlessly. "I'm just a traveler looking for work. The barkeep in town, Anders, mentioned that you might need some help."

Kaan lowered the crossbow but continued to eye Brant with suspicion. He was shorter than Brant, but older, probably in his forties. Out of habit from his fights, Brant always sized men up, and Kaan, despite the fact that he was almost a head shorter than Brant, looked as if he could handle himself. His shirtsleeves were rolled up at his elbows, and Brant noticed his strong forearms, heavily muscled and adorned with several scars. His curly brown hair was long, cut at the base of his neck, his headband, damp with sweat, kept the curly locks off his face, which was covered with fresh stubble. He wore the clothes of a simple farmer, and at a casual glance would have looked completely unassuming, minus the crossbow of course. But it was his eyes that drew Brant's attention. They were hard, suspicious, and Brant had no doubt that this man had seen violence before. "Where you coming from?" he asked gruffly.

"The Kul-brite mines northwest of here."

"Why did you leave?" he asked, stepping closer but keeping the crossbow at the ready. Kaan swept his dark eyes over Brant, appraising the newcomer just as Brant had assessed him.

"My father died," Brant said, shrugging matter-of-factly. "There was no place for me at the camp. And I did not want to live out my life in the mines."

"How old are you?"

"Eighteen."

Kaan finally seemed to relax. He stepped closer and raised his hand in greeting. But his eyes continued to convey the message that he was not to be trifled with. "My name is Kaan." They shook hands. "You look strong, and Anders is right. I could use some help. But I cannot pay you. All I can offer is a roof to sleep under and food to fill your belly. And if you don't mind that that roof I'm speaking of is the barn, then I'd be obliged to have you for the planting season. Keep in mind, I fought in the king's army. I don't know you, and trust comes with time, so rest assured that if you mean us harm, you will wish you hadn't come to my door."

Brant nodded his head silently, convinced that the farmer was not boasting. He glanced at the barn. It looked sturdy enough. "The barn looks fine. I'll be honest with you. I do not know anything about farming or raising animals. But I'm strong and a hard worker. And you need not fear my intentions."

"Fair enough. Most of what we do is manual labor, and I can teach you the rest." Kaan walked back toward the barn. "I'll show you where you can sleep in the barn. You can drop your possessions there and come inside and meet my children."

The first few weeks with Kaan went by quickly. Work started at sunrise and didn't stop until sunset. Brant was used to hard work, and he found that he enjoyed the change of pace from swinging a pick and hammer, although those practiced movements came in handy when chopping wood, one of his many chores. Brant learned to take care of the animals first and foremost. Kaan had three cows, a bull, two horses, four pigs, and ten chickens. They all needed to be fed and their stalls needed to be cleaned. On top of that Brant was required to keep their wood supply full. That meant he had to hike a considerable distance to find suitable trees, chop them down, limb them, quarter them, and bring the wood back. He used a wheeled cart pulled by one of the horses to haul the wood long distances.

After three weeks of getting accustomed to performing the household chores, Kaan brought Brant into the fields to teach him the basics of farming. They were well into spring and it was time to start plowing the fields. Brant learned that they grew potatoes, corn, and wheat. Kaan also had a small personal garden near the house where they grew a larger variety of foods, including onions, tomatoes, and turnips. In addition to running the farm, they had to harvest the vast fields of grass that covered the steppes to provide hay for the animals during the winter. The hay was stored in the loft in the barn. The horses were used to pull the plow, which cut into the soil, turning it and getting it ready for seed. It was often backbreaking labor, but there was something about the monotony of it that Brant enjoyed. It gave him time to think. He knew he could not stay at the farm forever, yet he needed to have a plan before venturing further.

It didn't take long for him to develop a relationship with Kaan and his family. His daughter, Jana, was kind and hardworking, taking care of most of the house chores and cooking. Tobias, Kaan's ten year old son was full of energy. Kaan spent a lot of time with Tobias, teaching him, as well as Brant, the skills of a farmer. And one evening, while he was teaching his son the basics of sword play, Brant learned that Kaan had not exaggerated about his ability to defend himself.

It was near dark. Jana was preparing a meal of grilled tulkick with fried onions and potatoes. Brant learned early on that whenever he left the farm to tend the crops or find wood to always take a crossbow, just in case he were to come across any wild game. The steppes were full of plump rabbits and tulkicks, a small ungulate that roamed the steppes feeding on the plentiful grasses. Brant was not great with the crossbow, but he was learning, and on several occasions had managed to shoot some rabbit and even a kip, a small wild chicken. They were bony, but Brant was proud nonetheless.

One could not always depend on a consistent supply of wild game, but this night they were going to eat well. Kaan had shot a tulkick that day and everyone was excited about having fresh meat for dinner. However, this was the time of day, just before dark, when Kaan spent a little time teaching his son the basics of sword fighting. Kaan had two blades racked by the door, one his infantry long sword from his days in the Dy'ainian Legion, and the other a lighter blade that he had purchased for his late wife.

Brant was leaning against the fence that housed the cows, watching the two move through the basic formations that they had been working on.

"Dad, this sword is too heavy," Tobias complained.

"That is good. It will build muscle. A swordsman must be strong to wield a blade. Now, try it again," Kaan instructed.

Tobias gritted his teeth and lifted the blade with both hands. Brant had to admit that the blade looked way too big for him. But he also knew from his days swinging a hammer that Kaan was right. He remembered his first days at the mines, and how heavy the hammer felt. But after a while it began to seem lighter, and he could swing it with more agility and force. He had gotten stronger, and the same would happen to Tobias if he continued to swing the heavy weapon. Kaan came at Tobias swinging his blade in a slow arc. He was trying to teach Tobias to not react naturally by backing away from the strike, and to counter the swing with an offensive move of his own. Tobias lifted the blade straight up, stepping forward just a touch. Their blades hit with a clang and Tobias grunted, pushing his father's blade down and away from him.

Brant grinned as Kaan stepped back, smiling at his boy. "Good. Now look what you did. When you stepped into my swing, blocking it, it allowed you to get close enough to attack me. You could kick me, shoulder charge me, or, if you were fast enough, reverse direction with your blade and cut me across my stomach. Good job, Son."

Tobias flashed a smile, but it disappeared quickly. "But, Father, I'm not fast or strong enough to do any of those things," he said with a frown.

Kaan walked over to his son and ruffled his curly hair. "Not now, but you will be. I have no doubt."

Tobias smiled and ran over to Brant. "Brant, did you see that?"

"I did. It took strength to block that swing. Well done."

"Why don't you give it a try?" Tobias said, handing Brant the heavy blade.

Brant gripped the leather handle and lifted the blade with one hand. The blade was heavy, but it was nothing compared to the hammers he had swung in the mines. He had to admit that the sword felt good in his hand, although he knew nothing about sword fighting.

"That is a good idea. Have you used a blade before?" Kaan asked, motioning for Brant to enter the dirt area they were using as a practice yard.

"No, never."

Bannerfall

"Let's start slow, with you following my lead so you can get used to the weight and movement," Kaan instructed. Brant nodded his head, lifting the blade before him.

Kaan started by swinging his sword down slowly and Brant met the attack by bringing his own sword to bear to block it. He then attacked Brant from the other direction, keeping his movements slow so Brant could follow him. They moved across the dirt as they slowly traded blow for blow, their blades meeting high, low, to the side, and directly in front of them. The sword was getting heavier, but Brant's strength allowed him to keep up so far with no problem. Even the vibration he felt when their swords clanged together did not hinder him much, accustomed as he was to the far stronger impact and heavy blows of pick and hammer on unyielding stone. Brant now realized how Kaan had developed such strong muscular forearms. Gradually Kaan increased the speed of his movements until both of them were sweating profusely. Finally he stopped and lowered his blade.

"Very good, Brant. I can see that working the mines has given you great arm strength. That will benefit you greatly if you ever want to be a swordsman."

Brant hadn't ever given serious thought to being a swordsman. Of course, most boys admired warriors and dreamed of becoming one. They imagined the feel of a long sword dangling from their belt and beautiful maidens swooning over them. He had to admit that when he had watched the wardens back at the mines, he had definitely been envious of their position and status. And he'd never really believed that he too could possibly become a swordsman. He chuckled softly. Just a few months ago he never would have thought he would be anywhere other than the mines. Now he was free from them. Maybe it *was* possible.

"Can you teach me?"

"We can start the process at least. Now, I want you to attack me. The blades are sharp, so use the flat of the blade for any sure strike. Don't hold anything back. Just do what feels natural."

Brant looked at Kaan with concern. "I don't think that's a good idea."

Kaan smiled. "Don't worry, you will not even touch me."

Brant's smile disappeared. His fights had given him an abundance of confidence, and he was not accustomed to anyone addressing him with such bravado. He had to admit that he didn't like it. "Very well, but I did warn you."

Kaan smiled, and calmly lifted his blade.

Brant came at him quickly, thinking there was no way for the older man to keep up with his speed. Using all his strength he swung his sword down towards Kaan's head. He wasn't trying to hit him of course, confident that Kaan could block the blade. But Kaan did not react as Brant had anticipated. Instead of lifting his sword to block the blow, Kaan rushed forward under the attack, smacking Brant's exposed belly with the flat of his blade.

Brant grunted but recovered quickly and spun around. He growled and swung his sword sideways, turning the sword in his had so he would strike Kaan with the flat of the blade. He was aiming for Kaan's midsection thinking there would be no way he could avoid the blow. He was partially correct. Kaan made no attempt to evade the stroke. Instead, he lifted his blade, blocking the blow. But then he used the tip of his sword and spun it around Brant's blade, using the momentum of Brant's attack against him and pushing the blade to the side and away from him. As Brant rushed by, he quickly smacked him across his thigh.

"Control your movements. You are attacking on strength and speed alone," Kaan instructed. "It is throwing you off balance. It is not always the bigger, stronger, swordsman that wins. Try to control your swings and stay on the tips of your toes."

Brant ran at him again, but this time he stopped, pulling up short, swinging his sword down toward Kaan's thigh. Kaan blocked the attack easily, reversing direction and angling his blade towards Brant's stomach. This time Brant's sword strike was controlled, his strong arms stopping the movement once it was blocked and his body adjusted, now staying on his toes to keep his balance. When Kaan's blade angled back toward him, he was able to leap back, narrowly avoiding it.

Kaan stepped back, smiling. "Very good. You controlled your movement that time. You are a quick learner."

Brant lowered the tip of his blade, his adrenaline dissipating. He would have to learn to control his anger. It was a good lesson. "It doesn't feel like it," he said, rubbing the bruise forming on his thigh. "You are very good."

"I'm decent. But there are many swordsmen far superior to me."

Bannerfall

"Like Kulvar Rand?" Brant asked, wiping the sweat from his brow.

Kaan laughed. "Yes, like Kulvar Rand. That man is the deadliest man I know."

"You've met him?"

"I have, when I was in the Legion."

"I too have met him."

"Who is Kulvar Rand?" Tobias asked, moving to stand next to his father.

"He is a Dygon Guard, and the best swordsman I have ever seen." He looked at Brant curiously. "How did you meet him?"

"He arrived at the mine where I was working the day my father died. There were twenty Dygon Guard there to pick up some Kulbrite."

"I see. But there is another warrior nearly as deadly with a sword as Kulvar. His name is Tolvanus, and he is captain of the guard in Kreb." Kaan laughed. "The man is small in stature, but you'd think he's a giant when he fights. He protects the king's chamberlain in Kreb."

"What is a chamberlain?" Brant asked. He was embarrassed he knew so little, but felt comfortable enough in Kaan's presence to ask.

"There are two of them…lords, appointed by King Enden Dormath to rule Kreb and Tanwen in his place."

"Supper's ready!" Jana yelled from the house.

None of them needed any urging, the smells from the kitchen had been whetting their appetites even as they fought.

***

It had taken nearly three weeks for the caravan to reach Lyone. True to his word, King Enden had sent his son, along with five hundred fresh troops, to the remote garrison. The trek had been long and tedious, with nothing for Prince Jarak to do other than stare at endless grasslands, dreaming of sweet Sofia's soft bosom.

He had only been to Lyone once, as a child, and he remembered very little of it. The garrison was built along the Pelm River, strategically placed at the only possible crossing point. Even so, a floating bridge had been built that spanned the river, and the garrison had been erected at the entry point into the lands of Dy'ain. The garrison was basically a keep surrounded by walls. The west wall had a large drawbridge that opened onto the floating bridge. The east wall had one entrance; it too was protected by a heavy gate built of thick timbers reinforced with bands of iron. The walls of the keep were forty feet high and ten feet thick, constructed of giant slabs of basalt that had been barged down from Elwyn. At any one time the garrison housed five thousand troops. The castle built in the middle of the keep was the home of Jarak's uncle, Daricon, and his family, as well as the families of the various officers that were periodically stationed there. Barracks, supply rooms, stables, and offices, surrounded the central castle, all protected by the keep's sturdy walls.

Lyone had been a war zone for over six Cyns. Dy'ain's relationship with Kael had been peaceful for the last two Cyns, but it hadn't always been that way. Under the leadership of a particularly brutal king, the Kaelians had tried to invade Dy'ain on numerous occasions, lured by the wealth of the Kul-brite mines. But each time they were kept at bay, and Lyone, reinforced by troops from Cythera, was the main reason for their failure. But when that Kaelian king had died, and his son took over, relationships had improved; the new king realized that trade during peace was much more lucrative than war. Occasionally the nomadic Schulgs attacked the outpost for no other reason than to test the sharpness of their blades, or to introduce the skills of warfare to their young warriors. But today the threat came from the Saricons, who had already conquered Fara. In fact, King Enden had signed a treaty with King Kaleck of Kael, and together their armies had kept the Saricons from taking any more land in Kael, and consequently from crossing into the lands of Dy'ain. Daricon Dormath had been placed at Lyone fifteen years ago when he was only twenty five years old, his sole responsibility to keep the western borders of Dy'ain safe. And now Jarak was to join him in this endeavor. He was not looking forward to it.

The caravan was quickly brought inside the keep's walls where the soldiers went about their duties with practiced efficiency. Servants appeared and took the horses, feeding and watering them before brushing them down for the evening. Supplies were unpacked; soldiers were dispersed to their barracks, and more quickly than Jarak thought possible everything in the courtyard was back to normal.

As the last of the carts were being moved from the courtyard, Daricon, accompanied by two officers, came over to greet them. Several servants had unpacked their bags and were standing behind Jarak and Serix waiting for their orders.

"By the fates, Jarak, it has been a long time!" Daricon exclaimed.

Jarak turned to see his uncle approach from the direction of the barracks. He was a tall man, with long arms and legs. He wore the armor of a Legionnaire officer, a golden cape fluttering behind him as he walked across the stone courtyard. At his hip was a long sword. He had a two day's growth of hair on his face, and his long dark hair was held back with a leather band, from which a few strands had escaped and clung to his sweaty forehead. Anyone could see that Jarak was related to him as they looked like father and son.

"Uncle, it is good to see you," he announced, as he held out his hand in greeting. The last time he had seen his uncle was nearly ten years ago. He remembered very little about him, and he felt a bit awkward at the moment.

Daricon grunted, slapping his hand away as if it were a sword. "Bahh! What is wrong with you, boy?" Smiling, he reached out and grabbed Jarak, holding him tightly in a bear hug. "In Argon's name you have grown. You look like a man."

"I am a man," Jarak laughed, his awkwardness crushed by the strength of his uncle's embrace.

Daricon released him, holding him at arm's length. "Well, we shall see about that," he said, his smile all but disappearing.

Jarak was impressed by his uncle's strength. Daricon had made quite a name for himself at Lyone, and was considered to be the best swordsman in the land next to Kulvar Rand. Like Jarak's father, his uncle was a Merger, and if the stories he'd heard were true he was a very powerful one.

"My Lord, it is a pleasure to see you again," Serix said with a bow.

"The pleasure is mine, Serix," Daricon replied. He reached out and shook the mage's hand. "And I must say that we could use your skill. Here, I'd like you both to meet Captain Hagen, and Colonel Lorth. They are my commanding officers."

Serix and Jarak shook their hands. Captain Hagen had a stocky build that looked powerful, his hazel eyes critically appraising them both. His hair was thick and black, cut short in the infantry style, and Jarak guessed that he might have some Schulg blood in him. Colonel Lorth was one of the largest men that Jarak had ever seen, nearly two heads taller than Captain Hagen. He looked extremely powerful, his trim waist accentuating his broad shoulders and large muscular frame. Both warriors wore the same Legionnaire armor and carried long swords.

"It is nearly time for supper. Let's get you two settled in and we can talk over a warm meal. A bath has been prepared, which I'm sure you could both use." Daricon turned to the servants holding their bags. "Take them to their rooms."

As the door shut behind him, Jarak looked about the drab room. He sighed in frustration. The room was small and lacked the more elegant furnishings and décor that he was accustomed to. *At least it was warm*, he thought, gazing at the blazing fire in front of the bed. There was an anteroom through an arched opening that housed the chamber pot and a large copper tub filled with steaming water. A table and two chairs were nestled in the corner of the room next to a door that opened onto a small balcony. On one wall was a large armoire flanked by two dressers with three drawers each. Plum colored tapestries embroidered with House Dormath's family crest hung on the wall flanking the fireplace.

Jarak moved to the balcony door and walked out into the cool evening air. The sun was beginning to set and he had to admit the view was beautiful, with streaks of red and orange brushed across the skyline. His room faced the river and all he could see beyond were the rolling grasslands of Kael.

His brief reverie was broken by the sound of some sort of commotion below him. He peered down over the railing. Below him was a training yard that separated one of the large barracks from the inner castle, and dancing around the cobblestones was a woman, her long auburn hair tied back into a single tail. She wore loose fitting black pants and a tan tunic cinched tight with a leather belt over a long sleeve white shirt. She held a long sword in her right hand, and appeared to be practicing various positions of swordplay, her feet smoothly gliding over the flat stones, her sword arm expertly going through the movements. He recognized her skill, as he himself had being trained in the same sword formations.

"Who are you?" he whispered to himself.

As if she heard him, she finished a spin, ending the movement perfectly, and stood up straight with her sword held erect before her. And it just so happened that she managed to end up facing him when she stopped. He got a good look at her face and he was struck by her unique beauty. Her body was more muscular, lacking the curve of full breasts and wide hips, than the women he was accustomed to, but it did not seem to detract from her femininity. Large brown eyes stared straight ahead with fierce concentration. The warm bronze of her skin was flawless, smooth and glowing in the soft light of the setting sun. And there was no denying that the fullness of her lips only enhanced her appeal.

He stepped back from the railing not wanting her to see him spying on her. *Maybe this won't be so bad*, he thought as he walked into the room toward his warm bath.

The vaulted dining room was spacious but simply adorned, like everything else Jarak had thus far seen. The accommodations at Lyone were nothing like the royal palace in Dy'ain. Though sturdy and useful, everything here was simple, lacking the fancy embellishments that were overly prevalent at the king's castle. A large oak table occupied the rectangular room, above which hung a huge iron chandelier with flickering candles that cast dancing shadows below. Six oil lanterns hung from iron hooks embedded into the stone walls, their orange light giving the room a warm glow. The large dining hall was further illuminated by two large stone fireplaces at opposite ends of the room, their heavy oak mantles simple and unadorned. Four foot logs burned brightly in their hearths, making the room feel warm and cozy.

One wall was dominated by a giant painting depicting an ancient battle. The opposite wall was almost completely covered by a heavy crimson tapestry expertly embroidered in gold thread with the symbol of Argon and Felina. The gold symbol was round with two intersecting lines, one pointing east and west, and the other north and south. The end of each line protruded just past the circle and ended in an arrow point. The arrows symbolized the all-encompassing power of Argon and Felina, extending in all directions. On each wall were two suits of silver armor, each statue holding a long spear, as if they were guarding the guests while they ate. Although the dining hall was relatively simple, and lacked the elegance of a royal castle, Jarak found it warm and comfortable nonetheless.

In attendance were Daricon and his wife, Mylena, their two young sons, Tye and Colgan, who appeared to be about eight and ten. Serix was also there, along with the two officers he had already met,

Bannerfall

Hagen and Lorth. But Jarak's eyes were drawn to the young girl sitting between the two officers. He recognized her. It was the same girl he had seen on the training grounds before his bath.

As introductions were quickly made, Jarak was not surprised to learn that the girl, Ca'tel, was the daughter of Captain Hagen. They looked very much alike, the same stocky, powerful build, wide face, and large green eyes. But somehow Ca'tel made it all look beautiful, while Captain Hagen had the harsher, more rugged look of a typical stoic military officer. Jarak had to admit however, that Ca'tel, despite her female persuasions, looked every bit as tough, and after witnessing her skill on the training yard, knew that she probably was.

After introductions, everyone sat down, eager to sample the warm rice soup that sat waiting for them. Jarak was pleased that he had been given a seat opposite Ca'tel. Wine was poured and conversation began almost immediately.

Daricon spoke first. "Jarak, I have just read the letter your father gave me. Did you read it yourself?"

Jarak took a sip of his wine. "I have not," he replied. "It was sealed."

"So you tried to read it?" Ca'tel asked bluntly, ignoring the warning glance from her father who sat next to her.

Jarak looked at her, giving her his best smile. "I did, Ca'tel."

"Call me Cat," she said plainly.

This time her father nudged her arm. "I'm sorry, my Prince. My daughter has not spent much time at court and I'm afraid she lacks the proper formality."

Prince Jarak looked around the room with his most charming smile. "As you can see, Captain Hagen, we are not at court, and I do not think that this *garrison* requires much formality." He then looked directly at Ca'tel. "Cat it is."

"This *garrison*," Daricon quickly replied, "at the command of your father, will be your home for the next three years, as it has been *my* home for the last fifteen. So I suggest that you treat it with respect. You will learn, *Prince*," his voice as hard as steel, "that these walls will become your best friend. They have protected our lands for hundreds of years. Your father has asked that I teach you how to lead, how to earn respect, and that I introduce you to the intricacies of war. He believes that as the future king you will need to learn these things, and you cannot do so through books and theory. I happen to agree with him." Daricon paused and drained the remaining wine from his goblet. His eyes bored into Jarak's. "Are you ready for this?"

Jarak looked about the table. All eyes were on him. He had no idea if he was ready for it, but he knew he had no choice. "I will do what is necessary." He wanted to change the topic of discussion, so he turned to Daricon's wife sitting quietly next to him. "Lady Mylena, I have heard about you from my father, but your beauty far surpasses what I've heard from court gossip.

Mylena smiled, looking up from her soup. "Thank you, my Prince. We are very excited to have you here with us." Jarak was not exaggerating. His uncle's wife was the most beautiful woman he had ever seen. Her most striking features were her stature and her hair, both atypical of the region. She was tall, nearly as tall as Daricon, with flaxen blonde hair, very rare in these parts. And her skin was much lighter, almost pale, with blue eyes like crystal clear ocean pools floating in her creamy flawless skin. Her features were angular, yet elegant, with high cheekbones and lips the color of a light red wine. Jarak noticed that she didn't wear any color around her eyes, or on her lips. Her beauty was unparalleled without added enhancements. He had heard rumors about how she and his uncle had met, and Jarak was beginning to wonder if they were true. It was rumored that she had Saricon blood in her, and by the looks of it that seemed like a realistic possibility.

"How did you and my uncle meet?" he asked, his curiosity getting the best of him. By this time the empty soup bowls were being taken away and an appetizer was set before them. It looked, and smelled, like some sort of white fish. It rested on a thick slice of fried bread, and a warm butter sauce was drizzled over the top.

"It was a long time ago," Mylena said. "My family and I were traveling from Fara to Eltus, fleeing the wars and the Saricons who had already taken my city. I was only fifteen at the time, but I remember it clearly. We were attacked on the road by a patrol of Saricons and my family was killed."

"How did you survive?"

"I was stabbed in the side with a spear," she said, indicating a spot along her waist where she had been injured. "I fell next to my father. I knew that I had to appear dead, or they would finish the job. So I didn't move; I lay sprawled over my father until they left. I was later found by your uncle, who was patrolling the road with a combined force of Dy'ainian Legionnaires and soldiers from Eltus."

"And her beauty entranced me even then, amongst the carnage," Daricon added.

"Thank Argon that you survived," Jarak added.

Mylena glanced up, her stunning blue eyes looking into him. "Yes indeed. I am very thankful."

"Pardon my ignorance," Serix said, speaking up for the first time. "But how did you two marry? I thought that the nobility could only marry within their station."

Mylena looked to Daricon to respond. "Even though she is not from Dy'ain, her father was a minor lord in Fara. We bent the rules some, her lineage being far below mine, but I did not care. Mylena was going to be my wife. I believe your father," Daricon looked to Jarak, "gave me some latitude considering the sacrifices I have made for our kingdom."

"I see. So, are you an Aurit?" Serix asked Mylena.

"Unfortunately I am not. I believe that our bloodline was too weak and it did not surface in me."

"What of Tye and Colgan?" Jarak asked.

"We do not know yet," Daricon said softly, "It is still too early to tell." The topic was clearly a sore spot for him. Jarak frowned, thinking that Daricon's choice to marry Mylena, despite her beauty, may not have been a smart tactical move. The power of the royal family was dependent on the Way, without it they would be open for usurpation. But he was right; it was still too early to tell. Aurit abilities usually manifested themselves during puberty, and the boys had a handful of years left before that stage in their life.

"I will be a Merger like you, Father," Tye, the older son, announced boldly.

"But I will be stronger than you, brother," Colgan said, elbowing Tye in the side.

Daricon and Mylena smiled. "That is enough, you two," Daricon scolded softly.

"Is it true that your family has bloodlines with the Saricons?" Jarak asked boldly.

He did not miss the looks that the two officers gave to their lord, who in turn did not look happy with the question. "That is a rude question for the dining table, Jarak," Daricon said, his voice a tense whisper.

Jarak did not miss the absence of 'prince' before his name. But he pushed further, continuing his line of questioning. "I'm sorry, I did not mean to be rude. I simply am inquiring. You look so different from us, and I have heard that the Saricons are tall and pale skinned with blonde hair."

"That is true," Mylena answered. "I have seen many of the fearsome Saricons." She paused for a moment, and took a sip of her wine.

"You do not have to speak of it," Daricon whispered to her.

Captain Hagen and Colonel Lorth both seemed uncomfortable, as if they knew something they should not.

"My mother was raped by a Saricon soldier when she was eighteen. She had been married to my father, a minor lord in Fara, for a year, prior to our holdings being invaded. My father was away at the time. I was the result of that rape. My father raised me as his own, despite my evident differences."

The room was deathly silent. Jarak looked down at his food and wished he hadn't asked the question. He had heard rumors that Daricon's wife did have some Saricon blood in her. Many people spoke ill of Daricon because of this, thinking it a slap in the face to marry one who carried the enemy's blood. But he had never considered the possibility of rape.

"I am truly sorry, Lady Mylena. I did not wish to bring up ill feelings. I hope you will forgive me."

She looked up at Jarak. "My Prince, you are forgiven. My Saricon blood is not who I am. Now, let us move on to more pleasant conversation. How is the food?" she asked.

Everyone, eager to change the topic, acknowledged the delicious food. Even Jarak thought the food was outstanding. "The food is excellent, Uncle. Who is your chef?"

Everyone in the know smiled, even Captain Hagen and Colonel Lorth, who thus far had remained silent and businesslike.

"You will meet her soon enough. She is a spirited one, and void of tact, but I cannot get rid of her. I'm afraid I would have a rebellion in my own castle," Daricon said, smiling.

"I can understand your reluctance. This food rivals that of the king," Serix added, swallowing a piece of the fish cake.

"It is the one thing we have here at this *garrison*," Daricon said, emphasizing the word as Jarak had done earlier.

Jarak noticed of course, but he did not take the bait, instead directing his attention to Cat. "Cat, where did you learn to use the sword?"

She looked up from her plate. "How do you know I can wield a blade?"

"I saw you from my balcony."

"I taught her, my Prince," Captain Hagen interjected.

"Captain Hagen is one of our best swordsmen. In fact he will be the one to train you," Daricon added.

"Thank you, my Lord," Captain Hagen said, nodding his head to Daricon, acknowledging the compliment, and the honor.

"Do you fight in the Legion?" Jarak asked Cat.

She glanced over at her father. "No, he will not let me."

"But we have female soldiers. I saw your skill. Surely you could pass the training," Jarak continued, trying to pay her a compliment.

His words seemed to make her angrier. But she said nothing.

"One day, my Prince, if you have a daughter, you will understand," Captain Hagen stated coldly.

Jarak looked at Cat and back to her father. Clearly this was a topic of contention for them both, and unwittingly he had just stoked the fires. The dinner table conversations had not been going well, and Jarak thought it best just to shut his mouth.

And that is what he did. Other than answer a few questions, Jarak remained quiet for the rest of the excellent meal. It seemed his arrogance and forthrightness may have burned some bridges, and hopefully he would be able to make amends.

***

Several weeks had passed and the crops they had planted were now breaking ground. He had to admit that it felt good to see the products of his labor. Things had progressed well and Brant was beginning to feel like part of the family. But he knew that his place here was only temporary, and he had already discussed his future plans with Kaan, who had recommended that he travel to one of the larger cities for work, and then return at harvest time. Brant wasn't so sure that was the best idea, remembering what Master Rand had said about staying out of the big cities. But it wasn't time to leave yet, so he still had a few weeks to figure it out.

Meanwhile, his sword work was progressing well. Brant found that he was an apt learner, quick on his feet and of course strong. And Kaan was a capable instructor, so it wasn't long before Brant was able, after a long bout of sparring, to eventually score a hit on him. It was after one of these practice sessions that Brant finally worked up the nerve to ask Kaan about his wife.

"What was your wife's name?" he asked, handing a ladle of cold water to Kaan as they rested after a long bout.

Kaan looked at him, pausing momentarily as his minded drifted to his wife. "Her name was Elana."

Brant took the ladle and refilled it, draining its contents in a few deep gulps. "My mother died giving birth to me. I never knew her."

"I'm sorry. I guess I should be grateful that my children knew their mother."

"How long ago did she die?"

"About this time last year."

"If you don't mind me asking, how did she die?" This time Kaan turned his back on him, looking toward Bone Peak in the distance, his thoughts traveling elsewhere. Brant waited a few moments. "I'm sorry, I did not mean to bring up bad thoughts."

"I know. It's just that it was a horrible death. I can hardly bear to think of it."

"Pretend I didn't ask."

Kaan turned around to face him, and Brant could see the cold anger and deep grief in his face as he recalled the day he had found her. "I found her body in the trees over yonder," Kaan said, indicating the location where her body was buried under a large oak tree. "She had been mutilated, but not by a wild animal. The wounds were precise; a sliced throat, puncture wounds across her entire body, skin ripped from her flesh. Even her scalp had been ripped off."

"In Argon's name who would do something like that?" Brant was horrified, and he was now sorry that he had asked.

"Not who, but what?"

"You think it was some sort of animal, or creature?"

"The wounds, although precise, were made by claws, not blades. I think it was a young kulg." Kaan could barely get the word out, so painful it was for him to relive the experience.

"What is a kulg?" Brant asked. He had never heard that name.

Bannerfall

Kaan sat down on the edge of a hay bale and motioned for Brant to do the same. "Do you know much about the Way?"

Brant only knew what Kulvar Rand had told him, which wasn't much. But he also remembered what Master Rand had warned, that he should not tell anyone that he possessed the Way. "I have heard of it, but I know very little," he said honestly.

"The Way is an inherited power. It is the ability to harness and then use the energy of one's auras. The power is bred into the royal families and its use is strictly forbidden to those without noble blood. There are many different forms of the Way. There are Mergers, who are people that have the power to use their own auras which enables them to be stronger and faster than others. And talented Mergers can even direct their energy into their weapons."

"I was told that is why Kul-brite metal is so precious, that it is the only metal capable of withstanding the energy of a Merger."

"That is true. Some very talented Mergers, the ones without the skill to become a swordsman, become scion forgers, the only blade smiths capable of forging Kul-brite weapons. Others who possess the Way become Channelers or Sappers. A Sapper has the ability to absorb energy from an Aura Mage, to cancel their spells and dissipate them harmlessly. A Channeler, on the other hand, can steal aura energy from others, and filter it to make it usable for an Aura Mage."

"Filter it? I don't understand," Brant said.

"I only know what I've been told. But my understanding is that not all auras are clean. If one is thinking unpleasant or evil thoughts, or doing a bad deed, or is simply a bad person, their aura will be dark. Negative. If an Aura Mage were to absorb such energy, it could impact them in a negative way, causing problems such headaches or illness. And over time the use of this dark energy can result in more severe problems, causing actual physical abnormalities."

Brant thought for a moment. "So a Channeler can take any energy, bad or good, and make it clean and useable?"

"That is correct. Then an Aura Mage can take that purified power and manipulate it into spells," Kaan continued. "A powerful Aura Mage, paired with a skilled Channeler, can make quite a team. When I was with the Legion and fighting in the west against the Saricons, I saw them work together on numerous occasions. It was something to behold."

"I would imagine so. But what does this have to do with this kulg that you spoke of?"

Kaan sighed. "Kulg's are evil creatures that were once Aura Mages."

"You mean they were once human?"

"Yes. It is believed that they became so addicted to power that they greedily sought more and more energy, any energy, disregarding the dangers of negative auras. Over time, the dark energy warped them, changing them. They are very rare, and I've only heard stories of them. But they do not look human anymore. They are rumored to have incredible speed and strength. It is said that no normal human can defeat one. Their incredibly sharp claws, as long as a man's fingers, have become their weapons, along with their ability to craft spells from the energy they hungrily devour. Their twisted and fragmented minds crave only one thing, the negative energy dispersed by the human body."

"I don't understand."

Kaan looked away. It was almost impossible for him to talk about, as his words gave way to images, images he had tried to repress, but were now released in his mind, and he saw again the reality of his wife's horrible death. Kaan paused as he struggled to maintain his composure. Then he continued. "When a person is frightened, in pain, suffering, or dying, they release negative energy. It is this energy that a kulg feeds on."

Brant gulped. "You mean they try to prolong the pain and fear so they can feed longer on their victim?"

"That is my understanding."

Brant didn't know what to say. He couldn't imagine anyone going through that type of horror, and when he thought of Kaan's wife having to endure that type of death, it made him sick to his stomach. But as he continued to digest this information, a stronger and more familiar feeling emerged. Anger. "I'm sorry." It sounded inadequate, but he didn't know what else to say. Then he thought of something Kaan had said earlier. "Why did you say you thought it was a young kulg?"

"Because it didn't try to kill all of us. A young kulg would be satisfied after one feeding, but not a mature one. An adult kulg would have killed us all."

Brant suddenly wanted to change the subject. "You mentioned you fought against the Saricons in the west. Who are they?"

Kaan looked at him with bewilderment. "You haven't heard of the Saricons?"

"No. I told you. I grew up in the mines and know very little about the world." Brant replied defensively. He didn't like to be reminded of his ignorance and was at first offended by Kaan's tone.

And Kaan picked up on it. "I'm sorry, Brant. I meant no offense. It's just that I assumed that everyone knew who the Saricons were. They invaded the lands of Kael thirty years ago and have been fighting against the Kaelians and our Legion the entire time since. The land west of the Pelm River is a war zone, and has been for a long time. The combined forces of Kael and Dy'ain are all that stands between us and these foreign invaders. And if they prevail, they will pillage our lands, rape our women, and create a life of persecution for our people.

"Persecution?"

"Yes. The Saricons worship a battle god named Heln, and they are not known for tolerance."

"I see."

"Come, enough of this serious talk. Let us eat."

Brant, always eager to eat Jana's cooking, walked with Kaan towards the cabin. But his mind was elsewhere, dwelling on kulgs, Mergers, and foreign conquest. He had a lot to think about.

A week later they were sitting at the table eating a steaming bowl of potato and rabbit stew and a warm flat bread called balter, made from the coarse flour of ground balt, a hearty grain native to the surrounding meadows. The bread was dense, but when dunked into the broth of the stew it softened, becoming a delicious amalgamation of flavors.

"This might be your best stew yet," Brant commented to Jana.

"Thank you."

"It is delicious," Kaan agreed.

"I wanted to make something special for your birthday, Papa," Jana said.

"Well, you succeeded," he said with a smile.

"Father, I made something for you," Tobias announced proudly as he set a small gift on the table. It was wrapped in brown cloth and tied with a leather string.

Kaan took the present and removed the cloth, exposing a carved symbol. It was a circle with an x in the middle. It was simple but well carved, the lines clean and not marred by many errors. The boy had done a nice job. "It is wonderful, Tobias. Thank you very much. I will hang it above the door for good luck."

"What is it?" Brant asked curiously.

"It is Goth's symbol. It represents harmony."

"I am not familiar with this Goth," Brant admitted.

"Have you not heard of the old gods?" Jana asked.

Brant shook his head.

"Goth is one of the old gods. He represents harmony in nature," Kaan explained. "Another is Morlock, keeper of the dead, and Bowgoul, god of justice and revenge."

Brant had heard the common curse phrase, *Morlock's balls*, and now he knew its reference. "So you are not Argonians?" They didn't answer right away and Brant sensed that his question made them feel uneasy.

"We are not. But I do not worship the old gods either," Kaan said quietly, as he stared at his near empty bowl.

"I like Goth," Tobias said. "Mother prayed to him often."

"That is enough, Tobias," Jana whispered.

"It is okay, Jana. Tobias, I thank you for the gift. It will always remind me of your mother."

Brant could certainly understand why Kaan would find it difficult to worship any of the gods after his wife's death. Goth had not saved her. Morlock now had possession of her. And where was Bowgoul? Certainly there was no justice for Kaan's wife, nor had Kaan been avenged for her tragic death. He thought it was a good time to produce his own gift.

"I too have a gift for you, Kaan. And I would like to thank you all for allowing me into your home." Brant had never bought a gift for anyone and he had to admit that it felt good to be able to do so now. Reaching under the table he brought out a rectangular wooden box a little larger than a wine bottle. "This is for you," he said, pushing the box across the table to Kaan.

"What do we have here?" he said, obviously surprised. He carefully slid the lid off the box, exposing a glass bottle filled with an amber liquid. His smile disappeared and he looked up at Brant. "Is this what I think it is?" he asked, recognizing the wax emblem pressed upon the bottle.

"It is."

"But how could you afford this?" he asked as he took the bottle out and cradled it in his hands.

"What is it, Father?" Jana asked.

"This is something that I've had only once, and I still dream of it. Again, I will ask you. How did you afford this?"

"I was a fighter in the camps, and the day before I left I fought a warden," Brant said.

"A warden?" Kaan asked, surprised.

"Yes. It's a long story. But a deal was made and Master Rand thought I deserved a parting gift based on my performance."

"You defeated a warden!?"

"No, but he felt I had earned the gold. I have had no use for it here, so I spent some on this," Brant said, indicating the bottle. The beverage he had purchased was a spirit called Sil and it was made from a cactus found only in the Sil desert. It was rare, and very expensive. But luckily, Anders, the barkeep in town, had a bottle available. It had cost him two gold dracks, an unbelievable sum for a bottle of liquor.

Kaan's smile was contagious, and everyone was soon beaming ear to ear. "Jana, quick, fetch some fresh cups."

She jumped up and ran to a shelf where they kept their mugs. She brought four to the table, setting them before each person.

"You two will just get a taste as you probably won't like it," Kaan said as he got up and poured a small amount into their mugs. Then he poured a healthier portion into his own cup as well as Brant's. He lifted his glass. "To friends and family." Everyone lifted their mugs as he toasted. Then they all drank.

Jana and Tobias immediately cringed, their faces wrinkled in distaste. But they knew it would be rude to spit out the small amount they were given, so they swallowed the burning liquid.

Brant held the liquid in his mouth for a moment, trying to analyze the flavor. The alcohol burned at first, but then the sensation disappeared and was replaced by a mild sweetness, followed by a flavor that he could not place. He swallowed and immediately his belly felt warm. The exotic flavors of the liqueur coated his tongue. They were flavors he had never before experienced. It was honey-like, with some sort of spice and a hint of smoke. The velvety liquid lingered in his mouth and he savored the experience as long as he could before swallowing.

Bannerfall

Kaan sat back in his seat, his eyes closed, he too enjoying the flavors before swallowing. "That is incredible," he whispered, opening his eyes. "Thank you, Brant."

Before Brant could respond, they heard a strange sound from outside. It was barely audible, but the uniqueness of it caught all their attention. It was a sound similar to one makes when they quickly move their tongues forward in their mouths, the wetness of the clicking giving the sound an eerie quality. They all sat up straight, listening intently.

The sound became softer, then louder, its pitch changing as it circled around the little cabin. It sounded as if whatever was making the noise was moving around the outside of the house at an astonishing speed.

"Brant, grab the sword! Kids, get against the far wall!" Kaan ordered as they all moved into action. Everyone sensed the alarm in the urgency of his voice, and followed his instructions immediately. The far wall he was referring to was the only windowless wall in the one room cabin.

Brant jumped up and grabbed the sword from its resting place near the door. Kaan did the same while double checking that the beam securing the door was still in place. Both of them backed up in front of the children, their swords held before them.

The sound continued, rising in volume. It was hard to describe, like a clicking sound underwater, wet but piercing.

"Father, what is it?!" Jana screamed, covering her ears against the eerie sound.

"I don't know!" he said tensely, then turned to Brant and whispered, "It's the kulg."

"Are you sure?" he asked softly.

"No, but I've never heard anything like that. And I've heard stories about them, how they make these horrible sounds before they attack."

Just then something crashed into the door, shaking it on its iron hinges. Jana and Tobias screamed.

"Promise me that you will not let them suffer as their mother did," Kaan whispered, lifting his sword higher.

Brant looked back at the children, Kaan's meaning clear. He didn't know if he could do it, but he knew he had to ease Kaan's fears. He nodded his head.

Bannerfall

The door shook violently again as another loud crash cracked the wooden beam that locked it, the sound of the splintering wood raking on Brant's nerves. And without even thinking, he brought forth his aura energy, the first time he had done so since he had left the camp. He could feel his strength and courage increase as the power flowed through his limbs.

The third hit was all it took. The wood beam snapped in half as the door was flung open. They were immediately assaulted by an overwhelming stench, the smell of death and decay, sour and putrid. And there, through their watering eyes, they saw, standing in the doorway, and silhouetted by the moon's glow, a tall figure shrouded in a ripped and torn black cloak, the worn garment fluttering listlessly around it. A hissing sound came from the creature as it floated through the doorway, its covered face, draped with the hood of the cloak. The children screamed louder and the kulg's hissing matched it, intensifying as their terror increased.

"Jana, Tobias, be quiet!" Brant ordered.

There was something in his voice that penetrated their fear. Instantly they were silent, and the kulg didn't like it. The beast made an eerie clicking sound as it crouched, spreading its arms out wide, impossibly wide. The creature was at least a head taller than Brant, with arms inhumanly long, its pale flesh and long clawed hands visible as it reached out beyond the dark cloak. Its hands, hideous and terrifying, were like gnarly driftwood branches sharpened to deadly points, covered with pale skin stretched tight over its bones. Yet despite the creature's repulsive appearance, Brant only saw a creature, a thing that had brutally killed his friend's wife. Any fear he had initially felt was now replaced by anger. The hatred he felt for the thing standing before him was palpable.

Before Kaan and Brant could act, the kulg raised its right hand, releasing an eruption of energy like crackling lightening, arcs of it flickering from one clawed finger to another.

Kaan glanced at Brant, their mutual understanding instant, born of the desire to protect the kids at all cost. In a blink Kaan shot forward to the kulg's right, while Brant, drawing upon his aura energy, ran to the beast's left.

A bolt of blue energy shot forth from the kulg's hand slamming into Kaan's chest, and launching him to the side where he struck the cooking counter with brutal force. Brant's unnatural speed carried him to the kulg almost instantaneously, his sword slicing sideways across the thing's outstretched arm. The blade struck true, but did little damage, slicing through the kulg's cloak and scoring a shallow cut across its arm. Before Brant could blink, he found himself flying through the air, his chest exploding in pain. He slammed into the far wall and crumpled to the floor. The creature was unbelievably quick, and incredibly strong.

Kaan struggled to get up as the kulg moved toward the children. Tobias, tears streaming down his face and trembling with terror, bravely stepped in front of his sister. But there was nowhere to go, the wall behind them blocking any escape.

"Stay away from them," Kaan growled, now standing awkwardly on an injured leg, his sword before him. His chest was scorched and his clothes hung from him, singed and smoking.

The kulg turned towards him, its movements jerky and unnatural. "Be patient," it hissed, its words barely recognizable. "You will all die in due time."

Kaan roared in fury and desperation as he attacked, his sword dancing before him. The kulg blocked the first strike with its long arm, the blade barely grazing it, but Kaan's second strike found its thigh, though the blade bounced harmlessly off it.

The creature made a sound that must have been laughter, then followed it up with a flash of its splayed claws, the dark talons digging deep across Kaan's chest and tossing him to the side as if he were a small a child.

Brant struggled to move as he lay at the base of the wall. He was hurt, and stunned, but something in him had begun to awaken. As he looked at the scene before him he saw flashes of color dancing around the room, making him dizzy. He shook his head, trying to clear it as he slowly stood. As he continued gazing, the colors were still there, but they were clearer, more acute. He realized that he was seeing everyone's auras, even the kulg's, whose dark colors of amber and gray danced around it uncontrollably. He squinted through the color and saw that Kaan had been knocked to the floor as the kulg approached the children, whose auras were now flashing bright blue with fear.

Brant concentrated on the kulg, trying to lessen the intensity of the lights. He looked for his sword and found it on the ground next to him. Reaching down, he picked it up. The weapon felt different, more like an extension of his arm. He stumbled forward, his body in pain, his mind dizzy, lifting his sword as he tried to focus through the dancing colors.

Then Tobias screamed. In a flash he could see again, although the colors of their auras did not go away, they just lessened, enabling him to see the kulg lift Tobias by the throat with one hand. Tobias's scream of fright had broken through Brant's dizziness.

Something surged within him, and Brant made no attempt to stop it, pushing incredible energy to his extremities. The power of his aura roared in his head, sounding like a thundering waterfall, and almost immediately his sword burst with an intense blue energy, and he launched his body forward, fueled by the aura energy firing through him.

But the kulg sensed the attack, dropping the boy and spinning to meet it, only to feel the force of a Merger's blade slam through its body, emerging out its back. The power of Brant's attack sent them both slamming against the wall behind them. Luckily, Tobias was lying on the floor, and Jana had just enough time to scoot out of the way. As they hit the wall, Brant felt his sword literally disappear, turned to dust by the intensity of the aura energy.

But the damage had been done. Brant scrambled away from the kulg, who was now convulsing against the wall as it struggled to stand.

"Brant!" Kaan yelled behind him. Brant turned around to see the farmer's sword fly through the air towards him. In his enhanced state it looked as if Kaan's blade was flying in slow motion. Brant's body, still burning with aura energy, more than he had ever before experienced, spun around easily, catching the blade with one hand. Anyone watching would only have seen the blur of his body as it moved with incredible speed. Without slowing, Brant continued his spin toward the kulg, who, incredibly was now standing, despite the terrible wound it had suffered. Everything happened in a flash. Kaan's sword, now in Brant's hand, also burst with blue energy, just as it struck the kulg's neck, and as the sword flashed into dust, the kulg's head parted from its neck, dropping to the ground and rolling several paces way.

This time the kulg's body slumped permanently to the floor, and it didn't move again.

Brant glared fiercely at the creature, his eyes wide as the intensity of his energy slowly faded. Then he slumped over, feeling completely drained. He was suddenly exhausted beyond belief. The floor welcomed him, beckoned him to lie down, to sleep, despite his desire to stay awake.

Bannerfall

He thought he heard Jana and Tobias yell their father's name, but the sound began to fade as the darkness overwhelmed him. The last thing he remembered before blacking out was the smell of the oak floor, and the vision of the kulg's sharp decaying teeth, pale, hairless face, and yellow eyes staring blankly back at him.

Chapter 4

Not much research has been done on the effects of the Way on the human body. I have heard of many physical abnormalities, some beneficial to the person and some not so much. I have personally seen only a few. We know for sure that harnessing negative energies, for a mage, can impact the user in a very negative way, creating not just severe headaches and sickness, but also mental illness or death. There are even worse fates as the negative energy can twist them into a blackness most physical and vile. But we know less about the effects of the Way on Sappers and Channelers. I have personally witnessed Channelers with minor deformities like larger eyes, pupils, or even entire eyes of unusual color, or complete hair loss. But I have heard tales told of Channelers and Sappers who had more severe abnormalities; issues like longer limbs, strange color hair, clawed hands, unusual voices, and many other rumors. I believe that these occurrences are quite rare, and typically concern individuals outside the noble families, outlaws who use the Way in secret and who have never been formally trained. It is something that I plan to research further.

Journal entry 31

Kivalla Der'une, Historian, Keeper of the records in Cythera, capital of Dy'ain

---

5088, the 14th cyn after the Great Change

    Brant opened his eyes and was assaulted by a pounding headache. He heard strained voices, saw flashing colors, and it took him a moment to sort through the stimulus around him, finally noticing Jana's face above him, yelling his name.

    He was on his back and his entire body was sore. Brant sat up slowly as Jana scooted aside; the aura around her was flashing bright red.

Bannerfall

Brant had to close his eyes and that was when he remembered what Kulvar Rand had said, that in order to control your aura sight, you had to learn to concentrate on something. Eventually you would be able to turn your towd on and off at will. So Brant concentrated on his heartbeat, the rhythmic thumping pounding in his head as he tuned out everything else around him, including the voices of Jana and Tobias, who were clearly agitated.

When he finally opened his eyes he could see much better, his headache had lessened and Jana's aura, although not gone, had dampened. Finally he heard what she was saying.

"Brant, are you okay!? It's father, he is badly hurt." She reached down and helped Brant to his feet.

"I'm fine…I think." Brant glanced around and saw the kulg's body and head near the wall. It seemed he had only passed out for a few moments. He looked to his right and saw Kaan lying on the ground, vicious slashes across his chest bleeding profusely. Tobias was kneeling beside him, several rags held tight against the wounds. Brant went to Kaan's side.

"Brant, can you help him?" Tobias asked frantically, his hands covered in blood. "He is losing so much blood." Tobias was crying and Brant felt helpless, unsure of what to do.

Kaan's eyes fluttered open. "Good, you are alive," he whispered.

"Besides the cuts on your chest, what else is hurt?" Brant asked.

Kaan grunted as he shifted his body. "I think I have some broken ribs and definitely some burns. But those injuries won't matter if we can't stop the bleeding."

Brant looked around and saw a kitchen knife that had been scattered on the ground. "Hand me the knife," he said to Jana. She grabbed it and handed it to him. Brant cut up the side of Kaan's shirt, ripping the garment off to get a better look at the wounds on his chest. There were three deep lacerations, starting on top of his chest and moving down and across it. Each one was deep and as long as his forearm, exposing the ribs underneath in a few spots. Brant had no idea what to do, and his facial expression showed it.

"Brant, you need to clean the wounds and stitch them up," Kaan stammered. "Use the liquor you bought me. Let me drink some and use the rest to kill any infection in the wounds after you've cleaned them. Jana, get the needle and thread. You are the most skilled so you will have to do it. Don't think of it as my flesh, think of it like you are sewing together two pieces of leather." Kaan closed his eyes, clearly tiring from the loss of blood.

Brant found the bottle of liquor on the floor, and luckily it had not broken. "Tobias, get some clean water and fresh rags," Brant said. "Jana, get the needle and thread."

In a few moments everyone had what they needed and stood around Kaan. As if he sensed them, his eyes fluttered open at their arrival. "Here," Brant said, "bringing the bottle to his lips." Kaan took a long gulp, followed by another. "Tobias, wipe the wounds as best as you can." Tobias plunged some cloth into the water and wiped at the wounds, Kaan flinching every time he brushed the cloth over the cuts.

"I'm sorry, Father," Tobias said through the tears.

"It's okay, son, you're doing fine."

Every time he wiped blood away, more seeped from the cuts. Brant knew that that was the best they could do, and if they waited any longer he would just loose more blood. "Okay, that is enough. Kaan, I'm going to pour the liquor on the cuts. You ready?"

"Do it," Kaan said.

Brant slowly poured the amber liquid into the gashes, creating a mixture of blood and alcohol. Kaan clenched his teeth, letting out a muffled scream, but he held his body rigid to keep the alcohol where it belonged. He knew that his survival depended on killing whatever type of rot might be under the kulg's claws. The bottle had been nearly completely full, so Brant was able to fully douse the cuts, but by this time Kaan had passed out.

"Is he okay?" Jana cried, her hand on her father's forehead.

"I think so," Brant said, his voice strained. "I think he passed out from the pain. That is good, perhaps he won't feel what you are about to do." Brant looked at her. "You need to stitch up his wounds so he won't lose more blood."

"I can't do this," she said through her tears, holding the needle and thread with trembling hands.

"Yes you can. Your father needs you. He will die if we can't seal these wounds. You are tough, Jana, you can do this. Take some deep breaths and begin."

Jana followed his instructions and took several deep breaths, trying to stop her hands from shaking. Then she went to work. She started off hesitantly, her unsteady hands, slippery from the blood, fumbling the needle. But Kaan never woke up, nor flinched, even when the needle pierced his flesh, and that helped Jana visualize sewing through leather or cloth instead of human skin. As she progressed in closing the wounds the bleeding gradually slowed, making it easier for her to finish the task. Finally, after what seemed like an eternity, especially to Jana, she tied a knot in the last stitch.

While she had been working, Brant had ordered Tobias to get a pot of boiling water going and to find some clean cloth. Brant had removed the kulg's body, dragging it outside where he planned to bury it later. Then they cleaned up the mess from the fight. Tobias allowed the rags he had boiled to cool sufficiently, then gently wiped away the blood from his father until, despite the three long gashes across his chest, he looked presentable. Brant considered moving Kaan to his bed, but was worried that the process of lifting him would reopen the wounds. So instead, they made his spot on the floor more comfortable, carefully sliding a blanket under him. They then draped another blanket over him and placed a soft pillow under his head.

After they had done all they could, they stood for a while, looking down at him, watching his chest slowly moving up and down.

"Is he going to live?" Jana asked, her eyes red and her face still streaked with tears. Tobias looked at Brant, anxiously waiting for an answer.

Brant had no idea if he would live or not, but he knew they didn't want to hear that. "He will make it. He lost a lot of blood. But you did a good job stitching him together. And Kaan is strong. Don't worry. He will not die."

"Brant," Tobias said, looking at him suspiciously. "How did you kill that thing? I saw your sword light up with blue fire."

"Let us not talk of that now. Jana, prepare some broth for your father for when he wakes. He will need it to regain his strength. "Tobias, come with me and help me bury that creature."

Kaan woke on the second day. He had a slight fever the first day, but by the second day it had broken, and it was early the following day that his eyes fluttered open while Jana was wiping his face with a wet cloth. She grinned with relief, and shouted for her brother who was busy cleaning the plates from their morning meal.

"Tobias, Father is awake!"

Tobias ran over and knelt by Kaan. "Father, how do you feel?"

Bannerfall

Kaan looked around slowly, his dazed eyes taking in his surroundings. He seemed to be attempting to piece things together. "What happened?" he asked groggily.

"We were attacked by a kulg," Tobias said quickly.

Kaan paused, as his mind struggled to recall the events, "I remember," he said softly. Brant killed it?" he asked, but it sounded more like a statement than a question.

"He did," Jana replied.

"Where is he? Can I have some water?"

Jana looked at Tobias. "Go get Brant. I'll get you some water, Father." Tobias ran out the front door while Jana poured some cold water into a cup. Kneeling before him she tilted the cup to his lips, allowing small amounts of the clear liquid to pour down his throat. "How do your wounds feel?"

He lifted the cover off his chest to take a look. The stitches were a bit irregular but they seemed to be holding his flesh together nicely, and the blood had coagulated, leaving only an encrusted residue along the sutures. The skin around the stitches was still red and puffy, but there was no foul smell so they were relieved the wounds seemed to be healing cleanly. "They are tender and are beginning to itch a bit, but they seem to be healing. You did a very good job, Jana. Thank you."

"Father, I was so scared," she said, lowering her head.

Kaan reached up and held his daughter's hand as he looked her in the eyes. "You saved my life. You should be proud. *I* am very proud of you."

She smiled. "It was Brant that saved your life."

Just then Brant entered through the front door with Tobias on his heels. "You're awake," he said, kneeling next to Kaan. "How do you feel?"

Kaan smiled. "Sore and hungry, but I'm alive, and happy about that. Thank you for saving my family," Kaan said seriously.

"I'm just glad I was here."

"Not to seem ungrateful, but I think there is something you need to tell me, young man."

Brant sighed. "Kaan, I'm sorry I didn't tell you, but I really don't know much about it."

"*It* being that you are a Merger," Kaan said sternly.

"Yes, but I only just found out myself what that even means. What happened with the kulg was simply an accident. I didn't know what I was doing. The power just came and consumed me."

"It's a good thing it did. I'm afraid if you hadn't energized those blades, they would have done little damage to that beast."

"I'm sorry I destroyed your swords."

Kaan waved the comment away, smiling. "Do not fret, Brant, I would gladly destroy a thousand swords to save my family. Are you of noble lineage?"

"No. Both my parents were poor and my entire life has been spent working the mines."

"Well, I have heard of commoners being born with the Way, but you're the first one I've met. Be careful, Brant, your power will put you in danger."

"I know; which is why I never said anything to you to begin with."

Kaan nodded his head in understanding. "Well, I thank you again for saving my family. I don't know how I can repay you."

Brant was silent for a moment as he wondered, a bit wistfully, what it would be like to have a close family. After a few moments he spoke. "You don't owe me anything. Besides, I have more bad news."

Kaan raised his eyebrows. "What?" he asked guardedly.

"There is no more Sil," Brant said solemnly.

Kaan laughed. "Well that is bad news." Then he got serious again. "But think about it…if we hadn't had that elixir, I might be dead. There's no better cure than a strong drink, and there's no better tasting one than Sil.

"Worth every coin," Jana added.

Kaan nodded his head in agreement. "But I'd give anything for a sip now," he sighed. Then he gave Brant a more serious look. "What will you do when you leave here?"

Brant pursed his lips in thought. "I guess I'll go south. I'll look for work in the small towns along the way. But if no opportunity presents itself I'll head to Cythera. I was thinking of joining the Legion."

"A sound plan. One more thing. Do you think you could help me up so I could lay in my own bed instead of this hard dirty floor?"

Jana and Tobias laughed, happy that their father felt well enough to start complaining. "Sure," Brant said.

Bannerfall

Together, they helped Kaan up from the floor. He was visibly exhausted as he strained to make his way to his bed. Once he was comfortable, he spoke to Brant again. "We don't have much work left for you, Brant. But I was hoping you'd stay long enough for me to get on my feet again. What say you?"

Jana and Tobias were both looking at Brant expectantly.

"Of course I'll stay." Jana and Tobias grinned unabashedly.

One month later found Brant walking the cart trail south, his bag slung over his shoulder. Jana had packed him some dried tulkick, several rounds of homemade cheese, and two loaves of bread. Kaan had told him that the nearest town outside of Bygon, Amorsit, was a two day walk from their home. Brant had to admit that he was going to miss them. He had enjoyed the work at the farm, and the camaraderie he experienced with Kaan and his family was something new to him. It was strange, he had only been with them for six months, but he felt closer to them than he ever had with his own father.

At several points along the road, more cart paths branched off, heading both east and west to other destinations. He saw a few travelers throughout the day, one heading north with a cart of potatoes, and the other, a family heading east to visit some relatives in a small town called Summerbell. Before the sun had fully set, Brant stepped off the path to make camp for the night. There was a patch about five paces in diameter where the grass was all laying on its side, as if it had been used as a camp site before or maybe where a herd of tulkick had bedded down for a night. As soon as he saw the ring of stones and the cold remains of a fire Brant realized that it had previously been used by other travelers. He collected some wood nearby and piled it up by the stones and just when he was about to lay out his bed role and start a fire the sounds of an approaching wagon turned his attention away from the task. Standing up he saw a small covered wagon approach with two people sitting in the front.

"Ho traveler, might we camp with you this night? There is safety in numbers and we have exhausted the sun's light."

As they neared, Brant noticed that the man that spoke was young, perhaps in his twenties, while the passenger, who had thus far remained silent, was withered and old, with a long gray beard and mustache that covered most of his face. The old man wore a thick gray traveling cloak and he leaned forward in his seat to get a better look at

Brant. Brant noticed that his eyes looked strange, nearly white, with centers streaked with brilliant blue like lightning bolts flashing in a gray tumultuous sky. Despite the shadows caused by the setting sun, the man's eyes stood out like blood on snow.

Brant shrugged. "You are free to join me. But I have little food, and I should warn you that I know how to defend myself." His bravado sounded lame but he had little experience with dealing with travelers and the thought of sleeping near strangers set him on edge.

The old man turned his head curiously and Brant thought he saw the faint flicker of a smile. The young man nodded. "Thank you, sir. We have food to share if it pleases you and rest assured, we are simple travelers making our way home from Cythera. We will be of no harm." The man got down from the wagon and proceeded to help the older man, who once stood on solid ground moved slowly but steadily toward Brant. The younger man unhitched the mules and set about preparing their camp.

The old man sat cross legged in the grass as Brant went about building the fire. It wasn't long before the flames were flickering high, the light of the fire chasing away the darkness that had finally settled in around them. The younger traveler carried a lantern and after several trips had four heavy wool blankets as well as a bag of supplies lying before the warm flames. The old man simply sat their staring at Brant.

"Mc name's Tilden and this is Angon." He reached out and shook Brant's hand. Angon didn't move or say a thing.

"I'm Brant."

Reaching into his bag he pulled out three apples, a loaf of bread, some other things that Brant couldn't see in the darkness, as well as a contraption that looked like a steel tripod. "Apple?"

Brant had already laid out several hunks of cheese, his dried tulkick and a loaf of bread. The apple sounded good and Tilden could read his expression clearly enough. Tossing the apple to Brant he went about setting the tripod over the fire, a hook and chain dangling from the center over the flickering flames. Brant ate the apple with relish. "What was your business in Cythera," he asked, trying to break the silence. He was not one prone to many words and he had little experience with casual banter.

"We travel to the city once a year to pick up supplies that cannot be purchased anywhere else. We are on our way home now," Tilden replied. "What of you? Where are you headed?"

"Amorsit. I'm looking for work."

"What can you do?"

Brant shrugged. "I'm a laborer. I know a little of farming. What is your line of work?"

"Me? I take care of Angon." Tilden looked at the old man and Brant saw him nod. "Angon is a healer."

"I see." Loosening up some, Brant offered them some food. "I have some dried tulkick, bread, and cheese if you would like some."

Knowing that not to accept would be rude, Tilden agreed to several pieces of tulkick, a hunk of a crumbly cheese, and half of the loaf of bread. Tilden proceeded to procure a wine skin, a stringy cheese that Brant had never seen, a small slab of cured ham, as well as a jar of honey and butter that he slathered onto the bread. They shared it all and in the silence they filled their bellies, the warmth of the wine in their stomachs and the soothing heat from fire on their skin breaking any tension that remained.

"How did you injure your back?" It was Angon who spoke, his voice soft and gentle. Brant was almost startled as it was the only thing the old man had said so far, and besides how did he know that is back was still hurting him? Ever since the fight with the kulg, Brant had had flashing pain in his lower back. He suspected the injury occurred when he was tossed against the wall of the cabin. The pain came and went, worse when he lifted things or worked hard all day. It was as stabbing pain that was still causing him considerable discomfort.

"How did you know I hurt my back?" Brant was suddenly guarded and Tilden sensed the change in his demeanor.

"I can see it. Your aura is angry around the injury."

Tilden jumped in quickly. "Angon, perhaps it's not wise…"

Angon silenced him with a raised hand. "He is a Merger." This time it was Tilden's turn to look uncomfortable, and wary, his posture alert. Brant noticed that his hand had dropped to his hunting knife sheathed at his side. "Leave the knife, Tilden. Brant is no threat."

Tilden seemed to relax a little, but Brant did not. "How can you *see* my injury and how did you know I'm a Merger?"

Angon ignored his question and asked his own. "You have not known long, have you?"

There was something about the man that emanated power. He had a sense of confidence that surrounded him and without thinking,

Brant found himself answering him. "I have not. I was told...recently. I know little of this...power."

"You are not of noble lineage." It was not a question but Brant answered it just the same.

Brant shook his head. "No."

Angon looked to Tilden. "Would you mind preparing some tylum?" Then he looked back to Brant, his strange eyes dancing with interest. "We can talk over a warm drink. Have you had tylum before?"

"I have not."

Tilden went about filling a metal pot with water and hanging it from the chain over the fire. "Tylum is a sweet drink made from a tylum pod," Angon continued. "It grows in Enoreth far to the south and is quite rare. Inside the pod are many white seeds, that when ground down to a powder and added to water and sugar, produce a smooth drink that is very delicious. It has a stimulating effect similar to coffee. I like to add a little ganth to mine."

Brant knew that ganth was a potent alcohol made from grain. "I've never heard of such a thing. But I am willing to try it." Suddenly Brant's mind flashed with bright colors as the auras of the two men in front of him blurred across his vision. Closing his eyes abruptly he leaned over as his mind swam with the disorientating colors. Closing his eyes had helped a little, but in his mind's eye he still saw flashes of colors that represented the auras of Angon and Tilden. Tilden's was barely noticeable next to Angon's shining aura. After twenty heartbeats the aura tracers had passed and he sat back up, opening his eyes to both of them staring at him.

"You will learn to control your towd. That is your aura sight. Think of something that you can mentally picture closing, like maybe a door or window shutters. As you practice closing the *shutters* to the sight, the flashes and disorientation will go away."

"How do you know this?"

"I am a Kynan." He said nothing more, as if it were enough to elicit a mighty response.

But Brant had never heard the word. "What is a Kynan?"

Tilden had poured the hot water into three cups and had stirred in the white tylum powder and sugar. He was just pouring in several capfuls of ganth when Brant had stated his ignorance of the Kynan. Stopping in mid-pour, Tilden glanced at Angon, his surprise evident. Angon seemed amused. "You have not heard of the Kynan?"

Brant knew that he lacked knowledge of the world around him, and it frustrated him greatly and angered him when other's pointed it out. "I said as much," he replied tersely.

Tilden handed them each a cup of tylum and Brant seemed to relax a little. "He meant no disrespect," Tilden added quickly. "It is just that Kynan is a word surrounded with silly superstition. For most people it is synonymous with demons and kulgs roaming the night, killing unsuspecting travelers. But those biases are based on ignorance and are far from the truth."

Brant took a sip of his tylum and despite his earlier flash of anger, a smile spread slowly across his face. The drink was simply incredible. It was smooth and thick, with a sweet buttery note countered with a warm bite from the ganth. "This is really good."

Angon smiled with him as he took a sip from his cup. "I'm glad you are enjoying it." Their conversation paused momentarily as they each drank their tylum. "I am Kynan, something rarely mentioned as people know not what it means. There are few of us left. In fact I am over three hundred years old."

Brant smiled at that as if it were a joke. But once he saw that Angon seemed serious, and that Tilden did not react as if it were funny, his smile disappeared and was replaced with a thoughtful look of his own. "You're serious?"

"I am."

"How is that possible?"

"Brant, I cannot tell you the mysterious of the world around you in one night sitting around a camp fire. But I will try to enlighten you some. What do you know of the gods?'

"Very little," he admitted. "I know there are old gods but they are no longer worshiped openly. I know that Argon and Felina are worshipped mostly throughout Corvell. That is the extent of my knowledge."

Angon sighed, as if Brant's lack of knowledge made it difficult for him to decide where to start. After several quiet moments he finally spoke. "Most people view the world through a lens of ignorance. People here, in Dy'ain, Kael, Gilia, and Layone, will have you think that the world and everything in it were creations of Argon and Felina, including the Way, the power that you yourself possess. But it is simply not true. Think of the world as you know it as a bag filled with sand, and the belief that that bag was created by Argon and Felina being just one grain. Our world is much older than that. Each grain of sand in the bag goes back many cyns ago, and each grain, or maybe two, being another idea or belief of how the world was created."

"I cannot wrap my thoughts around something that big," Brant interjected.

"Few can, which is why they focus on one grain of sand at a time. I am Kynan. We are scholars, we are healers, and we are wielders of the earth's magic. We have been around for many grains of sand, but even we have no idea how many thousands, or millions, of grains there are in this bag. The magic in our world is old and deep, entwined in its essence in a way that is difficult to understand. Over many grains of sand and thousands of cyns, we have been hunted, killed, and banished, our knowledge lost in the wind like a leaf caught in a storm. But it was not always this way. Long ago, thousands of cyns before me, the Kynan were the shepherds of this magic. We cultivated it and nourished it, but for reasons even I do not know, we slowly lost our power and way, and eventually we nearly became extinct. We are few now, shunned and hunted as demons in the night. But know this, the power that resides in you, is earth magic that created everything you see. The Way, as you call it, was not created by Argon and Felina, nor was it graced to the nobility by Argon and Felina, as many royal families would have you believe."

Brant was trying to digest all that Angon said but was having a difficult time coming to terms with the size of it, with the vastness of his words. "So do the gods exist?"

Angon paused for a moment as if he was thinking. "That is a difficult question to answer. But first, let me show you something." Without waiting for Brant to respond, Angon lifted his right hand and closed his eyes.

Brant had a sudden flash in his mind as his towd flickered on. He wasn't sure if he did it himself or if something Angon did triggered it, but suddenly he could see the auras of the two men opposite him glowing beyond the firelight. And Angon's hand started to glow a subtle blue in contrast to his warm aura made up of a hues of orange, red, and yellow. His lower back began to grow warm and the sudden sensation caused their aura's to flicker and turn dark, his towd turned off like a switch. Within moments the aching pain in his back disappeared, replaced with a minor tingling sensation that lasted for a few moments before it too vanished. "What did you do?" he asked in wonder, his hand moving to massage his newly healed back, expecting to feel pain. But there was none.

"I brought forth the power of the earth and healed you. It is not so difficult if one knows what to look for."

"So you are an Aurit?"

"Not really. But the power comes from the same place. Our auras pull energy from the earth, from the source, and when you draw upon it you are drawing forth power from the same source that I just tapped. I do not have the powers of a Merger, or an Aura Mage. My power is more closely aligned to that of a Channeler, but even that would not be accurate. I understand the true power; therefore I have fewer rules in its use and more flexibility in its delivery."

"You still have not answered my question. Do the gods exist?"

Again he paused as he drank from his mug. "Truthfully, I do not know. There are many worlds besides our own, all with many stories about their creation. The one thing they all have in common is that they don't seem to have a beginning. As a scholar who has traced the many stories back to their creation, all I find are more stories. Inevitably, the only thing I have learned about our creation is that I cannot find a beginning. Do I believe in the old gods? Do I believe in Argon and Felina? Simply put, no. But do gods exist? That is a question that I cannot answer."

They sat silent for quite some time, drinking from their mugs, staring into the fire, their thoughts alone. Finally Brant spoke. "Thank you for healing my back. I must admit that you have given me much to think about it. I feel as If my mind is drowning."

"It is a lot to…digest," Angon added. "It is a burden that I carry."

"Burden? What do you mean?"

"Knowing. Knowing things is a burden. What I have told you is just a scratch on the surface of what I know."

Brant nodded his head, thinking that perhaps he understood.

"Brant, I would suggest that you do not mention you have shared a fire with a Kynan," Tilden said, speaking for the first time in a while. "It may not bode well for you."

"You are really that despised?"

Angon nodded his head. "I'm afraid so. They think us evil…demons who bathe in the blood of their victims. Our knowledge contradicts what many believe, and therefore we are a threat. There is much more to this history, more than can be discussed in one evening. Just be cautious and wary in uttering the name Kynan."

They spoke softly and of more trivial subjects for the rest of the evening, sharing food and drink and enjoying the warmth of the fire.

When the morning came they ate a cold breakfast and parted ways with just a few words. "Friend Brant," Angon said, sitting forward in his wagon, "If you are ever near the village of Torset on the road to Tanwen, look for the large vylin tree just outside of town. You will see it clearly as it looks as out of place as a field of sallis flowers on a desert plain. Stop by and pay us a visit. I would enjoy talking with you more." Brant thanked him again and they left; the jostling of the wagon the only thing heard in the stillness of morning. Brant slung his gear over his shoulder and started on his trek once again.

On the second day, just as the sun was getting low on the horizon, he saw the town. Amorsit was nestled comfortably against a copse of trees. It wasn't large, typical of the small farming villages that were scattered across the steppes of Dy'ain. As he neared the town's entrance he saw several clusters of homes flanking a few larger buildings, one of which looked to be the town's inn. The other buildings appeared to be maybe a blacksmith shop, a pub, and some sort of market. As he got closer, he noticed that the entrance leading into the town was framed by two of the large buildings. One was clearly the town's inn, while the other had a sign before it that read 'Jon's Mercantile'. Each of the buildings along the road was equipped with a small wooden awning extending over the entrance. Lanterns hung from the support columns, their light flickering against the weathered wood of the buildings. To Brant they seemed quaint, but welcoming and comfortable. There were a few people about, some departing the establishments to more than likely head home for the night, while others were working, sweeping the entrances and cleaning horse manure from the tethered locations located all along the store fronts. Brant continued down the street, past the shops of a tailor, a blacksmith, and a tanner. There were also more homes scattered about, some extending along alleys which branched off on both sides of the road. At the far end of town, neatly placed among the trees that edged the small glade, were the larger homes of the more prosperous families of the town. It took him a surprisingly short amount of time to walk through the entire town and find himself back at the entrance to the inn. He knew that this would be the best place to look for work. He still had some coin left, and despite his refusal, Kaan had given him several silvers for helping his family while he recovered from his injuries. It wasn't much, but Brant knew that it was all he could spare.

Warm air enveloped Brant as he entered the inn. It was similar to, but larger than, the inn at Bygon. There was a bar directly in front of him and ten to fifteen tables were arranged on the wood plank floor before it. On opposite sides of the room were two large stone fireplaces, their crackling fires casting a warm glow around the room. Just less than two hands of people were seated at tables or leaning against the bar, drinking, eating, and talking. As usual, they turned to glance at the newcomer as Brant made his way to the bar. Suddenly his mind was bombarded by the flashing of the auras of the people around him and he stumbled, keeping himself from falling by placing his right hand on a nearby empty table. He knew he had to focus on something else, so he closed his eyes and again concentrated on his heartbeat, trying his best to control his towd. When he opened his eyes, the auras had diminished, but had not totally disappeared. He stood up straight, noticing the curious looks of some of the patrons. He smiled wanly, hoping to disguise his stumble as a trip, glaring at a nearby chair as if it were the culprit. The auras now appeared as only a subtle glow, and Brant was grateful that he felt no pain in his head. He closed his eyes briefly, one more time, creating a mental picture that he was closing shutters against the daylight sun. He silently thanked Angon for teaching him the mental trick, something he had previously attempted on a traveler he had met on the road just hours before. It had worked then, just as it had now, though it had taken a bit more effort with the larger numbers of auras in the inn. The light of the auras diminished, finally disappearing as his mental shutters closed. He took a deep breath to steady himself and walked to the bar.

The barkeep was an old man, his browned and weathered face creased with so many wrinkles that he looked as if he had lived in the sun for most of his lengthy life. His silver hair was thinning, and hung ill-kempt to his neckline. "Ho, stranger. What's your fancy?" he asked, his voice deep and hoarse, as if he had been yelling all day.

"Just passing through. My name's Brant. I was hoping to find some work if you know of any. And while I'm here I'd like a warm meal if possible."

The man looked him over briefly. "We have a hot pork stew. I must admit that it might be some of the best stew I've ever made. I braised it in wine and it's been simmering all day."

"You're the chef and the barkeep?"

The man snorted. "Not really, my wife does most of the cooking. But I cook the meat. It's sort of a hobby, but I will say that I prepare the finest meat dishes in these parts. My name's Borgan." They shook hands across the bar.

"It does sound good. How much?"

The old man looked Brant over again, perhaps appraising his wealth.... or the lack thereof. "I'll sell ya a bowl for two tiggs."

That was more than reasonable, and Brant strongly suspected that Borgan had lowered the price for him, clearly aware that he was not a man of means. "I'll take a bowl and a glass of water."

"Coming right up," he said as he walked through a swinging door behind him.

Just then Brant heard some commotion at the door and he turned to see four men burst through, laughing boisterously. They looked to be a little older than Brant, and one carried a jug in his hand. Stumbling around the tables they found a vacant one by one of the fires. They had clearly been drinking, and Brant watched them as they continued to pass the jug around, each taking another deep swig.

Borgan reappeared and set a steaming bowl of stew and a healthy slice of buttered bread before him, along with a large mug of water. Brant noticed his frown when he saw the new arrivals by the fireplace.

"Looks they are having fun," Brant said, nodding towards the fire.

Borgan sighed wearily, his displeasure obvious. "They come in often, usually drunk to start with. And it just gets worse."

"Can't you kick them out?"

Borgan shook his head in frustration. "Not so easy to do when the big one over there is the magistrate's son. Stay away from them. They are trouble."

Brant looked them over one more time. He didn't want any trouble so he turned his attention to the food. "Smells good," he said, digging into the stew. Borgan was right. The stew was the best he had ever had. He smiled through a mouthful as he laughed inwardly, realizing he had sampled so few stews, so by no means was he a reliable critic. But it was delicious. Borgan must have seared the pork over coals before he had braised it. He could actually taste the smoke from the meat and there was a complex flavor of savory herbs he could not identify, along with the subtle taste of the wine infused broth. His taste buds were very happy.

The boisterous newcomers gradually grew louder as he quickly consumed his meal. Five bites into his stew, a serving girl pushed through the swinging doors, smiled briefly at him, and made her way to the rowdy table. Brant was unaware that he had stopped chewing and was momentarily holding his breath. She was stunningly beautiful, with long lustrous black hair that in the lantern light looked like shimmering oil. Her tan smooth skin glistened with perspiration from her work and her green eyes, surrounded by long black eyelashes, dazzled with an inner light that, despite her obvious busy job, reflected a person who seemed to love her work. Brant liked her immediately.

Brant finally swallowed, glancing back as she attempted to get orders from the disorderly young patrons. It was obvious that they knew each other, their practiced banter painting a picture that they had all done this before. The magistrate's son, the largest of the four, attempted to wrap his arm around her waist and pull her onto his lap. She expertly slipped away from him, slapping his arm in the process. Brant heard her say, "Stop it Tage! What do you want to drink?" The young man mumbled something back.

"She's quite a sight, isn't she?"

Brant turned to see the barkeep looking at him with a smile. Embarrassed, he took a drink of his water.

"It's okay, son. She's not my daughter," Borgan said laughing. The barkeep looked back at the table, his voice now serious. "Someday though, those boys are going to go too far."

"Why do you say that?"

Borgan pursed his lips thoughtfully. Then he looked back at Brant. "I'm a good judge of character, young man. There is something rotten in that boy."

"Tage, the magistrate's son?"

"Yup, and the others aren't much better."

Brant was about to respond when the young serving girl appeared next to him, laying her tray on the bar. She sighed in frustration, blowing a wisp of hair from her face. "Borgan, can you get me two pitchers of your wheat ale?." Brant could smell her; subtle hints of rose petals. Suddenly he felt a lump in his throat.

"Sure thing. Thea, this is Brant, a young traveler hoping to find work in town."

Thea flashed Brant a welcoming smile. "Hello, Brant. How did you like the stew?" She was looking at his empty bowl, which he had wiped clean with his last slice of warm bread. Brant, momentarily speechless, was mesmerized by her smile. She laughed, a lyrical melody in Brant's ears. "Isn't it good?"

Finally Brant got his voice back. "It's the best stew I've ever had." And he wasn't lying.

"I'm glad you liked it. So you're looking for work? What can you do?"

Brant shrugged. "I'm strong and a quick learner."

She thought for a moment as Borgan placed two pitchers of ale on her tray. "Hey, Borgan, what do you think about E'rake?"

"I was thinking that too. But I hate to introduce anyone to that cantankerous man."

Thea looked back at Brant. "There is a man named E'rake that owns a small mine outside of town along the Skeen River. He may need some help. But I warn you, he is an unpleasant man who would rather bark at you than say anything nice."

Brant grunted nonchalantly. "If you had met my father you'd know that wouldn't be a problem."

"Well then, if you're interested, there is a path on the north side of town. You'll see it when you get to the wood line. That path takes you along the Skeen River to his plot. It's nearly a day's walk."

"Thank you."

Thea smiled, picked up the tray, and carried it over to the rowdy table.

"You need a place to bed down for the night?" Borgan asked.

"I could use one."

"Well, I have rooms out back. I can let you have one for a shike. If that's too steep I have a storage shed out back. You are more than welcome to bed down there for a tigg. It's drafty, but I have some blankets in there you could use."

Brant thought about it for a moment. He thought it better to conserve his money. "The shed will be fine."

"Let me know when you want to retire." Borgan turned around and grabbed two cups, filling them both from a barrel behind him. He set one in front of Brant and he started drinking from the other.

Brant pushed the cup away. "I don't have the coin to waste on ale."

"It's on me. I don't like to drink alone."

Just a few months ago and Brant would have been leery of the gift. This was the second time someone had given him something for nothing, but this time he did not react with suspicion, realizing that not everyone was like his father. Brant smiled. "Thank you."

They drank and talked for over an hour. The inn began to fill with more patrons as the evening progressed and Borgan was forced to shorten their conversation as he busied himself with pouring drinks and helping Thea get food from the kitchen. Yet somehow he managed to find time to refill Brant's cup. After a couple of hours, Brant was feeling pretty good. He was warm, his belly was full and he had an overwhelming urge to talk. Turning around on his stool, he scanned the busy room.

His eyes were drawn to more commotion from the table where the magistrate's son and his friends were sitting. Brant had been drinking more than usual, but they had begun drinking even before they came to the inn, becoming louder and more obscene as the night wore on. As Brant glanced at them, Tage, the magistrate's son, threw a clay jug against the stone of the fireplace, the noise of the shattering clay causing a momentary hush in the room. Once the crowd saw it was Tage causing the disturbance, they quickly resumed their conversations as if this were a normal evening event. Thea was at their table instantly, berating Tage while his cronies laughed. Brant was disgusted at their behavior, and he felt a flash of anger. But Borgan's warning rang in his ear and he subdued the urge to rise from his chair and teach the man a lesson.

Just as he was visualizing his fist crushing Tage's nose, the big man rose from his chair and stumbled towards the bar next to Brant. Tage was two fingers taller than Brant, with wavy shoulder length brown hair, green eyes, and a rare light complexion dotted with freckles. Brant thought he looked like a pompous aristocrat. He had that arrogant look that he had seen in some of the head wardens.

Bannerfall

"Hey Borgan!" Tage yelled through the swinging doors that went to the kitchen. Brant glared at him with disgust. Tage noticed his stare, and gave him a challenging look. "What are you looking at?"

Brant could smell his breath, heavy with garlic and ale. He narrowed his eyes. "Nothing."

Either he was too drunk, or just stupid, but he didn't get the insult. "Better not be," he said, his words slurred.

Borgan hustled through the door. "What do you want, Tage?"

"I want a bottle of Kaelian Red."

"I think you've had enough," Borgan replied.

Tage slammed his fist on the table, upturning Brant's mug in the process. Then he slammed his other hand down, a gold drack spinning on the table. "Get the damn wine!"

"You don't need to yell," Brant stated flatly, his anger slowly boiling to the surface.

Borgan looked at Brant meaningfully, warning him with a subtle shake of his head.

Tage looked at Brant. "What did you say?"

"I said you don't need to yell," Brant repeated, looking directly at him.

"Tage, don't worry about him. He's just passing through. I'll get you your wine. Go back to your seat and I'll bring it to you."

Tage shoved Brant in the shoulder. Brant was expecting it and he flexed his muscles, making his body rigid. Tage might as well have tried shoving a brick wall. "Don't push me...*farmer*," he spat out the last word as he glared disdainfully at Brant's clothes. Tage had expected his shove to razzle Brant, or at least knock him off the stool. But it did neither, and he was unsuccessfully trying to hide his uncertainty when he did not get the reaction he expected, in its place a stern man, his dark eyes boring into him as he tried to hold in his anger.

"You better do as Borgan says or this will not end well for you." Brant's jaw clenched reflexively as he used all of his will power to not lash out at the bully.

Suddenly Thea materialized at the bar, placing a tray of empty mugs on the counter. "Come on, Tage, let's go back to the table."

Brant wasn't sure if she had sensed a potential conflict, or if she was just doing her job. Or maybe she saw the look on Borgan's face. Either way, she successfully redirected Tage's attention elsewhere.

"Hey, beautiful," he slurred as he put his arm around her. "You coming home with me tonight?"

She tried to squirm away but he held her tight, turning her so they were both facing Brant. "Hey, *farmer*, do you think you'll ever get to bed a woman like this?"

Thea was now angry and she tried more forcefully to get out from his grasp. "You'll never bed me. Now let me go!"

Tage laughed derisively, his big arm holding her tighter. "Maybe not tonight, but I will someday."

"Tage, let her go," Borgan ordered.

"Shut up, Borgan. Go get that wine."

Brant could no longer contain himself. He stood up slowly from his chair and turned to face Tage.

"She asked you to let her go. Now do it." His voice was calm, but edged with violence, like the soft rumbling of thunder before a storm.

Tage released her, shoving her violently into the bar and knocking over the tray of mugs. Tage smirked. "What are you going to do about it?"

Brant was barely under control. His anger was clawing inside him, trying to break free. But, again he saw the look on Borgan's face, and he kept his fists at his side, well aware that Borgan did not want him to start a fight.

But then, out of nowhere, Tage slapped Brant across the face with the back of his hand, the force of the blow jerking his head to the side and destroying every ounce of will power that was holding his anger at bay. It surged forward and washed over him like a crashing wave. Brant turned his face and looked directly at Tage, his eyes narrowed and his face a mask of impending violence.

The big man was taken by surprise, thinking that the sudden blow would have been enough to cause the newcomer to back down and leave. But he had misjudged this young man. Instead of fear, he saw raw, unbridled fury in the eyes of the farmer, if that was indeed what he was. He knew he was about to be attacked, and instinctively launched his right fist forward in an effort to block the man's foolish response.

By this time Brant was so consumed with destroying the arrogant brat that his anger had eradicated any vestige of remaining caution. Perhaps the ale had helped wash it away. Now, in his mind's eye, the fist was coming at him in slow motion. Before Tage had even initiated the attack, Brant had instinctively surged aura energy into his body, concentrating a little more in his fists. In a blur, Brant side stepped the swing, following through with a vicious left hand punch to the man's kidney. Tage grunted, the force of the blow knocking him into the bar so hard that he bounced off only to find Brant's follow up right handed uppercut, hitting him so hard it shattered his nose and broke his jaw, launching him into the air where he landed several paces away.

The room was deathly quiet. Tage lay on the floor, silent and still. Brant's anger and power still surged through his body, his fists shaking with the energy. He glanced at Thea whose eyes stared back at him, wide with shock. In less than three blinks of an eye, Brant had unleashed such a concentrated act of violence and destruction that the people who watched seemed paralyzed with shock.

Borgan was the first person to react, running to Tage's side. "Tage, wake up!" he said, shaking his limp body. Tage still didn't move.

His friends slowly stood up from their table and walked over to stand in front of Brant. The young men looked to Tage and back to Brant, clearly uncertain of their next action. They, too, were stunned and showed no desire to attack. They had just seen him dispatch their friend with such fierceness and precision, that they had no desire to suffer a similar fate.

Thea ran over and joined Borgan at Tage's side. She put her ear to his mouth and rested her hand on his chest, hoping for any sign of life. But there was none. She stood up slowly and looked at Brant, "He's dead," she said quietly, her voice expressing mixture of dread and disbelief.

Brant's anger dissipated as quickly as it had come. He stepped back a few paces, his fists still shaking, but this time not from the power, but from fear. He had just killed a man.

The terrible reality of it what he had done hit him even harder when a patron in the crowd yelled for someone to summon the town's guard.

Brant's mind was racing. What should he do? Should he run for it? It was self-defense, anyone could see that. He was attacked first. But would that matter? He had just killed the magistrate's son. There was no way he would get a fair hearing. And where would he run? The town's guard was sure to have horses. He didn't have a chance.

Brant wearily sat himself down on a nearby stool, his mind made up. It was eerily silent. Then Borgan appeared beside him. "They are going to arrest you," he said.

Brant looked up at him and nodded his head dejectedly. "I'm so sorry. I didn't mean to. It was self-defense. He attacked first."

Borgan shook his head sadly. "I'll attest to that. But it won't matter. You killed him…and he was the magistrate's son."

"Should I run?"

"You could try. But they will catch you. They have dogs and horses. You wouldn't stand a chance."

"Then I have no choice."

There was a commotion at the door as three armed men, wearing Legionnaire armor, entered with swords in hand. Everyone pointed to Brant, who turned in his chair to face them. *It was going to be a long night*, he thought.

Brant had been dragged to a holding cell for the night. The guards had said nothing other than he would face the magistrate in the morning. The cell was located in a building on the far end of town, near the tree line, and it looked to be an office with several cells located in the back. There was another room off the main room that Brant guessed was where the Magistrate held proceedings. He didn't know it at the time, but any town in Dy'ain, with a population over five hundred, had a magistrate and a small contingent of Legionnaires. Towns with populations below that would fall under the jurisdiction of the nearest magistrate.

He didn't sleep much, wondering what would happen to him, and berating himself. If he hadn't used his Aurit abilities, he wouldn't be in this predicament. More than likely he would have simply knocked Tage out, not killed him. He didn't mean to hit him so hard. But he had been unable to control his anger.

The lock to the door clicked and Brant sat up. Two guards entered and motioned for him to stand. His wrists were still chained, and one of the guards grabbed the chain, yanking him forward. "Let's go," he said. "The magistrate is waiting."

The guards led him into the main room and through the side door that he had noticed the night before. They entered a room with a raised dais on one side and a series of chairs facing it. On the dais was a large desk and a comfortable leather chair. Behind the desk were several shelves stacked with thick leather bound books. Brant was grateful to see Thea and Borgan seated and facing the desk. They both looked worried.

At the desk, a red magistrate's cloak draped over his shoulders, a man sat with his head down reading. His short brown hair was streaked with silver. Looking up from his papers, Brant could see that his eyes were red and puffy. He had clearly not slept well that night. He had the typical look of many well fed aristocrats. His face was a little plump and freckles were scattered across his pale complexion. The magistrate didn't look like most dark haired dark skinned Dy'ainians. He wore a trimmed mustache and a beard that tapered neatly to point.

"Sit down," he said, his voice cold and emotionless. The guards motioned for Brant to sit in the single chair facing the raised desk. "State your name."

"Brant Anwar."

"Where are you from?" he continued, jotting down the information into some sort of ledger.

"I'm from the king's mining camps. I left last year after my father died."

"Where have you been since?"

"I spent half a year working on a farm near Bygon. Then I came here, just last night."

"Who's farm?"

"A man name Kaan."

"I know him. Bygon falls under my jurisdiction. He will vouch for you?"

"Yes."

"Where did you learn to fight?"

"I fought in the camps. My father taught me."

"Tell me what happened last night."

Brant was worried. The magistrate appeared far too controlled for someone whose son had just died the night before, by Brant's own fists. And now he sat before him acting as if this were just another case. Something wasn't right. "I was at the bar, eating and drinking, when the man, Tage was his name, came to the bar. He was drunk, and he challenged me. He shoved me and goaded me to fight."

"Are there witnesses to this?" the magistrate asked to the small audience. It looked as if Thea and Borgan were the only two with the courage to stand up to the magistrate and come to Brant's defense.

Borgan stood up. "Yes, sir. That is what happened."

The magistrate continued to write for a few moments as Borgan sat back down. His cold eyes again turned to Brant. "What happened next?"

"Tage grabbed the waitress, Thea, and was insulting her."

"How was he insulting her?"

Brant didn't want to repeat the man's words. But he had no choice. "He held her against her will, and he asked me if I would ever have a chance to bed a woman like her." Brant thought he saw the magistrate smirk through his otherwise stoic expression. "The barkeep, Borgan here, asked him to let her go. He was rude to him as well and continued holding Thea against her will. So I got up from my seat and asked him to let her go." Brant paused as the magistrate continued to write.

"And?"

"Then he backhanded me."

The magistrate looked up. "Witnesses?"

This time Thea stood up. "Yes, sir. It happened as he says."

The magistrate's eyes narrowed and Brant saw Thea shuffle nervously on her feet.

"Continue," the magistrate ordered, looking to Brant again.

"Well, then he swung at me again. This time I dodged the punch and hit him in the side and then the face. I did not mean to kill him, sir. I was just protecting myself. It was an accident."

This time the magistrate set his pen down and looked at Brant with undisguised malice. "An accident? You killed a man with two hits. And that man was my son. Now he may have been a drunk, and an idiot at times, but he did not deserve to die by the hands of some street fighter."

"I am no street fighter, I…"

"Shut up!"

Suddenly the door to the room opened and a man entered. Short and stocky, he wore fur lined leather clothes, and his chest was covered with a leather cuirass reinforced with plates of some sort of glossy black material. His skin was brown, as dark as tree bark, and his face was wide and almost flat. Long jet black hair fell from beneath the fur lined hardened leather helm he wore on his head. Brant could see the feathered ends of arrows jutting out from behind his back, along with the end of an unstrung bow which rose higher than the arrows, that was also stored in his quiver. He carried a unique sword tucked into his leather belt, the black scabbard narrow and slightly curved. The guard was not like those of the typical weapons used by the Legionnaires. Rather than being straight and simple, the guard was round, protecting the wielder's hand, and etched with intricate flowing lines. The handle itself was long and slightly curved, built for two hands, and wrapped with simple brown leather. Strapped to his right leg was a long hunting knife.

Brant saw the magistrate nod at the newcomer, then turn toward Brant. "Brant, you are accused of murder, and based on the evidence, I find you guilty. However, it seems, according to these witnesses, that it was self-defense. Therefore, in lieu of death, I sentence you to one year of slavery among the Schulg tribe. It just so happens that a member of this tribe arrived in town last night. That was just your luck," the magistrate said with an evil smile. "I sentence you to his care for one year."

Brant looked again at the stranger and the reality of his fate hit him. The man was a Schulg, a nomad, and he was here to take him away.

Borgan and Thea stood up. "Magistrate, you can't do this!" Borgan said.

"You know what they will do with him," Thea joined in. "He won't last the year!" she stormed.

The magistrate stood up, shoving his chair out behind him. "Sit down! Or I will arrest you too. This man!" he shouted, pointing at Brant, "has killed a man with his fists! He is a street fighter and his punishment fits the crime! And he will pay for that crime! Now, get him out of my sight!"

The Schulg tribesman came forward as the two guards lifted Brant up from the chair. They unlocked his chains and Brant instinctively rubbed his sore wrists. The Schulg stood before him looking him up and down, his expression deadpan. Then he reached out and grabbed his wrists, bringing them together in front of his body. Grabbing a thick leather thong from his belt, he wrapped it around Brant's wrists, expertly cinching it tight and tying if off. Then he reached for a rolled up length of rope at his belt, looped one end over Brant's head and pulled it tight. With a final grunt, the Schulg pulled the five foot rope and led Brant out of the room. It all happened so fast that Brant didn't know what to do. He was yanked from the room, and through the daze of shock he heard the fading sounds of Borgan and Thea's futile protests.

    They had been walking for half a day before the nomad slowed his horse. Brant's leash was tied to the back of the packhorse, and when the Schulg finally reined in his horse, the packhorse, which was attached to his horse, slowed as well. Brant was sweating profusely and his mouth was parched. He looked up as the Schulg dismounted, grabbed a water skin from his horse and walked to Brant's side.

    He handed Brant the water skin, grunting something unintelligible. Brant took the skin with both of his hands and brought the bag to his mouth, drinking greedily, the water washing away the dust from the road from his mouth. While he drank, the nomad withdrew something from a bag on the packhorse, and brought it to Brant. Taking the water skin away, he handed Brant what looked like a stick of dried meat.

    "What is it?"

    "Um'by."

    Brant had no idea what um'by was, but he was hungry. And by the looks of it, they were not done walking. They still had half a day until nightfall. He wasn't sure where they were going, but it looked as if they were traveling north, which Brant knew was the direction of Schulg territory. Brant ate his meal of what appeared to be some sort of dried meat. It was pretty bland, tasting mostly of salt, but he was hungry and ate it quickly. "What is your name?"

    The Schulg stood staring at him, his face emotionless. "Tangar," he grunted. "Your name?" he asked in Newain.

    "You speak my language?"

    Grunting, the nomad stepped closer. "Your name?"

    "Brant Anwar."

    Without warning the nomad punched Brant in the stomach. It was so fast that Brant had no time to even tighten his muscles. He doubled over in pain as the air in his lungs was violently forced out. That was when Tangar hit him in the face with a vicious uppercut. Brant flew backwards and landed in the dirt, coughing and trying to regain his breath.

    Tangar stood over him. "You fight for me," he said in stilted Newain. "Now up, we go three more days travel."

Despite the pain in Brant's nose, lips, and gut, he barely felt it through the anger rising up in him. Aura energy whirled around him and he pushed some into his arms and wrists, hoping to break the leather bonds cinched tight around his hands. But the angle was awkward and the bands were very thick, hardened by his sweat and the sun, and he could not break them.

Changing tactics, he channeled energy into his legs and suddenly kicked his right leg up, hoping to strike the nomad in the groin. He thought he had him, but at the last moment Tangar jumped up, using his own leg to deflect the blow. Brant couldn't believe how quickly Tangar had moved. But the power of his kick did catch Tangar off guard, as Brant's kick managed to throw his body backwards. But Tangar used the momentum of the kick to spin on his other leg like a dancer, dropping forward with his right knee and bringing it down hard on Brant's chest. Brant grunted from the weight and the pain. The Schulg then snapped his fist forward and struck Brant in the eye, knocking his head back into the dirt. Brant was dazed and groaning, the weight of the nomad still heavy on his chest, his bony knee digging into his sternum.

Tangar was looking at him, this time his eyes reflected something different…maybe surprise, or even respect. "Good. You have fight. You will need it. And no try to break bonds. Leather thick and wrapped around strong rope. You not break."

The next day began with a chance for Brant to escape. But, as fortune would have it, he would not be so lucky. It wasn't yet an hour into their travels when they were confronted by four men who were hiding behind one of the few copses of trees growing sporadically throughout the steppes. The morning, although brisk, was warming quickly as the waking sun's rays sought the cool air, gently massaging it with a rising heat. Neither Brant nor Tangar missed the morning light reflected off the surface of drawn swords.

"What do we have here?" a bearded man said as he stepped out from the trees to stand in front of Tangar holding a pitted long sword casually over his shoulder. Tangar pulled on the reins and his horse stopped ten paces from him. The brigand wore mismatched leather armor, scratched, rusty and dusty, mirroring his own worn and disheveled appearance. The three others looked similar. Two brandished long swords while the third held a spear.

Bannerfall

"Looks like a dirty shit eatin' Schulg," the man holding the spear sneered. His straight dark hair was trimmed short and he was unremarkable looking except for his large crooked nose, which looked as if it had been broken more than once, and not set correctly, if at all.

Tangar, without a word, dismounted and stepped forward away from his steed. His horse stood completely still. Brant, secured to the packhorse which was tied behind Tangar's horse, watched curiously. He was hoping that maybe they would kill Tangar and release him; after all he had nothing they would want.

The bearded man lifted his sword off his shoulder and pointed it at Tangar. "Hold on there Schulg," he said, practically spitting out the last word as if it were a bad taste in his mouth. Clearly these thieves did not hold the Schulg in high regard. "Don't move another muscle." Tangar obeyed, stopped before him, but Brant noticed his hand casually dropping to the hilt of his blade. "Who is that tied up?"

Finally Tangar spoke. "Prisoner. Step aside and you not die."

The man with the spear looked at their leader with mock surprise and both started laughing. That was when Tangar attacked. Brant wasn't expecting it, and neither were the brigands. Rushing forward the nomad drew his sword in one fluid motion, the mirror-like blade flashing in the sun as it took the astonished spear holder in the arm, cutting it cleanly in two. He fell screaming as Tangar continued his movement forward, his sword flashing as he blocked and cut, spinning and moving through the three men like a hummingbird. At least that's how it appeared to Brant as he watched the Schulg nomad dispatch each of the other three men, dancing from one to another like a hummingbird to the flowers. Brant was stunned at how quickly it had all happened. Within moments three were dead and the one that had lost his arm was still screaming on the ground.

Tangar wiped his blade clean on the shirt of the dead leader and casually walked back to Brant, ignoring the man whose howls were now becoming whimpers as he grabbed at the stump that was once his arm, trying in vain to stop the bleeding. He mounted his horse and they moved forward, the jerk of the rope snapping Brant out of his shocked immobility. They trotted by the dying man without a word.

The next three days were a monotonous blur, during which the nomad had spoken maybe ten words to him the entire time. They walked, ate, drank water, and slept. Brant was tired, but the trek wasn't grueling. The worst part, however, was the leather straps around his wrists. His sweat had soaked into the leather and during the day the sun would dry the bonds, and despite the supposed metal core, the leather shrunk some and cut into his flesh. By the end of the third day he could barely feel his fingers.

Finally they arrived at a Schulg village. Hundreds of tents, that looked very similar to the bilts he was used to, were scattered across a flat plain. One end of the settlement was sheltered by an outcropping of rock. A small stream flowed around the huge stone outcropping and meandered through the village. Small bonet trees peppered the area. At full growth they were only as tall as two men, but their splayed branches, thick with tiny green leaves, spread out as wide as they were tall, providing shade for their animals.

It was mid-day when they had arrived and Brant was first paraded through town before they finally stopped at one of the bilts, a tent-like structure similar to what they used in the mining towns. Brant got the feeling that he was being presented to the village, and that their stares were somehow appraising him, for what he had no idea. The bilt had been set up along the western edge of the rock outcropping. The roof of the structure was made of animal hides stitched together and smeared with some sort of fat or oil for weather proofing. The base of the bilt was formed with rocks stacked up to form a round wall that was about as tall as an adolescent child. There were hundreds of Schulg about, performing their afternoon tasks, chopping wood, tending to their horses, and preparing food for their suppers. Most of the villagers looked up from their tasks, briefly looking at Brant as they walked by, seemingly unconcerned that a stranger was being escorted into the village with his hands bound and tied to a leash.

Tangar removed the rope from Brant's neck and shoved him into the bilt. Stumbling through the opening, Brant moved away from the nomad, backing up against the far wall of the structure. The interior was simple. The floor was dirt, but much of it was covered with animal hides. There was an unlit fire pit in the middle of the room and on one end was a pile of furs, probably Tangar's bed. There were three wood tables covered with odds and ends, cooking utensils, knives, cups and other utilitarian possessions. Near the fur bedding was a weapons rack. It was mostly empty except for a bow and quiver, one curved sword, and a belt with a long knife. Tangar removed the quiver holding his bow and arrows from his shoulder and laid it against the weapons rack. Next came his sword, which he placed onto two pegs that held the sword upright. The only visible weapon that he now carried was his knife.

"Sit," Tangar ordered, pointing to a pile of furs near the fire ring.

Brant sat down on the furs while Tangar went about preparing a fire. Once it was lit, he tossed Brant the water skin and sat opposite him.

"You fight for me," he said again, his Newain choppy but understandable.

Brant shook his head, not understanding him. "What do you mean?"

"Schulg villages fight other villages. We win," he said pointing to himself, "we make coin. You fight for me."

"And if I don't?"

The nomad smiled. "Then fighter kill you. I find new fighter."

"I have to do this for a year?"

The nomad smiled again. "No, as long as I say."

Brant had a feeling there was no such agreement. "I am your slave?" he asked, knowing the answer.

"Yes." Brant looked over at the weapons on the rack. Tangar noticed his glance. "Go," he grunted. "Grab weapon." Brant new he was taunting him.

Tangar stood up and slid the knife from a scabbard at his side. Moving next to him, Brant eyed the silver blade with uncertainty. But Tangar motioned for him to put out his hands, which after a few moments he did, the desire to rid himself of the constraining bonds overriding any fear of the blade. Several flashes later and his hands were free. Immediately the blood rushed back to his fingers and his hands burned from the pain. Rubbing them, he slowly massaged the pain away until normal feeling returned to them while the nomad returned to his seat.

"What do I fight with?"

"Start with fists. Move to weapons. I train you so you don't die. I make money."

"Who determines the winner?"

"Winner not dead."

Brant had a feeling he was going to say that. "Where do I sleep?"

"Not here. Outside village. I take you in morning. I make food now." With that, Tangar stood and went about preparing supper. Brant looked about and noticed that very little light was shining through the cracks between the leather flaps that blocked the entrance to the bilt. It must be getting dark. He knew he had to try to escape. There was no way he was going to fight for him. He would be killed. Now he knew what Borgan and Thea were yelling about when he was dragged out of town. They knew he would be thrown into the ring and more than likely killed. He had suspected that the magistrate had something like this planned for him, and sure enough, he was right.

Tangar was paying him little attention as he went about preparing the meal. Brant figured that if he ran for it that he might be able to escape into the night. He did have an advantage. Tangar had no knowledge of his Aurit abilities. Maybe he could kill Tangar, or knock him out, and escape the village with no one else the wiser.

He glanced over at the weapons rack. The closest weapon to him was the belt knife. It appeared to have a bone handle of some sort. The blade was long, about the size of his forearm. Brant was a little worried though. His wrists were sore and his fingers were still tingling from the loss of circulation. If he couldn't hold onto the knife then he would have to resort to his fists. He was confident there, but he knew Tangar had a knife and his altercation with him a few days ago showed that he was no stranger to combat. He would have to take him quickly.

Taking a deep breath, he pushed aura energy into his legs and launched forward, reaching the knife quickly. But as fast as he was, Tangar was ready. In fact it looked as if he had been expecting the move the entire time. He spun with lightning speed as Brant lunged at him with the knife. But before he could reach the nomad, something struck Brant in the shoulder, causing him to stumble backwards. Brant looked down at his shoulder. A small knife was buried into it, no more than an inch in depth. But despite the relative superficiality of the wound, the stinging pain of it dropped him to his knees. He hadn't even seen the nomad move.

"It poison. Don't worry, won't kill. Just hurt."

Brant withdrew the knife and fell back on his haunches, the pain lancing through his body in what felt like stabbing electrical pulses. Tangar was right. It did hurt, a lot. Groaning with pain, Brant fell to his side, holding onto his shoulder and wishing the pain would go away. "How long…will…it…last?"

Bannerfall

"Half the night. You very fast. That is good. We eat soon." Then Tangar went back to preparing the meal, ignoring the sounds coming from Brant as he tried unsuccessfully to shut out the pain.

Tangar was right. About halfway through the night, Brant's pain began to gradually subside and he was able to finally fall into a fitful sleep. The morning came too quickly, however, and after a quick meal of cooked oats and water, Brant was taken to another location outside the village. He felt tired and his body ached. He assumed it was due to lack of sleep, residual poison, or both.

It took them an hour to get there and when they arrived Brant was greeted by a strange sight. A huge creature, easily two heads taller than he was, was stacking large stones from one pile to another. He was shirtless and wore only tan leather leggings. Three giant hounds sat nearby watching the beast move the stones. Behind the creature was a small cliff face, dominated by a cave entrance.

Brant pulled up short, eyeing the creature with uncertainty. The beast, if that's what it was, lowered a huge stone, squatting to use its massive legs to add the stone to the pile. Looking up, Brant made eye contact with it. The thing looked human, more or less, but was much bigger, and its skin was a light shade of mossy green. Brant could see that its eyes were green as well, though a brighter shade, almost iridescent. The beast's large forehead was hairless all the way to the crown, at which point a thick mane of long coarse brown hair grew, tumbling in disarray down to the middle of its muscular back. Its features were human-like, but its eyes were a little wider apart than normal, and its head was disproportionately large for his body. But the most unique feature was its wide mouth which reached almost ear to ear. Dark green lips framed rows of small sharp teeth making it look ferocious.

Brant's attention was then directed to the three hounds, as each one stood, growling ominously as they entered the clearing. Tangar shouted something in Schulg and they immediately quieted, lying back down and watching the big creature. Each hound was nearly as big as a mule and their thick fur grew in hues of gray, with streaks of brown and gold highlighting their flanks. Brant could see how it would provide perfect camouflage when hunting the grasslands of the steppes, which he figured they would be quite adept at.

Bannerfall

"Move," Tangar Grunted, pushing him toward the beast. "Gar'gon!" Tangar shouted into the cave. Immediately a large nomad ran from the opening carrying a long leather whip. He was big, round in the belly with a large head. His head was shaved except for a long thick tail at the crown tied with a leather strap. It hung to the middle of his back, flopping back and forth as he ran out to his master.

Tangar yelled something to him in Schulg and they conversed for a few moments. Then Tangar went and stood next to the creature. It was then that Brant noticed the long scars that covered its arms and chest, some red and raised, clearly recent results of Gar'gon's vicious looking whip. But what really stood out were the five sigils that had been burned into its flesh, the scar tissue slightly raised and puffy. Each was about the size of a child's fist and uniquely different, spanning his wide muscular chest.

"This is Uln," Tangar said, addressing Brant. "He fight for me."

"What is he?" Brant asked.

"I Varga," Uln said, its voice a deep throaty baritone. He spoke in stinted Newain. "You are?"

Brant was surprised that he could speak. He looked so animalistic. "I'm Brant. What is a Varga?"

Uln snorted. Brant wasn't sure if it was a laugh, or if he was angry. "You Dy'ainian, me Varga."

Brant had never heard of the Varga. But that didn't surprise him either. His knowledge of the world around him was limited to what he had heard or learned at the mine, and he had no formal education. Brant was impressed with the Varga's size and he had a hard time imagining fighting him. "Will I have to fight him?" Brant asked Tangar.

Tangar laughed. "You hope not. This is Gar'gon, help train you. These," he said as he pointed to the hounds. "My pets. Called nygs. You run, they kill you. Understand?"

Brant looked at the nygs warily. They were formidable looking animals and he had no doubt that he would not stand a chance against them. "Why is Uln moving rocks from one pile to another?"

"For strength. You join him."

"I don't think so." Brant was obstinate, not quite ready to give in to the nomad.

Tangar said something in Schulg and suddenly there was a loud snap, followed by excruciating pain flashing across Brant's back. He stumbled forward catching his fall with his hands, which had again been tied. Then he felt big hands on his shoulders, lifting him easily to his feet.

"Do not fight. Just do," Uln said.

Brant gritted his teeth against the pain as Tangar withdrew his knife and cut the bindings that bound his hands. The Schulg hadn't used the same bindings as before, just a simple rope, cinched tight and expertly tied. "Move rocks. Now. Use arms and legs, not back."

Brant stared at the two piles, the huge rocks taunting him. He had to find a way to escape, he thought. As if they heard his thoughts, the nygs growled, their deep rumbles destroying any thoughts of escape, at least for the time being.

For an entire month Brant was put through one grueling exercise after another. He moved stones, ran for hours while the dogs nipped at his heels, swung big steel rods into trees, strengthening his arms and grip. But the worst exercise involved a steep grueling hill, buckets, and sharp blades. The hill was a short run from camp. Hammered into the hillside was a well-worn trail, dug deep by the constant and tedious foot traffic up and down the slope. Merely climbing the hill would be easy. But he was forced to carry two buckets laden with stones. And attached to his bicep, wrapping all the way around his arm, was a metal band with a blade as long as his forearm attached to it, pointing straight down. The goal was to lift the buckets holding his arms out wide, while keeping the knife points away from the flesh at his sides. The exercise worked on core, shoulder, and grip strength. As soon as his arms lowered from fatigue, the knife points cut into his flesh. If he dropped the buckets, Gar'gon's whip flashed, causing more pain than the blades. He was forced to do this exercise three times a day. As he grew stronger, more rocks were added to the bucket. Uln had started off with his buckets completely filled to the top with heavy stones. But no matter how strong one became, sheer exhaustion would eventually prevail, and the buckets would lower. The resultant cut of the knife or lash of the whip would somehow provide enough incentive for one to stumble on, with steadfast determination, for another short distance,

Tangar worked with them both, training them in the use of various weapons as well as hand to hand combat. They worked on punches, blocks, throws, as well as wrist locks and submission holds that brought Brant back to his fight with the warden. Now he understood what Bargos had done to him. Tangar was extremely skilled and incredibly fast, and Brant realized that he could learn a lot from him.

However, during every second of his training Brant was trying to work out a way to escape. But the nygs were always there, watching them, their eyes taunting him to run. He was convinced they wanted an excuse to devour his flesh. A month into the training, Brant began to realize that he had better take Tangar's lessons seriously if he wanted to survive. If he couldn't escape, he would soon find himself in the ring where he would have to kill or be killed. He really had no choice until an avenue for escape presented itself. In the meantime he worked his body harder than he ever had. He grew stronger, faster, and became a better swordsman. Along with the sword he learned how to use spears, axes, hammers, and a Schulg weapon called an oswith, which had two blades with a handle in the center. From the handle, the blade, sharpened on one side, extended in both directions. Near the point, the razor edge continued a hand span on the other side before melding into the back of the weapon. When one grasped the leather wrapped handle, the blade jutted forward the length of a short sword, curving up at the end. In the other direction the blade covered the forearm, curving a hand length past the elbow. It was a very unique design. One could use the blade as a shield, blocking attacks with one's protected forearms. Offensive moves came from jabbing or slicing left and right like a normal sword. If a warrior fought with two oswiths, which the nomads generally did, he could block and attack at the same time. Anyone trained thus in the use of this weapon could become a deadly adversary.

Eventually Tangar began to teach him something that he called the Ga'ton. It was a series of body positions used to strengthen the body and mind and to prepare one for combat. There were twenty different positions, each transition from one to another designed to maintain strength and balance. At first Tangar performed the entire Ga'ton for Brant. He watched carefully as the nomad slowly moved from one position to another, the end of each movement accentuated by a sudden burst of speed and power, halting his body momentarily before moving to the next position. At each mark Tangar named the position. Brant tried to remember them, but when it was all said and done he could not bring them all forth, nor could he remember their order. There was Squatting Nyg, Swaying Grass, Leaping Tulkick, Setting Moon, and many others. But he had to admit that the movements were beautiful and powerful all at the same time.

"Now you try," Tangar grunted as he finished, a bead of sweat dripping from his forehead. "First move is Squatting Ngy. Then you move to Breeze over Water followed by Maiden's Thrust." Tangar stepped back as Brant tried to remember the starting position. He put his legs together and squatted into a seat position with is arms straight up. Tangar walked to him and tapped his back, straightening it. Then he pushed his body forward a little and roughly brought his arms further above his head. "Now, move forward in low crouch and strike both arms forward."

Brant tried to mimic his movement but failed miserably. "Show me again," he growled. And Tangar did.

After many tries Tangar finally felt like he had performed the move well enough. "Now, release breath and slowly step back, like this, and spin arms, ending with a sudden low strike with your right arm…Maiden's Thrust."

Brant released his breath and attempted the move. It was much harder than he thought and he felt like his boots were filled with iron. Tangar performed the move so smooth that it frustrated him greatly that he looked like a stumbling drunk in comparison. Frustrated, Brant stood up from his position. "You made it look much easier."

Tangar grunted his usual response. "Try again."

It went on like that for quite some time. Finally, after more tries than Brant could count, he was able to move smoothly through the first three positions. He was exhausted, and despite how hard he had been working on his stamina, his muscles felt tired and he was dripping with sweat. "What is its purpose?" he asked as he wiped the sweat from his eyes.

"Ga'ton bring you speed, balance, power, and strength. You work positions. You get stronger…you get faster."

And he did. Every day, intermixed with his physical exercise and his weapons work, they practiced his Ga'ton. After several months he was able to move through all twenty positions, albeit clumsily compared to Tangar.

Brant had been able to talk with Uln on several occasions. By the sounds of it Uln had been captured and fighting for Tangar for nearly a year. He had many scars to show for his fights, and on one occasion, as they sat near a fire waiting for their supper to be brought to them, Brant asked him about some particular nasty ones on his arm.

"How did you get those scars?" Brant asked, pointing to a series of crisscrossed white welts all covering his forearm. It looked as if something had shredded his flesh.

Uln narrowed his eyes and looked over at the dogs that were lying in the dirt nearby. "I ran. Hounds caught me. One did this, other two bite ankles. Flesh torn badly."

"Looks like it," Brant said. "What about those burns?" Brant asked, pointing to the marks on his huge chest.

Uln looked at him. "Let hope you find what mean." But he left it at that. "You learn fight, kill. You must. Save time for plan."

Uln clearly didn't want to talk about the scars, but Brant thought he understood the rest. He was saying to learn to fight to protect himself, so that he may live…and maybe, in time, he would find a way to escape. Brant nodded his head, looking into the flickering orange and red flames. "How far away is home?"

"Live west. Forests north Heyrith, in Kael."

"I've never heard of your people," Brant said, puzzled.

Uln shook his head, shrugging. "Reclusive. We hide in forests. Not want man."

"Not want man?" Brant repeated, unsure of what he meant.

"You," he said, pointing at him. "No trust. We like alone."

Brant knew he didn't mean him personally, but his people. He wondered what had happened between his people and the Varga to cause them to isolate themselves. "You have family?" Brant asked curiously.

"Family?" Uln clearly didn't understand the term.

"Umm, kids? Children? Woman?"

Uln wrinkled his forehead in thought, trying to understand what he was saying. Then it came to him, and he smiled widely. "Yes. I have woman."

"Well, when I escape, I will free you as well, so you can return to your family."

Uln smiled, as if it were a joke. But when he looked at Brant, his smile was not returned. Brant was dead serious.

Chapter 5

The Schulg are an enigmatic race. One the one hand, family is very important to them; yet with those outside the family realm they can be impulsively violent. One minute they are hugging their child. And the next instant they are slitting the throat of a stranger who inadvertently trespassed on their lands. Their history can be traced back thousands of years, when their ancestors crossed the Varos Mountains and moved south, presumably following the herds of tulkick, their main food source. From there they moved further south into Dy'ain, across the Sil Desert and into Torik. It is hypothesized that the Askarians in Torik, and the Schulg, came from a common ancestor. They have similar physical characteristics, but differ in their customs.

The migration of the Schulg into Dy'ainian lands led to a long history of wars and violence. Long ago, when the Schulg settled the steppes east of the Devlin Mountains, they had been relatively isolated. But as the Dy'ainian Kingdom grew, it encroached upon their lands. Bloody territorial battles were fought to possess the land. But once the precious Kul-brite metal was discovered in the Devlin range, nothing could stop the Dy'ainian war machine. Schulg villages were destroyed, their people slaughtered and scattered to the winds, forcing the nomads farther north. The Schulg population has been severely depleted from conquest and war. Now the Schulg mainly occupy the lands near Tanwen, and although both sides bear a mutual hatred and distrust of the other, they have come to tolerate one another. For though they technically live in Dy'ainian land, House Dormath knows to leave them alone. To do anything else would invite more war and death, and right now the Dy'ainians have the Saricons to deal with.

Journal entry 38
Kivalla Der'une, Historian, Keeper of the records in Cythera, capital of Dy'ain

Bannerfall

5089, the 14th cyn after the Great Change

Wounded soldiers lay scattered across the courtyard, moaning and crying out in pain, their bloody wounds wrapped in make-shift bandages as servants scurried about bringing water and fresh bandages to the few healers available. Daricon Dormath was yelling orders to servants and healers, directing aid to the most severely wounded.

They had been out on patrol when they were attacked by a Saricon scouting party. After a brutal battle they had managed to kill them all, but not without casualties. Fifteen men had lost their lives, and another thirty were wounded, some severely.

Word had spread rapidly that they had returned to Lyone, and it wasn't long before Jarak Dormath entered the courtyard, surveying the dead and dying with wide eyes, shocked at the sight of so much blood. He quickly located Daricon, guided by his loud commanding voice.

"Uncle, what happened?" Jarak asked.

Daricon, who was issuing orders to a servant, turned to face him. "We were attacked by a scouting party a day's ride from here."

Jarak looked about some more, taking in the many wounded men. He had been at the garrison for six months now and had gone on a few outings with his uncle, but luckily he had stayed behind on this particular trip, having made up a story about needing to train with Serix. Instead he had spent his time trying to court Cat, an endeavor that had not gone well since he had arrived. "How many dead?" he asked numbly.

"Fifteen so far, but more are sure to perish from their wounds. I need your help," Daricon said.

"But I know nothing of healing."

"Then learn!" Daricon snapped, his voice rising in frustration. "You can help in many ways. Bring supplies to the healers, talk with the men, comfort the wounded…"

"I am their prince. I should not be seen doing menial…"

"Menial!" Daricon stormed, stepping towards him, his eyes narrowing with anger. "Because you are their prince is why you should do it!" A few men glanced at them curiously as Daricon raised his voice. But the surrounding chaos and commotion drowned him out, and most were too busy seeing to the wounded to notice the nearby argument.

"You do not need to yell," Jarak said, stepping back from his angry uncle.

Bannerfall

"I do!" Then he lowered his voice, but to Jarak it mattered little, for his words carried the intensity of a kulg's claws scratching against stone. "These men are *your* men. They serve *you*. Talk with them and try to give them comfort as they suffer for their kingdom, as they suffer for you. Do you understand?"

Jarak knew that there would be no placating Daricon. "I will do my best."

"Good. Find Valen while you're at it. He is the head healer and will know best how to use you." Without a second glance Daricon turned and walked away, eager to see to his men.

Jarak scanned the scene, trying to figure out how to help. Just before him were three men lying on the stone ground. One had a blood soaked bandage wrapped around his thigh, while another was clearly unconscious, with blood still dripping from a deep cut on the side of his head. The third man had one arm in a crude sling and was trying to use his cloak to stop the flow of blood from his comrade's head.

Jarak walked to them, the man with the sling looking up as he neared. He recognized him immediately, bowing his head in greeting. "Is there anything I can do to help?" Jarak asked awkwardly.

The soldier looked up at the prince, seemingly confused. He appeared to be in shock as he cradled his friend's head in his lap, vainly holding his dirty cloak against the wound. "Umm, well, I don't know my Prince," the soldier said nervously.

"I don't think that dirty cloak is helping much. Let me get you some bandages."

"Thank you, my Prince. Manny is hurt pretty bad," the soldier said, removing the cloth from the wound. Jarak saw a wicked gash just above his ear, exposing the bone underneath. Manny's entire head was drenched in blood. It looked as if he had been struck by a sword.

"What is your name?"

"Liam, my Prince."

"Liam, how is your arm?" Jarak asked.

"I think it's broken, sir. But I'll be okay."

The man with the wound on his leg stirred, his eyes opening slowly. "Water," he groaned.

"I will return with bandages and water. Just give me a few moments." Jarak stepped away, quickly skirting through the crowd looking for a servant or healer to help him. He hadn't gone far before he saw a man leaning over a body. As Jarak approached he saw him remove the soldier's cuirass and begin cutting away his bloodied shirt. The man wore a loose muslin shirt and his short curly brown hair was drenched in sweat. As he cut the shirt away, a horrible raised welt became visible on his side where his breastplate had failed to protect him. The welt was black and purple and it looked like something was trying to break through his skin. The soldier was in shock, moaning as two other men held his arms firmly.

"Are you Valen?"

"Yes! Now leave me be! Can't you see that I'm busy!" he yelled as he quickly glanced up, his eyes opening wide as he saw Jarak. But he didn't curb his next words much. "My Prince, I am sorry. But I am busy at the moment."

"I see that you are. I would like to help and I need to bring some fresh bandages and water to some men. Where can I procure those items?"

"If you want to help then sit on this man's legs."

As if the wounded soldier had heard him, he began to thrash about, clearly unaware of what he was doing and trying to throw off the men that were restraining him. Jarak jumped behind the healer and attempted to keep the soldier's legs still.

"Good! Now try to keep him still. I need to feel his side and figure out where the rib is broken!" Jarak couldn't see what Valen was doing, but a couple of times the soldier reacted by jerking his body, his legs bucking underneath him. After a few moments the soldier screamed, jerking one final time before lying still. "You can get off now," Valen said as he stood. "Wrap his side tight," he ordered to one of the men that had been holding his arm. "Move him slowly and keep an eye on him. Let me know if he wakes or his condition worsens." Then Valen turned to Jarak. "Thank you, my Prince."

"You are welcome. Now, where can I get fresh bandages?"

Valen pointed to a cart on the other side of the courtyard. "You should find some there, and fresh water."

"Thank you," Jarak said hastily as he ran through the crowd towards the wood cart. The cart contained six wood buckets and a large keg filled with water, along with ladles and rolls of fresh white bandages. He grabbed a bucket, filled it with water using the spigot on the keg. Then he took a ladle and a roll of bandages and carefully made his way through the crowd of people, trying not to spill the water in the process.

Bannerfall

He found the three wounded men easily enough, setting the bucket down next to the man with the leg injury. "How is he?" Jarak asked Liam, nodding toward Manny. He filled the ladle, gently propped up the soldier's head, and brought it to his parched lips. The injured man swallowed gratefully as Jarak poured the water down his throat.

"Still unconscious," Liam replied, clearly worried. "But he's breathing."

"Good," Jarak said, drawing a knife from his hip and cutting a sizable chunk of cloth from the roll. Then he dipped it in the bucket and handed it to Liam. "Try to clean the wound. I'll cut a strip that we can wrap around his head and hopefully stop the bleeding."

Liam grabbed the drenched cloth and went about cleaning the wound as gently as he could. Manny moaned a few times as he dabbed at the raw flesh trying his best to remove any debris from the dusty road. "Thank you, sir," Liam said looking gratefully at the prince.

"You're very welcome. Jarak then turned to the man with the leg injury. Now, what is your name?" he asked.

"Reed, sir," he replied hoarsely. "Please, can I have some more water?"

"Of course." Jarak gave him another ladle full. "How is your leg?"

"Hurts, sir. Morlock's balls, that Saricon was tough. I stabbed him in the chest and he still came at me. Struck me in the leg."

"Let me look at it," Jarak said as he slowly removed the dirty bloodied bandage. It was pretty bad. The gash along his thigh stretched from his groin nearly to his knee and was as deep as the length of his longest toe. When the bandage was removed from the crusty wound, fresh blood poured from it freely. "I need to get this cleaned up and re-wrapped." He cut off another piece of cloth, dipped it into the bucket, and gently wiped at the wound, trying to clear away the blood. Then he remembered something he was carrying in his back pocket. He reached into it and withdrew a silver flask, its surface covered with beautifully intricate etchings. Rath had given it to him as a gift. He had hoped the golden liquid inside would give him the courage to talk with Cat, who he had been looking for when the wounded came pouring in over the floating bridge.

Normally, when it came to women he needed no such encouragement. But there was something about Cat that made his heart palpitate like a frightened bird's and caused his tongue to stumble over his teeth. He had yet to figure out what it was about her that got him so tongue tied. After all, she wouldn't even be considered his type. Most men would consider her average, her small breasts and narrow hips not enough to turn their heads. But when he was around her he couldn't stop staring at her. And when he wasn't around her he kept thinking of her, visual images of her filling his dreams.

Jarak uncorked the flask. "Reed, this might hurt a little. I'm going to pour some alcohol on your wound to clean it. You ready?"

Reed lifted his head from the ground. "Do it."

Jarak dribbled the golden liquid inside the gash and Reed instinctively jerked his leg. But the warrior was tough, and he grunted away the pain, keeping his leg more or less still despite the pain. Then Jarak quickly cut a strip from the clean cloth and tightly wrapped the wound. "Let's get some of this," Jarak said, indicating his flask, "on Manny's wound." Jarak moved next to Liam who had just finished cleaning the cut. They could view it better now and Jarak could definitely see bone through the flayed flesh and blood. He dumped the rest of the alcohol on the exposed flesh. "Push the skin together," Jarak said, "but don't use your dirty fingers. Use the edges of the wet cloth." Then he cut another strip from the linen and proceeded to wrap it around his head, the first wrap done slowly as they did their best to use the pressure of the bandage to push the flesh together and close the grisly wound.

Jarak stood, looking at his handy work. It didn't look too bad. "I better go check on the rest of the men. May Felina see you through this," he added. Argon and Felina were believed to be married, and depending on one's personal preference, one would pray to one or the other, or sometimes both. Men usually prayed to Argon before battle, but most prayed to Felina if they wanted healing. Jarak assumed it was because she was female. After all, men did most of the fighting, whereas it was usually a woman that would provide care and comfort if one were hurt or sick. It was a habit that he had picked up at a young age and he didn't think twice about offering her blessings.

"Thank you, sir," Liam replied sincerely.

Reed lifted his hand from his side, offering it to Jarak. It was dirty and bloody, but so was his. He took it. "Maybe someday I will have the honor of fighting beside you."

Jarak smiled for the first time. "It would be *my* honor. But get well first." Jarak cringed inwardly, ashamed that he had skirted his duty. He should have been with them...he should have fought with them.

Maybe he could have saved lives if he hadn't shirked his duty. But, despite his shame, he also felt something else. It was a sense of accomplishment. As he walked away he had a bit more spring in his step, uncharacteristically eager to help where he could.

It was later that evening, after supper, when Daricon sent a page to Jarak's room requesting his presence in the library. Jarak had spent the entire day tending to the wounded and providing what comfort he could to the dying. He was sweaty and his clothing was covered with blood by the time he dragged himself to his chambers. He had ordered a bath and requested supper in his room. He was physically exhausted and emotionally drained, and the promise of a hot bath beckoned to him. He had barely finished dressing after his bath when the page knocked and delivered the summons.

The library was located in his uncle's private chambers. Previously the room had been an anteroom with an attached storage room. To enter Daricon's private chambers one had to pass through the anteroom. Daricon had knocked out the wall between the storage room and the anteroom to make the space roomier. He then had his best craftsmen line three entire walls with heavy wooden shelves to hold his large collection of rare and valuable books. The edges of the shelving had been carved to represent leafy vines with delicate flowers, then covered in gold leaf. They shimmered in the bright light cast by the dancing flames of the fireplace which had been built into the fourth wall. Richly embroidered tapestries flanked the fireplace, and a large painting depicting Jarak's grandfather, heavily armored and riding a massive white horse, hung over the mantel. A large round oak table sat in the middle of the room surrounded by six sturdy oak armchairs upholstered in soft leather.

Jarak entered and saw Daricon standing, looking down at the table in the middle of the room. The chandelier above the table held six lanterns, each one containing three candles. Three more lanterns sat on the table and the roaring fire in the fireplace behind him provided a flickering orange light throughout the room.

"Uncle, you wanted to see me," Jarak said as he walked over to the table. Daricon was looking over a map covered with pawns representing troops. He looked up and smiled. Jarak hadn't seen his uncle smile at him for quite some time and it made him a bit apprehensive. "Have a seat. Would you like some wine? It's from Kael."

Jarak raised his eyebrows. "What's the occasion? And yes, I'd love some," he added as he sat down wearily.

"No occasion. I just wanted to tell you that I'm proud of you. You did well today. I overheard the men talking about you."

Jarak took the glass of wine. He was a little surprised. After all, Daricon had not been overly generous with praise since he had arrived. In fact it appeared that he was often more irritated than pleased with him. "Thank you, Uncle," he replied tentatively.

"You seem surprised."

"I guess I am. I feel like you've been disappointed in me since I arrived here."

Daricon smiled and took a sip of his wine. "You did not misinterpret my feelings. I have been angry at you."

"Why? What have I done?"

"That's just it, you haven't done anything."

"I don't understand. I've taken lessons in combat. I've attended military conferences. I've studied ledgers and maps with you and your officers. I've continued my mage training. All at your request. How can you say I've done nothing?"

"You have done all those things. But not with any heart in them. Jarak, your mind is elsewhere. It is clear to everyone that you'd rather be someplace else. But today, for the first time, you acted like a prince, and you did it well."

Jarak felt an initial flush of anger at Daricon's comments, but it quickly passed, as he realized that Daricon was right. Jarak took a long drink from his goblet, staring into the fire as he reflected on his uncle's words. When he had returned to his room to bathe, trying to process the jumbled events of the day, he had actually begun to look more deeply within himself. And as he washed the blood from his hands and arms prior to climbing into the steaming hot bath, he had stared at the blood in the wash basin, the swirling crimson a vivid reminder of the sacrifices that the soldiers, his soldiers, had given in defense of his family and home. Sitting in the bath, the hot water soothing his muscles and calming his mind, he tried to think about what he had done to deserve such sacrifices, and he didn't like the answer that surfaced. The fact was he had done nothing. He had made a promise to himself just then, laying in the soothing water, that when he stepped from the bath that he would try to change. As the water rinsed away the sweat and blood, it brought to the surface something different, cleaner in all aspects. He would try to do better. "You're right," he said finally. "I have not had my heart in my duties. I plan to change that."

"Good. Let us start tomorrow."

"What do you mean?"

"I am taking another patrol out in the morning. That scouting party was too close yesterday. I want a show of force and I want you to come with me."

Jarak saw images of all the men he had helped flash through his mind. If they could do it, so could he. How could he live a life of luxury, a life supported by the sweat and blood of others, if he wasn't willing to carry some of the burden himself? It didn't bother him before, but now it did. "I would be honored to join you."

Daricon smiled, lifting his wine glass. "To honor, courage, and new beginnings." Jarak tapped his glass to his uncle's. They both drank together, savoring the velvety smoothness of the fine wine, as well as a growing mutual respect.

"Tell me the plan," Jarak asked, leaning closer to the map on the table.

"Well, as you can see, we have our troops stationed with the Kaelian troops here and here." Daricon pointed to a line on the map that blocked the main roads crossing into the Eltus Peninsula and leading to the capital city of Eltus. There was a second line of troops, smaller than the first, barricading the roads leading to Lyone and into Dy'ainian lands. "Saricon troop numbers have been steadily growing, reinforced by troops from Fara. The scouting party that attacked us yesterday had made it through our lines. They are clearly trying to reconnoiter information. They have tested our lines numerous times over the last few weeks. I think they are planning something decisive. I'd like to reinforce our troops that are blocking the entrance to Lyone, as well as make a show of force."

"What time are we leaving?"

"The troops will be gearing up at first light. I plan to depart soon after."

"Will Serix be traveling with us?"

"Yes, he already knows."

Jarak tilted his head in wonder. "But how did you know I would agree?"

"I saw it on your face today. You were proud."

Jarak leaned back in his chair, smiling. "You are very astute."

Bannerfall

"I've lead men my entire life. One thing I can recognize a mile away is the aura that surrounds someone who is feeling proud of a task well done. You were shining like a lone star in a dark sky."

Jarak sat forward, raising his glass. "To lone stars. May Argon and Felina protect the brave."

They toasted, and drank to the morning adventure.

One hundred men in Legionnaire armor, helms, and bouncing lances rode into the lands of Kael. Jarak rode with Daricon and Serix in the front. He too wore Legionnaire armor but carried no lance, a weapon he had not yet become proficient with. He wore a long sword at his side and strapped to his horse was a short cavalry bow and arrows. One thing he always carried on him was his Mage Stone, which had been expertly set into the buckle of his sword belt. Accompanying the Legionnaires were six carts laden with supplies for the troops stationed on the front lines.

It took them a half day to reach the first picket line which was made up of fifty men camped along the main road to Lyone. It was mid-day and they were alert. Jarak noticed a few fires lit flanking the road, along with maybe twenty tents. Everyone was doing something; preparing the mid-day meal, gathering firewood, cleaning weapons, guarding the perimeter of the camp, or sparring in an open field. When they saw their column, everyone stood at attention.

Daricon dismounted. "Let's unload some supplies and take a brief rest." Jarak and Serix dismounted. Three soldiers hastened forward to see to their horses. "Jarak, order the men to take rest and have some quick rations."

"Thank you," Jarak said to the soldier who took the reins of his horse, leading it to the side of the road.

The man grunted. "My Prince," nodding his head in acknowledgment.

Jarak had never been given such a leadership role and he looked at Serix with uncertainty. Serix smiled and winked at him, which gave him a bit more confidence. Daricon noticed his hesitation. "Don't worry," he said, "tell Lieutenant Deklan and he'll take the lead."

Jarak took a deep breath and moved back down the line, finding the officer shortly. "Lieutenant Deklan, take four men and unload the supplies for the men here. Everyone else shall take a brief rest and quick rations. We will depart shortly"

"Very good, my Prince." Without a second glance the Legionnaire barked out orders and within a few moments the entire column was resting and eating dried meat and bread, washing it down with cold water.

Jarak found Serix and Daricon sitting by a fire talking with a soldier. When he approached the man stood and bowed. "Prince Dormath, it is good to finally meet you. My name is Captain Dalgard."

"Well met, Captain."

"Please, join us," he said, moving a short log near him. "I'm sorry we don't have anything more comfortable."

"It is fine. Thank you." Jarak sat down and Daricon tossed him a piece of dried meat.

"Have you seen any more troop movements behind the main lines?" Daricon asked.

Captain Dalgard frowned. "I'm afraid so. Just this morning several scouts came back and said they saw tracks no more than half a day's ride from here."

"Horse?" Serix asked.

"No, men on foot."

"Was it close to where we were attacked yesterday?"

"It was. It looks like the Saricon scum have been frequently crossing our lines. I'm afraid we just don't have the troop numbers to adequately block all access."

"For what purpose?" Jarak asked.

The captain sighed. "To gather information."

"I agree," Daricon added. "I think they are assessing troop numbers, movements, and supplies, whatever they can."

"Sounds like they plan on advancing," Jarak stated.

"Could be. But the question is, to where?" Daricon asked. "Will they send their army to attack us, here at Lyone? Or bring it east and cross onto the Eltus Peninsula and attack the Kaelian capital?"

"If they control Eltus, they control the Dynel Strait. I would imagine that would be important to them," Captain Dalgard suggested.

"What if they split their forces?" Jarak asked.

"Why would they do that?" the Captain asked. "It would weaken them."

Daricon looked at Jarak, who looked at everyone with uncertainty. Maybe he shouldn't have said anything. But something didn't sit right with him and it had been bugging him ever since he saw the map in Daricon's library. "Well, if they take their main army and head straight to Eltus, what will we do with our troops?"

"Depends," Daricon said. "If their main army heads to Eltus, then the Kaelian troops will have to retreat to the city."

"Will we be going with them?"

Captain Dalgard and Daricon both shook their heads. Daricon answered the question however. "We would not. We can't leave our border unprotected."

"And the Saricons know it. If my understanding is correct, we have been able to hold them off thus far because our forces have been combined. If they send the main force to Eltus, that will force us to split our forces just as they did. If I were them, I would attack Eltus with the main army and leave a small contingent here just to keep us pinned down."

Captain Dalgard looked at Daricon, a worried expression on his face. "What if you are right, my Prince, but instead of sending the main force to Eltus, they attack Lyone with the main force and cross into Dy'ainian lands?"

Daricon was deep in thought. "I don't think they would do that. They have to control the Dynel strait. We all know they want to control the Kul-brite trade. Without that trade route it would matter little if they took Dy'ain. They need Eltus first, then they can set their eyes on Dy'ain. Jarak, your thinking is sound. If they split our forces, they may be able to defeat us individually."

"But what choice do we have? We can't go with the Kaelians to Eltus and hope they don't attack the garrison. It's too big of a risk," Captain Dalgard said.

Daricon frowned. "You're right. We cannot do that. If they take Eltus, then they will certainly be heading into Dy'ain next."

"The real question is, do we try and make our stand at the garrison, or do we retreat to Cythera and make our stand there?" Jarak asked.

"Questions I'd rather not entertain," Captain Dalgard mumbled. The idea of giving up the garrison without a fight didn't sit well with any of them.

"Nor I, but we must think of the worst case scenario," Daricon said. "I'd rather not give up the garrison without a fight. If we had to, we could hold off a larger force for a week or two, hopefully delivering enemy casualties in the process. Then we could implement an organized retreat to Cythera."

No one said anything as they pondered the possibilities. After a few moments Captain Dalgard looked up at the sky. "You'd best be moving, Lord Daricon. You need to reach the next picket line before dark."

Daricon sighed, looking at the sun, now making its descent toward night. "You're right. Jarak, get the men ready?"

"Yes, sir."

Cat was becoming more nervous by the minute. How much longer could she go undetected? Her face wrap, hat, and the hood of her cloak had so far done an adequate job of hiding her identity. Sitting in the back of one of the supply carts had kept her away from the front of the line, specifically away from Prince Jarak who she knew would recognize her. After all, he had been clearly vying for her attention since he had arrived at the garrison over six months ago. *What did he see in me?* she thought. *I don't have the curves that most men prefer. Besides that,* she smiled inwardly, *I can probably wield a sword better than he.* She admitted to herself that he was physically appealing, but she also knew that a relationship with him could go nowhere. Technically she was the daughter of a lord, but her father's station was well below that of the prince, and their union would never be allowed. Besides that, she wasn't gifted in the Way, generally a requirement to marry into the royal family. She knew his type though. He wasn't the first man who had tried to bed her. He hadn't yet been too insistent, but she could see it in his eyes. Men were so easy to read.

The opportunity to hide herself within the caravan had presented itself the day before, and she had been ready. A new quartermaster had arrived at the garrison, along with two new assistants, and none of them knew who she was. One of the assistants, Tulvin, had been preparing the supplies the night before when she had presented herself to him with orders, handwritten from Captain Hagen. It was easy to for her to forge her father's signature, and the young man, being new, didn't question them at all. And even if he were to say something to the head quartermaster, it was unlikely that that would raise any suspicion, since he didn't know her either. So far it had worked perfectly. As far as Tulvin was concerned, she was simply someone assigned to him to help administer and deliver supplies. He had no idea that her sword was tucked between some boxes and that she wore hardened leather armor under her baggy tunic.

She was beyond bored with garrison life and had become increasingly frustrated that her persistent demands to join the Legion had been totally ignored by her father. Well, she would show him that she was capable. It wasn't as if she were hoping for trouble, but she wanted to experience being a Legionnaire, and if trouble presented itself, she would be ready.

The column had been making good time until a wheel on one of the carts broke when the axle cracked underneath from the weight of the heavily laden cart.

The wagon master, Jons, crawled out from under the wagon. Daricon and Jarak stood next to him waiting for his assessment. The rest of the column had already dismounted and were taking rest and water.

Jons shook his head, frowning. "I'm sorry, Lord Daricon, Prince Jarak, but the axle snapped. It must have been cracked already. The weight of the cart just finished the job."

"Can you fix it?" Daricon asked.

"I can, sir, but it will take a while. I always bring an extra axle. But I will have to unload the cart, lift it off the front wheels, remove the old axle and wheels and replace it with a new one. It will take a quarter day."

Jarak could see that Daricon was clearly frustrated. Jarak looked around, trying to get a feel for their surroundings. They would never make the next picket line before dark. He looked back at Daricon who seemed to be mulling over their options. "It's not a bad place to camp," Jarak said. "That outcropping over there," he added, pointing to a sheltered spot off the side of the road, "would provide some protection. Perhaps we should set up camp here while Master Jons fixes the wagon. Jons, can you have the wagon ready by tomorrow?" Jarak asked.

Jons scratched his dusty face, frowning again. It was obvious he was not looking forward to a sleepless night working on the wagon, but he knew it was his duty. He brushed his curly hair away from his eyes and stood up straighter, trying to appear confident. "I can fix it by tomorrow, my Prince. It shouldn't be a problem."

"Good. What do think, Uncle?"

"Well, we don't have much of a choice. Let's set up camp."

Bannerfall

With practiced precision the Legionnaires set up camp against the stone outcropping. The small cliff wall was about as tall as three men, and provided some shelter from the chilly evening breeze as well as protecting their backs in the event of an attack. Fires were lit and tents were erected, the four carts arranged along one flank providing more protection. There was a small copse of bonet trees that provided a convenient spot to tether the horses. By the time the men had cleaned, watered, and fed their animals, the sun had set and everyone had found a crackling fire where they sat to take their evening meal of beans, cheese, and bread.

A perimeter of torches circled the camp, along with guards stationed every thirty paces. Jarak, Serix, and Daricon sat around a fire, their single small tent nearby. A servant brought them a steaming plate of beans, departing quickly.

"How do you like our sleeping quarters?" Daricon asked, knowing full well that Jarak was not looking forward to sleeping on the hard ground. Serix smiled at the question, his mouth full of warm beans.

Jarak looked at the tent behind his uncle. "Why don't we at least have servants bring a more substantial tent, with mattresses? I do not see why we have to sleep on the ground like dogs."

"Dogs? So you think your men," Daricon said, pointing to all the fires surrounding them, "are dogs?"

"No, of course not. Don't put words in my mouth."

"I did not have to. They were your words. Will you not do what you expect your men to do?" Daricon asked.

"I will, but why should I have to?"

"Because if you don't, they will not respect you. How do you think they feel, tired and sore, sleeping on the ground, when they look at you and me experiencing the same hardships, day in and day out?"

Jarak thought about it for a moment. "I guess it would make it easier for them."

"Right. Especially if they know that we *could* have brought a bigger tent, softer beds, better food, and servants to cater to our every need. But we didn't. When you fight with your men, bleed with your men, and sleep with your men, you will earn their dying devotion, literally. All these men would die for me, and I for them. Do you think they would die for you? More importantly, would you die for them?"

Bannerfall

Jarak looked into the fire, thinking about Daricon's words. They were valid questions, tough questions…would he die for them? "I do not know, Uncle. You have given me something to think about." He looked up from his plate into his uncle's intense eyes. "I would like to think they would die for me. I am their prince. But you're right. What have I done to earn that kind of loyalty?"

"Yesterday was a start. Remember, they scrutinize everything you do," Daricon said, indicating the men around them. "Your words, your actions, everything is taken, digested, discussed, analyzed, and opinions are formed and spread throughout the army. I bet you that the entire Legion already knows how you provided aid and comfort to the wounded yesterday. That is the kind of action that will win their loyalty. But that loyalty comes with a cost. It is a two way road. You must return it. Being a prince is not enough. It is just a title, meaningless without the principles necessary to uphold it."

They finished their meals, talking quietly and discussing the plans for the morrow. Daricon wanted to inspect the lines and bring them new supplies. His main concern was to make sure that their scouts were continuing to patrol the area for any signs that the Saricons were trying to circumvent their troops and secretly move towards the garrison. He also wanted to get updates on the whereabouts of the Saricon forces and if they had increased their numbers. They needed information, and he was hoping to get it tomorrow.

Yawning, Jarak stood up from the fire, looking out at the darkness. "Time for me to retire," he said. "I'm going to take a piss and check on the horses. Be back in a moment."

"Be vigilant," Serix warned. "You know what happened yesterday."

Jarak nodded as he made his way through the scattered fires, saying hello to the men as he moved to the perimeter. He followed the line of torches that led to the horses tethered in the outer darkness. He passed by the guards that stood at attention along the perimeter.

Standing next to a tree, Jarak unbuttoned the flap on his pants, relieving himself as he stared absently into the darkness, his mind mulling over his uncle's words. A stick snapped and the nearby horses whinnied. Jarak buttoned his pants, turning on his towd. It was probably just an animal. He scanned the darkness again, this time the auras of the horses shined in the blackness. He saw nothing else, and turned to make his way back to camp. A flash of movement directed his eyes upward, to the top of the cliff face overlooking their camp. His heart jumped to his throat as he saw a handful of forms lurking in the darkness, creeping slowly to the edge of the wall, their auras firing orange and red.

Acting quickly, Jarak tasked the energy from the horses nearest him, then shouted as loud as he could. "Enemy! On the cliff wall!"

Just as he screamed the warning, he heard something crashing through the underbrush behind him. Spinning around, his towd still on, he saw six forms racing toward him from the darkness. They must have been hiding behind trees, their auras completely shadowed. But now he could see them clearly.

Reacting instinctively, Jarak shifted the energy from his tarnum into his left fist while simultaneously drawing his sword with his other hand. His heart was pounding wildly and he tried to concentrate on the spell, the task nearly impossible as his attackers rapidly closed the distance. Finally he broke through his mental paralysis, bringing forth the energy in a fiery blue rope of magical flames. He snapped his fist forward and sent the flames into the nearest opponent, surging the energy at the moment of impact as he had been trained to do. The man exploded in fire, flying backwards to his death. Keeping his arm spinning, he shot the fire chain forward again, the intense energy of the explosion blasting a second man off his feet. A third man appeared, sword raised and screaming maniacally. The man was huge and his long blonde hair billowed behind him as his long heavy blade came crashing down towards his head. Jarak lifted his blade to block the strike, the impact causing his arm to vibrate in pain. The man kicked out viciously, his boot hitting Jarak in his armored chest and catapulting him to his back. The Saricon warrior growled and jumped forward, his sword leading the attack. Frantically, Jarak scooted backwards, shooting his flaming fist forward, a ball of fire hitting the Saricon directly in the chest. The hot flames ignited his entire body and he stumbled backwards screaming, swinging his sword uselessly before him.

Jarak scrambled to his feet as three more attackers came at him. He had exhausted his tarnum but he still had energy in the mage stone at his waist. This time he tried a different spell. Converting the energy from the stone, Jarak reached out with his hand and wrapped invisible strands of it around the burning Saricon. With one powerful heave, he magically picked up the screaming man and flung him into the nearest

Bannerfall

attacker. There was a sickening thud as the two crashed together, their flaming bodies somersaulting across the grassy ground.

He was now out of energy and the two men were upon him. He lifted his sword and silently prayed that his training had been enough. One Saricon carried a heavy battle axe and he swung it sideways, yelling something that Jarak could not understand. This man was also large, and Jarak dropped low, almost to his knees, the axe narrowly missing the top of his head. He jabbed his sword forward into the man's thigh while jumping back in case he reversed the swing of his axe. The man howled in pain, but barely faltered. He screamed again, but this time Jarak understood the word. The Saricon had yelled "Heln", and followed his war cry with another giant step forward, his huge axe coming straight down like a woodsman splitting a log.

Suddenly another body was there, Jarak's savior leaping from the darkness and skewering the Saricon right through his abdomen. The swordsman spun by him, slicing his sword forward and out, nearly disemboweling the man. The Saricon fell forward just as the last attacker arrived, his two swords spinning as they attacked the man that had saved Jarak.

The swordsman was good, but so was the Saricon, who fought with two swords. They exchanged several blows before Jarak entered the fray, attacking the man from his flank, as the other warrior attacked him from the other side. Suddenly the Saricon screamed Heln's name and Jarak saw his eyes light up, literally flaring blue. Within seconds the Saricon was howling like a wild animal, his body moving impossibly fast, his two swords a blur of deadly steel. It was all they could do to avoid being struck, and finally the second swordsman was hit, the Saricon's sword slicing across his arm as he attempted in vain to avoid the whirlwind strikes. Jarak lunged forward, hoping to skewer the man in the back. But his sword was blocked as the warrior spun towards him with impossible speed. The Saricon, faster than Jarak thought possible, reversed the direction of his sword and struck Jarak in the side of the head with the pommel. His head spinning, Jarak stumbled to his left, the side of his face flaring with pain. Frantically Jarak attempted to scoot away from the crazed warrior.

"Time to die," the Saricon said in Newain.

Out of the shadows another warrior materialized. Daricon attacked, his Kul-brite sword flaring with green flames. They came together, their bodies glimmering in the darkness as the flames from

Bannerfall

Daricon's sword shed light on the combatants. Both warriors moved so fast that Jarak could barely see them, their forms blurs in the night. Daricon fought brilliantly; the green glow of his swords flames were reflected outward in lightning quick flashes as he skillfully wielded his weapon against the enemy warrior. The Saricon continued to scream insanely. Then suddenly he was silent, his violent screams now a gurgle as he dropped his blades to grab his neck, trying vainly to stop the flow of blood. The giant warrior stumbled, then fell heavily to the ground.

Daricon rushed to Jarak's side. "Are you okay?" His uncle's face and clothing were splattered with blood and Jarak could see the fire of battle still glowing in his eyes.

"I'm okay," Jarak said groggily as he slowly stood. He had a nasty cut across his cheek and a bad headache, but other than that he seemed fine. "Check the other Legionnaire."

Suddenly ten men were around them, forming a perimeter, swords and shields held protectively around their prince. Jarak looked back at the camp and saw a massive flash of light, lightning arcing through the darkness. It must be Serix enacting his spells. Jarak stepped towards the warrior who had saved him. The man wore a floppy brimmed hat and he held his left arm at his side. "Are you okay?" Jarak asked, stepping closer.

The man looked up and Jarak stopped in his tracks. This was no man. He recognized those eyes. It was Cat. "I'm fine," she said, clearly in pain.

"What are you doing here!?"

"We can talk about this later," Daricon said brusquely. "We have work to do. Men!" Daricon yelled. "Bring the prince back to camp!"

Everyone hustled back to the camp, guided by the light from the fires. The fighting was over, but the ground was littered with bodies, Schulgs, Saricons, and their own comrades, many pierced by the arrows fired by the attackers on the cliff face.

Legionnaires maintained their protective perimeter around Jarak while Daricon issued more orders. He wanted the enemy dead dragged away and burned. Perimeter guards were reset while soldiers searched for wounded. The scene was chaotic, but for the moment it looked like the skirmish was over.

Jarak noticed that his hands were shaking. He sat down on a rock by a fire and Cat sat down next to him. A soldier saw to her wound as they both stared silently into the fire. "You saved my life," Jarak said softly, breaking the silence.

"And you mine."

"Your father is going to be furious."

Serix moved past the perimeter guards, quickly locating Jarak. "Are you hurt?" he asked as he sat down next to him. "Bring some water," he ordered a nearby guard.

At his words Jarak realized how parched his mouth was. It felt like all the moisture had been sucked from it, and nothing sounded better than a cold cup of water. "I'm okay, just a cut."

A guard handed him a cup of water, and one for Cat as well. Jarak's hands were still trembling. "It's the adrenaline," Serix said. "It will soon pass. I saw your fire but I could not reach you. Tell me what happened."

Jarak drank deeply before he began the short tale. Serix didn't need to probe much with questions, as the events of the fight were still all too fresh in Jarak's mind. His words tumbled out quickly as he recounted the story. "I killed them, Serix," Jarak said softly, as if the reality of it was just sinking in. He drained the last of the water and sighed heavily.

"And it's a good thing. They would have killed you. You did very well, Jarak. Smart thinking when you tasked from the horses." Serix looked at Cat. "How is your arm?"

"Hurts, but the cut is not so deep." The soldier had cleaned the wound, smeared a salve on it and wrapped it with clean bandages.

Daricon slipped through the perimeter guards and tossed Jarak a wine skin. "Drink, it will help calm your nerves." Jarak gratefully obliged, quaffing several long gulps before he tossed the bag to Cat. She looked thankful, drinking heartily as well. "How are you holding up?" he asked Jarak.

"I'll be fine. How many attacked us?"

"Hard to say. We killed over fifty but some ran off in the night. There were Saricon and Schulg amongst the dead."

"Why would the Schulg fight with the Saricons?" Cat asked.

"Money…honor…who knows. They are tribal, each chief using his warriors for his own purposes. More than likely they were mercenary scouts."

"How many men did we lose?"

"Twenty nine. But it would have been more if you hadn't warned us. Serix here killed most of the bowmen on the cliff face before they could do too much damage. Nice job, Jarak."

Twenty nine warriors dead. Jarak thought of the men he had helped the other day, imagining them cut and bleeding on the dirty ground. So many. But he knew there would be many more. "Daricon, who was that Saricon that you saved us from? His eyes were glowing and he moved so quickly. Was he a Merger like you?"

"He was not. They do not have Aurits. What you saw was a power they call the Fury. It's an innate ability that some Saricons have, similar to our Way, enabling them to fight with incredible strength and speed for a short period. He was probably a war leader, or someone of high rank."

"Thank you for saving us," Jarak said.

Daricon stood, gripping Jarak's shoulder. "Get some rest. And Cat, get a tent from the supply cart and set it up here. I want you close to us. Your father would never forgive me if anything else happened to you."

Cat stood as Daricon and Serix left them, both having plenty of things to do. "Let me help you," Jarak said.

"I can do it."

"I'm sure you can. But I could use your company."

Jarak was being honest, and Cat could tell. Normally he was so flippant and confident, joking about everything. But now he seemed scared, almost vulnerable, and he didn't seem to be hiding it. And if she were being honest, she could use the company as well. Killing that Saricon had happened so quickly that she had barely any time to think about it, until now. And it made her sick to her stomach. "Okay, come on."

They walked together towards the supply cart. Four guards followed them from a discreet distance. "How did you pull this off?" Jarak asked.

"I forged my father's signature on a work order that required me to go with the new quartermaster's assistant on the trip. He was new and didn't know who I was. It was easy."

Jarak smiled, shaking his head in amazement. "I can only imagine what your father is going to do."

"I don't care. I want to be in the Legion."

"Well you saved my life. And you can fight. That has to count for something."

"He is so stubborn. I don't think it will matter."

They reached the supply cart and found a spare tent. The quartermaster's assistant was not there, which was good as Cat was in no mood to explain the situation to him. They grabbed the canvas tent and headed back to their fire.

"You know. I could talk to him. I am his prince. Maybe I could convince him…sort of order it. I do have the power to enlist men, or women, in the Dy'ainian Legion."

Cat stopped, looking seriously at him. "Would you do that?"

Jarak thought about it. He didn't' relish the thought of the conversation. But he did agree with Cat that she was of age and that she had every right to join the Legion if she wished it. She was talented with a sword, clearly tenacious and dedicated. It seemed to him that she would make a great Legionnaire. "I wouldn't look forward to it. But yes, I would talk to him, for you."

Cat smiled for the first time. "I would be grateful."

Smiling back, Jarak said, "Let's survive the night first. Then we can talk about it."

***

Rath sat by himself sipping chulo, a warm drink made from a strong alcohol mixed with sugar, warm milk, and various spices. The bar, a popular meeting place called Finns, named after the owner who had been running the place for the last twenty years, was located deep in the heart of the city, several blocks from Main Street. It was a place where people of all ages met for drinks, food, and entertainment. Rath had been working hard and he was hoping to have a few drinks, relax, and observe the patrons around him, one of his favorite pastimes. Recently he had been working for King Dormath, commissioned to organize and account for all military expenditures. He was honored to have been given such a task, the importance of the job weighing heavily on his young shoulders. He was now twenty, and despite his skill with numbers, and his penchant for research and knowledge, it was rare for someone his age to be given such an important position. Most of his days and evenings were spent in the king's library, reading and adjusting ledgers, recording data, and often finishing up late into the night. This night, however, he had promised himself that he would relax with a drink and maybe some conversation, forgetting the stresses of his new job for at least a few hours.

He sat at a table near the fireplace, its roaring flames blanketing him with warmth. It was now fall and the evenings were getting colder. One could almost feel the gentle touch of winter slowly turning into a silent embrace. The crowded bar was filled with the clamorous sounds of people eating, drinking, talking, and laughing, which Rath found surprisingly comforting, a welcome reprieve from the silent, tireless work he had been doing alone in the king's study.

Suddenly he recognized someone, and the man noticed him as well, their eyes somehow connecting across the crowded room. It was Banrigar, the big man who worked the door at the Black Cat. His huge head and scarred face made it easy to pick him out amongst the crowd. Rath found it difficult to maintain eye contact, and had to look away from his dark penetrating eyes. Subtly, he looked back, and Banrigar smiled, the corner of his lip raising slightly as he lifted his glass in salute. Rath nodded his head, doing the same, and they both drank from their cups. Rath noticed that he was alone as well. The man had always put Rath on edge and it didn't surprise him that he was alone, but maybe that was an unfair assessment. After all, he really knew nothing about him. He was big and scary looking, but he had always treated him and Jarak with respect.

There was some commotion nearby that drew Jarak's attention away from Banrigar. Three men sat at a nearby table carrying several pitchers of ale. They were clearly drunk and rambunctious, oblivious to the fact that their raucous banter might be annoying the nearby customers. In fact, a serving girl made her way to the table and politely asked them to refrain from yelling. Rath took an immediate dislike to them. The bar was loud, and lusty banter was not uncommon, but these three were taking it a step further. Two of the men looked to be brothers, tall and lanky, and wearing old and smudged clothes. Rath thought they might be artisans of some sort as he could see that their hands were heavily callused. Perhaps they were tanners or coopers, coming into Finn's for some fun. The third man was much larger, thick in the belly, with burly arms that looked like overstuffed sausages. His clothes were covered with white dust and Rath figured he might be a mason.

Bannerfall

The men laughed at the barmaid, ordering more ale and telling her to mind her own business. Frowning, her brows furrowed in anger, she stomped off towards the bar.

Rath continued to sip his drink, gazing around the room, and trying to ignore the obnoxious trio. Other patrons were eyeing them with frustration, but no one said anything, preferring their food and drink over confrontation.

As Rath finished his drink and prepared to order another, one of the men, the big mason, turned around and asked him something. He was obviously drunk, and his slurred words, despite his deafening volume, were hard to understand. "Want to hear a joke?" the man slurred. He didn't wait for Rath to respond nor did he take notice of Rath's irritated expression. "What does a leper have in common with Prince Jarak?"

Rath looked away, having heard the joke many times. Prince Jarak's brothel exploits were well known, and several jokes pertaining to his un-princely actions had been circulating the city for years now. "I've heard the joke before, now leave me be."

But the big man ignored him, delivering the punch line like it was the funniest thing he ever heard. "They both lost their manhood," he said, wiggling his little pinky in the process as if it would help Rath understand the joke better. His buddies laughed, consuming more ale in the process.

Rath continued to look elsewhere, ignoring the man.

"Don' you get it? You know, the prince's poker rusted off because he stuck it in to many wet holes." By this time the man was roaring with laughter, thinking his analogy even funnier than the joke. But his expression changed when he realized that Rath was not laughing with him. "Hey, I'm talking to you," the man said, his laughter taking on an edge of anger. "Whas' your problem? Don' you like jokes?"

"I like funny jokes. And that wasn't funny."

"It's hilarious. Prince Jarak is just a pompous cock anyway." Then he slammed his hand on the table, laughing boisterously at his own comment.

Rath did not normally allow himself to be pulled into futile arguments with drunken imbeciles. But the ale and his anger got the best of him. "He is not just a pompous cock," Rath snapped. "You don't even know him."

170

"And you do?" This time it was one of the big guy's buddies that spoke up, grinning lazily and caressing his mug as if it were the most precious of objects.

"I do know him. I'm his tutor."

The big guy, his mouth full of ale, burst out laughing, spewing the warm liquid all over Rath. "That is the funniest thing I've ever heard. You tell better jokes than me!" He howled with laughter, nearly choking on his ale.

Rath stood up quickly, wiping the liquid from his face. "You idiot! You spit on me! What do you know anyway, you're just a fat drunk!"

This time the man's smile disappeared and he stood up to his full height, towering a full head over Rath. Just a moment ago he seemed too drunk to stand or carry on a coherent conversation. But now suddenly he was standing on steady legs and his eyes narrowed dangerously, and before Rath could react, the man lunged at him, reaching out with his huge right hand to grab his tunic.

Rath's eyes widened in surprise as he stepped back to avoid the mason's meaty hand. But it never found his shirt.

Banrigar was suddenly there, his hand flashing out and gripping the big man's wrist, jerking it forward and knocking him off balance. Then, just as quick, he yanked the man's hand backwards, wrenching it hard over his shoulder in a violent and powerful move that lifted him off his feet and threw him onto his back, scattering his chair and the table in the process.

The mason howled in pain as Banrigar continued to twist his wrist. His friends prudently decided against involving themselves in the conflict; they wanted nothing to do with this fighter, and hurriedly scooted away from the table, while the rest of the crowd, now suddenly silent, watched on with fascination. "If you try anything more I'll break your arm," Banrigar growled. "When I let go of your wrist you are going to walk out of here with your friends. If you try anything else, I will kill you. Do you understand?"

Needing no further encouragement, the big man shouted his surrender. "Yes, yes, I understand! Just let go of my arm!"

Banrigar released him, and the man scooted away, holding his wrist as he stood. He glared at Banrigar as his friends joined him. "Now, pay for your drinks and get out of here."

Bannerfall

Each man reached into his pocket and tossed a few coins onto the table, and walked out of the bar as all eyes watched. Most were smiling, pleased at the justice meted out to the obnoxious trio, some even wishing they had been the ones who had dealt the punishment. Clearly everyone was happy to see them go.

Once they were gone the bar returned to its normal state, conversation buzzing around the confrontation they had just witnessed. Banrigar lifted up the chair and repositioned it by the table. He looked at Rath, smiled, and moved to return to his table.

"Thank you, Banrigar," Rath blurted out. "I didn't think he would attack me."

He looked back at him, the edge of his lip rising again in amusement. "Next time be careful who you anger. I might not be there to help."

"Sound advice," Rath replied as he sat back down. "Ummm...would you like to join me?" Banrigar hesitated. "I'm buying, it's the least I can do."

This time he turned to face him. "Let me give you another piece of advice. Never offer to buy someone drinks until you know how much they can drink." But he was smiling, and before Rath could respond he was sitting next to him. "Fighting always makes me parched." He was grinning from ear to ear, which looked awkward; his big mouth accentuated even more by the size of his large head. Rath had a feeling that the night was just beginning.

Chapter 6

My whole life I've studied war, conquest, and the impact that these two events have had on our history. As far back as I can remember, the Saricons have been a conquering people, invaders whose primary goals have been to destroy, pillage, and enslave. I will admit that these foreign invaders have been portrayed in a biased light. After all, as a student of history, it would not be fair if I did not look at the history of our own lands as a comparison. Are the Dy'ainian people so much different from the Saricons? Thousands of years ago our ancestors came to the shores of Dy'ain. They found the land already inhabited by the Schulg tribes. Did we not do to them the same as the Saricons are attempting to do to us? They desire our precious Kul-brite steel, and our fertile farmland, just as we desired the Schulg land, the land that the nomads had inhabited for thousands of years. And we took their lands by force, just as the Saricons are attempting to do to us. Despite our religious differences, and our obvious physical differences, it seems we are more similar than we'd like to believe.

The Varga are another example. The giants were once a mighty race living throughout the lands of Kael. Thousands of years ago our Dy'ainian ancestors were tribal, and some of the tribes, who later became the Kaelians, moved south. Over time their numbers grew and they slowly pushed the Varga north. They had also brought with them a sickness, a burning death, a disease that the Varga could not fight off, killing thousands. Their populations decimated, even the ferocious giants could not hold off the Kaelians.

So do we, the Dy'ainians, today, represent who the Varga and Schulg were thousands of years ago? It seems to me that we are now in the same position as they

Bannerfall

were a long time ago. Will we be conquered and subjugated by the Saricons? I don't know. But I can say one thing, that we, just like the Varga and the Schulg, will fight. It is our nature, as it was theirs, to do so. May Argon and Felina give us strength in the war to come.

Journal entry 38
Kivalla Der'une, Historian, Keeper of the records in Cythera, capital of Dy'ain

---

5089, the 14th cyn after the Great Change

Brant's first fight came after three months of training. He was moving through the sword forms he had been taught, his strong body guiding him smoothly through the positions. One hound sat nearby, the other two were watching Uln as he lifted a massive log, heaving it end over end.

Gar'gon was watching Uln while Tangar stood next to the hound watching Brant and correcting any missteps or improper arm positions. Then suddenly he told him to stop. Brant had been learning some rudimentary Schulg as Tangar had been conversing with him in that language, teaching him more every day.

"Fighters come into village tomorrow. You will fight."

Brant wiped the sweat from his brow. It was now the middle of summer and the mid-day sun was hot. His tunic was off and his muscular body was drenched in sweat. For the last three months, every hour, every day, was spent in training, learning new techniques of hand to hand combat, as well as ways to further strengthen his body. Much of each day was spent in physical training, while the rest was spent learning new fighting techniques. The giant hill became Brant's biggest adversary. Daily, he marched up the hill holding buckets laden with stones, his arms stretched out wide. His sides were scarred from the numerous cuts caused by the blades attached to his arms. But now he could ascend the hill several times, the buckets nearly full, without wounding himself. And despite his increased bulk, brought about by his intense physical training, he could run for hours in the heat and cover great distances. He ate meals of meat, grains, goat milk, and various fruits with honey. He also drank a disgusting green beverage. Brant had no idea what was in it, but Tangar told him that it would keep him healthy and strong. Brant had begun his training already fit and strong as an ox, but now nearly every ounce of fat on his body had been converted to pure iron muscle, his arms, legs, and chest resembled boulders over which his skin had been stretched. Not only was he powerfully built, but he could also move with incredible speed. Even Tangar had seemed impressed with his progress. "Tomorrow I fight?" Brant said apprehensively, knowing that the time had been approaching, He knew he was as ready as he'd ever be.

"Yes. Eat and drink well tonight. Get sleep. I take you to village in morning."

"Who will I fight?

"Don't know yet. But you must find anger," Tangar said, tapping his heart. "You must look for it here, or you could die."

Brant looked at the sword in his hand, the blade marred with chips and imperfections. But it was light and well balanced. There was a moment where he thought of lunging towards Tangar, and stabbing him through the heart. But he resisted the urge. Even if he could surprise and defeat the Schulg warrior, which he doubted, he knew he had little chance of surviving any confrontation with the hounds, who were always close by. He had to survive the fight. He would find that anger, and he would win.

The morning came quickly and Brant's restless sleep did little to calm his nerves. As he left their cave, Uln, who had already finished his morning meal, looked up at him earnestly with his large green eyes. "Do not die, friend Brant."

Brant gave him a waning smile. "I do not plan to."

Uln thumped his fist on his barrel-like chest. "Not hesitate, kill, or you die."

"Let's go," Tangar said, nudging Brant forward. Brant's hands were tied tightly together, and a leather strap with a length of chain connected his ankles together. He wore sandals with leather straps, soft leather leggings made in the Schulg fashion, loose fitting and stitched on the sides, and a vest made from the same leather. It was already warm and he needed little else for clothing.

After an hour of walking they made it to the village. This was the second time that Brant had seen Tangar's village, and this time it looked much different. The streets and public buildings were filled with Schulg nomads. There seemed to be twice as many people as before.

Bannerfall

Sensing his confusion, Tangar spoke in his own tongue. "This is Tullot Tribe. They come with fighters." Tangar pushed him through the crowd. It looked like most of Tangar's tribe was up and about, lighting fires and preparing meals, sharing drink and talking with the guests. The outlying area around the village was filled with bilts, surrounded by more tribesmen and their horses. They made their way to the far end of the village, everyone eyeing Brant, their expressions unreadable. It was obvious he was one of the fighters. They came to an empty circle of dirt about forty paces in diameter. Natural hillocks surrounded it, scattered with small rocks and shrubs. On closer inspection Brant could see that the small hills surrounding the circle were scattered with makeshift seats. Some seats had been dug into the hill, others had been created from rocks and logs stacked up into various chairs and benches. It was a natural arena. Most of the hills looking down into the clearing were not yet occupied.

Brant was pushed into the middle of the circle where he saw other men, chained and bound like him. They were looking at him, as he was them. They all looked fierce and strong. Several looked to be nomads, while others were Dy'ainian and perhaps Kaelian. But he saw one fighter that looked like nothing he had ever seen. He was short and stocky with disproportionally long arms which reached to his knees. His skin was gray and dry as if he had been baking in the sun. The fighter's neck was impossibly thick, starting from the base of his enormous head and angling directly to his shoulders. His head was shaved except for a thin strip of black hair that ran down to a thick patch of hair on his upper back. His face was human like, but differed in a number of ways. Everything about his face was bony and abrupt, with deep ridges and shadowy features. Brant saw sharp teeth in his wide mouth as he licked his dried lips with a thick gray tongue. The most unnerving part was its eyes. They were yellow, like a cat's, and Brant looked away when they caught him staring.

"What is that?" Brant asked Tangar.

Tangar smiled. "That's a Bullgon. Very rare. They live in the mountains. He is Chief Tu'rock's fighter. See the scars on his chest?"

Brant looked back at the Bullgon, who was now looking elsewhere. He could clearly see two raised brands just above his nipple. They looked like Schulg symbols of some sort, each one slightly different. They were the same scars that Uln carried, although he had five of them. "What are they?"

"The first one means 'honor', while the second one means 'courage'. Each one is earned after killing five men."

"So that Bullgon has won ten fights?"

"Fourteen fights. He will get his third brand today."

"Only if he wins."

Tangar smiled for the first time. "He is good at winning."

"Will I have to fight him?"

"Let's hope not."

Brant looked at the Bullgon again, appraising him. He was nervous, but confident. He would kill whoever he had to in order to survive. The Bullgon looked very formidable, but Brant had nearly defeated a warden, and that was over a year ago. Now he was stronger, and better trained.

Suddenly a horn rang out. Men, women, and children swarmed around the arena finding their seats on the hillside amphitheater. In a matter of moments the seats were filled by nomads, all eyes looking down, appraising the fighters.

"Take off vest," Tangar ordered.

Brant obeyed, and he noticed the other fighters doing the same. Most of the men had scars, and one, a tall man with long blonde hair, had a Schulg brand on his chest. He had never seen such a big man with such light blonde hair. He wondered where he had come from. Tangar dragged Brant to line up with the others, facing the majority of the crowd. Everyone was talking, but Brant's grasp of the Schulg language was not yet refined enough to pick up on the quick discussions.

"Turn around," Tangar said. The other owners were telling their fighters the same thing. A young boy with a bucket of something red moved down the line. Brant could see him painting something quickly on the backs of each fighter.

"What is that?"

"Blood mixed with red dust ground from rock. He is painting my symbol on your back."

"Symbol?"

"Symbol. It mean dog, or," Tangar was stumbling for the right word, "hound. Everyone bets. Need markers. Do not move." Tangar left his side and met with a handful of others nearby. They were talking and picking various things from a bowl. It only took a few moments and Tangar was back at his side.

Bannerfall

"What is going on?" Brant was glad that Tangar didn't seem to mind his questions.

"We each put in something valuable…gold, gem, diamond. We draw. Whoever's object we pick is who we fight. All the offerings then go to the chief who hosts the fight."

"Who am I fighting?"

"The big Saricon."

"Which one is the Saricon?"

Tangar looked at him. "You have never met a Saricon?"

"No." Brant was perturbed, as he had been with Kaan when he had said something similar to him. Apparently everyone knew who the Saricons were except for him.

Tangar lifted his head, indicating a warrior several men down. "The big one with light hair."

"He has a brand," Jonas said.

"Yes. He has won seven fights. You kill him, you get brand."

"I thought I had to win five fights."

"You do, or kill one who already has. Now be quiet" Tangar said. He then tapped the side of his head. "Prepare for fight."

Tangar told Brant that he was to fight third. Brant heard the sudden roar of the crowd and knew that the first fight had begun. Tangar then pulled him away from the arena behind several nearby bilts. He gave him some water and several pieces of urba, a round red fruit about the size of a child's fist. Underneath the bright red peel was a juicy red center, sweet but tangy.

"Fight start with no weapons. If no winner, or crowd or chiefs not like, weapons added. Do not show mercy, or you die," Tangar warned.

"What do you know of the Saricon?"

"Only hear of him. He strong, and fast. Don't know how skilled. You all those things, and smart," Tangar said, tapping his head. "You kill him," he added confidently. Tangar untied his hands. "Shake body, get warm. Move through Ga'ton."

That was a funny thing to say considering how hot it was. But he understood what Tangar meant. Brant shook his arms and rotated them in long wide circles, warming up his shoulders, back, and chest. He was already sweating, but he felt good. Then he slowly went through the Ga'ton, accentuating the end of each position with a burst of speed and power. His movements were getting more fluid and stronger, just as Tangar said they would. As he had progressed through the Ga'ton, Tangar had shown him its application. The movements of the Ga'ton not only helped with balance, strength, and speed, but they were also important positions in hand fighting as well as sword work. Brant's skill in the Ga'ton had improved, and each day Tangar had instructed him further how the positions could aid his fighting. It hadn't taken long for Brant to see the truth in it, thus he had worked harder than ever in improving his Ga'ton. As he concentrated on the positions he tried not to think about the upcoming fight. He knew that he had an edge on these men, that more than likely none of them possessed the Way. But he also knew that he had to be careful in using it. Kulvar Rand had warned him. He would have to use it sparingly.

By the time Brant finished the Ga'ton, Tangar informed him it was time. He guided Brant through the crowd into the center of the circle. Once there, he unlocked the shackles around his ankles. The crowd was howling but Brant heard only a muted roar. He looked at the Saricon who stood before him wearing nothing but loose leggings and sandals similar to his own. The big fighter was staring back at him, his face expressionless.

A Schulg stepped before them. "Start when horn blow. If you hear another blow, stop fighting. If you not stop, we kill you both," he said. Then he moved away. Brant took several steps back, trying to get some distance between them. Taking a few deep breaths, he widened his legs and brought forth his aura energy, pushing small amounts into his legs, arms, and fists.

Then the horn blew. The Saricon rushed him like a charging bull. One moment he was calm, still, emotionless…the next he was a ferocious roaring beast running at him with lightning speed.

Brant had only a few heartbeats to react. The man was a full head taller than him and more heavily muscled. It seemed obvious that he was planning on simply tackling him and using his massive weight and strength to pound him into the ground. So Brant did something that most fighters would never think of doing when facing someone that size. He crouched low, balancing on the balls of his feet, then shot forward, violently hurling himself into the Saricons legs. If he hadn't fortified his muscles with his aura energy the move would have flattened him, probably breaking his bones in the process. Instead, Brant roared and powered through the warrior, lifting him with one great surge of energy and using his opponent's forward momentum to turn sideways in the air, rotating backwards and slamming him to his back. The Saricon grunted as Brant rained fist after fist upon his face and body. Several blows struck home but he managed to use his meaty forearms to block most of them. Suddenly, in an explosion of power, the warrior managed to push his arms out, grab Brant's body and lift him in the air. He then felt the power of the Saricon's leg as he kicked out with his foot, catching Brant in his chest and launching him backwards.

    Brant miraculously landed on his feet, skidding to a stop as the warrior scurried to his feet. The big man wiped the blood from his lip, tasting it with his fingers as he sneered at Brant. Moving forward more slowly this time, the Saricon lifted his fists protectively before him. They traded blows and blocks, jabbing and punching. Brant had let his aura energy recede, saving it for an attack or a powerful punch. But he could see that his opponent had become more wary, having tasted his strength and power. But Brant saw an opening appear quickly when the warrior used his jab to set up a powerful right handed cross. He blocked the jab, the strength of the punch delivering a searing pain to the side of his arm, but saw the cross coming just in time. He ducked, narrowly avoiding the blow. Brant gave a low growl as he directed energy into his body, concentrating it in his fists; then he lunged forward, snapping his right fist forward and striking the Saricon in his exposed stomach. And though it felt as if he had struck a stone wall, Brant's enhanced strength broke through the man's formidable muscles, knocking the wind from him.

    The Saricon bellied over, but sensing another attack he continued forward, rolling across the ground and narrowly avoiding Brant's kick. Recovering quickly, he turned to face him. This time there was no sneer. They came together again. Fists snapped forward. They blocked and punched, their bodies dancing across the clearing. Brant took a couple punches to the side of his head, painful punches that wrenched his head to the side, reminding him of the power of the man he was facing. One solid hit from him and it would all be over.

    Two horn blows stopped them in their tracks. Both warriors backed away, their eyes guardedly watching one another. The Schulg that had begun the fight was shouting something into the crowd. Tangar appeared quickly at his side.

"Each man get weapon from rack," Tangar said, pointing to a weapons rack off to the side. There were two swords, one giant axe, one oswith, one hammer, and two spears. "What weapon you want?"

The axe was far too big. He was good with a blade, but he had practiced more with the oswith. He had also practiced very little with a spear. "I'll take the oswith."

Tangar grunted. "The crowd will like."

And they did. When Tangar brought Brant the oswith the crowd went crazy. Naturally, the Saricon took the axe. Brant had a feeling that the weapon had been placed there just for him.

They faced each other again. The Schulg came forward. "Only one live. Understand?"

They both acknowledged that they did. Then he blew the horn again. The Saricon resorted to his original tactic, feeling more confident with the axe in his hand. Running forward he swung the axe in a great sideways arc. He was incredibly fast for his size and it was all Brant could do, despite his energized limbs, to leap back and avoid the deadly blow. But he had no time to ponder his luck as the Saricon had quickly reversed his swing.

Acting on instinct, Brant shot more energy into his body and snapped his left foot forward, striking the warriors wrists as the axe headed his way. The Saricon howled as Brant broke his lead wrist, the axe falling to the ground. Following his kick, Brant lunged forward with the back blade of the oswith leading the way. Crouching low and moving incredibly quickly, Brant raced by the astonished warrior, the sharp blade slicing across his exposed belly.

The Saricon grunted in pain, his good hand clamping down over the gaping wound, in a futile attempt to literally hold himself together. Blood poured down his legs forming a crimson pool around his feet. But instead of faltering, the Saricon shouted a word that Brant had never heard. "Heln!" he screamed, and charged him with his bare hands.

Brant was so taken aback that he barely got his weapon up in time. Working the duel blades back and forth, Brant sliced the Saricon across his outstretched arms and chest as he backed away from the enraged and mortally wounded warrior. Finally he stumbled to his knees, bathed in blood from his countless wounds. He looked up at Brant for a few moments, then fell face first into the dust.

Bannerfall

The crowd roared and Brant dropped the bloody oswith to the ground. He had just killed a man for sport. He was angry. He was angry at the crowd for their bloodlust. He was angry at the men who had forced him to do it. But he was angrier at himself. He was angry at the exhilarating rush he felt from the power that surged through his body. He was angry at himself for how much he had enjoyed it.

Tangar walked over to Brant from the edge of the crowd. His face was his usual mask, showing no emotion whatsoever, but he nodded his head and grunted, acknowledging Brant's victory. Then the Schulg with the horn was beside him, holding a red hot branding iron. Tangar directed him to hold open his arms. Brant looked at the iron and back at Tangar and held his arms out wide, directing some aura energy into his chest in an attempt to reduce the pain. The nomad stepped forward and placed the red hot brand just above his nipple on the right side of his chest. He felt a brief searing pain, but the aura energy numbed it some. He grimaced but made no sound; he simply stared grimly at the nomad as the Schulg held the brand firmly in place. A wisp of smoke carrying the odor of cooked flesh rose from his chest. Then it was gone.

Brant looked down and saw a red, raised burn. Like the symbols he had seen etched on other elite fighters, it was the symbol for honor. Honor? He looked over at the dead Saricon. He didn't feel so honorable.

Over the next six months Brant trained, ate, and fought. He won eight more bouts and earned another brand. Earned? He found it disturbing that the term "earned" was used to describe how he had won his fights. He had killed nine men, and the brand signified that he had *earned* those victories. Perhaps he had. After all he had pushed his body further than he thought possible, training in weapons, strength, and endurance. Maybe he had worked harder than everyone else, or maybe he was just better. Obviously having the ability to Merg had given him an advantage. He had used it sparingly and thus far no one had seemed to notice. They just thought he was fast. The point was he didn't have a choice. He had not found a way to escape. The problem was the hounds. Even if he were able to get away they would easily hunt him down and kill him. He needed a way to eliminate them. But until then, he needed to stay alive, and the only way to do that was to continue to train and learn from Tangar, who was perhaps the finest fighter he had yet seen.

Brant had learned that Tangar was the sixth son of the chief of their tribe, who he had only seen from a distance at some of the fights. It had become fairly obvious that the Schulg were a war-like race, learning to fight as soon as they could walk. They were often at war with other nomads, taking land, slaves and women. Most Dy'ainians thought of the Schulg as one unified race, when in fact they were made up of hundreds of distinct tribes scattered across the steppes, each with their own chiefs and alliances. Some tribes even spoke slightly different dialects. Brant had learned many things when they had traveled an entire week to a distant fight. He had earned his third brand that day by killing the other chief's warrior. He had also earned a prominent scar that began from his right cheek and extended all the way to his shoulder, adding to the growing collection of battle scars he had collected over the last year.

His friendship with Uln had deepened during this time as well. They rarely spoke during the day, but in the evenings, sitting around the fire in their cave, the eyes of Gar'gon and the hounds constantly on them, they quietly talked. Tangar, as the chief's son, had other tribal responsibilities, so he was not always with them. But Gar'gon was always there, his long whip not far away. Brant had grown to tolerate Tangar, but he loathed Gar'gon. The stocky nomad had no redeeming qualities. It was as if he enjoyed causing them discomfort or pain. On the contrary, Tangar seemed to respect both Brant and Uln. He was not particularly kind to them, but neither was he cruel. He trained them, fed them well, and had thus far kept them alive, earning a lot of coin in the process. Brant had never seen anyone as skilled with a blade, or any weapon for that matter, as Tangar. He was not just extremely skilled, but his incredible speed and agility made it difficult for Brant to imagine anyone better, even Kulvar Rand. He had learned a lot from the warrior, but he knew there was much more the nomad could teach him, and the odds of him staying alive improved the more he was willing to learn.

Uln knew a little Newain, but over time they both learned the Schulg language and it was easier to communicate that way. Uln now had six of the strange symbols burned across his massive chest. But Brant never saw him at the fights and he wondered why. One evening around the fire he asked him.

"Why do you never participate in the fights?"

Uln looked up solemnly from the coals. Brant was still impressed at his size. The man he had fought in his first bout was the largest man he had seen, but this Varga before him was at least a head taller than the Saricon. His unnaturally green eyes had disturbed him at first, but now he saw something else. Beneath Uln's massively musclebound exterior, was something else, something gentle. Brant could see it in his eyes. "You so eager to die, Dy'ainian." Uln was smiling however.

"You think killing me would be that easy."

"It is never easy killing anything." This time the Varga was not smiling; he seemed to be thinking about something. He looked up again. "I am what you call champion. The Schulg call it Ull Therm, which mean Master Killer. Once one reach Ull Therm, you fight others who are Ull Therm. Last fight was five months ago. No one yet reach that rank." Uln looked at Brant's chest and the meaning was clear.

"So if I earn three more marks, then you and I will have to fight?"

"Yes, unless fighter reach before you and kill me."

"I would not fight you," Brant said adamantly.

Uln looked at him for a few moments. "You would rather die?"

"Of course not, but there has to be another way," Brant argued.

"I wish there was. But, friend Brant, if we ever fight in arena, promise me you will fight hard."

"Why would you want that?" Brant asked.

"I cannot die. I must see family again. I would not like, but I would try to kill you. It would hurt me badly if I knew I killed you and you not try. It would sully my victory and dishonor us both."

"And if I kill you?"

"It would be an honor to die by your blade. You are great warrior. I have never seen a human fight like you."

Brant smiled. "Well I've never even seen a Varga except for you."

Uln returned his smile. "I told you. We don't like humans. You are ugly, smell strange, and cannot be trusted. However, you are an exception; you are just ugly."

They both laughed, their minds drifting to other thoughts as they stared into the burning embers.

Three months later Brant stood before the Bullgon that he had seen at his very first fight. Brant now had four brands and the Bullgon had five. They each wore loose leggings and sandals, their bare torsos crisscrossed with scars. It had taken them over three weeks to reach this village and Tangar had told Brant that the fight had been arranged. Most of the time the fights were arranged through the random selection process, but sometimes the handlers arranged them, hoping to make a lot of money on the upcoming event. This fight had been in the making for some time as both warriors had made a name for themselves. It was a big gamble for each handler since one of them would lose a top fighter. However, if their man won they could earn an exorbitant amount on the fight. They were both willing to take the chance.

The Bullgon held a massive mace in his right hand, as if it were a child's toy. Stepping closer, the creature spoke, its strange yellow eyes gazing intently at Brant. "What is name?" he asked in stunted Newain, his voice deep and guttural.

"Brant," he replied, gripping his weapon of choice, an oswith, in his right hand.

"Well met. *Tuk antwok un kallum tor mylome.*"

"What does that mean?" Brant asked, not recognizing the words.

"It mean, *may the earth consume the blood of honor.* It Bullgon saying."

Brant liked the saying. It seemed fitting. He was surprised, however. The beast looked wild but he acted with courtesy and spoke about honor. "What is your name?"

"Tay'er."

Then the horn sounded. Tay'er stepped back and crouched low, raising his mace. Brant did the same, lifting his oswith, and they both began to circle one another. Neither fighter attacked right away, each assessing the other, looking for a weakness or an opening. Brant knew that the Bullgon's reach was going to be a problem as the creature's arms were much longer than his. But he was a Merger, and thus far he had been successful at hiding his power, using it in small doses to give him an edge. He had not yet fully tapped the Way, and he hoped he would not have to here.

Finally, after circling each other a few times, the Bullgon attacked, his long powerful arm swinging the heavy mace as if it were merely a stick. Brant knew that he if tried to block the weapon with the blade of the oswith, that it might shatter, or worse, break his arm. So he pushed his aura energy into his legs, to enhance their speed and power. He ducked and spun, avoiding the blow but not finding an advantage himself. It went on like that for about five minutes before blood was finally drawn, bringing howls from the watching crowd. Brant had jumped back again from the Bullgon's mighty swing, but this time a point of the spiked mace grazed his stomach, opening a shallow gash. The wound was not damaging as it had barely broken through the skin, but the sight of blood dripping from the wound was like a drug to the crowd and they screamed with new vigor, the sound deafening.

 Brant decided to use more of his aura. The Bullgon was not tiring and his short powerful legs and long strong arms were proving to be formidable defenses. He could not find an opening. He needed to even the playing field. Surging more energy into his legs, he shot forward like a rock from a sling, trying to get inside the reach of his opponent.

 Tay'er reversed the swing of his mace and shuffled quickly backwards, trying to maintain the distance between himself and Brant while continuing to attack with his weapon. But Brant was faster. As the reverse swing came at him, Brant, who was crouching low, was already inside his reach, his oswith angled up and blocking the mace on the shaft, rather than the heavy metal head, lessening the impact. Then he angled the forward blade down and sliced the Bullgon in the arm as he spun by him. But despite the speed of Brant's attack, Tay'er was able to punch him in the side with his free hand as he moved by. The entire attack and counterattack appeared as a blur of flashing weapons to those watching.

 The blow to Brant's side was a glancing one, but nonetheless bruised Brant's ribs. But Tay'er's injury was worse. His right arm was bleeding heavily from a deep cut under his arm, causing him to transfer the mace to his left hand, while his right arm hung uselessly at his side.

 They circled each other again, both wary of the other's skill. Then again the Bullgon shot forward, bringing his mace down quickly toward Brant's head. Brant, continuing to use his increased speed, tried to get inside the swing again, but was fooled by the Bullgon's ruse. Tay'er stopped his attack in mid-swing and snapped his stocky leg forward, catching Brant in the chest as he literally ran into his foot. His breath was ejected from his lungs and he found himself flying through the air. With a thud, he landed on his back. Coughing for air, Brant looked up and saw the mace descending toward him again. Rolling to the side, it missed him by a hair, upturning the earth in a shower of dirt. Brant directed energy into his right leg and snapped it forward, connecting solidly with the Bullgon's left arm causing him to drop the mace. He heard the crack of bone as the Bullgon howled in pain, giving Brant the opportunity to get to his feet.

Tay'er's arms now hung limply at his side. Brant faced him, still coughing as he tried to catch his breath. Each breath was accompanied by a stabbing pain in his chest. But he maintained his grip on the oswith with his right hand and the Bullgon had no weapon.

The crowd was screaming, sensing the approaching death. But then Brant did something they did not expect, and it sent a new wave of energy into the crowd. He dropped his oswith to the ground. "kallum tor mylome," he said to the Bullgon, his voice strained from the pain of his injured ribs. He wasn't sure if he was saying the words correctly, but he hoped they were the words that translated into *blood of honor*. He would not kill Tay'er while he held no weapon. They would end this bout with honor, just as they had started it. The Bullgon was unnaturally strong and fast, with longer arms and thick skin. Brant figured that his use of the Way evened the fight in hand to hand combat.

Tay'er nodded his head in understanding. His left arm hung useless at his side, but he lifted his right arm, still bleeding from his wound, and came at Brant. Brant ducked under the attack but the Bullgon reversed his swing so quickly that his knuckles caught Brant on the side of the head, causing him to stumble backwards. He directed aura energy into his head, chest, and arms, trying to numb the pain and re-energize his bruised and tired body. He was dangerously low on energy and needed to end the fight quickly.

Tay'er's arm descended again, but this time, strengthened by aura energy, Brant caught his wrist. He had practiced this move many times with Tangar and it came instinctively. Grabbing the Bullgon's wrist and hand in his iron grip, he twisted the Bullgon's arm down hard while turning his wrist upward and back, nearly breaking the bones.

Tay'er screamed and fell face first to the ground, his arm twisted back at an impossible angle. Brant knew that he would not give up, so he surged more energy into his arms and jerked hard, dislocating his arm at the shoulder. The Bullgon howled and the crowd screamed.

Brant released his grip and stepped away, his body tired, nearly depleted of energy. It took a moment, but finally Tay'er stood, his face contorted in pain, both arms hanging loosely at his side.

Bannerfall

"Finish it," he said.

"I will not kill you." Brant looked up at the crowd. "I will not kill him!" he yelled in Schulg.

Five nomads stepped from the crowd, Schulg bows nocked and ready. Tangar stood nearby. "Brant! You must! They will kill you both!"

"Do it," Tay'er groaned. "I do not want to die by a Schulg arrow. You give me honorable death." He looked around and saw the mace lying in the dirt, then reached down with his left arm, the one that was broken at the elbow. Cringing in pain he somehow managed to grasp it, holding the weapon low at his side.

Brant picked up his oswith. Then, without hesitation, and with great courage, the Bullgon somehow found the strength to raise his arm and attack him. Brant leaped forward and rammed the front blade of the oswith into the Bullgon's chest, just under his rib cage, angling the blade up and into his heart.

Dropping the mace, Tay'er brought his meaty fist to Brant's shoulder. He squeezed it once and then fell backwards, the oswith jutting from his flesh.

Brant had received his fifth brand on that day, later learning that the symbol meant 'killer', which Brant thought was fitting. He was a killer. Not by choice, but he had now killed eighteen men in the arena.

It took him nearly two months to heal from the wounds he received from the Bullgon, who had broken several of his ribs. Once they healed it had taken another month to get his body back into fighting shape. He now had five brands, one more closer to facing Uln. After he had fully recovered, Tangar had thrown him back into the circuit. Within another two months Brant had won five more fights, earning him the rank of Ull Therm. That victory was a double edged sword for Brant. He was happy to be alive, and he had to admit that he felt a great sense of achievement reaching that rank. But now he would have to face Uln in the arena. He could not imagine killing his friend. There had to be another way.

During these last few fights, Uln did have a challenge. A tough Schulg warrior, captured in war by an outlying tribe, had received his six brands, earning the right to fight Uln. But the Varga had won the bout, arriving late one evening to the cave with several fresh wounds, which were seeping blood through the bandages. The Varga had been gone for three weeks, the fight taking place in a village far to the north near the Sar'am River. Uln had not seen Brant during that time and was unaware that he had earned his sixth brand.

As Uln entered, Brant looked up from his meal, a savory meat stew with roots, rice, and vegetables. "It is good to see you," Brant said sincerely, though he wasn't smiling. He was grateful that the Varga had survived and he was happy to see him. But he felt a deep sorrow about what was to come.

Uln sat down as Gar'gon brought him a bowl of stew. "I am happy to be seen." Then he saw the sixth brand on Brant's chest, so recent that the flesh was still red and blistered. His face was expressionless, but Brant could see the sadness in his eyes.

Tangar was there as well, with another older man. Brant recognized him. He was Byn'ok, Tangar's father and the chief of their tribe, a stocky and powerfully built man, his stoic face covered with a long gray beard. Despite his age, his skin was smooth and his green eyes shone with energy. They both sat down and Gar'gon gave them each a bowl.

"Get the nord," Tangar ordered Gar'gon. For all practical purposes, Gar'gon was Tangar's slave, captured when he was a child from a faraway tribe. He had served Tangar his entire life and knew of nothing else. He grabbed several gourds filled with the alcoholic beverage and handed one to Tangar and the other to Byn'ok. They ate and drank in silence.

When they were finished, Byn'ok addressed Brant. "You have done well. Soon, you will fight Uln."

Brant shook his head. "I do not want to fight him. He is my friend. Is there another way?"

"You slave. You have no friends." Then he looked at his son. "You have honored our tribe. This has never happened before…two fighters from the same handler to reach such a rank. But you will lose one in coming fight. We need to make fight biggest the tribes have seen. It is only way for you to be compensated for the loss of one of these great warriors."

Tangar grunted. "The honor of my tribe is enough."

"Just the same, many tribes will come, many warriors. I will also invite others."

"Others?" Tangar asked, taking a long drink of his norg.

"Dy'ainian leaders. They will come to honor our tradition, to maintain peace. They will bring gifts as well. We will all win."

"Not all," Brant grunted. His Schulg was passable now, and he fully understood their conversation. Byn'ok ignored him.

"When will fight happen?" Uln asked, his deep voice echoing in the cave.

"Two weeks," Byn'ok spoke. "Need time for tribes and dignitaries to arrive."

Brant was thinking. Two weeks. He still had no plan for escaping. He glanced over at his friend and couldn't fathom plunging his blade into him. He had to find a way to escape.

The two weeks went by faster than Brant had hoped. Tangar had kept him and Uln apart for most of the time, training separately. They both slept in their usual spots in the cave, but their typical casual banter had diminished. After all, what do you talk about when you know you are soon to fight to the death? Neither of them had anything to say. Brant continued in vain to search for some way to escape, but Gar'gon and the hounds were ever vigilant. And at night, when they slept, they were shackled to an iron spike embedded in the stone wall.

The day before the fight presented Brant with his first glimmer of hope. Seven different tribes had slowly trickled in over the last few weeks, erecting a small city of bilts around Tangar's village. Several Dy'ainian nobles, members of the ruling council, had been sent by King Dormath and they had set up elaborate tents on the far side of town, guarded by Legionnaires and accompanied by a large retinue.

Ten fights had been scheduled, and the final bout would be between Brant and Uln. The day before the fight all the fighters were led to the ring and presented for all to see. New seating had to be built for all the chiefs and nobles and Brant noticed that more seating had been created near the tops of the hills above them. All the fighters were shirtless, their scars and brands visible to all. Brant looked about, trying to find the Dy'ainian nobles. It wasn't too difficult. They were sitting directly in front with Chief Byn'ok, eating, drinking, inspecting the fighters, and calculating the odds for their wagers. Uln presented something of a spectacle since few had actually seen a Varga. Brant guessed that the betting was moving in Uln's favor. But it mattered not; neither of them ever saw a coin. They were simply tools, slaves to provide entertainment for their masters.

Bannerfall

Brant's eyes wandered dully over the crowd, waiting for the inspection to end. As he glanced at the Dy'ainian representatives, his breath caught in his throat. He recognized one of the nobles sitting among them. It was Kulvar Rand and he was staring right at Brant. It had been over a year and a half since he had seen him and he certainly didn't expect to see him under these circumstances. Kulvar Rand made no attempt to show that he recognized Brant. He continued to eat and drink, talking casually to the men around him.

After a few moments they were escorted back to their quarters. For Brant that meant Tangar's bilt in the village. And since Tangar did not want Uln and Brant communicating before the fight, Uln was sent to sleep in Chief Byn'ok's bilt. The hounds were sleeping on the ground outside while Gar'gon prepared Brant a hearty stew. As usual, his wrists were chained together as well as his legs. Tangar had escorted him back, eaten a quick bowl of stew, and turned to leave. He would be up late entertaining the many guests.

Outside the hounds growled a warning. Tangar opened the flap to see who it was. Despite the anger, frustration, and sadness Brant was feeling about the impending fight, his appetite had not diminished. Feeling hungry, Brant directed his attention to the stew. He had to admit that despite his hatred for Gar'gon, the nomad was a good cook. Outside, a familiar voice distracted him from his meal.

Kulvar Rand stood before the bilt, his hand resting casually on his sword, the three hounds standing near the door growling ominously. He wore his Dygon armor and black cape, which Tangar immediately recognized. Everyone knew who the Dygon Guard were, especially the man known as Kulvar Rand. One could travel the steppes for years, visiting all the Schulg tribes, and probably never find a fighter more skilled than Tangar. But even he wondered if he could beat Kulvar Rand. He had dreamt of fighting him one day, and now he stood before him, his hand resting on his famous blade.

Tangar said something to the dogs and they stopped growling, backing up and sitting just behind the nomad. "Master Rand," Tangar said in Newain, dropping his hand to the sword tucked into his leather belt.

The movement was subtle, but it didn't go unnoticed by Kulvar Rand. A slight smile lifted the corner of his mouth. He had to admit that he admired these nomads. They feared nothing. And Tangar's name was not unknown to Kulvar Rand either. It seemed they knew of each

Bannerfall

other. "Tangar do Al'non," Kulvar Rand said in the Schulg language, addressing him by his full name to show respect. "I thank you for your hospitality. I am eager to see the fights tomorrow. I have heard much of your two champions."

Tangar was surprised and impressed that he knew his language. "The fight will be very good," Tangar said, wondering why the famous Kulvar Rand had come directly to his personal tent to thank him. "Is there something I can do for you?" Tangar said, sensing there was something else the warrior wanted to say.

Inside the tent Brant had stopped eating, listening intently to the conversation. He had recognized Kulvar Rand's voice right away. So Kulvar had recognized him at the arena. What was he doing here though?

"I was wondering if you would like to sell the Dy'ainian? It seems a shame to have two great fighters face off, as one will surely die. I will pay you five thousand gold dracks."

Stunned, Tangar was momentarily speechless. That was an enormous about of money, probably more than he would make from the fight itself. For just a few moments he considered the offer. But in the end he knew he could not accept it. There was more than just money at stake. If he cancelled the main attraction it would bring shame and dishonor upon his tribe. He could not do that, no matter the price. "I am sorry. I cannot sell. People," Tangar said as he indicated the thousands of people around them, "have come to watch. I cannot cancel the main bout. It would bring dishonor to my tribe."

For that brief moment Brant had thought that he might consider the offer. Just as quickly his hope was crushed.

Kulvar Rand was prepared for just such an answer, not really believing that he would accept the offer with so many people here to see the fight. But he had to try. He had taken a liking to the boy when he met him and he surely didn't deserve such a life, living in chains like an animal and being forced to fight in arenas for entertainment, the only eventual outcome being his death. "May I speak with your fighter?"

"For what purpose?"

"I know him. I met him years ago in the mining camps. I would like to wish him luck tomorrow."

It made sense, Tangar thought. The Dygon Guard escorted the Kul-brite caravans and Tangar knew that the young man had worked the mines his entire life. "You may," he said, gesturing for him to enter.

As Kulvar Rand stepped to the entrance, the hounds backed up, growling softly. "Your Nygs are quite impressive. How did you train them?"

"I found them when they were young. Raised them myself."

"Do you mind if I speak with him alone?"

"Gar'gon, my slave, is inside. He will stay with you. I have matters to attend. My hounds will remain outside."

"Very well." Kulvar Rand knew that the nomad was warning him. The hounds would rip him to pieces if he tried anything.

They both entered the bilt and as soon as Gar'gon saw them he stood up, ready to perform whatever duty his master required. "Gar'gon, this is Master Rand. He is here to speak with Brant. When he is done see that he departs safely."

Kulvar Rand looked at Brant, his face unreadable. Then he turned to Tangar. "Thank you. I shall see you at the festivities tonight."

Tangar grunted, turned, and left the bilt.

Kulvar sat on the opposite side of the fire, facing Brant. "It is good to see you, boy." Kulvar Rand had switched to Newain, hoping that Gar'gon did not speak it well.

Brant smiled wanly. "I wish it was under better circumstances."

"Tell me what happened."

Brant sighed and began the story. It didn't take him long and when he got to the part about his sentencing, Kulvar frowned. "What is it?" Brant asked, seeing his expression.

"I've met that magistrate before. He did not impress me, nor did his son."

"Well, your instincts were right. He sentenced me to a year with the Schulgs."

"How long have you been here?"

"I'm not sure exactly, but my guess is nearly two years."

Kulvar Rand sighed. "I wish I would have known of this earlier. Technically, your sentence is over and you should be free to go."

Brant sat up. "You mean I can leave?"

Kulvar Rand was shaking his head. "I'm afraid not. They will never let Dy'ainian law supersede tribal law. In their eyes, you are their slave."

"What am I to do? I cannot fight the Varga. He is my friend."

Kulvar Rand looked over at Gar'gon who was sitting on the far side of the bilt preparing the green drink that Brant consumed daily. He

Bannerfall

was paying them little attention. Kulvar nodded toward him, whispering softly. "Does he speak Newain?"

Brant shook his head. "Very little."

"I might have an idea. I'm afraid it's the best I can do considering the circumstances."

"What is it?" Brant asked eagerly.

Kulvar Rand reached into a pouch hanging from his belt and produced a small vile. "This is Nuru Oil," Kulvar whispered, afraid that Gar'gon might recognize the word. "The Schulg use it when they hunt. It's a poison." He looked back at Gar'gon who was busy preparing the drink. He gave the two an occasional glance, but didn't seem to suspect anything. When the nomad turned his back to reach for a mug for Brant's drink, Kulvar used the opportunity to toss him the vile. He caught it and quickly tucked it into his pants.

"How did you get it?" Brant whispered.

"It is readily available here. I bought some on my way to see you. Thought it might prove useful."

Brant thought about it for a moment. If he could poison Gar'gon, then maybe he could escape. But the hounds were still a problem. What if he could poison the hounds? That was the best idea. If he could do that, he reasoned that he could kill Gar'gon and escape. "I will see what I can do. Thank you for this. Whether I make it or not, I appreciate your help."

"If you do make it out of here in one piece, try to find me. I could use a man who survived the pits and became Ull Therm."

"I will."

Kulvar got up to leave. "And Brant, remember, if you use the Way tomorrow the two nobles with me will know."

Brant had forgotten about that. But what choice did he have? If he did have to fight Uln tomorrow, there was no way he could beat him without the Way. "If I have to fight, then I will have to take that chance. I cannot beat Uln without the Way."

"Then let us hope you escape. Good luck tomorrow, Brant." Kulvar turned and spoke in Schulg to Gar'gon. "I'm leaving now."

Gar'gon moved towards him. "Follow me. Don't want hounds to attack."

Kulvar looked at Brant one more time before he spun on his heels and followed the nomad out the door.

Bannerfall

Brant was thinking frantically. How would he get the poison into the hound's food? Usually Gar'gon fed them after they had all eaten, and he knew that it was almost time for their meal. The hounds were large and they required a lot of food. Typically they were given the less than savory pieces of meat, entrails, fat, skin, and bones, along with whatever other scraps remained from their meals. There was plenty of left over scraps in the village, as well as fresh game from the hunters that Tangar paid to provide more meat.

Gar'gon came back inside and Brant noticed that he was throwing the fat and bones from the soup into a big wooden bowl. Then came over to Brant. "Chain you to stone. Need to get scraps," he said. There was a huge stone in the corner of the room, near his bed, where he was chained at night, or when he was left alone. He reached down and grabbed the chain linking Brant's hands together, jerking him up hard. Brant had a sudden idea and he acted quickly. He surged aura energy into his right leg and rammed it with all his strength into the nomad's groin. Gar'gon was hit so hard that his heavy body was lifted from the ground. He groaned in pain and keeled over, and Brant, not wanting him to scream out, quickly wrapped the chain around his neck and propelled himself forward, spinning to the nomad's back and lifting him off the ground as if he were a sack of grain. Brant leaned forward, the weight of the Schulg on his back, and lifted him up off the ground. Gar'gon continued to struggle, gasping and gurgling as he tried desperately to breathe, but Brant pushed aura energy into his arms, constricting the chain ever tighter until finally Brant heard a snap and felt the nomad's body go limp.

Dropping the body to the floor he quickly searched for the keys to his shackles. He found them easily, attached to the chain clipped to Gar'gon's belt. He quickly unlocked his shackles, then ran to the hounds' food bowl, filling it with more scraps that he found. There was some dried meat and beans left over from their mid-day meal. Throwing everything into the big bowl, he withdrew the poison from his pants and dumped the entire contents of the vile into it.

He paused for a moment, took a deep breath to settle his nerves, and carried the heavy bowl to the bilt's opening. He placed the bowl on the ground and slowly pushed it forward. Once the bowl touched the flap, Brant heard the hounds growl. He kept pushing, using the weight of the bowl to nudge open the leather flap covering the entrance. Once the flap was open, Brant shoved the bowl harder, trying to get it beyond the flap so it would quickly close.

A few heartbeats later and Brant could clearly hear the dogs fighting over the scraps. The problem was Brant had no idea how long it would take for the poison to take effect. He ran over to the weapons rack and grabbed a sword and knife. The oswith was there but it was cumbersome to carry as the two blades made it awkward to sheath in any way. Next, he grabbed Gar'gon's coat and hat, and put them on. He tucked the knife and sword into his belt and ran back to the entrance, listening for any telltale sounds coming from the hounds. They were still eating.

He went to the tables where the meals were prepared and grabbed a small bag, filling it with any remaining food he could find. There were a handful of urbas, the small fruit that he ate before his fights, along with some stale bread and goat cheese. He stuffed the sack full and ran back to the entrance, listening intently. He didn't hear anything.

Drawing his sword, he used the tip to nudge open the flap. It was now dark outside and he could barely see a thing. But he didn't hear the hounds, and that was encouraging. Slowly, he emerged from the opening. There were a number of torches illuminating the paths between the many bilts in the village, shedding just enough light for Brant to see two of the hounds lying still on the ground. But where was the third?

His question was answered when a massive form shot from the darkness and struck Brant in the chest, the heavy fur covered body knocking him to his back. Instantly he felt claws tear into his flesh. Instinctively he lifted his arms in front of his face to shield it from the creature's jaws. Luckily the hound's jaws found only his left arm as they snapped down on it, ripping and tearing his coat and the flesh underneath. The hound was so strong and heavy that Brant could barely move. As if his life depended on it, which it did, he surged a massive amount of energy into his right fist and slammed it repeatedly into the hound's head. The third blow, delivered with as much power as he could muster, knocked the beast sideways, catapulting its body across the dirt. Brant scurried to his feet, looking quickly for the sword that had been knocked from his hand.

The hound had quickly regained its footing, but then suddenly faltered. It stumbled briefly as if it were drunk, then collapsed to the ground where it lay rigid and still. The poison must have finally worked. Brant frantically looked about, hoping the commotion hadn't attracted any attention. He didn't see anyone about. There was eating and drinking at the pit where the fights were to take place and Brant figured everyone was there as they celebrated the fights to come.

    He quickly inspected his wounds. Luckily the nomad's heavy leather coat had protected him from most of the hound's claws. His left sleeve was shredded and his arm was bleeding but he didn't have time to inspect it further. Blood stained his leggings where the hound's claws had torn through the cloth and found his flesh. The wounds stung but did not seem serious. Besides, he had just spent over a year fighting bouts to the death, and the numerous wounds he had suffered were testament to violent life he had been forced to live. He had certainly suffered worse injuries. Ignoring the pain he found his sword and sheathed it, picking up the bag of food and slinging it over his shoulder.

    In the darkness he hoped he would look like any other nomad. So he simply walked the paths that meandered through the various bilts, passing a few people as they sat at their fires eating and drinking. Several nervous moments later he found himself hiding in the darkness behind a rock, looking at the shadowed bilt where he thought Uln had been confined. Two torches were stuck into the ground, their flickering flames illuminating the entrance. Seeing no one about Brant ran over to the entrance. He didn't really have a plan. But how could he? He had acted quickly when Kulvar Rand had given him an option, and now he was just making it up as he went.

    Brant drew his sword, took a deep breath, sent some aura energy into his body, and pushed through the tent flap. He scanned the room quickly, his eyes darting around the interior. The bilt had been erected next to a rock face, most of which formed the back wall of the structure. Uln was sitting against the rock, a heavy chain securing him to the unmovable stone. A man and a woman sat at a fire in the middle of the room. Brant had no idea who they were, but he attacked without thought, knowing that to do otherwise would allow them to cry out for help.

    Before the couple could take a breath, Brant had reached them, attacking the man first as he stood and attempted to reach for his sword. Brant's sword flashed twice, cutting the startled man across the chest, the second swing slicing through his neck. The woman started to scream, but it only lasted a second as Brant reversed the direction of his sword arm and slammed the pommel of the blade against her head. She fell like a bag of rocks.

Brant ran to Uln who was now standing. "Where are the keys?"

"The man," Uln said.

He ran to the dead man and searched his body, finding the keys attached to his belt. Quickly he unlocked Uln. "Let's go. Grab a weapon. We need to start running."

Uln didn't hesitate. He grabbed an axe from against the wall and followed Brant out of the bilt. The area around the bilt seemed empty. The chief's bilt, where they now stood, was on a raised hill and they could easily see the party going on down by the arena "Looks like everyone there," Uln said.

"That is good. Let's go." Brant had no idea where they were going. He just knew that they had to escape into the night. They had to get as much distance between them and the village as possible. After that they could worry about where they were going.

Turning, they ran into the night, heading in the opposite direction of the arena, leaving an uncertain destiny behind.

Chapter 7

I've often wondered if there are others in our world with inherent powers like the Way. We know the Saricons have a similar ability called the Fury. But we had no knowledge even of them before several cyns ago. What other people's exist in our vast world with similar abilities? It seems feasible that others may possess some type of power that we have yet to see. It seems rather arrogant to assume that only one's own people would possess such powers. If such abilities are indeed given to us by Argon and Felina, why would they not also give them to others they created? But it seems that the question that eludes us is where did these powers come from? Did Argon and Felina forge the world? If not, who did, and why are we here? Where did these special abilities come from and why do only some possess them? I have not traveled as far north as Palatone, nor have I crossed the Varos Mountains. What wonders await us there? What types of people populate those lands? Would they too have been gifted with some strange power? There are so many questions, but alas I do not have enough lifetimes to search for all the answers.

Journal entry 54
Kivalla Der'une, Historian, Keeper of the records in Cythera, capital of Dy'ain

---

5090, the 14th cyn after the Great Change; present time

Six people sat around Daricon's table in his study. Maps and ledgers littered the table before them and Jarak stood in front of his chair leaning over the table to get a better look at the map. Serix, Daricon, Captain Hagen, Colonel Lorth, and a new captain, Endler Ral from Cythera, sat around the table discussing recent military matters. The young captain was a nobleman from Cythera and a skilled Channeler. He had worked with Serix during several battle campaigns

Bannerfall

and had been requested by Daricon to come to Lyone several weeks earlier. No matter what decisions they made this day, war was inevitable. For Serix and Jarak to be affective, they needed a Channeler. Endler Ral's father was a minor nobleman. House Ral made most of their income on trade and controlled over ten merchant vessels that sailed the Dark Sea all the way to YaLara and back. Jarak liked the warrior immediately. He was optimistic and he brought new energy to their discussions.

"So what do we know?" Daricon asked the men.

"It seems that Jarak was right," Serix replied, "I believe they will be splitting their forces. Our spies have indicated heavy troop movements to the east."

"It makes sense," Colonel Lorth added. "It is so simple, which is perhaps why it hadn't occurred to us. We needed a new perspective," he said, nodding toward Jarak. "But we still have the same problem. What do we do in response?"

"The real question is how many men will they leave here to attack the garrison?" Jarak asked, as he studied the maps.

"The Saricons must know our numbers and will send a large enough force to defeat us," Captain Hagen said.

"But surely we can hold them off with fewer numbers. Our walls are strong and when the drawbridge is up there is no way to cross the river," Captain Ral said.

"The way I see it is we have only three choices," Daricon said as he stood up and moved by the roaring fire. "We stay and defend our walls to the last man, we retreat to Cythera, giving up the garrison and allowing the Saricons into our lands so that we may face them at the capital, or we stay and fight, killing as many Saricons as we can before retreating to Cythera."

Jarak sighed, not liking any of the choices. Everyone was now looking at him. Over the last few months he had noticed the men, and the officers, including Daricon, were treating him differently. He had been at the garrison for over a year, and slowly he had changed, gaining confidence, and earning the trust of his men in the process. He still had a long ways to go, but it was a start. He wasn't sure if he was ready for it, but it was clear that they were looking to him to help provide an answer to their predicament. "I would rather spill Saricon blood on these walls than give them up to the enemy without a fight. Let us fight, and when the time comes that our defeat looks imminent, we shall retreat to Cythera where we will fight again."

The others nodded in agreement. "I agree, my Prince," Daricon said, moving back to the table. "Now, let us get some sleep. We have much work to do tomorrow to prepare for a siege."

Everyone stood up, said their good nights, and moved to leave.

"Captain Hagen, may I have a word please?" Jarak asked, forcing himself to remain calm. It had been several weeks since their attack on the road. He had promised Cat that he would talk with her father and he could avoid it no longer. Captain Hagen had been furious with her, not only because of the risks she took but because she had forged his signature. But he could not deny that she had saved Prince Jarak's life. Nonetheless, Jarak knew that the conversation he was about to have would not be easy.

"Of course, my Prince," Captain Hagen said, remaining seated. He looked slightly suspicious, as if he knew what was to come. Daricon, curious, moved back to the table and took his seat. It was his study after all and he had no intention of leaving his private rooms.

Jarak reached out and poured the captain and Daricon some more wine, refilling his own goblet in the process. He drained nearly a third of his goblet before proceeding. "I want to talk with you about Cat." Captain Hagen frowned and shifted uncomfortably in his seat. "As you know she wants to join the Legion. She is very skilled with a sword, and she saved my life. I must be honest with you and tell you that I feel obligated to grant her wish. It is the least I can do to honor her actions." Jarak had worked on his words for many nights, trying to figure out how best to appeal to the captain. He hoped that Captain Hagen would respond more positively to a request laced with words such as *honor* and *service*.

Captain Hagen did not respond immediately and Jarak looked at his uncle for support. Daricon leaned back in his chair and drank calmly from his cup, a slight nod showing his approval.

"My Prince," Captain Hagen began. "You do not have a daughter so I cannot pretend that you would understand. I have seen the atrocities of battle and my heart breaks in half every time I imagine my girl, her body broken and cut, sprawled across the muddy ground. Can you not understand why I would not wish it on her?"

Jarak stood up straight and looked away toward the fire, not able to meet his gaze. But then he looked back. "You are right; I do not have a daughter. But the death you speak of could happen to her right here within these walls when the Saricons arrive. Or it could happen to any daughter living in any of the frontier homes along our borders. She has as skill. She is a fighter. You know as well as I do that she will not be happy merely being someone's wife, producing children, and performing an endless succession of domestic chores. That is not her destiny. She *will* be a fighter, whether you wish it or not. You cannot keep her from doing what she wishes. She is of age, and I'm afraid that if you do not give her your blessings then she will leave you and join the Legion in Kreb, or Tanwen, away from you and me. I suggest we grant her wish and keep her close by, where we can watch over her."

Captain Hagen lowered his head in thought. Jarak glanced at Daricon who gave him a quick wink. "I know you are right," Captain Hagen sighed, his voice soft. "But I can't help but feel that if I say the words, if I allow her to join the Legion, that I am the one possibly signing her death warrant." Then he looked up. "Do you know what that feels like?"

Jarak sat down beside him. "I do not. But I have learned many things from you and my uncle since coming here. And one of them is that when you lead men, you must be willing to carry the burden of their deaths. We all face the dangers of war. You have sent men to their deaths. And I, no doubt, will send many more to the grave. Sadly, I never thought about it before, but now that burden sits heavy on my heart. I do not know if I'm ready for it, but you both have given me the strength to face the fact that men and women will die because of the decisions we make. But we will not let them face that danger on their own. For us to carry that burden, we must be willing to risk the same fate. Cat has the strength to carry that burden as well, and you or I will not be able to stop her. It is what makes her who she is…it is what makes her special."

Captain Hagen's eyes were rimmed with moisture. "She is special, isn't she?"

"I have not met anyone like her," Jarak responded honestly.

Suddenly the captain stood up. "I suspected at first that you were requesting this to win favor with my daughter. I have seen you with her and I know she can be very persistent." Jarak was about to speak when he cut him off. "But your words ring with truth. I have known that she would inevitably follow her dreams eventually. I was just hoping that she would change her mind, that perhaps the violence she experienced while saving you would persuade her to pick a new path in life. But I can see that I was wrong. I will give her my blessing. Now, if you will excuse me."

As Captain Hagen moved to leave, Jarak spoke up. "Captain, I want you to know that I will do whatever I can to keep her out of danger. She means a lot to me."

Captain Hagen turned slightly, but did not look at the prince. "And to me," he whispered.

Jarak's conversation with Captain Hagen had taken an emotional toll on him. He had been unable to think about eating, and now that the issue had been resolved, he realized he was literally famished. It was late but when he made his way down to the kitchens he saw that Jayla, the chef, was still working.

A long wood table was covered with flour and rolls of dough and Jayla was kneading more in a bowl. She was a large woman, in her sixties, with long gray hair pulled back out of her face and tied with a leather string. The wrinkles in her face made it look as if she were perpetually frowning. Over the last year Jarak had slowly developed a closer relationship with the woman. She was a cantankerous old lady, who on the outside appeared callous and mean, but Jarak had gradually learned that was merely a façade that concealed a warm and caring heart. One just needed to look deep and spend the time to uncover the layers to get to that soft spot. Most didn't bother, and Jarak was still digging.

"Good evening, Jayla," Jarak announced as he entered her kitchen.

She looked up and scowled. "The kitchen is closed."

"Even to your prince?"

She harrumphed and threw the dough down hard, kneading it like a fighter hitting his opponent's face. "Nothing's ready."

"I'm sorry to bother you, but when one can produce such culinary excellence you must surely be used to frequent visits from hungry patrons eager to sample your perfections." Jarak moved to the table and he saw, off to the side, a plate filled with fruit, cheese, and some dried meats. "What do we have here?" Jarak thought he saw her smile, but it disappeared quickly.

"That is not fit for a prince."

"It looks perfect for a prince," he countered.

"If you must," she sighed, "then sit and I will prepare you something fitting for your station."

Jarak smiled and pulled a stool over to sit at the table. They had gone through this banter on several occasions and he still wondered if she actually liked him or was just catering to his needs because he was the prince. He had never really met anyone who had the nerve to speak to him as she did, and who made him feel as if he were some peasant boy begging for food. But Daricon was right. She was such a fabulous cook that neither one of them wanted to do anything that might threaten her service with them.

Jayla went into the pantry and came back out with a handful of items, a cured tulkick leg, a fresh loaf of bread, and a crock of butter. She cut the bread into thick slices, spreading them with a liberal coating of butter. Jarak noticed specks of green in the butter and asked her about them.

"What's in the butter?"

"Rosemary."

Then she cut off thin slices of the smoked meat and laid them over one slice of the bread. Grabbing a clay jar off the shelf, she removed the wax covering, spooned out a generous helping of jam, and smeared it over the other piece of bread. Jarak could smell the rich fruity scent of the jam from where he was sitting.

"What is that? It smells delicious."

"Canton berries infused with vanilla."

Nothing from Jayla's kitchen was ordinary. Jarak marveled at her dedication and the time she spent preparing food for the lords of the garrison. She sliced some onion and tomato and layered them on the bread with the meat. Last she cut several slices of a strong cheese that Jarak recognized. It was called streak cheese from the streaks of green mold meandering through it. It had a strong taste that he knew would go well with the cured meat. Jarak smiled, knowing that Jayla knew the cheese was his favorite. Maybe she did like him. Finally, she set the sandwich on a plate and plopped it in front of him.

"There you go. Now leave me so I can finish my bread."

Jarak picked up the plate, bowing deeply to Jayla. "Thank you." And just as he was turning to leave, he thought he saw a glimpse of a smile.

***

Brant and Uln ran for over an hour before they finally stopped, looking up as the heavy cloud cover finally drifted away revealing a bright starry night. Uln was the one who stopped them, looking up at the stars.

"There," he pointed, breathing heavily.

"What?" Brant asked, looking up into the sky. He was tired as well. But they had both trained hard and he knew that they could run even longer.

"That star…my people call it Gota. It always in north. We must go that way," Uln said, pointing to the west.

"You want to go home," Brant said, aware of Uln's desire to return to his family. "How far is it?"

"Not sure…several weeks."

"We have different paths, my friend. But let us travel west until I reach lands I recognize. I have some friends that might help me. We will part ways there."

"How long?"

"Two days I think," Brant reasoned. He remembered that the trip from Amorsit to Tangar's village was a three day walk in the northeasterly direction, and that the road from Kaan's farm to Amorsit was a two day walk. But they would make better time if they ran due west. Then, when they hit Bygon Creek they could follow it directly to Kaan's farm. That was the best plan he could come up with.

"How are wounds?"

Brant took off his coat to look at the scratches and minor puncture wounds on his arm. They were not too deep, the thick leather of the coat had done a good job of protecting him from the hound's teeth. But he was worried about infection. He lowered his pants to get a better look at his legs where the hound's claws had scratched him. They were the most painful of his injuries, and when he looked at them he understood why. Each leg had several lacerations that ran the length of his thighs, and the open wounds, though shallow, were raw, irritated, and bleeding, exacerbated by his constant running. "I need to bind these somehow," Brant said.

"Rip off bottom of pant. Tear into pieces."

It was a good idea. Brant went about ripping the bottom of his pants off and tearing them into long strips. The cloth was old and worn and he could easily rip it. But it still wasn't enough. Uln did the same to his pants, and together it was enough to wrap around his thighs and at least seal the wounds. But he had nothing to clean them, and that worried him the most.

Once he was done, they ran off into the darkness, the bright star in the night always to their right.

***

Kahn Taruk pushed open the door and strode into the tavern, his long muscular legs taking him toward a private room in the back. Six large Saricons were with him; each warrior wearing armor in the Saricon style, pieces of steel plates protecting crucial parts of the body while a steel cuirass, adorned with Heln's horned symbol, graced the center. The men wore swords and axes, the weapons of choice for a Helnian. Strapped to the backs of three men were quivers filled with half a dozen throwing javelins, each weapon about half the size of a spear. The Saricons had perfected the forging of these weapons, the weight and balance allowing the warriors to use them with deadly efficiency and accuracy.

The tavern was full, filled with the evening crowd. Five off duty Saricon soldiers drank and ate their supper, but most of the crowd consisted of Kaelians, men and women who had decided to co-exist with the Saricon invaders.

The Saricons had invaded Kael and conquered Fara nearly thirty years ago. Enough time had passed that most of the Kaelians that stayed behind after the initial conquest now looked upon the Saricons as permanent fixtures. All the Argonians had been weeded out years ago; persecuted, killed, or forced to leave their homes and venture north to Eltus, or west to Heyrith. Either way, they were no longer welcome in Fara. Many Kaelians had converted, deciding that it was better to become a Helnian rather than forced to leave their homes. All vestiges of the Argonian faith had been destroyed long ago. Temples were leveled, statues destroyed, and paintings and tapestries burned. Helnian temples had been built upon the ruins, and now huge statues of their powerful god, carved from dark stone, could be seen throughout the city of Fara.

There were still pockets of resistance, however, small communities of Argonians who had refused to leave the city and who practiced their faith in secret. But these groups were by far the minority.

Bannerfall

The Saricons, true to their nature, had been successful in stamping out the Argonians, their violent persecutions enough to deter most to flee or convert. Besides, the Helnian faith was simple, lacked rigidity, and was straightforward in its concepts, making it an agreeable faith to most.

The owner of the establishment, a little man called Curly, scurried from behind the bar to greet the Tongra. "Good evening, Tongra. The room is supplied with ale and food and your guests have already arrived. Can I bring you anything else?"

"That will be fine." Kahn Taruk said nothing else, turned and moved down a hallway stopping at an oak door. They entered the large room, fanning out as they did. The room was generally used to entertain wealthy patrons. Tables could be set up for card games or soft couches could be brought in for lounging and watching whatever entertainment was provided. Today the large room, as per Kahn Taruk's instructions, was dominated by a large table in the middle surrounded by twenty chairs. Soft couches and side tables occupied the perimeter and a large stone fireplace was located to the right of the door, a huge fire blazing brightly. Sconces along the perimeter walls were lit, and candles, along with trays of food and drink, were scattered all across the center table.

Four people sat on the far end of the table eating and drinking, their hushed voices halting when the Saricons entered. All four of them stood, their postures a mixture of deference and alertness.

Thalon put his two fists together before his chest and bowed his head in greeting. "Tongra Taruk, it is good to see you." The rest of the assassins around him did the same, but said nothing.

"And you, Thalon. Please sit." Everyone sat, including the Saricons. "Let us eat and drink before we get to business."

Thalon smiled. "I hope you do not mind, but we have already started."

Of course he minded, but he said nothing, knowing that to do so would just be falling into the assassin's trap. The cocky man wanted to see him frustrated, and he would not give him the satisfaction.

He had met the others once before, but he did not acknowledge them. One was a female whose name was Lyra and Kahn Taruk knew she was an Aura Mage, just like Thalon. The other two were males, one quite large. The big man, thick with muscle, was Tulk, and he was a Merger. He had an oddly shaped head, large and blocky, with several scars covering his cheeks and forehead. Kahn Taruk noticed a large two handed sword leaning against the table near the man. The smaller man beside him was Ayden, who was a Channeler. Short white hair framed his narrow, almost feminine face. His eyes were almost all black, with only a tinge of lavender which gave him an eerie look, as if he were possessed by something ominous. They were known as the Shadows, assassins and mercenaries who worked for the highest bidder. And right now that person was Kahn Taruk.

They ate and drank, talking quietly, but keeping the conversation light. Kahn Taruk hated looking at them. Each of them appeared strange, different, not entirely normal. He knew that the magic they used had changed them, and not always for the better. Thalon's clawed fingers were all too obvious every time he reached for his mug, their sharp black tips tapping against the metal. The assassin's eyes were also different; large and oval, with lavender centers. The man's pale skin and bald elongated head made him the ugliest man Kahn Taruk had yet seen in Corvell. He wanted to bring forth his Fury and crush the man under his steel boot. But he needed him.

After the food and drink were nearly consumed, Kahn Taruk spoke up. "I need you to do something else for me."

"You paid us handsomely for the last mission. I am listening," Thalon said, tossing a grape into his mouth.

"I need you to go to Eltus. When you see my ships arrive, and anchor before the city, I would like you to burn the Kaelian navy."

Lyra, the female assassin, glanced at Thalon. She too had lavender eyes.

Thalon didn't say anything for a moment, drinking slowly from his mug, his elongated fingers, like the legs of a spider, encircling the cup.

"That would be nearly fifty ships," Thalon said casually.

"That is correct. Can you do it?" Kahn Taruk was worried that the task would be impossible, even for the Shadows. They were deadly and effective assassins, but could they destroy an entire fleet? He was hoping that they had the skill to complete the task.

"That would be a very difficult task. And very costly," he replied, emphasizing the word *very*.

"You did not answer my question. Can you do it?"

"Do you have the coin?"

"You know that I do."

Thalon took another drink of his ale. "I would not want to guarantee something that is unknown. Can we burn their ships? Yes. But I do not think we could completely destroy that many."

"How many then?"

He shrugged. "Perhaps half that. Here is the problem. As soon as we start to set fire to the ships with our spells, they will know we are using the Way. They will summon their own Aura Mages, Channelers, and Sappers and we would be destroyed."

"Perhaps there is another solution." Ayden, the Channeler, spoke up for the first time.

"You are Ayden, correct?"

"I am."

"What do you suggest?"

"I agree with Thalon. We can burn perhaps ten to twenty before we would be overwhelmed. But we may be able to render the other ships useless without burning them."

"How so?" the Tonga asked.

"Poison the crews."

Thalon smiled. But Lyra was not so sure. "How would we poison so many?" she asked.

"Most of a ship's crew sleeps on board," Ayden began. "Drinking water is stored on the boats. We slip aboard the ships and poison their supply. A skilled thief would have no problem sneaking onto the boats in the dead of night when most of the crew are sleeping. Even if we only kill half of the crew, it would be enough to keep the ship from being any danger. They would not be able to man it effectively, especially during battle."

"Timing would be difficult, but it may be a possibility," Thalon said, thinking out loud.

"I don't know," Lyra said, doubtfully. "The risks of detection are high. The four of us would have to sneak onto half of the boats, undetected, while preparing to burn the other half."

Kahn Taruk did not care how they would accomplish the task. He just wanted it done. The entire plan rested on the idea that the Kaelian navy would be nullified, allowing his own navy to bombard the city from the coastline while his troops attacked from land. Once they destroyed their navy and claimed the city, they would then control the Dynel Strait. Then they could focus on Cythera. Even as they spoke Karnack and his ten thousand men were on their way to the shores of the Pyres Mountains. From there Obaty, the Askarian nomad, would lead his army through the secret mountain pass, emerging months later on the other side along the eastern shores of the Bitlis Sea. At that point the plan called for the army to construct barges and sneak their troops across the narrow strait to the lands of Dy'ain. Karnack would then secure the lands east of the capital city of Cythera. Meanwhile, Kahn Taruk would have already taken the city of Eltus and transported his men by ship through the Dynel Strait to offload along the shores of Dy'ain near the capital city. Both armies would then converge on the city. He had a few other secrets up his sleeve, but everything rested on Karnack's army securing the east undetected. "I have something that may help," he added, looking over at one of his men. The big Saricon reached under his cloak and produced a round clay ball about the size of an infant's head. Kahn Taruk took it from him and placed it before Thalon.

"What is it?" the assassin asked.

Kahn Taruk smiled. "A Tynell. Inside it are two substances, that when mixed produce a violent fiery explosion."

"I have never heard of such a thing," Lyra said, leaning forward to get a better look at the ball.

"Of course you have not. It was created by our alchemists and no one else has the knowledge to produce them," Kahn Taruk added with pride.

"Alchemists?" Thalon said, clearly unaware of the term. "I have heard of no such word."

"It matters not. Our knowledge of such things is far beyond yours," he said. "What matters is that when these are dropped onto the ships, they will create fiery havoc. So, I will ask one more time. Can you dismantle the Kaelian navy?"

Thalon looked at Ayden, then Lyra, who looked away, still not willing to commit to the idea. But Thalon didn't care. With their spells, and these new Saricon weapons, the chance of success suddenly got better. "We will do as you ask. We want five thousand dracks before we leave for Eltus and another five thousand after we complete the job."

Kahn Taruk sat back in his chair. The sum was a king's ransom. Even the stoic Saricons sitting next to him looked shocked by the sum.

Lyra looked back at Thalon, wondering if she heard him correctly, but knowing that she did. Tulk tensed, easing his meaty hand towards his sword, worried that the Tongra would be so angry that he'd attack. Tulk knew that Saricons were prone to quick and sudden violence and he did not want to be caught unprepared.

Thalon stared at Tongra Taruk, his lavender eyes revealing nothing.

Finally the Tongra spoke. "I agree to your sum." Then he leaned forward, his huge arms pressing down on the table, his blue eyes narrowing. "But if you do not succeed in this task, I will make it my personal mission to hunt you down and kill you, all of you. In Heln's name I will crush you, and no amount of aura magic will save you. Do you understand?"

Thalon smiled, but the others did not. "We understand."

***

It was mid-day and Tangar sat on his horse, looking down expectantly at the trackers before him. Two men inspected the ground, conversing quietly as they analyzed the disturbed earth. Fifty men sat on horses behind him.

They had been following the trail since daylight. Tangar estimated that Brant and Uln had escaped at least four hours before the bodies were found. At that point it was too dark to set out blindly after them. They had to wait until the sun came up the next morning. That meant that they had at least a half day's lead on them, but also that they had been running for many hours. He knew they were tired and hungry, and on foot. They would find them.

Tangar was beyond furious. Brant had killed his slave, the hounds he had raised since birth, and had humiliated him in front of all the tribes. He would make them pay dearly for what they had done. And then there was that Dy'ainian scum, Kulvar Rand. Tangar had been so angry when he found out they had escaped that he had confronted the Dygon Guard immediately. Swords were nearly drawn, but his father, Chief Byn'ok, would not allow his guests attacked without proof or provocation. But Tangar knew that the Dy'ainian Lord had something to do with their escape. It was too coincidental that he had visited Brant that night, and that soon after he poisoned his hounds and escaped. Where else would he have obtained the poison? When Kulvar Rand had been confronted he had defended himself by saying that the poison was common amongst the tribes and that Brant had probably just found some, or perhaps stolen some. But he knew that was not the truth. It couldn't have been. Brant didn't spend any time in the village for just that reason. And he was always chained or under constant surveillance. Kulvar Rand had helped him escape, and he would pay for his treachery, alongside Brant.

Tangar looked at the setting sun. It was going to be dark soon. "How far away are they?" he asked in frustration.

The scouts stopped talking and looked up. One spoke. "We think they are a half day ahead of us. I think they are heading for the river."

"And how far away is the river?"

"We will reach it mid-day tomorrow. They might reach it before dark."

"Will we be able to catch up with them tomorrow?"

One tracker grunted, looking at the one who spoke. "It will be more difficult to track them if they reach the river. But yes, I believe we will find them tomorrow, tomorrow evening at the latest."

"Get on with it then."

The trackers mounted their horses and moved forward, their vigilant eyes scanning the signs left behind by the men. Luckily, the big Varga left deep imprints in the grass and they could follow their trail easily enough.

The sun had nearly disappeared when Brant stopped jogging. He was exhausted and his legs hurt badly. Uln pulled up short, sucking in deep breaths. He too was tired, but he had not been wounded and he looked at Brant with concern. They had entered a small copse of trees and Uln inspected it briefly, moving back to Brant who had peeled a piece of fruit, handing a chunk to Uln. They both ate their meager rations, savoring the sweet juices that only briefly quenched their thirst. But it wasn't enough. They needed to get to the creek.

"I think we should sleep for a couple of hours. This spot looks good," Brant suggested.

Uln nodded in agreement. There was a small bonet tree nearby that looked like an ideal place to bed down. The branches drooped low, almost to the ground, creating a natural shelter big enough for two people. Uln walked over to some nearby trees and ripped off branches, showing a great display of strength. He laid the leafy bows against the outside of their shelter, creating another layer of protection from the outside elements. Soon, the Varga had created a simple enclosure, protected by dense foliage. Hopefully it would be enough to maintain their body heat. The evenings on the steppe could get pretty cold. They crawled inside and were asleep in moments, the last vestiges of the sun's light vanishing behind the horizon.

They had slept longer than they wanted, their exhausted bodies refusing to heed their intentions. With only several hours left before daylight they took off hastily, hoping to get to the creek as soon as possible.

Shortly after they left they were jogging through another small copse of bonnet trees when suddenly Uln, with a great surge of speed, jumped in front of Brant. Something struck him, spinning him sideways and to Brant's left.

"Kite'ens!" he roared, lifting his axe before him and crouching lower in the tall grass.

Brant noticed a small sharp object sticking from Uln's left shoulder but he had no time for further inspection as three strange forms materialized from the grayness of dusk following several thrown projectiles. One struck Brant a glancing blow on his thigh, opening a shallow cut, and he was able to avoid the second missile by ducking low.

Whatever it was moving towards them Brant had never seen before. They had detached themselves from the nearby trees and attacked very quickly. Being tall and lanky, their skin looking exactly like the bark of the bonnet tree, they were able to blend in perfectly with the trees common on the steppes. Patches of green covered their entire body and to Brant it looked like some kind of moss. They had three long fingers that looked like gnarly sticks sharpened to points and their heads resembled stumps of different shapes, a row of sharp teeth visible even in the early morning darkness. Each one carried a long crude spear with a white bone tip and their long loping strides brought them to an attacking position very quickly.

One jabbed its long spear forward in a powerful lunge hoping to catch Brant off guard. Ducking from the projectile weapon had put Brant in a good low position. He was tired from running and didn't want to risk using the Way, afraid it might drain him too quickly. Sidestepping the attack, Brant grabbed the spear handle and attacked the creature with his stolen sword, striking the thing two times across its long thin torso. It felt like he had hit a tree, the power of his strikes reverberating up his arm. And the creature was strong. Faster than Brant thought possible the Kite'en, if that's what it was called, yanked his spear from Brant's grasp and whipped the opposite end around, striking a glancing blow on Brant's side as he pivoted away from the attack. Brant struck the creature again, hitting it hard in the thigh, but it had little effect. His sword didn't seem to be doing any damage, barely cutting into the creature's hard skin.

"Go for glowing green spot!" Uln roared, fighting against two of the beasts off to his left.

Brant hadn't seen a glowing green spot at first, but as he spun and attacked the creature, he caught a flickering green light under some sort of hard carapace on its stomach. You couldn't see it when looking at the creature straight on, but when it turned, or Brant did, he could barely make out several narrow gaps in its hard exoskeleton that shed small vestiges of a strange green light.

It would be a tough spot to hit, Brant's blade barely fitting between the slots to begin with. They fought on, both exchanging attacks for defensive maneuvers. The thing was fast with long gangly arms enabling it to attack Brant from a distance. He had to get inside the thing's defenses and penetrate the gaps in its abdomen. The Kite'en made a strange gurgling sound just before it kicked out with its right foot. Brant side stepped the attack and leaped in close, aiming his blade for the glowing green opening. The creatures gurgling turned into a high pitched screech as Brant's blade found the slot, pushing into the thing at least a hand span before the beast spun and jumped away, pulling Brant's sword with it.

Weaponless, Brant glanced at Uln as the Kite'en jumped away screeching, trying to dislodge the sword from its side. Uln had already dispatched one creature and Brant saw him unleash a barrage of powerful swings with his axe, cutting into the remaining creature's legs and arms like a logger felling a tree. The Kite'en was screeching and desperately trying to evade the devastating onslaught of the powerful warrior.

Brant ran forward hoping to take down the injured Kite'en and finish his work, remove his sword, and help Uln finish off the last beast. But as he neared the frantic creature Brant glimpsed an even bigger shape hurtle towards him from his periphery. Reacting on instinct, Brant channeled a little energy into his legs, using the burst of strength to catapult himself out of the way. Tumbling, Brant came to his feet to face the new threat. His cuts on his legs hurt but he had bigger problems to face. And it was definitely bigger. Another Kite'en, nearly three heads taller than Brant, missed him by a hair and came to its feet quickly. This one held a long bone in each hand, the head heavier and carved into a sharp edge. To Brant they looked like bone axes. Gurgling loudly, the thing bolted forward.

Brant was tired and weaponless, afraid to use the Way, worried that he might drain himself completely. Crouching, he readied himself for the attack, thinking of nothing else he could do.

And then Uln crashed into the creature, their bodies rotating and tumbling through the tall grass. Brant saw Uln's massive body rise up from the grass and his small axe descend again and again, the creature howling and screeching eerily the entire time. Brant realized just then that there was no way he could've defeated Uln without the use of the Way. He was simply too big and strong.

Fifteen strikes later and the Kite'en lay still. Uln stood up to his full height, the rising sun in the distance silhouetting his giant form. Brant walked over to him.

"Is it dead?"

"Yes."

"What were those things?"

"Kite'ens. They blend in with tree, very dangerous."

"And the green spot?"

"It's heart."

"I've never heard of them," Brant said.

"They rare. Live in surrounding forests. Only venture to steppes when food scarce."

Brant saw Uln's injured shoulder. "Are you okay," he asked, indicating his muscled arm.

Uln glanced at his shoulder, seemingly forgetting the projectile sticking from it. It was small, or at least it looked small in his colossal shoulder, and chipped from some black stone. It had three blades in the shape of leaves and the edges looked very sharp. Uln reached up and removed the weapon with a grunt, dropping the bloody thing to the ground. It looked to Brant that it had only penetrated his hard skin an inch or so. "It not serious. You hurt?" Uln asked, looking at his bleeding leg.

"The old wounds opened up. And I got a scratch on my leg and a few bruises. I'll be fine. Thanks for saving me. How did you know of the attack?" Brant realized that the projectile that barely hurt Uln could have killed him. Not to mention the fact that Uln had killed three to his one. He would be dead now if it weren't for the Varga and his axe, which seemed like the perfect weapon against these beasts.

"I heard them."

"I didn't hear a thing."

Uln smiled. "You are Dy'ainian."

Brant was used to Uln's jabs about his race and ignored him. "Just the same, thank you for saving my life, twice."

Uln stepped towards him, placing his giant hand on Brant's shoulder. "You rescued me. Didn't have to. I see family again. For that, friend Brant, I will always be in debt."

Brant nodded, not sure of what to say. He looked over at the creature he killed and moved to get his blade. "Let me get my…"

"No sword. It gone," Uln interrupted.

Sure enough Brant could see that his sword was destroyed. Whatever the thing's heart was made from reacted violently with the steel of the blade. It was no longer usable, the steel melted and bound in the things hard exoskeleton. "Let's get going. I want to reach the river soon and clean these wounds and hopefully get them off our trail."

"Lead on, friend Brant."

It was late morning when Brant and Uln finally reached the slow moving stream. They had rationed the food that Brant had taken and they were now down to two hunks of bread. Panting heavily, they both stood at the edge of the creek. Brant tossed Uln a piece of bread while he ate the other.

"This is where we part," he said, breathing deeply from the long run and biting into the hard crust of the bread.

Uln nodded and swallowed his portion in less than three bites. "Thank you, friend Brant."

Brant nodded and smiled. "Good luck. I hope you find your family."

"Good luck to you," the Varga said, extending his huge hand. Brant shook it, his own hand looking like a child's in comparison. "You need anything…I help. My home deep in Heyrith Forest. Look for me there."

"How would I even find you?"

Uln smiled. "You not. I find you."

Uln patted Brant on the shoulder, turned, and ran to the edge of the stream. It was a large creek and the section before them was fifteen paces wide but not very deep. Brant watched the Varga push through the sluggish current easily, his massive legs cutting through the water as if it were air. Once on the other side, Uln turned and waved before disappearing into the brush that flanked the water.

    Brant took a moment to inspect the wounds on his legs, which had become very painful. He walked to the edge of the creek and untied the bandages around his thighs. They were dirty and sweaty, and caked with blood. He didn't like what he saw. The flesh was red and puffy, but at least the bleeding had been reduced to a mere trickle, and it did not yet smell of infection. But that could come soon. They needed to be cleaned. Sitting at the creek's edge, both of his legs submerged in the cold clear water, he let the slow current wash away the dried blood and dirt. Then, painfully, he used his fingers and gently rubbed the cuts to clean them out further. Dried blood broke free like a crumbling dam, and fresh crimson poured from the wounds, mixing with the water, and swirling momentarily before washing down stream. Grabbing the dirty strips of cloth, he washed them in the creek as best he could. He knew he couldn't dally any longer. Standing, he retied the wet strips around his legs, the fresh blood staining the cloth immediately. He was tired and weak, and his thighs throbbed with pain. But he couldn't stop. He knew that Kaan's farm was somewhere south of his location, and if he followed the creek he would find his friends home soon enough. That is if the creek before him *was* Bygon Creek, of which he could not be sure. But he had no other plan.

    Using his hands as cups he gulped down a generous amount of water. He no longer had the energy to run, which was fine with him as the terrain along the river was not always easy going. Many times he had to climb over rocks or logs, up steep embankments or push his way through the dense brush that grew along the creek's edge. He had set off at a fast walk, following the creek bed and walking in the water as much as he could in hopes of throwing off the trackers that he knew would be following them. Tangar would never let them go, especially after he had killed his hounds. And the Schulg had some of the best hunters and trackers in all of Dy'ain. They were behind him, he had no doubt.

    Ten Dygon Guards led by Kulvar Rand rode their tired steeds into the town of Amorsit. They had been riding hard for the entire day, stopping for a one hour break at mid-day to take food and rest the animals. When the sun dropped behind the horizon they had set up a quick camp. Kulvar ordered the men to sleep for six hours before they would mount up again and head out. He was hoping to reach the town by late morning. They had made good time and found the town in full swing. The sudden appearance of ten warriors, dressed in silver armor, with the instantly recognized black and silver symbol of the Dygon Guard, caused quite a stir. It wouldn't be long before the town's own guard arrived to greet them.

Kulvar Rand looked about until he saw the sign for the local inn. "Dismount and tie up the horses. We will get food and water here." He glanced over at two young men mounted beside him. Both wore the typical breaches, tunics, and cloaks of a traveler. They were not Dygon Guards, but servants they had brought with them to the fights. "Corben and Swil, please feed and the water the horses. Then come in and join us."

"Yes sir," they said in unison, dismounting and tending to the horses.

The men, following his lead, did as instructed. One warrior, tall and middle-aged, with jet black hair shaved short like all the rest of the men, walked over and stood beside Kulvar. There were no ranks among the Dygon Guard. All were equal, except for Kulvar Rand. He was their leader, chosen by the king, and everyone knew it, but even he held no formal title. All the men were allowed to speak freely, without worry or repercussion.

"Sir, are you sure about this?" His name was Kade and he was the best swordsman in the guard next to Kulvar Rand.

"I am. We are the king's men required to uphold the law. That boy had served his sentence and was being held unlawfully."

"I know. But we may find ourselves facing Tangar and his men. He will not let them go."

They both finished tying their horses to the wood beams provided for just that. "That boy is tough," Kulvar responded, "but he will need help. It is our job to provide that."

"Even if it means fighting fifty Schulg warriors, one of them the son of a chief? King Enden may not be so happy if we break the truce we have with the nomads over one man…and a criminal at that."

"He is no criminal. And don't worry. If it comes to a fight, I have a way to avoid unnecessary deaths and still uphold the treaty."

"How?"

"Blood Rite."

"You will challenge Tangar?" Blood Rite was a system of justice that the Schulg adhered to above all other traditions. It was the ultimate competition of martial skill whereby one would challenge another to combat, the winner earning Blood Rite, allowing them to take ownership of the loser's possessions, including wives, children, land, and weapons. Warriors did not challenge others lightly, since losing would mean one's death as well as the loss of everything one owned, which would all go to the victor. Not to mention if you were to challenge someone you had to be of equal rank or skill, avoiding the one sided fights that would be prevalent if more skilled fighters were allowed to challenge anyone.

"If I must. Now let us eat and rest. I want to talk with the magistrate."

Kade shook his head, not understanding his loyalty to a young man that he barely knew. But he said nothing else. The other men had already entered the inn when Kulvar and Kade pushed through the heavy door. The lunch crowd had not yet arrived but there were a few people about drinking ale and wine. Most of the patrons were already staring wide eyed at the ten Dygon Guards sitting at the tables beside the large stone fireplace where a roaring fire kept the cold at bay. The well-disciplined men were stoic in expression and posture, sitting and talking quietly amongst themselves. Kulvar walked over to the bar while Kade joined the men.

A pretty serving girl was stacking cups of water on a tray while a man behind the bar filled them with a big pitcher. His men would not drink, not while on a mission, although they knew very little about the mission, or why their leader had left the Schulg camp at daylight, racing west as fast as he could.

The girl smiled when she saw him. "Hello, sir. I'm bringing these waters to your comrades now. Would you like anything else?"

"Have they ordered food yet?"

"They have not."

"Do you have anything warm that you could quickly procure for thirteen men?"

"We have a wonderful bean soup, and biscuits, with butter and condor berry jam." Condor berries were a sweet black berry that grew along the stream beds. They were small and it required many of them to make anything, but they were juicy and sweet for their size.

"That would be perfect. I will cover the cost."

"I will attend to it right away." Then she left to deliver the waters.

The man behind the bar, finished with the task of filling the thirteen cups, greeted Kulvar Rand. "Good evening, sir. I'm Borgan and the proprietor of this establishment. Is there anything else I can do for you? It's not often we get the Dygon Guard in town. Are you just passing through or looking to stay the night?"

"Well met, Borgan. I'm Kulvar Rand." At the mention of his name Borgan's eyes widened momentarily. Be he regained his composure quickly, cleared his throat and poured himself a mug of ale from a cask behind the bar. "We are moving through quickly. But I have a few questions that I was hoping you could answer."

"Sure, I hope I can help. Would you like to share some ale with me? I hate to drink alone."

Kulvar Rand smiled. "No, thank you. We are on business at the moment and we won't be staying long."

"Very well," Borgan said, drinking deeply from his mug, hoping to calm his nerves a bit. He, well everyone for that matter, had heard many tales about the famous swordsman, but never thought he'd meet him in person. "So, what can I do for you?"

"Have you ever encountered a young man named Brant? He would have passed through town over a year ago."

Borgan took another long drink of his ale, nearly choking on it. "Yes, sir. I remember him very well. I liked the lad. But he got into some serious trouble."

"Such as?"

"He got in a fight, right here where you're standing. I've never seen anyone move so fast or hit so hard. He killed the man with two punches."

"Who started it?"

"Tage for sure. He was the magistrate's son. True to form he was drunk, insulting Thea, my server, and getting obnoxiously rowdy. Brant ignored him pretty good until he grabbed Thea over there." Borgan pointed to the pretty waitress now serving the warriors big bowls of soup with fresh biscuits slathered with butter and jam. "Tage slapped Brant in the face, and when he went to hit him again Brant side stepped the punch and hit him twice, knocking him over there," he continued, pointing to the ground three paces away. "He was dead before he hit the floor."

"Sounds like self-defense. What happened next?"

"He was arrested and found guilty. The magistrate stayed his execution since Thea and I spoke up for him. But he sentenced him to one year of slavery with the Schulg nomads. I'm sure he is dead by now."

"You were there during the sentencing?"

"I was."

"Good. And no, he is not dead. The day before last the Schulg tribes held a great event, a fight between two Ull Therm. Brant was one of them."

Borgan was shaking his head in disbelief. "Morlock's balls I knew that lad was tough. But Ull Therm, I cannot believe it." The Schulg fights were well known, and even though very few Dy'ainians ever saw them, they had heard many stories told of the few warriors who actually reached the rank of Ull Therm. They were almost as famous as Kulvar Rand.

"I was there. Several nobles, including myself, were sent by the king to attend the event. I met Brant almost two years ago in one of the camps and I recognized him immediately. We are trying to find him now. I assume he has not been here?"

"He has not."

"Did he ever mention anyone nearby that he knew?"

By this time Thea had made her way back to the bar. "Borgan, can I get four red ales."

"Sure. Thea, I would like you to meet Kulvar Rand."

Thea looked at Kulvar, her eyes wide in disbelief. Then she smiled at the Dygon Guard. "Yeah, and I'm the Queen."

Kulvar smiled and Borgan cleared his throat. "I'm speaking the truth, girl, this is Kulvar Rand."

Thea, her smile disappearing, looked back at Kulvar, her cheeks turning red. "Really?"

Kulvar nodded his head.

"I'm so sorry, sir. I..."

Kulvar put his hand up, smiling the entire time. "It's okay. Borgan said that you met a young man over a year ago named Brant. Do you remember if he ever mentioned a friend, or family, someone living nearby that he might visit if he were in trouble."

"Brant is alive?" She asked, clearly shocked.

"He is...as far as I know anyway. But we need to find him."

Thea thought for a moment. "I don't recall him saying anything about anyone. He was just passing through looking for work." Then she paused, thinking back. She looked over at Borgan. "You remember at the trial when the magistrate asked Brant if there was anyone who could vouch for him?"

Borgan thought back to over a year ago. "Yes, that's right. He mentioned a man that lived near Bygon."

"You remember his name?" Kulvar asked.

"I'm sorry, I do not," Borgan said.

"I think it started with a K, but his name is eluding me," Thea added.

"Bygon is a day's ride," Kulvar said, thinking out loud.

"If you leave now and ride hard you may get there before dark. Go to the inn and look for Anders. If anyone in town can help its him."

Kulvar thought it over. He and his men had ridden hard the previous day, but they were now rested and would soon have full stomachs. The horses were likely tired, but he knew they still had another hard ride in them yet. He also knew that Tangar and his warriors would not rest until they found Brant. He wouldn't have a chance if Tangar found him first. He would have to postpone seeing the magistrate for another day. He needed to find Brant.

"We will rest a bit longer before we leave. Any chance you have any cold rations we could purchase from you? And we would be grateful if we could refill our water skins."

"Of course. We have some cured ham and day old bread. Will that work?" Borgan asked.

"It would. Prepare it and tally the cost. We will be departing soon."

"I will take care of it right away," Borgan replied.

"Thank you for your help," Kulvar said as he turned to leave.

"Sir," Thea said, causing him to turn around. "I hope you find him. I liked him. He was a good man."

Kulvar gave her a reassuring nod. "I will do my best."

***

Brant was stumbling now, his legs nearly giving out on him. He had been running for a day and a half and his injured legs were barely plodding along. There was no more food but luckily plenty of water available from the stream he was following.

Suddenly he came to a clearing and he felt a surge of hope as he recognized the land. He could see that the area showed signs of work. There were a handful of tree stumps, the wood clearly cut with an axe. He had been there before. In fact he had chopped down several of the trees himself, limbing and cutting the logs into smaller sections. He knew from experience that he was not far from Kaan's cabin and that he could make it there before dark. Picking up his pace, he followed the cart trail, new energy, built on hope, bringing life to his tired limbs.

His mind was in a daze when he finally walked into the clearing that housed the cabin and barn. Brant was no longer thinking clearly, but it was obvious that it was evening, so it was no surprise to see light emanating from the windows and smoke spiraling into the air from the rock chimney. Jana was probably preparing supper. Stumbling forward he leaned his weight against the side of the house, using his fist to pound on the door. He registered a quiet commotion inside, hearing hushed conversation and nervous commands from Kaan.

"Who is it?!" Kaan shouted from inside.

"Brant," he whispered, too tired to yell.

"Who?" This time his voice was less guarded, as if he had heard him but couldn't believe it.

Brant took a deep breath. "Brant!" Suddenly the door was open and Brant nearly fell forward, catching himself on the door frame. Kaan was looking at him with wide eyes, his crossbow held at his side. Brant smiled feebly. "Good to see you," he whispered.

Kaan grabbed him and helped him inside, moving him to a chair. "Jana, get some cold water. Tobias, get some water boiling." His children, seeing his concern and the shape Brant was in, silently went to work. "In Goth's name, what happened to you?"

Brant could barely sit up straight. "It's a long story that will have to wait. Can I have some food and water first? I feel as though I might pass out."

Jana was already bringing him water and a bowl of bean soup with bread and several slices of cured ham. "Here Brant," she said. "I will cut you some apple as well."

"Thank you," he said, almost inhaling the food.

"What happened to your legs? They look a mess."

"Nyg attack," he muttered through mouthfuls of soup.

Kaan had heard of the reclusive hounds, but had never seen one. They were rare and very dangerous. "What!? And you lived?"

"I had poisoned it. Kaan, it's a long story and I cannot stay long. My presence here is putting your family in danger. I just need to rest a bit, eat, and clean my wounds."

Jana came back and gave Brant a cup of water and some apple slices. He ate them quickly, washing them down with the cold water.

"Danger from whom?"

"The Schulg."

"They are coming here!?"

"I do not know. I was made the slave of the chief's son and forced to fight in the pit. I escaped and I'm sure they are after me."

"When did you escape?"

"The night before last."

"You've been running the entire time?"

"Yes. Do you have any clean bandages? Alcohol? Or something I can clean the wounds with?"

"Of course. Tobias, how is the water coming?"

"It's close," the boy called out from the kitchen.

"Get what's left of the roll of cotton and cut it into strips. And grab that healing salve," he ordered, turning back to Brant. "You're in luck. After the kulg attack I promised myself that I would have good healing supplies on hand. I used the few coins I had left to purchase this salve in town. It's supposed to be a Schulg remedy for infections."

"Thank you," Brant said weakly, enjoying the irony of that. He wiped his soup bowl clean with his last slice of bread. "Do you have a knife? I want to cut these bandages off." The strips of cloth tied around Brant's leg were nearly black from dirt and blood. Dry and encrusted, the knots were nearly impossible to untie. It would be easier to cut them away.

"Jana, get us your sheers."

Several moments later Jana was kneeling at Brant's side. "Let me do it," she said. Slowly and gently she cut the fabric away on both legs, revealing long gashes, puffy and inflamed. They looked worse than he had imagined.

"They don't look so good. We need to clean them and rub that salve deep into them. It's going to hurt."

"Do it."

"The water is boiling, Father," Tobias shouted from the kitchen as he cut the cotton fabric into strips.

"Good, pour it into a bowl and bring it here. We will need some clean cloth as well as the strips," Kaan said.

Tobias carried over the bowl of hot water and the cotton strips, then went back to get the salve. Kaan grabbed a cotton towel, dipped it into the hot water, and proceeded to clean both legs. Brant cringed, and the cloth was soon saturated in fresh blood as his open wounds began bleeding again. But gradually the cuts were cleaned of the remaining dirt and dried blood, exposing the red and swollen flesh. Kaan sniffed the wounds, crinkling his nose at the subtle odor of infection.

"Well?" Brant asked, already knowing the answer.

"It's not bad yet, but they are infected. We need to apply the salve. It's going to hurt bad," Kaan repeated, looking to Brant to make sure he was ready.

Brant gripped the edges of the chair. "Let's get it over with."

Kaan grabbed the jar of salve, and looked at Brant. "Here we go." Brant said nothing, nodding his head for him to do it. Kaan smeared a large amount of the thick greenish paste onto his hand and went to work, smearing the gooey substance over and into the wounds, so the healing salve could penetrate them, causing fresh blood to again drip from the cuts. But the salve also acted as a coagulant, mixing with the blood and forming a dark paste that oozed out of the lacerations. Throughout the process Brant cringed, stiffening from the pain, but said nothing. Kaan continued to work, applying the salve to all the cuts on both legs. After a few minutes he was done.

Finally Brant spoke. "That hurt."

"I bet. Let me see your arm. Then I will wrap your legs in the clean cotton."

"Very well," Brant said, lifting his left arm before him. Kaan cleaned the puncture holes, using the last of the salve to massage into the wounds. Then he grabbed the fresh cotton strips and wrapped up his arm and both legs. After a few moments he was done.

"Let's hope that medicine works," he muttered, standing up and looking satisfied with his work.

"Thank you, Kaan. Can I ask one more favor before I leave?"

"Leave!?" Jana said. "You are in no condition to leave."

"She is right," Kaan added.

Brant was shaking his head. "I must. You are in danger."

"I was in danger before. And if I recall correctly, you saved our lives. You cannot walk far in your condition," Kaan added.

"You cannot leave," Tobias said, inserting himself in the conversation.

Brant smiled, but shook his head. "Believe it or not, I've been through worse. I will be fine. But I will need food and water for the road. Do you have any to spare?"

"Of course, but you are not going anywhere."

"I'm sorry, Kaan. But you cannot stop me. I will not put your children in danger," he said, his tone firm. Brant stood up but gave no indication that his wounds were causing him pain. "I could use a weapon if you have anything to spare."

Kaan saw that he would not be able to persuade him to stay. "I have my crossbow and my long knife. I'm sorry I have not had the coin to replace my swords."

"Can I use the knife? I promise to repay you."

"As I've said, you saved my life, and the lives of my children. I owe you everything. Take what you need. Jana, prepare a food bag. Tobias, fill a water skin for Brant," Kaan ordered as he moved to his bed to grab his hunting knife. The long blade was sheathed and attached to a thin leather belt that had been hung on the bedpost. He handed it to Brant who cinched the belt around his waist.

"Thank you," he said.

Kaan nodded. "Where will you go?"

"To Amorsit. I have some unfinished business there." Brant wasn't exactly sure what he was going to do when he made it to the town, if he made it at all. But he knew he had served his time and he wanted to see the look on the magistrate's face when he walked into town. Besides, he knew the town had a small force of Legionnaires and perhaps they would uphold the law and help protect him. He was hoping that if Tangar did follow him that he wouldn't be stupid enough to attack an entire town to retrieve him.

Jana handed him a cloth bag filled with food and Tobias gave him a full water skin. Then he hugged him tightly, his small arms wrapped around his waist. "Be careful, Brant." Jana hugged him as well.

"You both take care of your father. Don't worry. I will see you again."

Brant reached out and shook Kaan's hand. "Thank you, my friend."

Kaan nodded grimly. "You be careful."

He turned and walked out the front door, Kaan and his family following. The sun was still visible, but barely, its soft golden rays still fighting off the onset of darkness.

Suddenly, as if they had been waiting for him to exit, a horde of nomads on horseback rushed from the far side of the creek, crossing it in great splashes. Kaan yelled at his children to get into the house while he reached around the door frame to grab his crossbow, joining Brant who was standing in the middle of the clearing.

Fifty mounted nomads stood before them, the whinnying of the animals and the creaking and rattling of the leather and metal harnesses disturbing the peaceful evening. Tangar rode forward, his face with its typical stoic expression, devoid of emotion. He held his short bow in his hand, an arrow nocked and ready.

"Did you really think you would get away?" he asked, speaking in Schulg.

"I had to try," Brant answered, also in Schulg. "Do not hurt them. They are not part of this. I will go with you."

Tangar looked at Kaan who was aiming the loaded crossbow at his chest. "Who are they?"

"No one. I just met them and they offered me food and water."

"Strange that someone you just met holds a crossbow at fifty mounted warriors," Tangar said flatly. He then switched to Newain, "Lower the crossbow," Tangar ordered. Kaan looked at Brant, who nodded his head. He lowered the weapon but kept it at the ready. "What is your name?" Tangar asked.

"Kaan. What do you want?"

"I think you know what I want. Tell your children to come out."

"I will not..."

In a blink Tangar's arm came up and an arrow shot across the clearing, slamming into the tip of Kaan's right shoulder and cutting a deep gash in his flesh. He stumbled back and dropped his weapon.

"No!" Brant yelled, moving to help Kaan stay on his feet.

"Tell your children to come out," Tangar said again, his voice a harsh whisper. "I missed on purpose. It won't happen again."

Kaan was biting back the pain. "Jana, Tobias, please come here." Both of the children ran from the house to hold their father. Jana looked at his shoulder, a trickle of blood dripping from the wound. "Father! What have they done?" she cried.

"I will be fine," he said through gritted teeth.

Tobias stood before his father holding a small kitchen knife in his hand. "Brant, what do I do?" he cried, tears streaking the side of his face.

Tangar smiled for the first time. "It seems they know you after all. That is good. I need to replace the slave you killed. And the price I get for these children may make up for the deaths of my hounds."

Brant stepped before them. "You will not take them," he whispered, drawing the knife from his side.

"You think you can kill fifty Schulg warriors?"

Suddenly there was commotion behind Brant and the nomads' horses shifted nervously, instinctively stepping backward. Ten mounted warriors rode up the cart path, dust and debris scattering behind them as they galloped into the clearing. They quickly spread out behind Brant, facing the nomads.

Tangar's horse pranced nervously but the Schulg held his position, his face impassive. Kulvar Rand slowly trotted his horse forward until he was next to Brant. Looking down, he winked at Brant, then returned his steady gaze to Tangar.

"Greetings, Tangar, son of Byn'ok," he said softly, his tone menacing.

"Have you come to further insult your king?"

Kulvar Rand tilted his head, puzzled by the comment. "What do you mean?"

Tangar spat on the ground. "You came to our village as a guest, then helped one of our most valuable slaves escape. And now you are here to help him when all we want is our property back. Your king will not be happy."

"You are right, my king may not be happy with what I've done and am about to do. But he," indicating Brant, "is not your slave, nor is he your property. He is Dy'ainian and he was given to you to serve out a sentence of one year. That year is long over and he is now free according to our laws. You did not pay for him and I am here now, as a servant of the king, to uphold his law."

Tangar shifted uneasily in his saddle. "You have ten men and I have fifty."

Again, Kulvar Rand tilted his head, but this time he smiled. "I have ten Dygon Guards."

As if on cue the ten warriors behind him drew their swords in unison and hefted their cavalry shields, the movements smooth and practiced. Each man's Kul-brite sword reflected the morning sun's light, flashing a warning that they were dealing with the Dygon Guard. Brant and Kaan, sensing the conflict, grabbed Jana and Tobias and moved them against the house and out of the way.

"I have always wanted to see whose is superior," Tangar whispered.

Kulvar Rand saw his opening. "Perhaps you can. I challenge you to Blood Rite."

All the nomads behind Tangar looked at their leader, not expecting to hear such a challenge. Tangar looked uneasy for a split second, but he quickly smiled. "You are not Schulg, and yet you want to challenge me to Blood Rite...all over one man?"

"Not one man. I challenge you for all the men here. If we fight, you will all die, and I may lose men as well. I challenge you personally to prevent that from happening."

"You are of noble blood. Do you understand what would happen if you lose?"

"I do. You would earn rights to all my weapons, armor, and my holdings."

Tangar nodded. "I would require the value of your land in coin. Do not forget that your wife and children would be mine as well."

"I understand, but I have neither so it is of no consequence. However," Kulvar Rand said, drawing his blade from his hip. "This sword would be yours and the value of this blade far outweighs anything you have to offer."

Tangar looked at the polished silver blade. He knew of Kulvar Rand's sword. All warriors did. "Do not be so quick to assume," the nomad said, drawing his own blade, "that you are the only one with a blade of value." Kulvar Rand's eyes widened momentarily as he recognized the silver polish of Kul-brite steel. Tangar's sword, although forged in a design favored by the nomads, was a Kul-brite blade.

"How did you get that?" Kulvar asked. The king of Cythera used his precious steel to forge powerful weapons for his Dygon Guard, but for others to have such weapons they would have to possess great wealth, generally far more than what a Schulg nomad could ever come by.

"It is a long story. One that you will never hear." Tangar had always wanted to fight the famous leader of the Dygon Guard. The unanswered question of who was better had always gnawed at him. But now that the opportunity had arrived he was not entirely sure if wanted the answer. But he could not deny a Blood Rite challenge. His men would never allow it. Besides, if he won, he would suddenly become the richest Schulg in existence. He would have more than he had ever dreamed. "I accept your challenge on one condition."

"What is it?"

"You cannot use the Way. Blood Rite is a challenge of skill and the use of the Way is not allowed. Will you swear not to bring forth your noble powers?"

Kulvar Rand already knew that he could not use his powers. "I will."

"Will your men swear on their blades that you will not use it?"

Kulvar Rand knew what he was asking. Tangar, not having the Aurit abilities himself, could not see one's auras and so would never know if Kulvar broke the rules and used his power. But the other Dygon Guards could see his aura and would know if he broke his word. He also knew that they would not break their own word, nor would Kulvar Rand. Too much honor was at stake to win with anything but skill alone. "They will swear."

Each man behind him said the words, "we swear", banging their sword against their shield once.

"Very good. Let us begin." With that Tangar stepped down from his horse. He unbuckled his leather armor and removed it, taking everything off until he was bare chested, wearing nothing but his leather leggings. He held his Kul-brite blade in his right hand. The blade was of Schulg design, long, slightly curved, narrow and razor sharp on one side. At the tip the sharp edge followed the back side of the blade for several hand spans before expertly blending into the backbone of the silver shaft. The handle was long, wrapped in brown leather, and two handed, the guard protecting the hands round and simply adorned. It was a beautiful weapon, unadorned, simple and elegant, made to kill, not to hang on a nobleman's wall.

Kulvar Rand followed suit, removing his armor and shirt until he was standing bare chested and holding his famous blade.

Bannerfall

Brant stepped over to Kulvar, concern evident on his face. "You do not have to do this for me," he said. Brant was worried. He had seen Tangar fight. Tangar had trained him for nearly two years. He had never seen anyone move with such speed and precision. Kulvar Rand was a legend, but it was hard for Brant to imagine anyone skilled enough to beat the nomad.

"I do need to do this. It is my job to protect our citizens."

"But he might kill you. And if he does he will take everything you own."

"If I am dead it will not matter," Kulvar Rand said with a twinkle in his eyes. Then the twinkle disappeared, his black eyes turning to deep pits, drowning out any doubt. "But do not worry for me. I am not going to die." Kulvar Rand's words sent a chill down Brant's spine and it was as if death had entered the clearing. Brant stepped away as Kulvar Rand moved forward, standing before the nomad. He lifted his blade to his forehead. "I swear to uphold the rules of Blood Rite. May honor, courage, and skill decide the victor."

Tangar did the same, reciting the exact words. Then they begin to circle one another. What happened next was something that Brant would probably never witness again. Tangar moved forward quickly, his blade coming down towards the Dygon Guard. Kulvar Rand's blade flashed once, twice, and three times, his body gliding forward in a blur and spinning away from the nomad.

Tangar stopped and dropped his sword, his right arm sliced deep across his bicep. His free hand moved to his throat, crimson waves gushing from the wound, his hand futilely trying to stop the flow. Then he fell forward to the ground. It had all happened in a heartbeat.

Tangar's stunned warriors stared at Kulvar, barely registering what had just happened. Several moments later two warriors dismounted, walked toward Tangar's body and lifted it up. They laid his body across the back of a pack horse, mounted their steeds, and rode slowly off across the river without saying a word.

They had left Tangar's horse, weapons, and armor, the Blood Rite demanding it. The Dygon Guard dismounted and tied their horses to the railings of Kaan's animal pen. Greeting their leader, they helped him with his armor and clothes as if what they had just witnessed was a bygone conclusion.

Kaan and Brant approached as he was strapping his armor into place. Kaan was holding his hand to his wounded shoulder, the blood from the gash seeping through his fingers. "I don't know what to say," Brant mumbled. He had never before seen such a display of skill, what little of it he actually saw. It happened so fast.

"You do not need to say anything," Kulvar Rand replied.

"But *I* do," Kaan added. "You saved my life as well as Brant's. He was going to take me and my family. Thank you for not allowing that to happen."

"You are welcome. As I said, I am the king's man, as you are his subjects. It is my job to uphold his laws. Let's take a look at that wound."

"Soon enough," Kaan agreed. "I would be honored if you would allow my daughter to prepare a meal for us all. I killed a tulkick yesterday and we have an abundance of potatoes and onions. Besides, you have ridden hard and it will soon be dark. I do not have much room but the barn is better than sleeping on the road. What do you say?"

"My men and I would be honored. But I insist on paying for the food and hospitality." Kaan was just about to protest but Kulvar cut him off. "Please, I know that times are hard. Besides, I would be paying for the meal and lodging in town anyway. And I would like one of my men to see to your shoulder. I insist."

"Very well. Jana, Tobias, please get to it," Kaan asked his children. They left without a word, realizing the importance of their task.

Kulvar looked at Brant. "In the morning I would like you to come with us."

Brant looked at the Dygon Guard. "For what purpose?"

"I told you before. I could use a man like you, a man with your special skills." Brant and Kaan both knew what he was referring to, but they said nothing. "A war is coming, Brant, and men like you will be needed. What do you say?"

Brant was uncertain what role Kulvar Rand had for him, but he had nothing else to do and nowhere to go. There was nothing for him anywhere. Perhaps he could create something. He needed a purpose and he felt he might find that purpose at Cythera. "I will go with you."

Kulvar Rand smiled. "You will use the nomad's horse. We will leave early." The warrior turned to let his men know to set up camp in the barn.

"I don't know how to ride."

Bannerfall

Kulvar Rand turned back around, looked at his groin, and smiled. "Well you're going to learn."

Kaan saw the look, and despite the pain from his wounded shoulder, laughed out loud. Brant didn't know what was so funny. But he had a feeling that he was going to find out soon enough.

Bannerfall

Chapter 8

Why are wars fought? The answer to this question continues to elude me. I understand that there are always reasons why men think they need to go to war. History is filled with countless examples of wars fought between nations for power, religion, trade, land, or simply to right perceived wrongs. But are they really necessary? When we strip down the causes what do we really find? Almost every war I've ever studied could have been avoided if men simply discussed their grievances rationally. But therein lies the crux. Can men conquer their base instincts such as greed, anger, and desire, reigning them in enough to discuss alternate solutions besides death? Thousands, perhaps millions across our lands, have perished, and for what? So one king can control a river vital for trade? So one idea, perceived to be righteous, can be spread throughout the kingdoms? Or because one ruler shamed another? None of it has ever really made sense to me. The cost of war, not just in lives, but in coin, should be a deterrent for most conflicts. But it's not. I believe I understand why. The men that make the decisions to go to war, that may profit from it, are not the men who are fighting the wars. Generally speaking, the rulers who choose warfare over dialogue are not the ones whose bodies will rot on the battlefield, while worms and crows eat their decaying flesh.

But let's get back to my original question. Is war ever necessary? Despite my misgivings, I believe there are times when it is unavoidable. What must one do when one's lands are invaded, the conquerors dead set on rape, pillage, and destruction? What must one do when a group of people attempt to eradicate another, or force their ideas upon them, taking away the right to choose? The answer is simple. They must fight. There is no other answer, their course of action set into motion by the very invaders who brought death to their lands.

Journal entry 79
Kivalla Der'une, Historian, Keeper of the records in Cythera, capital of Dy'ain

---

5090, the 14th cyn after the Great Change

    King Enden Dormath sat casually at his large oak table listening to his advisor, Kivalla Der'une. His wife, Queen Irstan Dormath, sat to his left while the captain of his Sentinels, Tul'gon, sat on his right. Also in attendance was General Veros, commander of the Cythera Legion.

They were sitting in King Enden's favorite room. It was the place he went to relax, to ease the stresses of his position. The room was cozy rather than large and pretentious. The walls were lined with racks filled with every conceivable weapon that could be found in Belorth and Corvell. He even had several cab're's, the knife-like weapons forged by the Askarian nomads, and a beautifully crafted oswith forged from Kul-brite. Where there were no weapons leather bound books filled shelves, tomes collected from the many kingdoms surrounding Dy'ain. The high ceiling was dominated by massive wood beams crisscrossing the span of the ceiling, the center one anchoring an impressive chandelier built from the white horns of the loryn, a huge four legged herbivore that lives deep in the Lorien Forest far to the north, feeding on the plentiful plant life that grew there. Loryns sported two horns, each as long as the height of a man. Twenty of these horns had been connected at their bases, the long sharp points spanning outward and held together with bands of iron. At the ends were iron oil lanterns, made by the king's best blacksmiths, their flickering flames casting dancing shadows in the rafters above. They all sat in hand carved chairs lined with soft leather.

"My King, our scouts were unable to ascertain their exact numbers," Kivalla replied, attempting to answer the question posed by King Enden, who had hoped his longtime advisor would have more information on the strength of the Saricon forces. "But we know that the Saricons have now split their forces, leaving a small contingent of men behind to attack the garrison. The majority of their army has nearly reached Eltus and will be storming their walls shortly." Kivalla was thin and unassuming, his hair as dark as night and showing no signs of his forty seven years. His clean shaven face and smooth skin belied his age, perhaps due to the many hours spent inside, sheltered from the harsh elements outside the king's quarters. Kivalla was from Rygar to the north and had been recruited by King Enden many years ago, when he was just twenty six.

"They have split their forces, holding enough men behind to keep our troops from helping the Kaelians," Veros stated, his voice deep and commanding.

"That seems to be the case," Kivalla added, "and the letter from Daricon mentioned that Prince Jarak was the one who had surmised this possibility. By all accounts, your son is doing well," Kivalla added.

Queen Irstan looked at her husband, but said nothing. If Kivalla were not mistaken her look suggested she was not happy with the king. Perhaps she was angry that he had sent Jarak to Lyone. After all, the garrison was always a dangerous place, now more than ever.

"That is good. What is Daricon's plan?"

Kivalla looked to the queen and back to King Enden, not eager to share the next bit of information. "It seems, my King, that Daricon and Prince Jarak have decided to hold out at the garrison as long as they can, keeping their losses to a minimum. They want to hurt the enemy as much as possible before abandoning the garrison."

"And will my son be present during the attack?" the queen asked, her voice soft but carrying the keen edge of a Kul-brite sword. She was a beautiful woman, with long dark hair and skin the color of honey, smooth and soft, repudiating her age of fifty five years. Many people whispered that she had found a spell that countered the negative effects of age. And despite her lithe petite form, she was a powerful Aura Mage in her own right.

Kivalla coughed, clearing his throat. "He chose to stay behind...to take part in the fighting."

King Enden looked at his wife, her face a mixture of anger and sadness. Despite her frustration with him for sending Jarak away, King Enden was proud of his son's progress, and equally proud to hear that he had agreed to stay behind to fight with his men when he could have easily run back to Cythera, something he probably would have done a year ago. The decision to send his son away had not been easy, knowing the danger he may have put his son in, as well as having to deal with the wrath of his wife. But by all accounts Jarak was becoming a man, a prince that his people could follow and respect. He just hoped that Argon saw fit to protect him so he could see him again. "That is good," the king said, avoiding the icy glare of his wife. "He will learn a lot, and besides, my brother Daricon will protect him." Everyone knew he had mentioned that last part for his wife, and perhaps to convince himself as well. "What of Kulvar? Have we heard from him?"

This time Tul'gon spoke. "Word came in yesterday. The nobles you sent in response to Chief Byn'ok's request have returned. But Kulvar Rand was not with them."

Bannerfall

"Where is he?" the king asked.

"It turns out there was a problem at the fight. The two fighters that were supposed to face off in the final bout, both of whom were Ull Therm, escaped the night before. I guess there was a confrontation between Tangar and Kulvar soon after."

"About what?" This time it was the queen who asked the question, clearly interested.

"Tangar, the chief's son, accused Kulvar Rand of helping the prisoner escape. Master Kulvar left early that morning and has not returned. We do not know where he went."

King Enden sighed. The Schulg were a volatile race, prone to violence and rash behaviors. He didn't like anything that could potentially cause political strife between Dy'ain and the nomads. He hoped that Kulvar hadn't done anything that could potentially break the precarious truce he had worked so hard to procure with Chief Byn'ok.

"Do we have any news on any troop movements entering Dy'ainian lands?"

Everyone looked to General Veros. "Other than the imminent attack on the Garrison, we have not had any reports of any Saricon troops entering our lands."

"But we must assume that their attack on Eltus is just a precursor to their invasion of Dy'ain," Kivalla added. "My guess is they want to occupy Eltus so they can control the Dynel Strait. They must also defeat the Kaelian navy before they venture into the Dark Sea and attack Cythera. They want control of our Kul-brite trade."

"I agree," General Veros said. "That is the tactic that I would employ if I were in their position."

"Can they defeat the Kaelian navy?" the queen asked skeptically. Everyone knew that the Kaelian navy was all but invincible.

"They do not have the ships or the skill to do so," General Veros replied.

But Kivalla was shaking his head. "Do not underestimate the Saricons. Many people have done so and suffered for it. They have huge transport ships, each capable of carrying nearly five hundred men. And their navy, although smaller than the Kaelian's, includes ships from the conquered island kingdoms of YaLara and Argos, and as you know those seafarers know their way around a ship. I agree that a naval confrontation with Kael would not end well for them, but they are an intelligent and resourceful enemy, and if there is a way to win they will find it. I suggest we make our plans based on a possible Kaelian defeat. That way there will be no surprises."

King Enden leaned forward in his chair, resting his strong forearms on the table. "Let us assume then that they defeat the Kaelians. My guess is that after they take the garrison, which we know they eventually will, that they will take that force into Dy'ain and make their way here. But what of their main army? The shortest route would be to ship men and supplies from Eltus to our shores. What are your thoughts on this?"

Everyone leaned forward and looked more closely at the map spread across the table. Kivalla spoke first. "They have few options. If we use our navy to protect our coast, including the Bitlis Straight, then they only have one path before them. They must land along our coast and unload their army."

Queen Irstan looked carefully at the map. Then she pointed along the eastern shores of the Dark Sea. "Can they land their forces here?"

"They could," the king answered. "But we would know of it. Besides, that would mean they would have to travel across the Sil Desert and then find a way to cross the Bitlis Sea to attack us from the North. I do not see that happening."

"I agree," General Veros said. "We will have the advantage of knowing where they will attack."

"One more thing," the king said. "I would like runners sent out alerting all Legionnaires that war is coming. If the Kaelians are defeated, we will order most of our troops from all garrisons and outposts. I want everyone ready."

"What of our troops in Kreb and Tanwen?" Kivalla asked.

"Send word and have half of each contingent return to Cythera," the king ordered.

"That will weaken our northern and western borders," General Veros cautioned.

"True, but holding those borders will be inconsequential if we cannot repel the Saricon horde," King Enden added somberly. "Now, prepare the orders and get some rest." With that, the king stood, ending the meeting. Queen Irstan stood with him, and together they left, heading for their quarters.

***

Bannerfall

Jarak crouched next to Serix, nervously watching the Saricons through a screen of brush on the far side of the river. Daricon had been right. The small army of Saricons had been assaulting the garrison wall from the far side of the river for two days, using catapults of a strange design to fling round clay balls that exploded with fiery flames when they landed. They had never before encountered incendiary projectiles such as these. Luckily they had plenty of water and most of the garrison structure had been constructed of stone, and with a quick relentless effort they were able to put the flames out before they did significant damage. At least for now.

But he had warned them that they would try to cross the river in small groups, hoping to assault the garrison on the Dy'ainian side so the defenders would have to split their defense to protect both the eastern and western walls. So scouts had patrolled the river's edge religiously, looking for any signs of enemy movement preparing to cross the river. Today, just three hours ago, a scout had returned proving Daricon's hunch to be correct.

Captain Hagen and Jarak led five hundred men to the river's edge, slowly creeping forward under the cover of dense brush and low lying trees that grew thickly along the river's edge. The Saricons had picked a good spot to cross, one the Dy'ainian scouts figured would be a likely crossing point. The river bent before them, narrowing and then opening up to a wide slow current. The immediate ground before and after the bend was mostly sandy, but interspersed with fields of smooth river rock, and littered with fallen trees and debris that had been washed down the river over the years. It would be a good spot to cross and regroup on the near side.

Captain Endler Ral had joined them as well, and being the only Channeler they had, he made sure he was near Jarak and Serix. Jarak looked at the captain, then at Serix, hoping to gain some confidence from them and help calm his nerves. Endler felt his gaze, and sensing his unease gently squeezed his forearm. "Stay close to me," he whispered. "I should be able to hold enough energy for you both. But remember…"

"Don't rely on it," Jarak finished his sentence, giving him a weak smile.

"Exactly. You will do fine. Argon and Felina will watch over us. Just remember your training and stay close to Serix and me."

Jarak nodded and looked down the line. He was looking for Cat but he could not see her. She would be near her father, and despite the fact that Captain Hagen was the best swordsman there, he was still concerned about her.

They had silently watched the Saricons as they slowly moved their men across the river in large barges, each hastily built raft carrying twenty men. There were very few places along the Pelm River that offered any spot for a sizable force to cross. This was one of them, along with several others further west of the garrison where the river was narrower.

Jarak counted a total of two hundred men, and once the last barge had crossed they fanned out in groups of ten, slowly moving towards them, alert and ready. They were smart. He was hoping they would stay grouped together in a tight formation, but they did not, knowing that they were in the open and susceptible to attack. The Saricon warriors were huge, wearing banded mail, animal furs, and carrying long swords, axes, and war hammers. About half carried shields while the other half wore a strange quiver on their broad backs, the tips of short spears rising above their heads. Jarak had never seen weapons such as those.

The plan was simple and Jarak was glad they held the element of surprise. He and Serix would attack with fire, signaling for their archers to release their arrows. At that point, it would turn into a melee and their larger force should prevail.

Jarak's heart was pounding. He had never faced anything like this before. True, he had fought valiantly when they were attacked on the road, but that was the extent of his experience. Before, he had been ambushed by surprise. He didn't have time to think about the consequences. But now, waiting silently in the brush, watching the hulking warriors advance towards them, his mind went through every possible scenario, the negative outcomes pounding down his resolve. He came to the conclusion that he was not fond of having to wait before engaging in battle.

"They are close enough," Captain Ral whispered. Reaching out, he began to task aura energy from the enemy, slowly building it up, holding it in his chest. Jarak was impressed. They were still too far away for him to task, but by the looks of it Channelers were able to draw energy from a more substantial distance. Or maybe Captain Ral was just more skilled than most.

Serix, who was on Jarak's left side, leaned in close. "Pull energy from Endler until your towd is full. Then follow my lead. You know the spell. Just concentrate. When we move forward be cautious of their throwing spears. I've heard they are incredibly accurate and they can throw them much farther than expected. Remember, do not accidently draw energy from them. Their auras will be angry and filled with malice. Draw from Endler, he will filter it for you."

Jarak was too nervous to respond, so he merely nodded in agreement, then slowly began to draw the energy from Endler, dragging it from his aura and storing it in his towd. Endler's aura was a brilliant white, the filtered energy building with power as he pulled it from the advancing army. Jarak and Serix were able to continuously draw energy from him as Endler drew more of it from the approaching men.

Once Jarak's towd was full, he sat up on his knees, the screen of brush concealing him from the approaching enemy. Using both hands he concentrated on forming a ball of fire between them. It took only a few moments before energy surged from his hands, coming together in a swirling ball of intense red orange heat. Focusing on the task, Jarak pushed more energy into the sphere, condensing it into a tight ball, encasing it by weaving strands around it, until the ball could hold no more power. It was a tough spell to perform, but one Serix had forced him to practice on many occasions. And now he was thankful, silently berating himself for any disparaging words he had mentally slung at Serix for making him work so hard.

Serix had already finished. In his right hand he held a large glowing ball, flickering flames dancing all around it, eager to explode in destructive power. "Ready?"

The soldiers surrounding them gripped their weapons tighter, knowing that battle was upon them. The bowmen readied their weapons, arrows nocked, with several more stuck into the ground beside them for fast deployment.

Jarak took a deep breath. "Do it."

Serix stood up quickly and threw the fireball at the closest group of men. Jarak followed his lead, aiming for another group further to his right. Traces of fiery light arced through the air as the flaming spheres descended on the enemy.

The Saricons frantically threw up their shields for protection. But it mattered not; the balls exploded in intense heat, the impact unraveling the strands and releasing their power, blasting through shields, armor, and flesh. Dozens were instantly incinerated, while the spreading flames more slowly killed or injured others.

The scene turned to chaos as a rain of arrows flew from the brush from which hundreds of Dy'ainian archers had stood up to release their shafts, following the first volley quickly with two others. The battlefield exploded in pandemonium as men screamed, orders were shouted, and scores of Saricons fell, quivering arrows jutting from their flesh. But the Saricons were skilled warriors, and once they saw the attack, had closed formation, the men with shields holding the front line while the warriors that carried the spear-like projectiles stood crouched behind them. Arrows slammed into the shields, some hitting their mark and dropping the warriors to the ground. But then, with practiced familiarity, those behind the front line drew the short spears from their backs, flinging them with both expert skill and tremendous power into the Dy'ainian ranks, flying with such speed and force that they barely saw them coming. And those that managed to heft their shields up in time were nearly knocked to the ground as the heavy steel points slammed into them, busting through the shields as if they were made of thin wood. Several Legionaries suffered broken arms from the impact, and they were the lucky ones.

"Move forward!" Captain Ral yelled, drawing his sword and lifting his shield. Jarak drew his sword, as did Serix, and they pushed through the brush into the open, running alongside Endler Ral. The Legionnaires ran at their flanks, shouting Argon's name. There was just enough time before the two forces came together for Jarak to create another spell. He hurriedly drew more energy from Endler, using his free hand to wrap invisible strands of it around a large downed log before them. There was a lot of driftwood scattered around the battlefield and Jarak grabbed the log closest to the Saricons. Directing it with his hand, he lifted it, heaving it forward as he ran and hurling it lengthwise into the approaching Saricons. The power of the attack crushed six men, burying the ones behind them under the combined weight of the log and their mangled bodies. Then they were upon the invaders, slashing down with swords and axes, killing the enemy as they struggled to get to their feet. But more Saricons surged forward and the fierce fighting continued.

Farther down the line Captain Hagen withdrew his sword from the chest of a dead Saricon. He was splattered with blood and the grime of battle. He looked quickly to his right, silently thanking Argon that his daughter was still there. She was engaged and battling a massive warrior, but he had no opportunity to help her as more fighters attacked. All he could do was hope that he had trained her well, and that the men around her would protect her, as they did each other.

"Heln!" an enemy warrior bellowed, his huge axe descending towards Hagen just as a Saricon spear smashed into the warrior to his left, puncturing his armor and bursting out the other side. The force of the blow knocked his lifeless body backwards several paces. Hagen's flank was now exposed, but he had no time to worry about that as he hastily lifted his shield to take the axe blow, which descended with such force that it nearly broke his arm.

Then he heard a scream that caused his heart to lurch in his chest. Risking a glance to his right he saw Cat knocked to the ground, a Saricon standing above her readying another blow. Growling with fury, adrenaline firing through his muscles, Captain Hagen snapped his foot out, connecting solidly with the Saricon's chest, knocking him backwards several paces. He knew it would do no real damage, but he didn't care, he just needed a few extra seconds. Lunging to his right, he jabbed his sword into the thigh of the Saricon that stood over his daughter. Then, with incredible speed, fueled by self-preservation and fear for his daughter, he changed direction and leaped back towards the warrior he had been fighting, lifting his shield at the last second to take the blow he knew was coming. This time, he lessened the force of the impact by angling the shield down and away from him, simultaneously stepping in closer and viciously ramming his sword into the Saricon's chest. His sharp blade broke through the banded mail and found his heart, killing him instantly.

Cat had been scooting frantically away from the warrior, her sword held protectively before her ready to block the downward stroke. It was then that her father, faster than she thought possible, had stabbed her attacker in the thigh before reengaging his own opponent. The man before her howled and grabbed his injured leg, temporarily thwarting his attack. He had given her a moment of reprieve, and she capitalized on it. Spinning her legs under her body, she jumped up on her knee, her sword arcing across the Saricon's leg, slicing him just under the metal plate on his thigh, opening up a deep red gash above his kneecap. Howling for a second time, he withdrew his right leg, only to find her sword reversing direction, this time cutting across his stomach, where her blade opened a terrible cut below the protection of his armor. He stumbled backwards, his eyes wide with pain. But his pain quickly turned to fury and in two heartbeats he had lifted his axe, screaming maniacally, and bringing the weapon down towards her head.

Cat hadn't a moment to think; she reacted solely on instinct, remembering the training her father had drilled into her since she could lift a sword. He had always taught her that, when fighting a man in armor, especially if he were larger, to always look for openings. The body, he instructed, had several weak points. The inner thigh where the femoral artery ran was always a key target, along with the neck and head. The heart of course was always a target, but that was usually protected. The spot that many warriors forgot, and which was typically vulnerable, was the spot just under the armpit. As he lifted his huge axe, Cat pivoted to his side and jumped forward, aiming the sharp point at the soft spot under the arm. She was lucky that he was left handed, giving her a proper attacking angle with her right hand. Like her father, she too was incredibly fast, and her blade found its mark, plunging in deep. She had angled it perfectly, slicing between his ribs and piercing his heart. Just as quickly, she withdrew her blade and the man fell to the ground with a heavy thud.

Before she could catch her breath another Legionnaire had fought his way to her, and together they surged forward, trying to keep her father on her left flank.

Farther down the line, Jarak fought like a crazed man, knowing that to do anything else would mean his death. He had suffered a small cut on his right arm, he was drenched with sweat, and his armor was splattered with blood. He had killed well over a dozen with his spells, although he could not be sure, and just recently had dispatched an enemy with his sword. His own men fell around him, their screams muffled by the howls of the Saricons. Serix was on his left and he knew that Captain Ral was on his right, sensing him but no longer able to see him. He had exhausted the energy he had pulled from Endler Ral and was too focused on staying alive to get more. Drawing energy while fighting was possible, but Jarak did not have the experience yet and was worried that any lapse in concentration would end in his death. But he could feel the Channeler's aura energy and was prepared to draw on it when he could.

Suddenly the man he was fighting, reacting to a yell behind him, pivoted away, revealing a giant Saricon with long blonde hair encrusted with blood, rush at him with amazing speed. Jarak barely had time to lift

Bannerfall

his sword. Nonetheless he had just enough time to catch a glimpse of his attacker's eyes…and they were glowing green.

The man, evidently one of their leaders, had enacted his Fury. Jarak lifted his sword, madly trying to block the sword wielded by the warrior. They exchanged several blows, their swords clashing together, but Jarak could not match his strength and speed. The Saricon's blade sliced across his cuirass, the force of the blow denting his armor and throwing him to the side.

Two Legionnaires, sensing his danger, rushed in to cover his flanks. But the crazed Saricon was screaming the name of his god, his body and sword nothing but a blur of movement, and within moments they were both dead, and he turned his attention again to Jarak.

His brave men had given him several moments of reprieve, and he used it to task more energy from Captain Ral. He knew he didn't have time to construct a complicated spell, so he did the first thing that came to him. It was a simple spell that all beginning mages learned and he could enact it almost instantly. Just as the Saricon's sword came at him, Jarak lifted his sword to block it, simultaneously pushing his left arm forward, propelling a small amount of energy into the warrior's chest. To the armored Saricon it would have felt as if an invisible fist had just punched him. It did no real damage, but it caused him to hesitate, just for a moment. Jarak wasted no time. He thrust his sword forward into the stunned warrior's stomach. His blade sunk into his flesh, but then he saw stars as the man's fist found his jaw. He hadn't even seen it coming, but in a flash he was stumbling away, his sword left behind in the man's gut.

In his daze he saw a bright flash of lightning, followed by the smell of cooked flesh assaulting his senses. Falling to his knee he put his right hand out to stabilize his body.

"Are you okay?" A voice came from his left. It was Endler Ral. Jarak momentarily shook off the dizziness, and looked up, half expecting to see the crazed Saricon, his sword lifted and ready to cleave his face. But that didn't happen. In fact, the Saricon war leader lay sprawled and unmoving on the ground, his body blackened and smoking in spots. Serix stood before him, residual lightning arcing across the fingertips of his left hand.

Endler helped him to his feet. "I'm fine, I think." Around them the fighting had suddenly stopped. It was surreal to Jarak. For what seemed like an eternity, even though he knew it was mere moments, the chaos and sounds of war had echoed in his head, and now, his body drained, it was eerily quiet.

Serix stepped toward him, his armor covered in gore. But he seemed unhurt. He lifted Jarak's chin, inspecting the damage. "A nasty cut, but I think you'll be fine."

If Jarak could have seen his face, he probably would have been shocked. The powerful punch had opened a deep ragged cut along his jawline, which was bleeding profusely, painting the side of his face and neck crimson. Luckily for him, it looked worse than it was.

"Let us see to our wounded," Captain Endler suggested, stepping away to do just that.

Serix stepped closer to Jarak. "I know you are tired. We all are," he added, dropping his voice to a whisper. "But now is when you should walk among your men, talking with them and checking on their well-being. They will see you wounded, and your courage and strength will make them proud, a feeling they desperately need right now, with so many of their friends and comrades dead around them."

Jarak took a deep breath to steady himself. His chin hurt, but clearly others were much worse, and despite his drained body he knew that Serix was right. "I will do my best." He stepped away on shaking legs, hoping that he had the energy to do as Serix suggested.

"And Jarak," Serix said, forcing him to turn and look at him. "You did well. I am proud of you. Your father would be proud of you. I am honored to have fought with you." Serix bowed his head before he turned away to deal with the horrors of war.

Jarak made his way through the battlefield. He was tired, drained both physically and emotionally, but no amount of exhaustion could compare with the devastation that he saw around him. Bodies were strewn about, lying at awkward angles, covered in the gore of battle. Vacant eyes, expressionless, devoid of that once present spark that signified life, stared back at him. He tried to ignore them, focusing instead on the living. He made the rounds talking with his men, and providing what aid he could before moving on. Officers were organizing the removal of the dead, stacking the enemy warriors in big piles to be burned. Their own men would be buried with honor higher up on the banks, away from the floodplain. They had a lot of work to do.

Suddenly Cat appeared beside him looking worried when she saw his jaw. He had been holding a piece of his cape that he had torn off against the wound and it was saturated with blood. But he smiled when he saw her, the images of the dead finally replaced with something akin to joy, and an immense relief that she was alive.

"Are you okay?" she asked. She tried to hide it, but Jarak could tell that she was gratified to see him; perhaps feeling the same emotions as he, that they had both made it through the fight intact.

"I'll be fine," he said. "Better than some. How are you?"

She took a deep breath. She was covered with the same sweat, grime, and dried blood of battle that all those who had taken part in the fight had endured, but she seemed to be uninjured. "I'm alive." That was all she said, not wanting to bring up the memories of the battle.

"My Prince, I am happy to see you," Captain Hagen said, bowing his head as he approached. Unlike his daughter, who had only been splattered relatively lightly with the visual evidence of battle, he had generous streaks of blood across his cuirass. His face, too, was smeared crimson, though it looked as if none of it was his own.

"And I you. How did it go on this side?"

Captain Hagen frowned. "We lost more than you would have thought considering we outnumbered them five to one. I'll hand it to the Saricons...they know how to fight."

Jarak nodded his head in agreement. "Let us see to our men so we can get home. I'm sure Daricon is eager to hear what happened."

"Yes, Sir," the Captain replied, stepping away to issue orders.

Cat looked up at Jarak. "You better get that stitched up."

"I will. I want to see to my men first."

She looked at him seriously, appraising him, and if Jarak hadn't known better he would have sworn she was looking at someone else. Smiling again, she turned to help her father.

***

Brant was told that the trip to Cythera would take them a week. The morning they left Kaan's cabin they stopped at Bygon to resupply. Every day they rode hard, stopping in the evening to camp and rest the horses. Brant had to clean his wounds several times each day and reapply fresh bandages. The salve seemed to be working and the pain was slowly receding. The lacerations, not so deep to begin with, slowly closed up and started forming thick scabs.

Bannerfall

Brant now knew what Kaan and Kulvar Rand had been laughing about the night before they departed. They had only been half way into the first day when he started to feel a slow ache grow along his inner thighs and buttocks. That ache grew until it felt like a blacksmith was pounding on his inner thighs, each jolt of the horse a powerful swing of the hammer. Brant did not complain, knowing that to do so would cause him to lose respect amongst the toughest fighting men in all of Dy'ain. The Dygon Guard rode hard each day, their eyes ever alert, their expressions revealing little emotion. Idle conversation was minimal. They were all business.

On the third evening of their journey they had again set up camp after the long day's ride. Ten warriors sat around several fires, the sun having long ago bedded down for the night. The warriors carried a tightly woven waterproofed cloth that Brant had never seen before. They rolled them up tight, along with their sleeping blankets, and carried them on the back of their saddles. On evenings when rain was unlikely, they simply laid them out on the ground to provide a dry place to lay their blankets. If rain looked imminent, then they would erect small tents from the cloth, each one large enough for two men. They had spent countless nights setting up camp and they went about their chores with practiced precision, saying very little, each man knowing his role. This night was clear, with a cloud of sparkling stars illuminating the night and casting soft shadows on the ground.

Brant had begun to feel a bit out of place. The men were not unfriendly but none went out of their way to talk with him. But then again they did not talk much amongst themselves. They had just eaten a meal of cooked beans with salted ham and slices of bread. Brant looked across the fire to Kulvar, finding the courage to break the silence. He had been thinking about this since the fight with Tangar.

"Master Rand," Brant began, not sure what to call him. "How did you beat Tangar so easily?"

At their fire sat Kade, second in command, along with two other warriors, Dayd and Horst. They were both big men, their dark hair shaved short exposing their scalps. Brant had noticed that all the Dygon Guards had their hair similarly trimmed. But they looked very different despite that commonality. Dayd was the ugliest and toughest looking man Brant had ever seen, with a scrunched up face and narrow eyes surrounded by deep lines, etched from years in the elements; most prominent among them were those across his forehead that made him look as if he were permanently frowning. His large mouth and huge jaw looked fitting compared to the size of his massively thick neck. Brant had no doubt, however, that Horst was a man the ladies swooned over. Like Dayd, his neck was also thick and muscular, but it supported a smooth skinned handsome face with wide intelligent eyes, and irises a brilliant green.

Kulvar Rand looked up at Brant, his dark eyes noncommittal. He shrugged. "I was better." Kade looked at Kulvar as he stirred the fire with a stick, perhaps wondering if he would elaborate.

"But how? I had fought and trained with Tangar on many occasions. He was an amazing swordsman. And everyone spoke of his prowess as if he were a god. But you killed him with three strokes of your sword. How did you do it?"

This time Kulvar did elaborate. "I have no doubt that Tangar was a skilled swordsman. I too had heard tales spoken of his skill with a blade. But most skilled warriors have not learned to kill quickly. They might think that every move and position they learn is for that purpose, but the reality is that most sword forms focus too much on stroke and counter stroke and not enough on the death stroke. They practice their sword movements religiously, mastering the dance, perfecting each strike and counter, as if it were an art form." Kulvar paused, gazing thoughtfully into the fire, then looked back at Brant. "We," he said, indicating his men, "train to kill, and to kill quickly. It is not about fancy moves and displays of skill. Tangar was expecting a great display of skill, and if I would have obliged him you would have seen a dance equal to none. But he was not ready for what he faced, and he died for it."

Brant was digesting his words. "Can you teach me?"

Kulvar pursed his lips, as if weighing his options. "I can."

The next night as the men lit the fires and began preparing the evening meal, Brant faced Kulvar in a nearby clearing. His wounded legs itched a little but they were healing nicely. Brant could feel the men's eyes on them as they went about their evening chores, seeing to the horses, laying out their bed rolls, and preparing dinner. Kulvar held his sword in his right hand, the blade angled low, while Brant held Tangar's blade. The weapon was beautiful, balanced perfectly and razor sharp. He marveled at its weight and how light it felt in his hand. He stood, momentarily oblivious to all else, and stared at the blade, smiling.

"What is it?" Kulvar asked.

Brant looked up from the silver sword. "I've worked in the Kul-brite mines my entire life but I never thought I'd actually hold a Kul-brite forged blade. It is hard for me to fathom the value of this blade. I wonder where Tangar got it."

"I wonder the same. I'm sure there is an interesting tale behind it. Now, let us begin. I am not going to teach you anything specific yet. First I want to see what I have to work with. Let us start out slowly. I want you to match my speed and follow my strikes and counters. I need to see what Tangar has taught you. If your injuries become painful, let me know."

Brant had suffered far more serious wounds in the arena, and had managed not only to fight through the pain, but to kill his opponents in the process. The scars that covered his body were testament to that. Any pain he felt from the cuts on his legs could easily be ignored. Brant had killed many men in the pit, the images of their deaths would flash through his mind when least expected. They came in his sleep, and sometimes while awake. He could not erase the memories of all the men he had killed. But facing Kulvar now, knowing it was not a fight to the death, caused him more trepidation than he would have imagined.

Kulvar lifted his sword. "Ready?"

Brant lifted his blade in response, nodding his head to indicate he was ready. Kulvar came at him quickly, his sword moving left and right. The combatants moved across the clearing, their Kul-brite blades coming together again and again. Brant followed his moves easily enough, performing the strikes and counters as Tangar had taught him. Kulvar came at him low, high, and from the sides, and every time he was there to meet him, blocking and spinning his blade in offensive maneuvers of his own. Tangar had taught him well, and his skill and experience in the pit was showing itself. Then Kulvar picked up speed, and power, the strikes coming harder and faster. But still Brant was there, their blades clashing, the strikes resounding in the clearing.

Suddenly Brant's sword was knocked to the side and Kulvar's blade was resting on the side of his neck. Brant froze, the edge of the razor sharp blade drawing a thin line of blood. Then it was gone, the blade facing the ground, the same position as when he started.

"What did you do?" Brant asked. He was confused. They had been fighting hard, and he had been keeping up, then suddenly he was as good as dead.

Bannerfall

"You are very good, Brant. I am impressed. You are fast and strong, and you know the correct forms. Tangar taught you well."

"Not well enough. What did you do?" he asked again.

"I will show you." Kulvar sheathed his blade and went to his horse. He removed a steel ball with a hole on one end. It looked to be about the size of large fist. Then he went over to Kade who handed him a stick as tall as a man. He had been carving on the stick since they had arrived that night and now it was smooth, one end carved down to a smaller point.

Kulvar walked over to Brant and tossed him the metal ball. Brant had already sheathed his blade so he caught it with both hands. It was heavy. "This ball," Kulvar said, "weighs about as much as a blade." Then he took the ball from him and set it on the ground. Taking the tip of the stick, he shoved it into the hole, pushing it in until it was wedged tight. Then he pivoted the other end of the stick and handed it to Brant. "Lift it up. But do it with one hand."

Brant stepped back; using his right hand he gripped the stick several feet from the end and attempted to lift the ball from the ground. The steel ball, its weight now stretched across most of the six foot pole, seemed ten times heavier. His grip tightened and the muscles on his forearms strained with the effort. Slowly, the ball rose several feet into the air, its weight bending the pole into a slight arc. He managed to lift it about waist high before he was forced to drop it.

By this time the men had gathered around them. Kulvar smiled. "How does that feel?" he asked.

"Heavy," Brant said, unsure about the point of the lesson.

"Now, grip it at the very end and carry it to that tree," he added, pointing to a small bonet tree, "and hit the ball against the trunk."

Brant looked doubtful. He was barely able to lift the steel ball and he had choked up on the stick several hand spans. Now he wanted him to lift it further back on the stick. He wasn't sure if he could. Gripping the stick tightly, he lifted with all his might. The ball rose a few inches off the ground. Straining, he tried harder, his forearm shaking. When he had the ball a foot off the ground he quickly started towards the tree. But he had scarcely taken two steps before he was forced to drop the ball, his forearms burning with exhaustion. "It can't be done," Brant said, rubbing his forearm.

Kulvar smiled and strode purposefully forward. With his right hand he gripped the stick, lifting it quickly to waist height. Then he moved to the tree, the heavy ball dancing on the slightly bent pole. He then stopped, braced his legs, and swung the ball into the tree. The heavy metal thudded into the trunk ten times before he finally dropped it.

"How did you do that?" Brant asked as he stepped towards him, clearly amazed.

"I trained to do it, as have my men."

Kade joined them by the tree as the rest of the men departed, going back to their evening tasks. "But rest assured that we cannot hit the tree ten times," Kade said, smiling. "Most of us would be lucky to perform that task five times." It was the first time Brant had seen the man smile since he had met him. "Each one of us went through what you're going through now…disbelief. We thought we were strong, and we were, but not strong enough, in the right places at least. In fact, I'm impressed. None of us could even lift the ball off the ground with the stick when we first tried. You are indeed stronger than most."

"So what is the lesson here?" Brant asked, trying to tie it all together.

"Wrist strength is the key to being a deadly swordsman. Everything you have demonstrated to me is important. You need to know the proper moves, the correct counters to various attacks, but if you want to be deadly, seriously deadly, you have to strengthen the power of your forearms. I was able to kill Tangar, and beat you moments ago by using primarily my wrist. I used a subtle but extremely powerful movement to knock aside your sword and have my own at your neck. Think about it, Brant. If I'm strong enough, I can use the tip of my blade like that steel ball. With just a flick, I can redirect your blade, and with another flick I can find your throat. The movements are so inconspicuous that you barely feel them."

"Until it's too late," Kade added.

"Will you teach me this?"

"I said I would. But I cannot teach you the moves until you strengthen your wrists. You are as good a swordsman as I have met, as skilled as some of my best men. But if you were to fight any one of them, you would be killed. Strengthen your wrists and forearms, then I will teach you."

"I will do it."

Kulvar turned to Kade. "Grab the ring." Kade left and went to Kulvar's horse. "Pick up the stick again," Kulvar said, turning back to Brant. "This time choke up on the handle about half way."

Brant reached down and grabbed the middle of the stick. This time he easily lifted the metal ball off the ground. "That is much easier," he said.

"The closer you grip the stick to the ball, the easier it will be. You will have to slowly work on your strength, moving your hand further back on the stick as you gain strength." Kade walked back to them and handed Kulvar a steel circle slightly larger than a man's head. There was a chain on one end which Kulvar attached to a tree branch. The circle dangled before Brant at about waist height. "Now, lift the ball so it's in the center of the circle." Brant did so. "Now, using your wrist, flick the ball left and right, up and down, hitting it against the metal ring." Brant did as he was instructed, the weight of the ball rapidly taking its toll on his tiring forearm. The metal rang out eight times before Brant was forced to drop the ball.

"That is very difficult," he said, rubbing his arm.

"It is. You will need to do this with both arms, until you can control your movements and hit the ring in all directions while gripping the end of the stick. Then I will teach you how to use this new strength."

Brant picked up the ball with his left hand, ringing the bell only twice before he had to drop it to the ground. His left arm was definitely weaker.

"Do not fret. You are stronger than any of us were when we started. It will come. Now, let us eat."

Brant looked at the stick on the ground. "Go ahead without me." He gripped it again, putting the ball in the center of the ring.

Kulvar Rand and Kade turned away, the ring of the metal behind them bringing a smile to their typically aloof expressions.

They traveled hard that entire week. Every evening Brant and Kulvar trained using the metal ball. He was definitely getting stronger, but realized that it would be months of hard work before he was strong enough to hit the tree five times.

When they arrived at Cythera Brant stared in awe at his surroundings. The massive city, constructed of white stone, had been built along the Dark Sea overlooking the Bitlis Strait, the narrow neck of water separating the Dark Sea and the Bitlis Sea. On a clear day one could look across the strait and see the edges of the Sil Desert. The grasslands surrounding the city were filled with numerous shops and dwellings, creating almost another town in itself. Several small rivers flowed from the Devlin Mountains across the steppes, merging together outside the city, where it meandered like a snake to flow into the Dark Sea. Along its banks hundreds of homes had been built before it passed in front of the north wall of the city, forming a moat that could only be crossed when the drawbridge was dropped. Beyond the outer village were several dozen farms, their expansive crops of grains and corn swaying in the evening breeze.

Kade and the rest of the Dygon guard were sent into the main city while Kulvar directed Brant off the main road to the city, and onto another road that flanked the river along which a large number of impressive homes had been built, large buildings constructed of heavy stone, surrounded by rock walls and expansive gardens.

"Where are we going?"

"I have an estate here, along the river. You will stay there while I report to the king," Kulvar replied.

"Are all the homes here owned by noble families?"

"Yes. Property along the river is quite costly. Most of the homes you see are owned by noble families or wealthy merchants."

"Are you from here?"

"No. My family is from Tanwen. We have homes here, in Cythera, as well as Kreb. We own land throughout Dy'ain and need to be able to manage and maintain our holdings. I live here most of the time as Cythera is my home base. But when we bring Kul-brite shipments to Tanwen and Kreb I will visit my family and my homes there."

Brant could not comprehend the amount of wealth required to maintain that many homes. And the homes they were riding by were huge, most several stories and constructed of sturdy stone. Windows were adorned with intricate shutters and an assortment of colorful flowers bloomed from stone planters along the sills.

They rode past several intersecting roads lined with more homes before Kulvar pulled up next to a house that dwarfed the others. A stone wall as tall as a man surrounded what looked like a three story mansion. An iron gate blocked the entrance and through the vertical bars Brant could see beds of flowers and exotic pruned trees lining an entrance to a large oak door, intricately carved with twining vines surrounding a beautiful leaded glass window.

A young boy, waiting beyond the gate, opened it for his master. Kulvar and Brant rode into the area beyond the gate, a small round courtyard paved with rare white marble, veined in threads of silver and gray. Several servants were there to take the horses. Two paths followed along the wall's edge. One led directly to the main entrance, while the other looked like it led to the rear of the home. They dismounted and one servant led Brant's horse down one path along the wall's edge, presumably to stables that must have been located somewhere in the rear of the estate. Kulvar held the reins of his own horse.

The young boy who opened the gate bowed before them. "Greeting's, Master Rand. Welcome home."

"Thank you, Ari. This is Brant Anwar and he will be our guest. Will you please make sure that he has several changes of clothes and put him in the room facing the river." The second servant had taken Brant's few belongings from the back of the horse and was now holding his bag, standing behind Ari. Ari was perhaps fifteen years old. He was dressed in simple yet clean clothes, such as those worn by a house servant. His wavy hair was dirty brown, cut just out of his eyes and long over the ears and neck. His light freckles, unique in these parts, gave him a kind quality, and combined with his pronounced dimples exemplified a young innocent boy.

"Of course, sir. Welcome to Rand Estate. It is a pleasure to meet you, Master Anwar," Ari said, bowing low to Brant.

Brant smiled awkwardly as Kulvar looked on with a smile. "Please, Ari. Call me Brant. I am no master."

Ari looked to Kulvar to see if that was appropriate. Kulvar winked at him. The boy's smile broke through his proper façade, but he quickly reverted to his professional demeanor. "Very well. Brant, if you will please follow me. I will lead you to your room."

"I need to meet with the king. I will not be back until late. Please make yourself at home," Kulvar said to Brant. Then he looked at Ari. "Ari, please show Brant to the training yard and make sure he has what he needs."

"It will be done."

Brant turned to Kulvar as he mounted his horse again. "Thank you, sir. I appreciate the hospitality."

"You are welcome, Master Brant," Kulvar said smiling. Then he turned his horse and rode out the gate.

"If you will please follow me," Ari said, leading Brant towards the main entrance, the servant in tow carrying Brant's dirty bag. *Well this will be different*, Brant thought. He couldn't help but smile in anticipation.

Brant's room was immaculate; nicer than anything he had ever experienced. And *he* got to sleep there. He was having a hard time coming to terms with the fact that he was Kulvar Rand's guest, sleeping under the same roof as the most skilled swordsman in the lands, perhaps in all of Corvell. His bed was huge and the feather filled mattress softer than anything he had ever slept on. The furniture was elegant, yet simple and functional, the wood polished to a brilliant sheen. But the most impressive part of the accommodations was the balcony. A double door opened out onto a narrow balcony overlooking plush gardens and the river beyond. The sun was setting, silhouetting the giant towers of the city, the tall spires tipped with fluttering flags. Gazing at the imposing city before him, with all its grandeur, made him feel insignificant, as if he were a worm in a farmer's field.

Brant made his way downstairs. He wanted to look around outside and find the training area that Kulvar Rand had mentioned. He found Ari soon enough. Or perhaps Ari had found him, materializing from nowhere. Either way, the young boy led him outside, taking him through the gardens to the stables on the northern side of the property. Once there he showed him the weapons rack inside the expansive stables and explained to him that Master Rand usually practiced on the cobble stone courtyard in front of the large building. The space was large and flat. It would be perfect.

Ari was just about to leave when Brant asked him a question. "How long have you been working for Master Rand?"

The young boy turned and smiled. "Since I was ten. He found me in the streets and took me in."

"You were an orphan?"

"Yes."

"How old are you now, Ari?"

"I'm fourteen."

Brant was surprised. He looked much younger. Perhaps it was his frail build but Brant would have guessed he was no more than twelve. But age can sometimes be hard to determine. After all, Brant was nearly twenty one but most people would guess he was approaching thirty. He had been forced to grow up faster than the average child, and his many years working the mines and then fighting in the arena had given him a more mature physical appearance than one his age. "What kind of work do you do here?"

Ari shrugged. "Anything that needs to be done. I clean, serve his guests, whatever he needs. Most of the servants here were once orphans, children found in the streets. He has given us a home and a purpose. Master Rand is a great man."

Brant couldn't disagree. From what he had witnessed so far he was indeed a man to emulate. Maybe someday he could be like him, helping others and serving a just king. "Thank you for showing me around."

Ari bowed his head. "You are welcome. Let me know if you require anything else. Would you like dinner brought out here or served in your room?"

Brant looked back at the weapon's rack in the barn. "I think I'll eat out here if you don't mind."

Ari bowed again. "As you wish." Then he turned and walked toward the main house.

***

It was the fourth day of the siege and they had agreed the night before that they would start a staggered retreat in the morning. The servants and non-combatants would leave first, taking carts filled with provisions, weapons, supplies, and anything else they did not want the Saricons to get their hands on. Then, throughout the day, the Legionnaires would retreat in groups, until none were left. Despite their retreat they had accomplished their goal. They estimated that they had killed five Saricons for every death they sustained.

The Saricons had continued to assault the western wall. Several times a day they marched men across the bridge, a shield wall before them, pushing forward through the onslaught of arrows and spears descending upon them from the defenders above. And although the enemy could throw their short spears with deadly accuracy even from behind the shield wall, the drawbridge was up and the span from the end of the floating bridge to the castle wall continued to elude them. On several occasions, however, the enemy managed to hit the wooden gate with their explosive clay balls, only to be extinguished by brave defenders, risking their lives by leaning over the edge to dump huge metal containers of water, attached to pivoting gears, over the edge of the wall. They were of ingenious design, and had been placed every several feet along the outside of the barbican just above the wooden drawbridge. They could be filled with water, and then turned with handles, the buckets pivoting on oiled gears, dumping gallons of water at a time on the gate, extinguishing the fires before they could fully ignite the wood. But the constant force of the fiery explosions were beginning to weaken the gate. It was time to leave.

Jarak was on the barbican with Serix and Captain Ral, creating devastating damage to the Saricons with their magical onslaught of a relentless barrage of lightning bolts and fireballs that rained down upon them. The Saricons had no defense against the calamitous power of the Aura Mages. Nonetheless the defenders had to be vigilant. The Saricons were extremely accurate with their throwing spears and several nearly struck Jarak, the displacement of air as they flew by reminding him to keep his head below the battlements. Jarak was dismayed to see some of the heavy spears find their marks, nearly impaling a handful of his men and knocking the brave warriors from the wall to the ground below.

Just as he ducked to avoid a spear, a warrior crept toward him from the stairs on the inside of the wall. He crouched low, having witnessed the efficiency of the Saricon spears. "My Prince, you are requested at the kitchen. Chef Jayla says it's urgent."

Jarak frowned. He had never been summoned by the chef before and he could think of no reason why she would need to speak with him. Whatever problem she had could be solved by another. But he also knew she would not request him if it were not important. After all, despite his efforts to get to know her, she rarely spoke to him. He had to admit his interest was piqued.

He quickly made his way to the kitchens and found Jayla and several servants filling wood boxes with supplies. They were part of the second wave leaving and they would be departing soon.

"You asked for me," Jarak said as he entered.

The two servants bowed as Jayla looked up from the box. "I need you to see something," she said, moving past him and down the narrow hall. He used to get perturbed with her brusque attitude and apparent insolence, but not anymore. Now he found it almost amusing.

He followed her down the hall coming to steps that went to the cool cellar below. She descended and he followed.

The large room was damp and musty, but nearly empty. The dark room was dimly lit by several small lanterns, casting dancing shadows among the beams and discarded barrels throughout the cellar. They had already boxed up most of the supplies and what was left behind would be staying.

"Why am I here, Jayla?" Jarak asked. He was becoming impatient. For what purpose did she need him to leave the fighting to join her in some dank cellar?

She said nothing, directing him to a wall to which she moved a large wooden shelf that was attached to some sort of bracket that allowed it to role perfectly flush with the wall, revealing a crude hidden opening. Jayla grabbed a nearby lantern and looked back at Jarak. "Follow me."

He did just that and they stepped into a small room, the lantern she held aloft giving off plenty of light to view the space. It was a simple square room about the size of a small bedchamber, but what he saw on the far wall stopped him in his tracks, his eyes widening in surprise. "In Argon's name I cannot believe it."

"I didn't know who else to tell. I thought I should inform you," Jayla said softly.

Before him stood an altar. There was a small table against the wall and on the table was a large statue of Heln, the Saricon god. The black painted figure was about the size of a child and expertly carved from wood, depicting a muscular man holding a two handed sword before him. Heln's head was covered with wavy hair that cascaded down the sides of his neck and over his massive muscular chest. Jarak had seen images of Heln before and there was no mistake…he was looking at an altar to Heln. He stepped closer and saw a heavy, leather bound tome, Heln's horned helm symbol depicted in red against a black background. It was their religious book, and Jarak knew from his history classes that they called it their Torgot.

Jarak stepped closer and opened the black book. It was clearly written in Drak, the Saricon language. He knew a little Drak, but not enough to decipher anything. "This is an altar to Heln," Jarak said, turning to face Jayla. "You don't know anything about it?"

"Of course not," she said, tapping her forehead twice with two fingers, the Argonian religious gesture for Argon and Felina. "I am Argonian."

"Does anyone else know of this?"

She shook her head. "Just me. I found it accidentally while packing up my wares."

"Good. Keep it that way. Tell no one. Let us go," Jarak said as he walked past her and out of the room. They closed the secret opening and ascended the steps. Once in the kitchen, Jarak turned to Jayla again. "Thank you for informing me. Safe travels tomorrow and I'll see you back in Cythera."

"And to you, Prince," she said, bowing only slightly. "And be careful. There is something not right about all this."

Jarak couldn't agree more. "I will." Then he turned and left, his thoughts disturbed as he thought about the implications of what he had seen. Who had set up an altar to Heln? It made no sense. Did they have a spy in their midst? Jarak wasn't sure what to do. But right now his main goal was to leave the garrison with as few casualties as possible. He would deal with the altar and what it meant once they were safely on the road to Cythera.

Chapter 9

I've always been fascinated with Scion Forging; the ability to create Kul-brite weapons and armor. Very few people possess the skills and attributes necessary to become Scion Forgers. There are therefore very few, making them extremely valuable. I know of only three in the entire Dy'ainian Kingdom. Amori, from Cythera, came from a small noble family in Kreb, to the northwest. Since he was a Merger, he had been guided towards the path of either becoming a Sentinel, or, if he were skilled enough, a Dygon Guard. But he seemed to have two left hands when it came to wielding a sword. So, he became apprenticed to the king's blacksmith in Cythera. It was there that his skill with metal was developed, his Merger abilities allowing him to surpass the talents of his master in a few short years. From Cythera he was sent back to Kreb to apprentice under Caleren, the most famous Scion Forger, who, like most Scion Forgers, had learned his craft similar to Amori. After all, as a male noble gifted with Merger abilities you would more than likely end up serving the king with a sword. But if you were not skilled in that arena, then you have few choices, being a Scion Forger one of them. But those talents were even rarer and more often than not male nobles that lacked martial skill would end up working in the family business. Lastly, there was Ethrean, from Tanwen. He was the oldest of the three, nearly sixty winters, and by all accounts was having a difficult time mustering the strength to continue to forge. It won't be long before he will have to retire.

  Each man, not suited to the dance of the blade, had something that other Mergers did not. They were all able to use their auras to develop an understanding of the metal that no other blacksmith was able to do. This unique ability, which had been developed over time, enabled them to more easily heat, bend, and manipulate the incredibly hard steel. My understanding is limited but my research suggests that these craftsmen, during the forging of the weapon, give the blade an affinity for aura energy, infusing the steel with a need for it, as well as enabling the metal to actually enhance the power of any aura energy sent into it. The greater the Scion Forger, the stronger *the blade and the more power it can handle. These forgers may disagree, but, from what I've learned, I believe that a blade forged by Caleren is unparalleled to any other. Perhaps there are other Scion Forgers in other lands, with skills equal or better than our own, but there is much we do not know.*

Journal entry 99
Kivalla Der'une, Historian, Keeper of the records in Cythera, capital of Dy'ain

---

5090, 14th cyn after the Great Change

Keltius leaned against the railing of his ship gazing at the large city of Eltus in the distance, the gentle sway of the Dark Sea rocking him in a cradle of contentment, its waves and currents as natural to him as the winds and updrafts of air are to the hawk. The swarthy man was born of the sea. He had lived his entire life on the island nation of Argos. While still a boy he had become a deck hand, working on one merchant ship after another, learning the skills of navigation and maintaining a merchant vessel. Finally, after years of service on many ships, a rich merchant he had known for years offered him his own boat, transporting cargo across the Alsace Sea and sailing as far north as Tanwen.

Keltius was born under the rule of the Saricons. Years before his birth the Saricon horde had invaded the island nations of Argos and YaLara. He had been told that the people of Argos, including his father, had fought against the foreign invaders. But for the small nation of Argos that was like trying to run into a hurricane. They fought valiantly, but in the end the Saricon horde took the island nations, slaughtering any who would not convert. Keltius' father had been killed, and his mother, fearing for her life, and the life of her son, had converted. So Keltius, like his mother, had become a follower of Heln, and he had been serving the Tongra of Fara, Kahn Taruk, for the last fifteen years, transporting supplies and men when needed.

He looked to his right and left, the flickering deck lanterns of Tongra Taruk's fifty anchored ships sparkling in the darkness. He had never commanded so many, but was eager to prove his maritime skill as well as his loyalty to the Tongra. Two days ago they had unloaded ten thousand Saricon warriors, led by Karnak, along the eastern shores at the base of the Pyres Mountains. From there, Obaty, their Askarian guide, would lead them through the dangerous mountains along a secret path known only by the reclusive Askarian nomads. He was told it would take them a month to traverse the secret pass and emerge along the southern edge of the Sil Desert. Karnack's orders were to lead his men across the Bitlis Sea on barges and claim the Dy'ainian lands north of Cythera. Then, once they had destroyed all resistance and cut off Cythera's reinforcements and supply lines, they would then converge on Cythera.

    Keltius was glad to see the stinking Saricons go. Even though he had lived among the hulking race his entire life, they still put him on edge. They were intelligent, and deadly in battle, but quick to anger, choosing steel over diplomacy to solve problems. Keltius could fight if need be, but he preferred negotiation to combat, which was perceived as weakness by the Saricons.

    Now he was waiting. King Kaleck and his queen had been murdered over a month ago, setting Kahn Taruk's plan in motion. With House Kaleck no longer in power, Eltus had initially experienced a period of chaos as rival nobles fought for control of the city. But spies reported that they had hastily formed a temporary ruling council of nobles which was now governing the Kaelian people until the Saricon threat could be ended. Only then would they have time to choose which house would then rule Kael. The last thing they needed was civil war while foreign enemies were invading their lands. The Saricon armies were presently marching across the Kaelian Peninsula, and if their scouts' estimates were correct, would be arriving at the city's gates the following day. He had been informed by the Tongra that when he arrived off the coast of Eltus that the Kaelian navy would not attack, that they would be worrying about more pressing matters. Keltius was skeptical about how an attack could be avoided, but he figured he would find out soon enough. When the sun rose the next day, the Kaelian's powerful navy would sail from their harbor to defend their city. If that happened, his armada would most likely be defeated. True, they had large strong ships of a Saricon design, but they could not match the speed and maneuverability of the Kaelian navy. All he could do was trust that whatever the Tongra had in mind would come to fruition tonight or the next morning. If not, they were doomed.

Just when he was about to turn away to head to his cabin for his evening meal, a bright flash caught his eye. Another sailor who was nearby coiling lengths of rope stepped to the railing. "Did you see that, Captain?"

Keltius looked closer. There it was again…another bright flash of orange light. "Looks like fire," the captain said. More flashes lit up the sky, and soon, even at their great distance, the docks and boats could be seen as growing flames illuminated the scene with fires sprouting up throughout the docks. "It has begun."

***

Thalon flew across the dark sky, the surging wind he had conjured spinning below him, lifting his body and hurtling him forward. He had three more of the clay balls remaining. He knew that Lyra was on the far end of the docks dropping her own explosive projectiles onto the ships below. He didn't have much energy left in the fly spell but it would be enough.

The scene below him was chaos. Crewmen scurried about, shouting in alarm, awakening from their slumber and vainly trying to extinguish the flames. The incendiary weapons of the Saricons were quite effective. When they landed they exploded in pyroclastic fireballs which hurled serpentine rivers of fire across the decks. Thalon had been aiming for the bases of the masts and so far he had been deadly accurate. Sheets of fire shot up the masts, quickly igniting the coiled ropes and rolled up sails before spreading to the rest of the ship.

Gliding over another boat he dropped his projectile, the clay ball exploding in hot fire, engulfing two sailors near his target. Their screams were cut short as the deadly flames quickly charred them beyond recognition. Two ships later, he turned towards the docks and aimed for the predetermined area, hoping that Tulk and Ayden would be there as planned. He hadn't entirely mastered the finer points of the fly spell and he was coming in pretty fast. The section of the dock where they had chosen to meet was located away from the Kaelian navy, near the wharf and the smaller fishing boats. Cargo boxes and kegs were stacked up along the wharf ready to be tallied and picked up by the merchants that had purchased them.

Thalon only had a few moments before he hit the dock. Glancing quickly around he saw several bodies sprawled across the docks. Good, he thought. Tulk and Ayden must have already dispatched any workers, guards, or fisherman in the vicinity, giving him a safe spot to land. Preparing his muscles, Thalon bent his legs and released the energy of the spell just before he hit the wood planks. As his feet touched the wood the momentum of his body caused him to trip up, slamming his body into its hard surface. Rolling across the dock, he lessened the impact some. But it was a hard landing.

He stood up painfully. Luckily nothing seemed broken.

"Nice landing," Tulk, the giant Merger said as he materialized from behind the boxes, his sword dripping crimson. Ayden stood beside him, his black eyes blending in with the darkness.

Thalon ignored Tulk, and with practiced ease he tasked energy from Ayden, storing a small amount in his tarnum. "How did it go?"

Their job had been to sneak aboard the ships that were anchored in the harbor. There were fifteen of them and they had to start early in order to get to them all. Tulk had silently rowed a small boat to each ship, and from there Ayden climbed to the deck and poisoned the water supply. He had dispatched a few men that were about but most were sleeping. There were few that were more stealthy than Ayden, and he used every ounce of skill, avoiding guards when possible and silently killing some when necessary. It had taken them both most of the night, which was why Thalon and Lyra had not planned on starting their fire attacks until very late. The results of Ayden and Tulk's work would not be witnessed until later, perhaps not until morning when the remaining ships that had not been destroyed sailed out to meet the Saricon Armada. But they would quickly be dead in the water as their crews succumbed to the deadly fast acting poison. Not everyone would die, but it would be enough to make the war vessels obsolete as they would not have the man power to run the ships affectively.

Suddenly they heard a whoosh of wind as Lyra swooped down toward them from the darkness. She dropped to the dock, lessening the impact by rolling forward and somersaulting to her feet, her short bow in her hand.

"Much more graceful," Ayden said with a smile.

Thalon glared at him. "Shut up. She has practiced more."

Out of habit Lyra tasked some energy from Ayden as she stepped towards them. "Well," she said. "That was fun."

"How did it go?" Thalon asked.

"I set fire to nine ships."

Bannerfall

"And I was able to burn eight."

"We were able to poison the water supply of all fifteen ships," Ayden said. "I was not detected."

Everyone knew that Ayden was the most gifted thief of them all. He had spent his whole life working the streets of DosDronas in Layona. As a boy he had survived by stealing, which had caught the attention of the local thieves' guild, who recruited him in his early teens. He quickly became one of their most profitable thieves. He had learned he was a Channeler at the age of sixteen, but he knew nothing of his true abilities. As time went on he learned some things about the Way on his own, but it wasn't until he met Thalon that his full powers had been unlocked. They had been inseparable ever since.

The docks were now in pandemonium. Seventeen ships were engulfed in flames and their frantic crews, the ones that hadn't yet been on board, rushed down the docks to try to save their ships. But they were too far gone by now. Thick smoke rose into the night air but the huge conflagration drove away the darkness. The remains of the navy, including the unmanned ships, their crews killed by the poison, would be defeated easily enough by Keltius's armada if they were able to rally after the destruction from the fire and poison.

"We better go. The guard will be here soon as well as their Aura Mages," Thalon warned.

As if on cue, a score of warriors wearing the official armor and green and gold capes of the City Watch rushed down the main dock. They were at least a hundred paces away, their attention drawn to the burning boats. Not one guard looked their way since they were so far away from the flaming destruction of the ships. This was why they had picked this particular rendezvous location to begin with. Suddenly a single warrior at the rear of the column stopped at the intersection of the main dock, looking down the dock to his right, and then to his left, right toward them. Even at the distance they could tell that this was no ordinary guard. He wore silver armor and he wore a fluttering cape of gold.

Thalon saw him smile. He must be an Aura Mage, his towd turned on, enabling him to see their auras as if they were shining stars. And, they had just tasked energy from Ayden, making their auras even brighter.

Bannerfall

The Aura Mage shouted something to the men in front of him and twenty guards reversed direction and started running down the dock toward them. Each man carried a spear and a long sword.

Their escape plan had been simple. Thalon and Lyra, after tasking more energy from Ayden, would enact the fly spell again and fly away to safety. Meanwhile, Ayden and Tulk would use their small boat to escape into the darkness. They had a prearranged spot along the coastline, just west of the city where they would meet. There they had horses and supplies and they would ride to meet Kahn Taruk, who by that time would be at the main gate of the city.

But now they had a problem. Thalon and Lyra couldn't leave Tulk and Ayden, whose boat was tied off thirty paces down the dock toward the fast approaching men. They would not have enough time to get to the boat before they were overwhelmed. They would have to take care of these guards before disappearing into the night. But Thalon was worried. A lot of things could go wrong. Ayden could be killed and then they would not be able to task any clean energy from him, trapping them behind enemy lines. Or it would take them too long to kill these men and more guards and Aura Mages would come to aid them, overwhelming them in the process. But they had no choice. They had to kill them quickly.

Thalon quickly enacted a plan of action. "Lyra, lightning! Ayden, stay close! Tulk, once we hit the front lines cut a swath through and get to the boat! We will handle the Aura Mage! And Ayden, we will need more energy from you to escape so don't row too hard!"

The guards were now close enough to throw their spears. Thalon pulled energy from his tarnum and quickly wove a protective shield before them. It was crudely done as he didn't have the time to bind it properly, but it performed adequately, trapping the spears in mid-air, as they slowly sank through a dense, yet invisible, substance. In reality, the spears were trapped in his shield, and as the power unraveled, the spears sank slowly, finally dropping harmlessly to the planks below.

Lyra, wasting no time, put her hands together, also drawing energy from her tarnum. Concentrating on the spell, she spun the power into crackling energy, blue arcs shooting between her hands. Then she screamed and sent the energy forward, directing as many bolts as possible into the charging ranks of men. Five crackling lightning bolts struck the men in the front, their power catapulting the men backwards as the remaining energy arced across their armor, catching more men behind them in the devastating spell.

Ayden drew his two short swords and reached out with the Way, sucking in large amounts of energy form the charging men, quickly filtering it and making it clean for Thalon and Lyra to use. Tulk stood next to him, his legs spread wide. He was grunting like a wild animal and soon the guards would find out just how dangerous he was.

Ayden felt Thalon draw more energy from him and just moments after Lyra's lightning halted the charge, a large cone of burning fire shot forward from his hands, killing any guards who had survived Lyra's magic.

There were six men left when Tulk charged. Ayden ran behind him knowing that he needed to stay out of his way. The little Channeler could not keep up with the Merger. Tulk drew large amounts of aura energy into his legs and arms and shot forward like a loaded spring. The remaining guards didn't know what hit them. His huge two handed sword flashed left and right, his body a blur of death.

But as Tulk was just finishing off the remaining guards, a new threat was floating slowly and silently above them. The Aura Mage glided toward them, his body straight and erect. He grasped a glowing ball of fire in his right hand. Thalon and Lyra saw him at the same time. They had only enough time to share a quick look before the ball of fire was arcing towards them. They both dove to either side, knowing that that was all they could do.

Thalon was lucky. He was near the edge of the dock and when the ball landed, the massive explosion sent a shock wave in all directions. But by that time he had hit the surface of the water, dropping below the protective cover of the sea as flames surged above him.

Lyra was not so lucky. She landed on the wood planks and frantically rolled toward the stacked barrels nearby. But the shock wave picked her up and hurled her into the barrels. She felt the skin on her back singeing and the force of the impact stunned her. Slowly she regained her senses, trying desperately to shake the dizziness from her head knowing that the mage was still there. The question was did he have a Channeler or a mage stone? If so, then he would have more energy to use and they would be in serious trouble. But if not, they still might survive the night.

Tulk had cleaved the last man's face in two, withdrawing his deadly blade so quickly that he was already stepping toward their boat when his body hit the floor.

"Not so fast." The voice came directly in front of them as the Aura Mage dropped from above to stand on the dock ten paces away. Ayden was five paces behind Tulk and they both froze, their swords held at their sides.

The man before them was wearing silver armor embossed with House Kaleck's symbol, a ship silhouetted by a shining sun. Ayden new that Lyra and Thalon had killed the king and his son. So who was this man? The royal families were often large so he could be anyone; maybe a cousin or a distant relative. But, by the looks of the powerful fireball he had just witnessed, this man was most definitely a skilled mage and probably had close ties to the ex-royal family. His hair was short and he wore a trimmed pointy beard on his chin that matched the color of his dark eyes.

Ayden could sense that Tulk was about to charge. The mage seemed to sense it as well. "Don't, Merger," he said, his voice threatening and supported by lightning arcing across his right hand. "I would like nothing better than to kill you. But I think we will want to question you. And know that we have men that are very skilled at getting information."

Lyra was in agony, flashes of stabbing pain piercing her back, but she had finally regained control of her senses. Yet despite the severity of her burns she could still walk. Crouching behind the tumbled kegs she looked upon the scene. Thalon was nowhere to be seen and Tulk and Ayden were about twenty paces before her seemingly conversing with the mage. She could see lightning dancing around his hand. He must have a mage stone as there was no Channeler about, except for Ayden, who would never allow the mage to pull energy from him.

Lyra looked for her bow and saw it tangled amongst some barrels. She could see that the bow string was now charred and had become unstrung. Quietly, she reached into a pouch on her belt and removed her backup string. Crouching, she put the edge of the bow against her foot and used her weight to bend it, hooking the loop of the string to the notch on the bow. It was a light bow, made for short distances, so she had no problem attaching the string without standing. She searched for an arrow in her quiver and only found two that had not been damaged by the flames. She nocked one and looked between the cracks of the barrels again.

The mage raised his right hand before him, more lightning arcing across his fingers. She could see Tulk twitch, as if he were losing the mental battle that was keeping him from attacking the mage.

"Don't do it," Lyra whispered to herself as she drew back on the bow. She knew that the mage would kill them both if Tulk moved. She also knew that she had a tough shot. The man wore armor and her bow was not powerful enough to pierce it. That meant she had to hit him in the face or perhaps an arm or leg. She took a deep breath, slowly releasing it between her lips, and silently opening her fingers to free the arrow. The short bolt shot forward and just when she was sure it would hit his throat, the man stepped back, raising his arm higher as if he were about to release the spell. The arrow hit him in the chin, the impact of metal on bone jerking his head to the side and opening a deep gash from his chin to his cheekbone. Stumbling, the mage regained his footing and turned to face the new threat, hoping to renew the spell that he had momentarily lost. But all he saw was a blurred shadow before everything went black. Tulk stepped away from the body as the mage's head thudded to the wood planks.

Lyra stumbled from behind the barrels, her bow held low at her side. Ayden assumed the arrow must have come from her. He rushed to her side and held her up as she was about to collapse. "I cannot create a spell," she stammered. "I need to go with you."

Ayden and Tulk quickly helped her into the boat. There was no sign of Thalon. The dock was nearly two paces above the water, so even if Thalon had survived the explosion there was no way he could have climbed back onto the dock from his position. He would have had to find another spot from which to pull himself out of the water. But they couldn't wait any longer. More guards would soon arrive. They had to hope that Thalon had escaped and would meet them at their rendezvous just up the shoreline. So, without looking back, Tulk grasped the oars with his powerful arms and quickly heaved the boat out into the water. Within moments they were moving rapidly away from the dock and into the protection of darkness.

***

Bannerfall

It had taken Brant only three months until he could hit a tree more than five times while keeping the metal ball at waist height as he held the end of the pole. He had worked at it at every possible moment. Early each morning he would get up and run, work the ball, and move through the sword positions. There were several occasions when he accompanied Kulvar and the Dygon Guard on Kul-brite transportation missions, and even then, when he wasn't leading the wagons, attending to the horses, or helping prepare the meals, he was working with the steel ball. Sheer determination had paid off, and one evening, while camping along the side of the road returning from Tanwen, he had done it. He had struck a tree seven times with his right hand and five times with his left.

His typically stoic Dygon Guard companions, most of whom had taken a sincere interest in his progress, clapped and cheered at his success. A few were sitting by the fire, resting from the long ride. But most were up sparring with swords. The Dygon Guard trained constantly, whether on a mission or not. It was something that had been ingrained into their psyche since they had begun training at the Warden Academy, to be at the peak of their physical fitness and to always have a sword ready to grasp in their hand. Kulvar made sure that the keen edge of their training was never dulled.

Kulvar clapped him on the back, smiling from ear to ear. "Well done, Brant. I would have thought it would take you longer, but I should have known better. A man with a will can move mountains."

Brant smiled with relief and satisfaction as he rubbed his sore forearms. "Will you teach me now?"

"I will. But not tonight. It will be dark soon and we should arrive at Cythera tomorrow. Let us begin then."

"I would like that. Thank you."

Kulvar was still smiling. "Come. Let's eat." They made their way to a fire surrounded by smiling Dygon Guards who congratulated him with pats on the back and kind words. The guards were tough men, quiet men, not typically ones to engage in casual banter, thus difficult to get to know. But Brant was somewhat comfortable with that, as he too was not prone to idle conversation. But he had slowly woven his way into the fabric of the close knit warriors. Kulvar had hired him as a driver and overall camp helper. The king had agreed, knowing that having a man who had reached the title of Ull Therm as a driver for their Kul-brite carts would not only provide more protection but would free up a Dygon Guard to fight if the need ever arose. It was a win win situation for everyone and Brant was more than willing to work for the king in that regard. He was not one of them, he knew that, but it was clear that they at least accepted him…at least most did. There was one young warrior who seemed distant, and there were numerous times when Brant caught him staring at him as if he were some sort of pariah. His name was Kay'il and he rarely spoke. But his looks and stares spoke volumes. It was obvious that he was not happy with Brant's presence.

Brant and Kulvar sat beside the fire and he couldn't help but notice Kay'il's cold stares. They were handed a bowl of rabbit stew and a thick slice of hard bread. Brant ate it quickly, trying all the while to not think about the glares coming from Kay'il.

Everyone was hungry and it didn't take long before they had consumed their meals. "I'm going to check on the horses," Kulvar announced as he stood up from the fire. It was now dark and Brant watched him blend into the darkness, heading for the small copse of trees where the horses were tied.

Kay'il ripped off a piece of dried bread, eating it slowly as he looked directly at Brant. "Why are you here?" he asked. They had never spoken before, and based on his behavior Brant figured there would be some sort of confrontation at some point. It looked as if tonight would be the night.

"What do you mean?" Brant responded, knowing full well what he meant.

He chewed slowly on his bread. "You should not be here. You do not have noble blood."

So that was it. Kay'il, like many nobles, saw commoners as beneath them. The other guards around the fire said nothing, curiously watching to see how the encounter played out. The Dygon Guard didn't make it a habit to defend one another, rather allowing, and expecting, each man to take care of their own personal issues. "I'm sorry you feel that way. You are right, I am no noble. I was in need, and Kulvar helped me. I will find my path soon, so there is no need to worry. I will not be here long."

"Do you know why he helped you?"

This time Kade spoke. "Kay'il,…that is enough."

There was no formal ranking within the Dygon Guard, but everyone knew the unofficial one. Kulvar was their leader, there was no doubt of that, and Kade was second in command, not just because of his superior skill, but because of his extensive experience as a Dygon Guard. Next to Kulvar, he was the most senior.

But Kay'il did not stop. "You remind him of his son. You should leave. I think your presence is bringing up painful memories."

Brant was caught off guard. He didn't know that Kulvar had a son. But now that he thought about it they did look similar. Both of them had that strong dominant chin, and dark hair, although Kulvar's was cut close to his scalp, and despite the difference in their eye color, both had piercing cold eyes. "I did not know he had a son. He has never spoken of it."

"That is because he is dead. He died when he was about your age, along with his mother."

"How?"

"The sickness swept through their town while he was away. They were dead by the time he returned." Again Kade interjected, "Now, that is enough talk of this. It is true, you do look like his son. But," Kade said, turning to Kay'il, "it is not our place to question Master Rand. He has his own reasons for the choices he makes, and whether you agree with them or not, Kay'il, is inconsequential. His choice in taking Brant in and helping him has done nothing but strengthen us in the process."

"I'm sorry, Kade, but I do not agree. He risked our lives to rescue him. And now, with the death of Tangar, he may have brought further danger upon us. Tangar's father is sure to want revenge. I am not so sure that Master Rand's decision was the best one."

"You may be right. But by all accounts Brant is strong, an adept warrior, a man of honor, and despite his lack of noble blood, he was given these gifts by Argon for a reason. Perhaps you are not looking at the big picture as is Master Rand. Master Rand has never let us down before. He obviously believes that rescuing Brant was worth the risks, and so far, knowing Brant's character, I agree. Now, enough of this talk."

Kay'il looked at Kade but said nothing, his eyes pivoting to Brant's as he tore off another piece of bread. Brant was too preoccupied with his own thoughts to notice Kay'il's malevolent glance. His mind drifted to Kulvar and he wondered if Kay'il was correct in his assessment.

***

Bannerfall

It had taken two weeks of constant bombardment to finally break through the city gate. They had pounded the walls with firebombs, launching hundreds of tynells, their explosive projectiles, over the walls to the buildings beyond. Keltius, after defeating what was left of the Kaelian navy, assaulted the city from the water's edge. Large catapults had been erected on the foredecks of his ships and they slung large clay firebombs at the city walls. The Kaelians bravely fought to defend their city, but in the end they could not hold out against the constant barrage of shelling. They had no defense against the flaming projectiles which destroyed whole sections of walls, and flattened the buildings and homes within the city. Raging fires spread rapidly, completing the devastation.

The main gate, now a wreckage of its former self, was blackened and bent, the steel reinforcements twisted amongst the thick timbers. The Kaelians had fought valiantly to protect the gate. But, eventually, the Saricons were able to hit the gate directly with a huge firebomb. The already weakened and charred wood sundered on impact, the massive explosion pushing the gate inward. The Kaelians sent a rain of arrows, spears, and stones onto the Saricons, who rushed forward with a huge battering ram to knock aside what was left of the damaged gate. Saricon warriors surrounded the men holding the ram, holding their shields aloft to protect them, but many of the attackers still perished under the onslaught. But when one fell, another took his place, until finally they were able to use the ram to smash through what was left of the gate.

Tongra Taruk stood eagerly behind his men as they poured through the gate in a river of steel and rage. He held his giant battle axe with one hand and felt the adrenaline rush through his body. Kahn Taruk was weary of the siege…he was eager to bloody his axe.

He charged through the gate with his men and quickly surveyed the scene. It was what he had expected. The defenders along the walls had joined forces with their men on the ground, forming a defensive wall of steel beyond the gate. Within their defensive wall was utter chaos. Panicked civilians screamed and Kaelian soldiers shouted orders as fires continued to rage through the ruins of homes and buildings. Two weeks of bombardment had left the city in shambles.

Kahn Taruk had seen if before. There would be one last push to destroy the invaders. But they would lose, and they would die. Hundreds of civilians, not willing to convert, would be killed as well.

But others, about a third, would convert and pledge their loyalty to the mighty Heln. Then they would rebuild the city in Heln's name. But Kahn Taruk was not thinking of the future; his muscular chest heaved as he breathed in deeply, his heart pounding with anticipation. All he wanted right now was to fight.

Hefting his battle axe he moved forward, his men flanking him with swords, axes, and shields held high. Arrows and spears came at them. Saricon shields came up in unison, forming a defensive wall as the projectiles slammed into them. With practiced precision they quickly dropped their shields to allow the men behind them to hurl their heavy javelins. The Kaelians used their shields as well, lifting them in defense, but they were much less effective. The heavy spears of the Saricons, thrown with incredible strength, found their targets. And when they struck the Kaelians' shields, they struck with such force that scores of the Kaelians were knocked to the ground.

"Charge!" Tongra Taruk yelled in Drak.

The two groups came together in a thundering clash of steel upon steel. Kahn Taruk swung his huge axe down, connecting solidly on a Kaelian shield. The power of the strike contorted the shield, cleaving a fold down the middle. The man behind the shield howled, his arm broken by the force of the blow. Kahn then kicked out with his right foot, knocking the man backward into the throng of warriors behind him, then followed the kick with a sideways arc of his axe, which struck another defender who was battling a Saricon warrior, cleaving his body nearly in half. He fell to the ground, his body unnaturally contorted. Despite the carnage, the Kaelian defenders continued to surge forward, spears and swords coming at the Saricons from all angles.

Kahn Taruk felt his Fury rise to the surface and he howled like a wild animal, the power of it surging into his limbs. Red fire flared from his eyes and he suddenly felt invincible. It was a strange phenomenon, but when he was possessed by the Fury, he saw everything in hues of reds and orange. And those around him appeared to be moving in slow motion as his own body, enhanced by energy, moved with incredible speed and power.

His men, sensing the power of his Fury, angled away from him, their axes and swords directed at the enemies on his flanks, enabling him to surge forward, his body and axe a blur of motion. They needed to stay out of his way and give him room to kill. This was not the first time they had experienced their Tongra's Fury, and they knew what to do. Nothing could touch Kahn Taruk. He perceived every attack before it could occur, his body and axe spinning, blocking, and attacking almost simultaneously. Blood sprayed as his silver axe cut its way through the brave Kaelian warriors as his own soldiers frantically did their best to help him cut their way through the defensive line. And the Saricon assault was more than effective. The defenders were tossed aside like children, their bodies cut and bleeding.

Suddenly a warrior appeared, attacking the Tongra with a speed matching his own. He was a Merger, probably one of the few remaining from one of the noble families. During the two week siege, Kahn Taruk had sent in the Shadows, who had assassinated as many of the remaining Aura Mages as possible. They had targeted anyone known to possess the Way, but they were bound to have missed some. It had cost him a fortune, but he had to admit that the Shadows were proving themselves to be a valuable asset. Working with mercenaries, however, was always unpredictable. One had to assure their loyalty by paying the highest possible price. If not, they could be bought by one's rivals and turn against you. Kahn Taruk knew that paying the exorbitant fees demanded by the Shadows accomplished two tasks; they not only performed their duties as required, but they had no motivation to double cross him. And the Tongra also knew that Thalon and his assassins hated the Argonians. They hated everyone from Corvell. It had been their own people after all who had hunted them down and tried to kill them just for being different, their own people who had made them what they were today. That hatred, and Kahn Taruk's coin, had guaranteed them to be powerful allies.

The Merger came at Kahn Taruk with incredible speed, his polished silver sword erupting with green fire. The Tongra quickly thrust his axe forward, catching the sword on the front of his axe between the two blades where they connected to the thick handle. As the sword struck the Tongra's axe the green flames flared even brighter, slicing through the steel and dropping half of Kahn Taruk's axe blade to the ground. But the Tongra had anticipated that could happen, having fought against the famous Kul-brite blades before. With lightning speed he angled the axe head to the right, turning the remaining deadly blade away from himself, as he spun his weapon around and used the blunt end to deal a devastating blow to the swordsman's chin. His head jerked sideways, his jaw broken, and Kahn Taruk quickly reversed the weapon again, spinning around and using the single remaining axe blade to strike the surprised swordsman in the face. Stepping over the bloodied fallen warrior, Kahn Taruk roared, his Fury raging inside him. Rivers of blood ran along the cobblestones as the Saricon horde slowly but inexorably overran the Kaelian defenders, the enraged Tongra, his fiery eyes flashing red, leading the way.

***

Karnack squatted next to Obaty, gazing at the seemingly endless Sil Desert below. They had descended the northern reaches of the Pyres Mountains and now squatted upon a cliff face, the ten thousand strong Saricon army spread along the mountain trail behind them, taking a much needed rest. It had taken them a little over two months, and the trip had not gone without difficulties. The trail was arduous, and certainly not meant for an army to traverse. Days had been spent clearing the path in several locations, where the thick trees and brush had nearly obliterated the trail, making travel nearly impossible. The extra time and effort required to clear the path had caused them to nearly exhaust their provisions. More time, then, had to be spent hunting to supplement their meat rations. By the time they had reached the end of their journey, roughly fifteen men had been lost. Three had fallen to their deaths as they traversed a particularly narrow rocky section of the trail along a steep cliff. The loose rocks made for unstable footing, and one misplaced foot, especially when men were tired and hungry, could lead to sudden death. Six more men, who had somehow wandered off the trail during a blinding snowstorm, were never seen again.

The worst loss of life, however, occurred on a night when the full moon had been covered by a thick layer of clouds, revealing only a faint halo of light which did nothing to diminish the darkness. Six men were killed while everyone was sleeping. They were set upon by three Gullicks, rare yet dangerous beasts that inhabit the high elevations of the mountain ranges across Belorth and Corvell. Twice the size of any man, the bear-like creatures are covered with a thick coat of white hair. Quicker and five times more powerful than any known bear, they have adapted to the harsh environment of the high mountains. Though vicious, they are not evil like some other creatures; they are simply animals trying to survive the harsh conditions in which they live. The creatures had stalked the men silently, then striking with incredible remained relatively small and fairly stable, anywhere from five to fifteen. When one was born with the gift, they were taught early how to train and handle the torgs, as well as how to fight from their backs.

"Soon, KeeAysa, you and your riders will serve Heln's cause," Karnack said.

"That is good. We are tired of waiting. We want Argonian blood." The torg, sensing her emotions, growled softly, its large paws shuffling with anticipation, the black claws gouging the gray stone.

***

They were four days into their retreat from Lyone before Jarak found the time to talk with Prince Daricon about what he had found. It had been nagging at him for days, but the staggered retreat from the garrison had been chaotic, despite their planning. Food and supplies had to be carefully monitored and transported up and down the long line of people. And not all were warriors who had been trained for, and were accustomed to strenuous marches. In addition to the warriors there were several hundred men and women who were servants or family members of the officers. They had to constantly run scouting parties in front of the line looking for any possible attack from brigands or Schulg nomads, while simultaneously maintaining a defensive retreat at the rear of the column. They assumed the Saricons would not leave the garrison and follow them so quickly, but they couldn't be sure.

Prince Jarak had been riding hard, leaving the rear of the column several hours ago. Cat was among that group and he had wanted to check on her while inspecting their food and water supplies. He saw Daricon at the head of the column and galloped over to him, reining in his horse abruptly as he drew near. The middle aged lieutenant, Bal'tour, rode beside Daricon.

"How would you assess our supply situation?" Daricon asked, smiling.

"It is fine," Prince Jarak replied, ignoring him. He knew that Daricon was aware of his feelings for Cat, but he wasn't going to play into his game. "We will need to procure some more beans by tomorrow but the water supply looks good. Bal'tour, will you excuse us for a moment. I wish to speak with Lord Daricon in private."

"As you wish, my Prince," he replied, turning his horse around to find someone to ride with down the column.

Daricon looked at him. "What is it?"

"I've wanted to talk with you but we've been so preoccupied." Jarak hesitated before continuing. "I saw something at the garrison that is disturbing."

Daricon pursed his lips. "Oh?"

"Down in the cellar. Jayla found a secret door."

This time Daricon looked surprised. "A secret door? I've been at the garrison for fifteen years and I've never heard of such a thing. Where did it lead?"

"To a room. It was a shrine to Heln."

"Are you certain? There are no Helnians here, nor have there ever been at the garrison."

"I am certain and obviously that is not true. There was an altar along with their Torgot."

Daricon spit on the ground in disgust. "Their book was there?"

"Yes. What do you think? Who could have built such a room without anyone knowing?"

Daricon was silent, looking ahead across the expansive steppe, deep in thought. Endless grasslands speckled with small groves of trees spread out before them as far as the eye could see. Finally he looked back at Jarak. "Who else knows of this?"

Jarak shook his head. "No one. Just Jayla and I."

"Let's keep it that way. Obviously we have a spy in our midst. I need to think on this. But for now, there is nothing we can do. We will soon arrive at Cythera and we will have plenty of work to do to prepare for a possible siege. I will need you vigilant, and be aware of anything out of the ordinary. If you hear or see anything strange, make sure you let me know."

"I will. It has me worried, Uncle. I mean, how long has the spy been there and for what purpose? I do not like the unknowns."

"Nor I." But Prince Daricon said no more, his thoughts already occupied by the implications and possibilities.

***

Brant gave a subtle jerk of his wrist which belied its great power, knocking Master Rand's sword to the side, then flicking the blade back around to hit him in the chest, the tip of the blade scraping along his armor.

Bannerfall

"Well done!" Kulvar Rand exclaimed, stepping back and smiling. They had been working on the move for quite some time and finally Brant had broken through his defenses. For three months they had been training together, Master Rand showing him the intricacies of real sword work. They did the usual; working on conditioning and sword forms, but the real focus of their work was training to use the power of the wrist to create openings, and then using that same power to exploit them.

This secret style of swordplay had been created four cyns ago by Kilt Rand, another Dygon Guard and distant relative of Master Rand. It had fittingly been named the Kilting Way. It was not typically taught to anyone outside the Dygon Guard. But Master Rand made an exception with Brant. He taught him that with sufficient speed, knowledge, and power, a true swordsman could end a duel in a few heartbeats. That was of, course, unless your opponent had also been trained in the Kilting Way.

"Thank you," Brant said, lowering the tip of the Kul-brite blade. Master Rand had allowed him to use the blade when they trained at his estate. They had gone out on several more missions, moving more Kul-brite than they had in a long time. The king had secret hiding places for the steel, and Master Rand was stockpiling it for the coming invasion. He did not want the Saricons to get their hands on it. When they weren't on missions procuring and transporting Kul-brite, they were training and helping prepare the city for a possible siege. So far all they knew was that the Saricons had conquered Eltus and destroyed the Kaelian navy. As of now they had no reports of any Saricons moving towards Cythera. At least not yet.

"Now, let us try using the Way," Master Rand continued.

Brant nodded and widened his legs, concentrating on his aura. They had not been practicing this skill for long and Brant still had a lot to learn. But he was improving, and under the meticulous eye of Kulvar Rand he was improving at a faster than normal rate.

Kulvar's eyes narrowed as he focused on his own aura, surging the explosive energy into his muscles. In a snap of the fingers he was attacking. They danced for several moments, their swords flashes of light as they spun around, attacking, countering, and attacking again. They continued their sword dance across the cobblestones, their feet a blur of motion, while their swords clashed with such incredible speed they sounded as if five black smiths were continuously hitting hammer

Bannerfall

to anvil heartbeats after one another. Anyone listening to the cadence would never guess that it was a duel. It was simply too fast.

By this time Ari had come from the house, attracted by the sound of the duel. He leaned against the stables, his eyes wide as he tried to visualize the fight, but the bodies of the warriors were moving too fast for someone who was not a Merger to witness.

Suddenly Kulvar's blade knocked Brant's aside, allowing him to smack the side of Brant's arm with the flat of the blade. The move was barely detectable, but it had been enough. If he had hit him with the razor sharp edge, his forearm would have been split open.

Brant stepped back for a moment, narrowed his eyes, and attacked again, surging more energy into his limbs. But Kulvar Rand was there to meet every strike, and once again was able to knock his blade to the side and whip it back this time to hit him in the thigh. Without stopping, Brant growled in anger and came at Master Rand again. This time he surged more energy into his legs, hoping to use the extra speed to get past his defenses. It didn't work. In fact, it made things worse. Kulvar stepped back quickly as Brant rushed forward, his enhanced speed shooting him forward like a rocket. Never stopping, Kulvar spun like a top, avoiding Brant's sword, his own blade leading the way to hit Brant in the back, nearly knocking him to the ground.

Now Brant was furious. The familiar anger breached its cage and new aura energy stormed through his body. Without thinking, he directed it into his blade, the Kul-brite steel all but begging for it. Blue fire burst from the blade and he jumped forward, his blade moving so fast that all one could see were the tracers of light left behind.

Now Kulvar's blade instantly erupted in green fire as the two blades came together. Again, they danced across the courtyard; their fiery blades striking each other so many times that an observer would be unable to count them. Brant gritted his teeth together, allowing the anger to push more energy into his limbs, pushing them to new limits. His sword flared brighter, the Kul-brite steel seeming to come alive, humming as if with joy. Brant was relishing the powerful, almost ecstatic sensations he was feeling. Until it suddenly evaporated, replaced by a blackness that nearly overwhelmed him as his head snapped back from Master Rand's kick. Somehow, Kulvar had angled Brant's blade away, and snapped his foot forward, hitting Brant so hard that it nearly broke his jaw. Brant stumbled backwards, his anger slipping away like water in a drain.

"Brant!" Kulvar yelled, "stop!"

Brant dropped to a knee, overwhelmed by exhaustion, his body suddenly feeling the need to collapse to the ground. His jaw hurt like hell and his nose was bleeding, maybe broken. He looked up at Kulvar, suddenly feeling like an admonished child. He had lost control, allowing his anger to manipulate him. "I'm sorry," he whispered.

Ari was at his side, trying to help him stand. Kulvar was furious, his dark eyes boring into him, increasing his feeling of shame. "What happened?" He stormed.

"I got angry…and…it took over."

"I could have killed you," he said, his voice dropped in volume but did not lose its intensity. "I did not know you could Fuse. Has this happened before?"

"Fuse?"

"It means you have the ability to manipulate your aura in conjunction with Kul-brite steel. Mergers who can Fuse can bring forth energy in their weapons. Few, however, have that ability. Now, have you done this before?"

"Yes," he whispered. He was so tired. If it weren't for Ari helping him stand, he would probably lie down on the ground and fall asleep. "While I was staying at Kaan's home we were attacked by a young kulg. I used it then. I destroyed two of his swords but killed the kulg. I did not know what it was. I'm sorry I said nothing. I know now I should have."

"Brant, if I am to train you properly I must know what you are capable of. And," he emphasized, "you have to learn to control your anger. That will most definitely get you killed. You need to rest now. You used so much of your energy that you nearly passed out. I thought you were going to destroy the blade. I'm sorry about the kick, but it was necessary."

"I deserved it. It won't happen again."

"See to it. Now, Ari, take Brant to his room to rest. We will speak of this again." Kulvar Rand took the sword from Brant's hand as the young boy led him to his room.

As tired as Brant was, sleep eluded him. He felt horrible about the previous evening's events, and spent most of the night worrying about it. And his nose and jaw really hurt. Luckily, neither were broken, but his jaw ached and his nose was swollen and turning a light shade of purple. When morning finally came, he dressed and washed his face with cold water, then made his way to the kitchen. There were two servants about prepping for the day's meals. The sun had barely risen so breakfast was not yet ready, but Brant grabbed a sweet muffin made the previous day, along with an apple, and headed out to the training yard.

Like everyone else at Master Rand's estate he had daily tasks to perform. When he wasn't traveling with Kulvar Rand it was expected that he pull his own weight, which for Brant was a forgone conclusion. The idea of doing nothing while eating and sleeping under someone else's roof was something he would never entertain. So he spent the next three hours cleaning the stables and feeding and grooming the horses. Next he oiled and polished all the practice weapons and armor. By that time he was really hungry so he made his way back to the kitchen, grabbed some bread, cured ham, and another apple, and quickly returned to the stables. Now it was time to train.

Master Rand had what he called a Kilting Dummy. It was a heavy log about the height of a man with stout pieces of wood about the length of a man's arm sticking out from it at different angles and heights. The entire structure was too heavy to lift but could be moved using the two wheels positioned on the edge of its base. When it was tilted on edge, the wheels caught, and it could be moved about with relative ease. The days were becoming shorter and the leaves had begun to turn shades of red and gold. But the days were still relatively comfortable. The sun was out and the air was cool and crisp. It was a great day to train. So Brant wheeled the dummy out into the middle of the courtyard and stood it up, the wooden posts sticking out in all directions and elevations. Before practicing with the sword, Brant wanted to perform the Ga'ton, eager to put his body through the strenuous movements. He had been working on the forms for over a year now and was performing admirably. His strong body and focused mind carried him through the movements with smooth precision. Remembering back he thought how much he had improved. When he first started he couldn't even remember all the positions, let alone perform them. It took him many months before his body was able to hold the positions and carry him through the movements. But over time his muscles attuned to the forms and slowly, with great effort, he was able to perform the entire Ga'ton with graceful and powerful movements. He finished the forms and relished in the warmth flooding his muscles and the sheen of sweat covering his body. Now he was ready to practice the sword forms. He grabbed a Kilting Way practice sword, which was a basic blade with added weight at the tip.

Staring at the structure, he visualized the moves he had been working on. Then he started slowly, using the tip of the heavy blade and his powerful wrist to strike each of the wood arms, moving up and down and across the dummy. He pivoted left and right and moved around the dummy, all the while his blade flicking into the wood appendages with a thud. Then he switched hands, working his left just as hard as his right. It wasn't long before he was sweating, and that was when he picked up the pace. Gradually the rhythm became faster, the thud of steel on wood the only sound in the courtyard. He switched to a two hand grip, adding to the power of his strikes. Faster and faster he went as his sword continued to dance all across the structure, the heavy blade smacking into the wooden arms. Although the blade was dull, the constant sparring with the dummy had created worn grooves across the arms and it wouldn't be long before they would have to be replaced.

His body could move no faster without using his aura. So he narrowed his eyes and concentrated on his aura, electrifying his body with its power. Now he looked like a hummingbird, its wings a blur as it flitted from flower to flower. The strikes of the heavy sword on wood became so rapid that the sounds blended together into what sounded like one long *thud*, the intervals between each strike unrecognizable to the human ear.

Eventually one of the arms succumbed to the constant barrage of strikes and split almost in two, hanging an awkward angle. Within several heartbeats Brant had reduced his speed to normal, until finally he stopped, his body drenched in sweat.

"I will have to take that from your pay."

Brant turned around and saw Master Rand approach from the main house. He was smiling, which was good. Maybe the conversation they were about to have wouldn't be so bad. Brant smiled back. "Fair enough."

"You've improved a lot. To be honest you are as good as most of my Dygon Guards, perhaps better than some."

"Thank you," Brant said awkwardly, both because he was not accustomed to praise and he still felt ashamed about his behavior the night before. "I want to tell you again that I am sorry for losing control last night."

Bannerfall

"I know you are," Kulvar Rand said. "I'm not angry with you. I'm concerned. If my striking you several times was all it took to bring forth that anger, then I'm worried that you will not have the control necessary for battle. If you were fighting a duel against a skilled swordsman, he would surely exploit that anger, which could potentially get you killed. And, if you were fighting next to a fellow warrior, your lack of discipline would not only get you killed but it could potentially be fatal for the men on your flanks." There was a bench nestled among some flowers and shrubs near the edge of the courtyard and Kulvar sat down on it, directing Brant to do the same. "You must learn to control this anger."

"I know...it...um...rises up so quickly...it's hard to control it as I don't recognize it until it's too late."

"Where does this anger come from?"

Brant thought about it for a moment, delving into his memories and trying to figure out why it was always just below the surface, ready to break free from the muck of his psyche. He looked down at the ground for a moment, but then the answer came to him quickly. "My Father," Brant finally said, looking up at Kulvar Rand. "He was not a nice man. He treated me poorly and never showed me any act of kindness. I do not think it mattered to him what would become of me."

"And that angers you?"

Brant paused for a moment. "Yes, it does. Each time you hit me with your sword I pictured my father doing it, and...well, I lost control."

This time it was Kulvar who paused thoughtfully. "I too had a similar issue, but my anger was not directed at my father, but at Argon."

"You were angry at your god?"

"Yes. You may have heard that my wife and son died years ago of the fever that passed through Dy'ain. I was away at the time. I never even got to say goodbye. Why would Argon allow my wife and child to die such a senseless death? I have served him my entire life, and that is the payment that I receive. It made me very angry."

"Your anger seems justified."

"As does yours. But it did me no good. It ate me up and I became less of a man."

"How did you deal with your anger?" Brant asked, hoping for some insight on how he could control his own.

"I had a very wise man help me," Kulvar answered with a smile.

Bannerfall

"Who was that?"

"My father." Kulvar laughed at the irony.

"Well, what did he tell you?"

"Many wise things. But the one thing I remember most was when he told me that if you are patient in one moment of anger, you will escape a hundred days of sorrow. It is true, you know. When you act out of anger you are not likely rational, and it only brings you grief and more anger. If you embrace only anger you will fall into a hole of bad choices from which you cannot climb out. I was up to my neck in grief and anger. But I dug my way out. I learned to forgive, and my anger left me." Brant thought back to his incident with Tage and couldn't agree more with Kulvar's words. If he had been able to control his anger, he never would have killed him, thus he would never have set the ball in motion that ended with him fighting in the Schulg pit. So many bad things happened because of that one action sparked by anger. Kulvar looked at Brant, his eyes serious. "Can you learn to forgive your father?"

Brant looked away, pondering Kulvar's words. "I do not know," he finally said, looking back at Master Rand. "But I will try."

"That is good," Kulvar Rand said, smacking Brant on the leg and standing up quickly. "Now, let us test this new resolve of yours. Go to the house and get the Kul-brite blade."

Brant smiled and ran to the house, leaving Kulvar to his own thoughts, drifting from images of his father to his wife and son. *He is a lot like my son*, he thought, trying to imagine his own son at Brant's age.

***

Cat had to admit that she felt out of place. She had finally been allowed to join the Legion, but it wasn't her recent admittance to the military that had her stomach churning with nervous energy, it was the fact that she was no longer stationed among the troops from Lyone, soldiers that she had known for years, who knew her, and more importantly her father, as well. Now she stood in a line, wearing Legionnaire armor, holding a long spear and listening to Sergeant Lynel yell instructions at them as he paced up and down the lines. She was surrounded by men, most who seemed indifferent to her. There were several, however, who glanced boldly at her with undisguised desire.

Bannerfall

There were only two other women in her three hundred man battalion and one would have to look twice to recognize that they were female. They were both big and stocky, their female attributes well hidden by their armor. But Cat, despite the armor, was lithe and sinewy, her narrow waist and hips clearly a sign of her gender. Most knew who her father was and figured that was why she was there. Most of the men, and even the other women, did little to hide their sneers, and their whispers were often just loud enough for her to hear. Many comments seemed to suggest that she was allowed into the infantry because of her father's standing, or even more scandalous, and ridiculous, that she had somehow earned her entry by bedding down with the powers that be. There were some, however, who were not unpleasant toward her. They didn't go out of their way to befriend her, but they at least spoke with her on occasion and didn't take part in the insults. But few could deny her skill with a sword, and it didn't take long before her talent added fuel to some of the recruits' anger. Most didn't think a female belonged in the military, and when they realized that she could best them with a blade their humiliation just made things worse. She was hoping things would eventually get better. After all, they couldn't get much worse.

As a new recruit she had been training for the last three weeks, ever since they had arrived from the garrison. She already knew how to fight in hand to hand combat, better than many of her instructors. But she had almost no idea about how to fight in formation using shields and spears. The work had been grueling. Her day began with early morning formation training combined with long marches. There was a short rest for lunch, followed by more drills and practice. Then, after a quick dinner, the training would again resume, halted only by the setting sun. Although she was exhausted, both physically and mentally, she had actually enjoyed the martial training, enthusiastically soaking up a vast amount of new skills, techniques, and information. Today they were performing their first live formation drills with wooden practice swords and blunt tipped spears. Despite the lack of real weapons, it was very dangerous. No one pulled their strikes and it wasn't uncommon for recruits to get injured or to even break bones.

Following the screaming sergeant's orders the recruits broke up into their platoons. They were outside the city walls on the training grounds adjacent to the northern wall. There was plenty of room there for their mock combat, and after several minutes the officers had each platoon facing another. The lead platoons were backed by reserve platoons making their formation two lines deep. Normally, in battle, their infantry might be four lines deep, but for training purposes they were keeping it simple. Cat's platoon was the front line of her team, which equaled two platoons, and as she gazed at the recruits facing her she prayed to Argon that her nerves would calm.

 She glanced to her left and right and noticed most of the fifteen men in her platoon looked like she felt, nervous. The only soldier who appeared calm, almost eager, was a man named Boris who stood on her right. She didn't know him well but he seemed to treat her fairly. He saw her look at him and he winked back. "You ready for this?"

"I think so."

"Be careful of Torrin, he has it out for you."

 Cat looked across the fifteen paces to the soldiers facing her and saw Torrin standing among them. The tall warrior caught her eyes, his lips curling up in a wicked smile that looked more like a sneer. And sure enough he was positioned in the line directly opposite her. She had defeated him once in sword practice and ever since then he had gone out of his way to ridicule her. Now she was facing him in formation and that worried her. Formation fighting was nothing like a sword duel. You fought side by side, protecting one another's flanks, jabbing forward with your spear until you lost the weapon or it broke, at which point you used your infantry sword, all the while holding the line while using your shield to protect those beside you. Your movement was limited and you had more than just yourself to worry about. Your job, besides keeping yourself alive, was to protect the men, or women, that flanked you.

 There were twenty platoons positioned throughout the training ground and not one man or woman said a word. The tension and nervous energy was thick. Handfuls of officers were positioned all around the platoons and their job was to monitor the fighting. Anyone struck in the chest with a spear was required to withdraw from the fighting, and if they failed to do so the officers would pull the offender clear under a barrage of insults followed by extra work details for their dishonesty. Sword strikes to the torso were also considered kills. But those were the only restrictions of combat. It was 'anything goes' after that. Everyone knew it wasn't a perfect replica of an actual battle. That wasn't the point. The point of the drill was to have the recruits experience the actual chaos of battle, how it felt to have spears and swords coming at them, trying to stay alive, and protect their comrades, while attempting to stay in formation.

Bannerfall

"Ready!" the sergeant yelled.

Cat lifted her shield and readied her spear. Hundreds of others did the same thing in unison. She took several deep breaths, staring at Torrin over the edge of her shield.

"Charge!"

All fifteen warriors of her platoon shot forward, followed by the reserve line behind her. Their role was to fill in the positions vacated by fallen comrades. If their formation broke, they would lose. The officers would sound a horn which would signal the end of the exercise. The side that had the most soldiers remaining would win the bout, earning the rest of the evening off. Needless to say, everyone wanted to win.

The two platoons came together in a tremendous clash of wooden shields and blunted spears. Spears flew forward over enemy shields searching for targets. Torrin's spear just missed her head and she was jarred backwards a few steps by the strength of his shield charge which nearly knocked her into the man behind her. Cat was not as strong as most of the men and she was forced to rely on her speed and cunning. She jabbed her spear at Torrin, but it missed, hitting the man behind him directly in the forehead. He fell to the ground, stunned, and an officer quickly jumped in and dragged him out of the fray. Instead of withdrawing her spear she snapped the weapon sideways hitting Torrin in the side of the head. It wasn't a killing stroke but she was confident that it had hurt him. Suddenly the man to Torrin's left brought the edge of his shield down on the shaft of her spear, snapping the weapon in half. He then brought his spear back before ramming the blunt tip forward, attempting to strike her chest while her own shield was occupied with Torrin's. Clearly the two had worked out a plan. They were ganging up on her.

That strategy might work for one on one combat, but it was a stupid plan when fighting in formations. The man was so preoccupied attacking Cat that he failed to notice Boris's spear coming at him and was too slow to avoid the strike. Boris quickly shoved his spear forward and over the man's shield, striking him squarely in the chest, knocking him off balance and throwing off his aim as his spear whistled harmlessly over Cat's head.

"You're out!" an officer yelled as the man howled in frustration, jumping to the back of the formation and out of the melee.

Torrin growled in anger as his spear was ripped from his hands by a soldier to Cat's left. By now most of the spears had been lost, knocked from the warrior's hands or even broken, and the remaining solders now fought with short infantry swords. Cat had thrown her broken shaft at Torrin. He blocked it with his shield, but she was able to simultaneously draw her wooden practice sword. There was no one to fill the gap to Torrin's left as the warrior closest to him was frantically defending himself. Torrin's line had lost more fighters than Cat's line, and despite their reserves, had widening gaps in the front line. So he was forced to fight furiously to avoid the strikes from Cat and Boris. It appeared to Cat that Boris was taking an extra interest in Torrin, perhaps noticing that they had attempted to gang up on her, or maybe he just didn't like him. After all, he was not well liked by most.

"Push forward!" Boris yelled, eager to exploit the gaps in the line before them. Swords and shields banged together as her platoon used their greater numbers to push them back on their heels. Cat growled and used her speed to duck, block, and strike, focusing her attention on Torrin but being careful to watch the flanks of her comrades. Several times she lunged to the right and left, blocking blows meant for her comrades, while using her speed to strike at Torrin, always looking for an opening.

Being forced to cover more ground, Torrin leaped back and forth along the line, yelling maniacally as he narrowly avoided strike after strike coming at him from all angles. Cat had to give it to him; he was fighting bravely and skillfully. But then she saw her opening. Boris came at him high with his sword forcing him to raise his shield and expose his mid-section. Cat glanced to her left and saw one of the few remaining spears descend towards the man on her left flank. She had to make a choice. She could jab her sword forward and strike Torrin in the chest, or lunge to her left with her sword and deflect the spear meant for her comrade who was preoccupied with another fighter. It had to be her sword as she didn't have enough time to get the shield in the right position to intercept the spear. Without further thought she pivoted to her left, snapped her sword forward, and deflected the spear just enough to cause it to go harmlessly above his head. With relief that her deflection was true, she noticed her comrade on her left quickly glance at her before jabbing his own sword forward to strike the spear wielder in his exposed stomach.

Torrin growled as he blocked Boris's strike, his eyes widening momentarily as he realized he was exposed. He saw Cat turn her attention from him to an opponent on his right. He narrowed his eyes, capitalizing on his opportunity, and lunged forward hoping to hit Cat in the side.

Her peripheral vision caught his movement as he came at her. Cat, like her father, was known for her quickness and agility. He had given her the nickname. Everyone thought it referred to her real name, Ca'tel, but in fact it referred to her speed and agility. She fought on her toes, her knees slightly bent, her center of gravity low, enabling her to change direction quickly. As she deflected the spear away, she lunged back to her right, ducking incredibly low beneath Torrin's sword, and popping up on the inside of his sword arm, a feat aided by her diminutive size. It had happened so quickly that he didn't even have time to wipe the gloating sneer off his face before Cat's fist, the one holding the wooden sword, struck him under the chin, snapping his head back and knocking him to the ground.

"Get back in formation!" Boris yelled to her right.

Cat lifted her shield to block another soldier's strike as she scooted back a few steps. Feeling a moment of relative safety with her comrades beside her, she had a quick moment to smile as she pictured Torrin's face just before she struck him.

Then the horn blew and everyone stopped fighting. Stepping back and away from the platoon they were fighting everyone finally had a moment to survey the damage. Cat counted fifteen men left on her team from the original thirty, every one of them panting and sweating as they tried to catch their breath, some bleeding from various 'non-lethal' blows to their bodies. The opposing team had only eight men remaining. They had won.

A thin man with a dark beard tapped his sword on her shield. It was the man that had fought on her left, the very same man she had saved from the spear strike. "Nice work," he said. "I'm Ballin."

"Thanks. I'm Cat."

"I know."

Then he walked away. She was suddenly exhausted and her wooden sword felt as if it were made of lead. Her arms burned with fatigue but she still managed a smile as she glanced over and saw several men try to rouse Torrin. She had knocked him out.

"Don't think that'll make him like ya," Boris laughed.

Cat smiled. "He nearly had me. Thanks for your help."

Boris shrugged. "Just doing my job." Then he walked off to get some water.

Job, Cat thought. It was her job now as well and the reality of it suddenly struck home. For the first time she wondered if she had made the right decision in joining the Legion. After all, it would be no easy life.

Chapter 10

What is it that makes someone heroic? Is it bred into them, as many of the nobility believe? Is it taught, similar to teaching someone how to read and write? Or is it a trait that any person, noble or commoner, can possess? Perhaps it is a gift from Argon and Felina? Perhaps we all have a penchant for altruistic behavior that just needs to be nurtured by the right circumstances or mentors. I do not know the answer but the selfless acts of some people have always inspired me. I've witnessed various acts of bravery and have read about many more, and every time I always wonder how I would react in the same situations. Would I show bravery while facing adversity and danger? Could one tell if one would rise to the occasion just by looking at them? I think not. Heroes can come in any size and shape. Clearly, a warrior, trained to fight, who gives up his life protecting his people is a hero. But so is a child, homeless and starving, who faces his or her problems head on and spits in the face of adversity. A widow raising her children alone while running a small farm is also clearly a hero.

War is a terrible thing. The dark shadow of it suffocates everything, but always there is a glimmer of hope, a flame lit by heroism. The dark hand of death accompanies war, but always, whether it's a farmer protecting his family, a young boy picking up a blade in defense of his home, or a Dygon Guard standing before a horde of Saricons, there are heroes to beat back the darkness. I hope that if I'm ever faced with choosing between the fear of death and an act of heroism, that I act heroically, that my actions will help bring light into the darkness. I would hope that I would act heroically, but to be honest I do not truly know. My future actions are unknown to me, and that alone brings me great consternation.

Journal entry 101

Kivalla Der'une, Historian, Keeper of the records in Cythera, capital of Dy'ain

Bannerfall

5091, 14th cyn after the Great Change

    King Enden Dormath, wearing full battle armor, stood upon the western wall looking out to the Dark Sea. It was mid-day and the fall skies were clear. Off in the distance along the western shore were dark shapes, nearly a hundred, their billowing white sails dropping as their anchors dropped into the water. They were miles away and just specks on the horizon, but he could tell, even at such great distance, that it was a sizable force. The Saricons had arrived.

    Jarak was also in full armor, armor fitting for the future king of Dy'ain. The silver polished steel was in sharp contrast to the black cape he wore. Daricon and Jarak, along with the remaining forces from Lyone, had arrived in Cythera nearly a month ago. Every moment of every day since then had been a whirlwind of preparation. Scouts had been sent west, and south, constantly looking for signs of the Saricons. A few days ago they had returned with grave news. The small army of Saricons that had taken the garrison was now on their way to Cythera, destroying anyone and anything in their path. Scouts had also been sent north and they had not yet returned. King Enden wondered when they would arrive with news of reinforcements from Tanwen and Kreb, and their absence had given him considerable trepidation. After all, the ships on the horizon were not trading vessels. They were outfitted for war.

    "What do you make of it, Father?" Jarak Dormath asked.

    "Hard to say at this distance," the king said. "I have scouts out now. But my guess would be that there are around a hundred ships. Each ship can carry no more than two hundred men."

    "Twenty thousand," Jarak added.

    Daricon came up the steps along the inner wall and joined them. His face was red as if he had been running. "I was just given word. How many?" he asked, squinting as he gazed along the coastline.

    "Could be twenty thousand men, but I'll know more when my scouts return," the king replied. "We can't forget the twenty five hundred coming from Lyone. You did well reducing their numbers, both of you."

    "What are our numbers?" Daricon asked.

    "Within the city we have ten thousand Legionnaires not including my Sentinels. We should be seeing reinforcements from

Tanwen and Kreb soon," King Dormath replied, trying to sound hopeful.

"How many Legionnaires will we be getting from Tanwen and Kreb?" Jarak asked.

"Two thousand each," King Enden Dormath replied running his hand through his long hair. "I put a call out to all the provinces requesting retired Legionnaires. That should bring in another couple thousand."

"Let's not forget our Dygon Guard. Fifty of them are worth a thousand men," Daricon said, trying to lift the spirits of the weary king. Clearly the stress of the coming conflict had kept King Dormath from sleeping well; he was obviously worn out.

"That is true."

"Brother, let us all eat together this evening in the great hall. We need to rest. I've had Jayla working on a special dinner since yesterday. You have not met her yet, but I think it wise that you taste her cooking first." Daricon was smiling and Jarak joined in, the thought of the brusque headstrong woman meeting his father was quite amusing.

"I agree, Father. Her food is fantastic."

"Very well. But after dinner I want all the officers to meet in the council hall. We will need to discuss the information brought to us by our scouts and what to do about this fleet."

"It will be done," Daricon said.

"Are we going to send our fleet and army out to meet them?" Daricon asked.

The king sighed. "That will be the focal point of our conversation this evening. Now, if you will excuse me. I need to meet with my quartermaster." King Dormath strode from the battlements and made his way down the steep stairs of the inner wall.

"You should bring Cat tonight," Daricon suggested.

"She has guard duty tonight patrolling the eastern wall."

Daricon shrugged. "Perhaps another time. I'll see you this evening." Patting Jarak on the shoulder he followed his brother, leaving Jarak gazing out to the ships beyond. It was a foreboding question. Would they be able to withstand the Saricon horde when so many in the past had not? He did not like the idea of inheriting the position of king when he had no kingdom to rule.

Bannerfall

It was near dark and Jarak was in his quarters preparing for the evening meal when he received a summons. His father had requested his presence in his study. He was nearly ready, wearing a beautifully tailored shirt, tunic, and breeches, all made of soft gray cotton and hemmed with silver thread. The tunic was trimmed in bright blue silk and the center was adorned with House Dormath's symbol embroidered in silver. It was cinched tightly around his waist with a black belt, his Mage Stone embedded in its polished silver buckle. He wanted to hurry as he had planned on paying Cat a surprise visit on the wall before he made his way to dinner. Now he would be pressed for time and more than likely late for dinner.

He quickly made his way through the palace passing several guard rooms in the process. The Sentinels were on alert, which was customary for the elite warriors. But now there was a more palpable feeling of danger with the Saricons so close, and that had put them on edge. No one wanted anything to happen to their king on their watch. Jarak greeted the last guard standing before the locked door of the king's study. The warrior acknowledged his prince with a bow, unlocked the door, and stepped aside.

Entering the well-appointed and luxurious room, he found his father sitting in a soft leather chair by the roaring fire. There was a second matching chair beside him with a small table, its legs carved into realistic replicas of a wolf's paws set between them.

"Father, you asked to see me."

King Enden Dormath looked up from a ledger. He still appeared tired, his sunken eyes surrounded by dark circles. But his worn appearance was in sharp contrast to the rich colors and textures of his clothing. He wore a long royal robe of gold silk, the hem trimmed with plum colored velvet on which had been embroidered a golden filigree of intricate scrollwork. The trim around his neck and cuffs was made from the pelts of tarangers, small rare animals that lived in the bonet trees found aplenty in the Dy'ainian steppes. The animal's fur was gray and brown with streaks of white and extremely soft. But the reclusive creatures were very smart and difficult to catch, making their rare fur quite expensive. The queen and king preferred the furs over any others. His long dark hair, streaked with wisps of gray, was pulled back from his eyes and held in place with a small gold band, engraved in patterns of branches and leaves.

Bannerfall

The king smiled and motioned for Jarak to sit. "Thank you for coming. I wanted to tell you how proud I am of you. The officers and the men who were at Lyone have expressed admiration and praise for your skill in combat and perhaps more importantly, your character. I know it was tough for you there, but by all accounts you have grown into a man worthy of the Dy'anian throne."

"Thank you, Father, but you have already told me," Jarak smiled.

The king waved him off. "I know, but let me relish my pride. You have performed beyond my expectations."

"Thank you. I must admit that I originally did not agree with your wisdom in sending me to Lyone. But once there, I realized that the only way to learn to lead was to actually lead. I will admit, however, that Daricon deserves much of the credit. He taught me much."

King Enden nodded his head. "He is a great teacher and a worthy man. But remember, he only showed you the road. You are the one who chose to walk it. Do not discount what you have done."

"I will not, but I still have a lot to learn."

This time King Enden laughed. "As do I. You will never know it all, and that is half the battle."

"I suppose you are right. Was there anything else, Father? I have a quick errand to run before dinner."

"As a matter of fact there is," the king said as he stood from his chair and walked over to the wall. His back was turned to Jarak so he could not see what he was doing. When he turned around and walked back, Jarak could see he was holding a sheathed blade. "I have a gift for you."

Jarak stood, his eyes taking in the sheathed weapon held in his father's hands. The weapon was a long sword, its sheath black and unadorned. The pommel was wrapped in black leather interspersed with silver wire. The wrap was perfect, clearly done by a master. The cross piece was silver, adorned in the middle with a dark stone with red veins, the ends slightly flaring forward. The inset stone, which Jarak noticed was on both sides of the cross piece, was a calimite, his birth stone. But it was the end of the pommel that caught his eye. Engraved into the metal was a beautifully rendered depiction of House Dormath's symbol, crossed swords before a mountain, the rising sun's rays shining behind the peaks. The emblem was quite small but carved in such intricate detail that one could see the designs carved into the handles of the crossed swords along with ridges and valleys of the mountain peaks.

It was obviously the work of a master artisan. "You had a sword forged for me?"

"Not just any sword." With that the king drew the sword from the scabbard and held it before him. Jarak stepped back in disbelief. It was polished to an incredible sheen, the Kul-brite steel vibrant, reflecting the subtle light from the room off its mirror-like surface. "This is a Kul-brite blade made by Caleren. It does not have an equal. In the pommel is a Mage Stone, and not just any Mage Stone. When held by an Aura Mage, the wielder can use the energy stored in the Mage Stone to bring forth fire across the blade."

Jarak's eyes were wide with astonishment. "You mean like a Merger can? Like Daricon's blade?"

"Yes. The fire is limited to the amount of energy stored in the stone. You can task energy and fill it like any Mage Stone. But it will not create any other spell. Master Caleren linked the stone to the exact steel in the blade. I don't know how he did it, but there is no other like it. Here, take it," he said, handing the blade to Jarak.

Jarak reached out, holding the blade gently before him with awed reverence. He marveled at the workmanship. It was simple in design, but more beautiful than any ornamental blade he had ever seen. It was light and balanced perfectly. Jarak looked closely at the base of the blade, his eye noticing a small mark.

"That is Caleren's mark."

Jarak saw a decorative C with a similar T next to it, the lines curved and fluid. "What does the T stand for?"

"His last name, Tandon."

"Father, I don't know what to say," Jarak said, unable to take his eyes off the magnificent weapon.

"You deserve it. It is a fitting blade for the future king of Dy'ain. Guard it carefully. That blade is worth more than you want to know."

Jarak took the scabbard from his father and sheathed the blade. Then he un-cinched his belt and ran it through the scabbard, quickly buckling it back on. "Thank you, Father," he said, reaching out and hugging him briefly. They had not hugged for a long time and it felt a bit awkward for them both.

As Jarak turned to go the king put his hand on his son's shoulder. "You must always honor that blade and this House."

"I will. I promise."

Bannerfall

"Good. Now be off. Say hello to Cat for me and try not to be too late for dinner," the king added, winking at his son.

Jarak didn't know what to say, so he said nothing. He smiled and left the room, eager to show Cat his new sword.

***

The sun had just set and Brant was exploring the main street in Cythera, a wide boulevard lined with shops, inns, and various businesses. For all the months he had lived at Kulvar Rand's estate he had only ventured into the city a few times. Master Rand was busy with his Dygon Guard. They were helping with preparations, training recruits, and even scouting the outlying areas looking for any signs that the Saricons were on their way. It had only been a day since the Saricons had landed on their shores but so far they were holding up a half day's march west of Cythera.

Brant thought to take an evening for himself and explore the city. The first thing he noticed was that the city was definitely on high alert. Typically at this time in the early evening the area would be swarming with people, but now the city was relatively quiet, with people moving about quickly, anxious to attend to their errands and return to the security of their homes. The usual lively hum of voices interspersed with the clatter of horses' hooves and carts along the cobblestones had been replaced by nervous whispers and furtive conversations. The presence of the Saricon army caused a suffocating feeling of foreboding that hung over the city like a heavy fog. Legionnaires were everywhere, patrolling the streets and the city walls in large numbers and helping move stores and weapons. There was a nervous energy in the air. Few had ever imagined that anyone would have the courage, let alone the strength, to attack Cythera. After all, the magnificent city had never been attacked by a foreign army.

Brant had asked Kulvar Rand why the Legion hadn't gone out to attack the invaders before they arrived at their gates, or why the navy hadn't been sent out to confront the invading armada. Master Rand had replied that both options were probably being considered. It made sense to Brant. Why not take the fight to them before they get trapped in their own city? It was something the king and his advisors were probably discussing as he was walking down the street, mulling over the options himself. They were hoping to get information from their scouts this evening.

The previous night he and the servants, along with Master Rand, had packed their important possessions so they could be ready to quickly retreat inside the city walls when the Saricons arrived. Brant didn't really have much to pack, so he helped the servants fill a couple crates for Kulvar, filling them with important documents and papers, sufficient clothing, bags of gold, and an assortment of weapons and armor.

When they finished packing Kulvar had asked Brant to follow him. He had led him through the large house into a room, its walls lined with intermittent shelves which were filled with books. It was a large room with several tables, each surrounded by six to eight soft chairs, occupying the center of the space. Randomly placed around the perimeter of the room were a number of stone statues draped with suits of armor. There were at least eight that Brant could see. Some wore full plate armor while others wore hardened leather armor embossed with intricate designs. Each suit was unique in some way, but they were all beautifully designed and crafted. In the empty spaces between the shelves were hung a variety of weapons from all over Belorth and Corvell…swords, spears, Saricon axes, Schulg oswiths, and he even had an Askarian cab're. The ceiling of the room was twice as tall as a man with massive wooden beams spanning the distance. It was a one of the most magnificent rooms Brant had ever seen. Kulvar Rand led him to one of the sculptures against the far corner. They were staring at a unique, but simple, suit of armor. The chest plate was constructed of hardened leather, in the center of which a steel plate had been inlaid, and etched with the symbol of a wolf's head. Leaning against the statue was a sword that Brant recognized. It was Tangar's sword, the Kul-brite blade he had been practicing with. There was only one shoulder guard secured to the armor and Brant asked Kulvar Rand its purpose. "Why only one guard?"

"This was my son's armor. He liked his sword arm free. He wore the pauldron on his left shoulder allowing for more protection there while giving him freer movement with his sword arm." Kulvar paused, his eyes distant, as if remembering a long ago image. Then he blinked and looked at Brant. "I'd like you to have it, along with the sword."

Brant didn't know what to say. Just three years ago he would never had thought he'd even see a Kul-brite blade let alone carry one. "I can't. The sword alone is too valuable."

"That is true. But as you know I didn't pay for it. I have a blade, and a sword such as this should not collect dust in my library. You are a swordsman, and a Merger. Carry this blade for as long as you wish," he said, handing the sword to Brant. "My son would like you. You are much like him, you know. I know he would rather you wear the armor than have it sitting here, collecting dust, useless to anyone. Please, take it."

Brant was speechless. He tucked the scabbard into his leather belt, resting his palm on the handle. It felt as if it were part of him. He had trained with this blade and he had to admit that when he wasn't holding it, or wasn't near it, he longed for it. Smiling broadly, he looked at Kulvar, his eyes filled with undisguised joy. "Thank you. I shall wear them with honor."

"I know."

Brant smiled, remembering Kulvar Rand's words, his hand resting on the pommel of his Kul-brite blade as he slowly meandered down the street. He didn't venture anywhere without his armor. It fit him perfectly and he had to admit that it gave him a sense of a safety. Thinking of Kulvar's son, he wished he could have met him.

***

Jarak found Cat on the east wall. Torches had been lit all along the battlements and Legionnaires stood on alert looking out across the Bitlis Strait that separated the Dark Sea from the Bitlis Sea. A guard had been stationed every twenty paces. Each warrior was armed with a sword and shield, the latter leaning against the wall beside him. Behind each guard, next to a bin of bolts, lay a crossbow. Originally Cat had had little experience with the weapon. But she had been training hard with the crossbow, and thankfully, which was why they were used on the wall, one did not need much practice to be accurate with the weapon.

She heard him approach and turned, the look of utter boredom on her face quickly disappearing. She smiled, obviously happy to see him. Jarak marveled at how her face could appear both beautiful and strong. "Well look at you," she said, admiring his regal attire. Typically she saw him wearing either his armor or the more practical apparel of a warrior. She was unaccustomed to seeing him clothed in the fine garments he had donned for this evening.

"Thank you, my lady" he said, bowing theatrically before her, "I will take that as a compliment."

"What are you doing here?" she asked, looking around as if she might get in trouble. "You know I have duty tonight."

"Cat, I am the Prince of Dy'ain. I don't think you're going to get in trouble."

"Maybe not. But I don't want any of the men to think differently of me because I know you. It's hard enough fitting in being a woman. Did you know we only have a hundred and fifty five female fighters in the Legion?"

"I did not. But I bet you are the most beautiful," he added, smiling. Ever since they had both shed blood together the night of the ambush, they had begun to develop a growing friendship. But Jarak was not just interested in developing a friendship and he made every attempt to make that clear. So far she had either ignored his advances, or admonished him for them, and had, as yet, shown no inclination to reciprocate. But he wasn't willing to give up.

She looked away, ignoring his comment, and moved back to her post along the wall. He joined her, gazing out into the darkness, the rolling waves of the Bitlis Strait before them. "I hate this duty," she said, as she continued to gaze beyond the wall.

"I imagine so. It doesn't look terribly exciting. How long do you have to stay on the wall?"

"Until sunrise."

Jarak shook his head. "Perhaps I should say something to your commander."

She looked at him, her eyes set. "No. You will do no such thing. I can't have you interfering or the men will think I'm weak."

He put up his hands in mock surrender. "Okay, no problem, pretend I never said it."

"Why are you dressed like that anyway?"

"My uncle prepared a dinner for us. Just my family and his. Jayla is cooking and my father and mother have never tasted her food."

"When is it?" she asked, knowing that dinnertime was long past.

"Now," he said with a mischievous smile.

"Then what are you doing here?"

"I should think that is obvious."

She glared at him, but it didn't really hold any weight; a faint smile betrayed her best efforts to look annoyed. "Won't they be mad?"

He shrugged. "Maybe. But I can eat dinner with them anytime. How often do I get to stand along the city wall talking with a beautiful woman in armor?"

This time she played along. "I should hope never."

"I think I will stay awhile. Do you mind?"

"No, if I am to be honest, I would enjoy your company."

"Good, then you shall have it." He smiled at her and this time she returned it.

***

"Let us just start," King Enden Dormath announced impatiently, his hands resting on the table. "Jarak is visiting that girl, Cat, and you know he will be late."

Queen Irstan Dormath smiled, knowing her husband to be correct in his assessment. But this time she was not concerned with his absence. She had not met this 'Cat' yet, but had heard good things. Any woman who could wield a sword and join the Legion was not Jarak's typical female interest, and if she wasn't his typical interest, then it was all the more likely that she would like her. She was happy that her son had finally found someone who could keep him interested for so long. By all accounts he had been attempting to court her for over a year.

Daricon, however, did not look too happy, but he forced a smile and nodded his head. "Very well, let us begin. I'm sure he will arrive eventually." Daricon's wife, Mylena, sat to his right, while their two sons, Tye and Colgan, sat on his left. "Jayla has prepared for us a cold chata soup. I think you will enjoy it." Chata was a green vegetable with a mild flavor, but Jayla's recipe included the addition of several spices that gave the creamy soup an intensely savory and spicy flavor.

King Enden looked up. "A cold soup? I've never heard of such a thing."

"Nor had I," Mylena responded. "But trust me, you'll love it."

They all dug in, and after several swallows King Enden and Queen Irstan were in total agreement. "It is lovely," the queen said. "Such an exquisite texture. I wonder how she did it."

"I agree," the king added. "This is quite delicious."

Bannerfall

They finished their soup with gusto, and the bowls were quickly removed as the main course was brought to the table by several servants.

Daricon looked periodically towards the entrance of the dining hall, where two guards stood attentively. Jarak had still not arrived.

"He will or will not be here, Brother, do not fret it. I gave him the sword today and he is probably showing it to Cat. Perhaps he will join us for dessert," the king added.

Daricon nodded his head. "Perhaps. I just wanted the family to be together tonight. Difficult times are upon us and we may not have many chances to dine like this. I'm just disappointed."

"I understand, trust me," Kind Enden added with a knowing smile. "But let us not allow this wonderful meal to get cold. What do we have before us?"

***

"I have something that I want to show you, Cat," Jarak said. "My father just gave it to me."

They had been leaning against the battlements talking, enjoying each other's company. She stepped back and looked at him. "What is it?"

Jarak drew the sword and held it before her, the pommel on one hand and the flat of the blade on the other. Even in the dim light of the flickering torches the polished blade looked as if it were glowing.

"In Argon's name," she whispered, her hand coming to her mouth in shock. "He gave you a Kul-brite blade?" She had only seen a few of the blades before. The night they were attacked she had witnessed the effectiveness of Daricon's blade and she knew that King Enden had a similar weapon. She also knew that every Dygon Guard had a Kul-brite blade, the cost of outfitting fifty men with such a weapon hard for her to comprehend.

"He did," Jarak said. "And inside the pommel is a Mage Stone somehow linked to the steel in this blade. I can task energy and fill the stone like any Mage Stone, but this stone allows me to bring forth fire along the blade."

She looked at him in wonder. "You're kidding! You will be able to use the sword like a Merger?"

"Well, not exactly. I can't use the energy to make me faster or stronger, but it will fuse energy into the blade like my uncle's ability can."

"That is incredible. Have you tried it yet?"

"No, not yet."

"Maybe you should," she added mischievously, eager to see the weapon flame.

"You think?"

She smiled and stepped away from him. "Do it."

Jarak gave her a *you asked for it* look and held the sword straight into the air. The stone was full; it had probably been filled with energy by Serix. So Jarak merely concentrated on it just as he would if you wanted to use the Mage Stone in his belt. Instantly he felt the energy and urged it into the blade. In a blink the sword lit up in lavender fire. It happened so fast that Jarak almost dropped the weapon to the ground. It felt as if the stone and the metal of the blade were one, fused together, and that the steel was pulling the energy from the stone, the lavender fire blazing brighter. Jarak decided to try something, just to see if it would work. Pulling more energy from the stone, he concentrated on a short but powerful burst. A gout of fire shot from the flaming blade three paces into the air before receding back into the sword. Noticing that he was quickly draining energy from the stone, he cut it off and the fire disappeared just as quickly as it had appeared.

Cat was giggling with astonishment. "That is amazing," she cried. Several guards on either side came running towards them, their swords drawn and shields held before them.

"Everything is fine," Jarak told them, sheathing his blade. "It was just me," he added.

Both of the guards saw who it was and sheathed their weapons. One of them, the older of the two, spoke. "Sorry, my Prince, we were not sure what created the fire."

"Thank you for being so vigilant. You may return to your post." The guards bowed and walked back to their positions on the wall.

He looked back at Cat and she was smiling from ear to ear.

***

"So what we have prepared for you is tulkick tenderloin medallions braised in a wine and mushroom sauce served with creamed telmu root and roasted turnips.

No one needed any urging and within moments they were well into their meals.

Bannerfall

Queen Irstan was speechless. "I don't even know what to say," she stammered, savoring a tender morsel of the flavorful meat. "Where did you find this cook?"

"She lived in a village near the garrison. They were attacked by a rogue group of Schulgs and nearly everyone in the village was slaughtered, except for her and a few others who had managed to hide in a root cellar. She was found several miles from the village, wandering aimlessly with a serious head wound. She didn't remember what had happened to her. We took them in and she started off cooking for the troops. But her talents were soon discovered and I quickly commandeered her to cook for us. Best decision I ever made."

"What happened to the nomads?" King Enden asked. It was his duty to protect his people and it pained him knowing that he had failed to do just that.

"We hunted them down and killed them," Daricon replied. "It took us two weeks to find them."

"Well done, my brother." King Enden took a sip of his wine. "I wanted to thank you for all you have done for the kingdom. You have sacrificed much living at the garrison. But by all accounts I could not have picked a better commander to guard our western border." Queen Irstan suddenly coughed, interrupting the king's words. Her cough quickly began to sound as if she was choking and her eyes grew wide with the realization that something was terribly wrong. King Enden put his hand on her back. "Are you okay?"

Daricon leaned forward. "Perhaps she has something in her throat."

The queen coughed again, this time more violently, as if she were trying to dislodge something in her throat. But she was shaking her head. "I...don't...feel so..." but she couldn't continue as the violent coughing worsened. She lurched back, away from the table, as if that would somehow make it stop.

The king's eyes mirrored concern and fear for his wife, then sudden panic as he too began to cough. His hand went to his throat as the same choking coughs wracked his body.

"What is it!?" Daricon said, jumping up from his chair and running around the table to his brother.

"What is going on?!" Mylena's voice rose in fear. "Sons!" she screamed, "Do not eat or drink anything else!" The two boys immediately dropped their eating utensils, their eyes wide with fright.

By this time King Enden and Queen Irstan had fallen to the floor, their limbs twitching uncontrollably and their violent coughing echoing in the dining hall.

Daricon stared at the king and queen, so stunned by the sight that he did not know what to do. Within seconds Mylena was beside him. "What do we do?" Her eyes were wide with fright.

"I don't know," he said grimly.

And that was when their choking coughs suddenly ceased and their bodies stopped twitching, filling the room with an eerie silence.

"In Argon's name," Mylena whispered, her hand to her mouth in shock.

Daricon finally was able to move and he knelt down to put his hand to his brother's neck, feeling for a pulse. There was nothing. He did the same to Queen Irstan with similar results. Shocked, he stood up, an expression of stunned grief on his face. Within moments, however, his countenance turned to one of anger.

By this time four guards had arrived, having heard the commotion from the dining room, and were now standing beside them, their hands on their swords, and like Daricon and Mylena, unsure of what to do. Finally Daricon stood and faced them. "They have been poisoned. Follow me to the kitchen. Post guards on all exits and do not let anyone leave the palace."

***

Thalon, Ayden, and Tulk, were hiding in the darkness of the alley. Word had reached them quickly that Prince Jarak had not arrived at the dinner. That did not bode well for their plans so they had to quickly adjust them. But they had planned for every possible contingency and none of them were worried. They had an extensive network of spies within Cythera enabling them to have eyes and ears nearly everywhere. The last they had heard was that the prince was somewhere on the eastern wall. He would be heading to the palace soon and when he did he would have to pass by their location.

"Do you think he will be alone?" Ayden asked.

"I imagine so," Thalon whispered back. Tulk said nothing, his massive form leaning against the stone wall. There were a few people about, but the streets near the palace were mostly empty. Most of the city's night life was closer to Main Street, which was nearly six blocks away.

***

Brant stood on the street, watching the people around him as they bustled about, eager to join their friends in the local taverns and eateries that lined Main Street. He was looking up beyond the roofline to the palace which had been built on the main hill within Cythera. He could just make out the tall towers of the palace, the white flags of Dy'ain fluttering in the night breeze. He had never seen the palace grounds before. Perhaps he should take a look he thought. He was in the mood for a quiet walk anyhow.

***

Prince Jarak was moving at a quick pace hoping that he could at least make it to dinner for the last course. He was nearing the palace when suddenly three cloaked forms emerged from a side alley. He stopped, his hand resting instinctively on the pommel of his blade.

"Good evening, Prince Jarak. Nice night for a walk?"

It was dark and there were no torches lit nearby. But the sky was clear and the moonlight enabled him to see well enough. Immediately he turned on his towd and did not like what he saw. The man that spoke was an Aura Mage, while the smaller one was a Channeler. The big man on the left was more than likely a Merger considering the ease at which he held the giant sword in his right hand. Serix had taught him how to read auras, and a man or women with the Way carried a distinct aura pertaining to their particular skill. They were clearly not interested in a chat, their drawn blades ominously reflecting the moonlight. "Who are you?" Prince Jarak asked, drawing his sword as he spoke. The Kul-brite blade took on a bluish hue, the polished steel reflecting the blue moonlight as if it were a mirror.

"My my, what do we have here? I did not know you possessed a Kul-brite blade," the mage said.

"Leave now and maybe you will not feel its edge," Jarak said, trying to sound confident. He was nervous. The only energy he had was stored in his Mage Stone and that was only enough for one spell. And he had already used most of the energy stored in the stone that was embedded in his sword. Reaching out with his towd, he looked for anyone nearby from whom he could task. There was no one.

"I think not," the man replied calmly. The two men near him slowly spread out, flanking him on both sides. "Do you know who we are?"

"I do not." Jarak's mind was churning. Three Aurits stood before him. He doubted they were from any royal family. If they were they wouldn't be about to attack him. They must be commoners. He knew there were rare cases of commoners being born with the Way, but he had never met one. Perhaps it was because they were persecuted, often hunted down and banished or even killed. A commoner with such unique ability would probably not make it known.

"We are the Shadows."

Now he was worried. Everyone had heard of the assassins but no one knew who they were. Now there were three of them standing before him. He would be hard pressed to defeat them alone if any of the stories he had heard were true. "What do you want?"

"I should think that is obvious. Your mother and father are dead as we speak. You were supposed to be with them. If you had been, you would be lying on the ground next to them. That, of course, is why we are here. We have come to kill you."

Jarak stepped back in shock. His mother and father were dead. He didn't want to believe it, but there was something about the three before him that led him to believe they were telling the truth. Why would they make it up? "Who is responsible for this?"

The man's face was hooded, but for some reason Jarak got the feeling that he was smiling. "Someone who had the most to gain. But enough talk. It is time to die."

Just then Jarak sensed another person nearby, his towd touching his own aura and bouncing back. The newcomer's aura was fiery, on alert, and more powerful than anything he had ever felt except for his father's or uncle's. He could not task anything from him. But he had no time to ponder who the man was or why he was there, for in the next second the big man with the sword was attacking, his body moving faster than he could follow.

Jarak had no choice but to use the last of the power in the sword's stone. There was no way he could fight a Merger, so he was hoping that the lavender flames would disable the big assassin, and then maybe, just maybe, he could handle the mage and his Channeler.

Jumping back, he pointed his sword at the attacking Merger; lavender flames shot forward, striking him in the chest and knocking him off his feet.

Then, drawing power from his Mage Stone, Jarak wove the energy into a defensive shield. And just in time. The Aura Mage pushed his right hand forward releasing a jet of orange and red fire which slammed into the shield, dispersing harmlessly to the side.

"Well done, Prince," the mage said.

Slowly the Merger staggered to his feet. His chest, protected by hardened leather armor and bands of steel, was scorched. His clothes had burnt and his neck and chin were blackened, the skin bubbling and flaking off. He groaned in pain, but when he planted his feet firmly on the ground, Jarak knew he was in trouble. "That hurt," he hissed through clenched teeth.

"Are you going to be okay?" the mage quickly asked his comrade.

"No," Tulk grunted. "But I will live. I'm sorry to say you will not," he growled, lifting his sword towards the prince.

"We have a newcomer," Ayden whispered to Thalon, sensing the new aura before he did. "And he possesses the Way."

As if he had been introduced, Brant appeared from the darkness, his Kul-brite blade held low, his wary eyes analyzing the situation. He had arrived just in time to see Tulk attack the prince, the fire from Jarak's blade knocking the Merger to the ground. Not knowing what was happening, but seeing a lone man facing three attackers, all gifted with the Way, he decided to intervene, the familiar anger rising within him. Obviously something important was occurring, the four men before him were Aurits. But the fight seemed far from fair. And from what he could see, this was clearly an unprovoked attack, which angered him further. "What is happening here?"

Thalon looked at him. "Bad timing, my friend. You see, we are about to kill the Prince of Dy'ain, and now you will have to die with him."

Brant gripped the hilt of his blade tighter, looking at Jarak. "Are you the prince?"

"Yes."

Brant turned back to the assassins. "In that case, you will find I am not so easy to kill."

Bannerfall

"He is a Merger," Ayden said. Tulk, sensing the confrontation, tightened the grip on his blade, his feet adjusting so his weight was on the tip of his toes.

Thalon nodded his head and the big Merger shot forward like an angry bull. Brant, his limbs rushing with aura energy, met the charge head on, his Kul-brite blade dancing before him. In the fighting pit Brant had to conserve his aura, using it sparingly and in small doses so as not to bring attention to his powers. But now he could harness its full potential. This was the first time Brant had used the full power of his aura in actual combat and he relished the feeling as energy coursed through his body, firing in exhilarating pulses throughout his muscles. Brant's body reacted on instinct, his mind focused and his training taking over. Tulk's blade whistled towards his head, the powerful strike aimed at decapitating him. Gripping his blade with both hands, his strong wrists directing it, Brant met the strike. The Kul-brite steel slid down Tulk's blade, shaving metal off in a shower of sparks. Then, with one powerful forward snap of his wrists, the assassin's sword was knocked back two feet. Without stopping, Brant stepped forward, his powerful wrists flicking his blade up and across the Merger's throat. Tulk's eyes widened in surprise at the speed and power of the attack. Leaning back in desperation, Tulk was able to barely avoid the death stroke. However, Brant's blade whizzed past his neck opening a small gash below his chin. Tulk shuffled back, punching out with his left fist hoping to catch Brant off guard and give him time to readjust. Sensing the frantic attack, Brant tucked his shoulder and head, catching the blow on his shoulder guard and deflecting much of its power. The Merger was extremely strong, and the blow, despite the fact that it had merely grazed him, hurt like hell. But Brant didn't flinch. He released his two handed grip and flicked his razor sharp sword forward and low, slicing the inside of the Merger's thigh. Howling in pain and rage, Tulk desperately gripped his sword with both hands, and hopping backwards he brought the blade down towards Brant with all his strength. As Tulk's blade descended, Brant pivoted to the side, his own blade shooting forward and flicking the assassin's blade harmlessly away, while following through with a devastating arc that took the killer in the neck. Tulk's headless body stumbled backwards, falling to the ground with a thud next to his head.

For the others watching, the duel had taken no more than a few heartbeats, the Merger's enhanced speed nearly impossible to follow. But when Tulk's body hit the ground, the scene turned chaotic.

Bannerfall

Thalon drew more energy from Ayden, converting the energy into a spell that he could launch relatively quickly. Ayden stepped forward, ready to protect Thalon in case Jarak attacked, which was exactly what he did since he had no other options. Their swords came together several times, sparks erupting as the inferior steel of Ayden's sword struggled to maintain its integrity. Jarak was a decent swordsman to begin with, and with his recent training with Captain Hagen, he was turning into a proficient fighter. But Ayden, trained in the streets, an assassin and killer for most of his life, had the upper hand. Deflecting the Kul-brite blade and hoping his sword wouldn't break under the impact, Ayden spun towards Jarak, drawing his dagger at the same time and running the blade across his left arm. Jarak howled and jumped back.

"Down!" Thalon yelled. Ayden, who had fought with Thalon for years, dropped to the ground just as an electric bolt of blue energy shot from the mage's hand to strike Jarak in the chest. The prince's body jolted and fell backwards, landing hard on the cobblestone street.

But neither of the assassins expected the fierce and powerful onslaught that came next. Brant, after he dropped the Merger, kept his body moving. He was moving incredibly fast, but for a Merger things appeared to be happening at normal speed. Seeing the prince fall he growled and Fused, his sword erupting in blue fire. Targeting the mage first, Brant's body became a blur of motion, the fiery sword sweeping towards Thalon's mid-section.

Thalon saw only the tracers of blue flames. In a panic, and with no time to do anything else, he angled his sword before him hoping to deflect whatever was coming his way. The mage was a skilled swordsman, perhaps even better than Tulk, but he was no Merger, nor had he expected to face one who could Fuse. After several frantic exchanges, the fiery blade snapped his sword in two; the hot steel carving through his chest down to his abdomen as if it were cutting through butter. Continuing his movement, Brant spun to the right, his sword swinging downward towards the Channeler.

Ayden caught the movement of the sword with its blue fire, but could do nothing against such a fast opponent. Jumping back, hoping to evade the attack he knew was coming, Ayden threw his dagger side armed.

The blade struck Brant in the thigh, nicking his flesh and dropping to the cobblestones with a clank. But the wound would not stop him. His anger, under deadly control, pushed him forward. As his fiery blade came down, Ayden desperately raised his own sword to block it. To no avail. The flaming Kul-brite blade cut through the inferior steel, striking the assassin in the face, and cleaving his head in two. When the body hit the stones, Brant cut off his aura, and the flames disappeared.

He was tired, the full use of the Way had taken its toll. But the prince was in worse shape. As he ran to him he hoped for the best. His heart soared when he saw the young prince move, groaning in pain, but alive.

Brant kneeled next to him. "Are you okay?"

The prince's chest and clothes were scorched. "No," he groaned, getting to his knees. "Did you kill them?" he asked, looking up.

"Yes."

"Who are you?"

"It doesn't matter. We need to get you to safety. Let me help you to the palace."

Jarak was shaking his head. "No."

"But..."

"Listen," Jarak interrupted. "That mage told me that whoever was responsible for my parent's death was someone who had the most to gain."

"And who would that be?"

"Well, if I were dead, which was surely their intent; it would be my uncle, Lord Daricon."

"You think he poisoned your parents?"

"I don't know," Jarak said in disbelief. "I cannot believe it. But until I know, I am not safe at the palace. Do you have any place to hide me?" He was now standing, his face pale. He was clearly in severe pain.

"We need to get you to a healer," Brant said.

"Not yet," Jarak said, cringing from the pain. "Get me to safety first."

"The only place I know is outside the city."

"That will do. But we need to make a stop at the eastern wall first. I have someone there who will be coming with us." As Jarak stood, he swooned from the pain, nearly falling over. Brant grabbed him, wrapping his strong arm around his waist. The prince leaned into him, his own arm around his shoulder. "Let's go. More assassins will come after me once they learn the first attempt failed. Thank you, by the way."

Brant grunted acknowledgement, and together they moved as quickly as they could down the dark street.

***

Brayson pulled hard on the reins of his horse, coming to stop at the peak of a hill, his eyes straining in the evening grayness as the sun sought its nightly resting place. Being a scout, his eyes were good, and his heart nearly jumped from his chest when he saw thousands of men, large muscular Saricons, moving stealthily through the grasslands beyond. What were they doing here? He was on his way to Tanwen, heading north, hopefully to find out where Cythera's reinforcements were. He did not expect to find an enemy army moving in their direction. As far as they knew, the Saricons were days away, amassing their army south of Cythera. But now it looked as if they had somehow amassed an army around them, and that they were advancing, hoping to surprise the Dy'ainians.

"We must warn them," he whispered to his horse, jerking the reins hard to the right to turn his horse around. Suddenly the horse whinnied in fright, and Brayson felt the beast tremble under him.

"You won't be going anywhere."

Brayson looked to his right and blanched at what he saw. A huge creature, larger than his horse, crept silently towards him, mounted by a large female Saricon carrying a long heavy javelin. Although the beast was a massive creature, it made no sound as it slowly moved forward. Its fiery red eyes and its deep throaty growl sucked away any resolve he might have to stand up to this threat. He had never seen anything like it. It had the head of a wolf but the body of a bull in its prime, strong rippling muscles flexing beneath short black fur.

Without thinking, he urged his steed to his left, the terrified animal needing no encouragement. Churning up soil, the horse and rider bolted through the grass trying to distance themselves from this strange enemy and get to Cythera to warn them of the advancing army. But they made it only five paces before the javelin slammed into the back of Brayson's shoulder. Miraculously he was able to hold onto the reins, his terror giving him the strength to hang on. But it mattered not. A huge form, another rider and its beasts, leaped from the shadows, the front paws of the powerful animal striking the horse and rider head on. The creature was so powerful and heavy that it slammed them to the ground, their bodies sliding across the grass, dirt and mud spraying into the air. Ripping its claws across the horse, the creature disemboweled it, while simultaneously clamping its massive jaws around Brayson, shaking him violently, and tossing him aside like a discarded child's toy.

Brayson landed in the grass, his body cut and broken, his mind straining to maintain consciousness. Rolling over, he looked up at the night sky, straining to breathe as blood filled his throat, dripping from his mouth onto the cold ground.

The torg's head and the face of a Saricon warrior, blue tattoos streaked across her face as she peered down at him from the side, filled his blurred vision. It was the last memory he had before the heavy metal point of another javelin pierced his heart, killing him instantly.

In the dead of night, Karnack and five thousand of his men quietly surrounded the city, cutting off Cythera from any communication. The plan had worked perfectly. All Dy'ainian eyes were on Kahn Taruk's army along the southern shores, unaware of the Saricon army moving stealthily from the north. Even if they were watching north, they would never have seen the Saricons as they maintained their distance, hiding in the tall grass and trees that surrounded the city.

Once they had destroyed the Schulgs on the eastern shores of the Bitlis Sea, they had built barges and transported a thousand men across. Among them were the five Shadow Riders. The advance army had set up a perimeter along the shore, killing anyone who came near. They had to make sure that no word of their approach would reach Cythera, nor even the cities of Tanwen and Kreb to the north. The Shadow Riders could run down even the fastest horse, killing any and all who ventured near. No one could escape them, and they had already proven their effectiveness by eliminating all scouts and witnesses to their arrival or movement. While those thousand guarded the Dy'ainian shore, the rest of the ten thousand made their way across. It was a slow process, but by the third day they had all reached the western shores.

Karnack had previously left five thousand men stationed along the main road from Tanwen to Cythera, preventing any chance that reinforcements would arrive from the Dy'ainian northern outpost. The other five thousand crept to the city, arriving at night. Once in position, they had sent one of their spies, a young scout from Argos who was a devout Helnian, into the city. Any Saricon walking the streets of Dy'ain would be spotted immediately, but a dark haired Argosian would blend in easily enough. Using their network of spies, he would pass the word on that Karnack's army was in place.

Word had come back that the king and queen were dead. The ball was now rolling. Karnack looked to the two officers on his right. They crouched amid the gently swaying grasses that covered so much of Dy'ain. Two thousand Saricons were scattered throughout the grasslands, eager to bloody their blades. Three thousand more men formed a perimeter around the city. Anyone who approached, be it a scout, merchant, or farmer, would be killed on the spot. The city was now cut off from all communication. And the beauty of it was that the people and rulers of Cythera had no idea.

"We will sneak into the outlying homes surrounding the city and kill everyone. But make sure you send a group of men to block the city's main gate. I don't want anyone fleeing into the city for asylum. Everyone outside the city must die. Then we will wait."

"What are we waiting for?" one of the officers asked. He was a young Saricon, barrel chested and shorter than most of his race. But like the rest, he looked fierce and imposing.

Karnack smiled. "For our invitation."

***

Something didn't seem right to Kulvar Rand which was why he was making his way to the dungeon. Word had found him quickly regarding the death of his king and queen and the imprisonment of the chef. He couldn't believe they were dead and something about the situation felt wrong. Why would a chef poison the king and queen and then stay and help the staff clean the kitchen? Wouldn't she have fled? He wanted to talk with her personally before he passed any judgment.

The palace was on high alert, grim faced Sentinels were blocking every exit, along with a large contingent guarding the main palace gate and a dozen more walking the wall that surrounded the royal home. There were four more guarding the entrance to the dungeons below the palace.

"I need to see the prisoner," Kulvar Rand said, addressing the Sentinel who stood before him.

"Yes, sir," the Captain of the guard replied, fishing out the key ring attached to his belt. "Follow me." Everyone knew who Kulvar Rand was and Dygon Guards in general were given free reign. He led him through a long hallway containing a series of locked doors, each illuminated by a burning torch. Coming to a door at the end of the hallway he unlocked and opened it, stepping aside so Kulvar could enter.

"I want to talk with her alone please," Kulvar Rand said.

The guard nodded, handing him a torch from the wall. "I will be just outside."

Kulvar Rand grabbed the torch and entered the dark and dingy room. The guard shut the door behind him. The stench of decaying vegetables, sour sweat, and human excrement accosted his senses. Orange light from the torch cast shadows across the sparse and damp room. In the corner, sitting on a stone bed, was a heavy set old woman. She looked up when he entered.

"Who are you?" she croaked, her voice strained and tired, parched from lack of water.

"Kulvar Rand, leader of the Dygon Guard. Do you know of me?"

"Yes, I've heard the name." Her lined and weathered face appeared haggard, but her eyes reflected defiance. "What do you want?"

"The truth," he said, stepping closer.

"I've already given that."

"Humor me."

She shrugged. "There is nothing to say. I did not poison the royal family." She looked resigned, almost sad. "I was asked to cook a meal for Lord Daricon and King Enden's family. I was honored to do so. Halfway through the meal guards came to arrest me. They beat me and shoved me down here in this disgusting hole."

"Who asked you to do this?"

"Lord Daricon of course. I was his chef at Lyone."

"Who served the food?"

"Several servants."

"So you prepared the meal, then gave the dishes to servants who delivered them?"

"Yes."

"Did you know any of the servants?"

"I did not, but I would not know them anyway. I am not from here and am unfamiliar with any of the king's servants."

"I see." Kulvar Rand paced the room, thinking.

"I had no reason to kill the royal family. What gain would I receive? I was a chef, nothing more. I liked their boy a lot, Prince Jarak. It saddens me that he is dead."

Kulvar Rand stopped pacing. "He is alive. He did not make the dinner."

Jayla's eyes lit up in surprise, her hands coming to her mouth. "Really? That is good news. I am happy to hear that."

Kulvar Rand was a good judge of character. This woman was genuinely surprised, and happy that the prince was alive. There was no doubt. It made no sense that she was the killer. She had no motive. Something was amiss. "Something doesn't seem right," he whispered, more to himself than anyone.

"Ask yourself this, Master Rand. Who has the most to gain from the deaths of the royal family?"

"What do you mean?"

"At the garrison I found a secret shrine to Heln hidden in the storage cellar. I showed it to Prince Jarak and no one else. Whoever created that shrine is more than likely involved in these deaths. I ask you again, where to the stands of evidence lead? Who has the most to gain?"

Kulvar Rand stopped in his tracks, as a thought occurred to him. "Stay strong. I will do my best to get you out of here." Then he turned and walked to the door, knocking so the guard would open it.

Master Rand followed the guard down the hallway to the anteroom. Before leaving, he addressed the captain. "Make sure she is given food and water, and not hurt. Do you understand?"

"Of course, sir."

Then he left without another word.

***

Tongra Taruk, sitting tall on his horse, gazed at the vast city of Cythera. His plan had worked perfectly thus far. Karnack's troops had surrounded the city and cut off all access, which was a good thing too, as several scouts had been apprehended trying to get through. The Saricons had been forced to kill them, along with several groups of civilian traders. They could not risk any word reaching the city. As far as the occupants knew, his army was still stationed miles away along the coast.

No one yet realized that they had traveled all night under the light of the stars and had linked up with Karnack's forces. Nearly seven thousand Saricons and a few thousand conscripted men from Argos and YaLara were spread out behind him. Their numbers, now combined with Karnacks, was around fourteen thousand. Slowly and stealthily they had inched their way forward, surrounding the outer city. While they had made sure that no Dy'ainian scouts had made it through their lines, they were able to get their own messengers back and forth with ease. Word had made it to Tongra Taruk that his spy inside had successfully killed the king and queen. But the young prince had somehow gotten away, and Thalon and most of his crew had been killed. That was an interesting turn of events. Tongra Taruk had hated paying the assassins so much coin, but he had to admit they had been very successful, up until now that is, when he needed them the most.

Right about now Kiltius and his armada would be sailing towards the city. If his man inside did his job, then soon the gate would be secured by the Saricons, and once secured, he would flood the city with his horde, slaughtering all who resisted, sparing only those who converted. He knew from experience that very few would convert, at least at first. But they would eventually find themselves bowing at the altar of Heln…they always did.

***

After grabbing Cat from her post on the wall, the trio made their way to the main entrance. The gate generally stayed open until late in the night. It wasn't uncommon for people from the community outside the city to venture inside for drink, food, and sport, returning home late in the evening. Twenty Legionnaires guarded the entrance and a thirty more stood upon the barbican protecting the gate. There were several fail safes in place. If they were surprised, the men on the barbican could drop the portcullis, blocking off the entrance to the city. Then they could use the gate mechanism to shut the gate behind it. Any enemy trapped behind the portcullis would be cut to pieces. The mechanisms to run the portcullis and the gate were protected inside the barbican.

As they neared the entrance, the prince, still in severe pain, slowed. "I need a way to cover my face. You two hold me up like I drank too much. The guards see that all the time and won't think twice about it. But I don't want them seeing my face just in case they recognize me…and Cat, lose the Legionnaire cape and armor.

"You can use my cloak," Brant said, unclipping it from around his neck and handing it to Prince Jarak. While the prince was putting on the cloak, Cat had stepped into the shadows of an alley to take off her cuirass and cape. She used the cape to wrap up the armor, slinging it over her back like a sack. Now she looked like a typical townsperson carrying supplies from the city.

Suddenly a flash of orange and red lit up the sky as a fireball shot into the darkness. It was extremely bright against the darkness and Jarak recognized it as a spell.

"What is that?" Brant asked.

"Spell. Looks like a signal," Jarak replied.

"And it's coming from the gate," Cat added.

Prince Jarak put his arms around them both. "We need to get out of here. You ready?"

They both nodded and started walking. As they neared the guards Jarak lowered his head and dragged his feet, stumbling purposefully and causing Brant and Cat to adjust to his awkward gait. Then he started mumbling a song, acting like a drunken farmer.

Walking by a smiling guard, Brant kept eye contact with him, rolling his eyes as if to portray his frustration in having to take care of a drunken friend. "Little too much to drink, tonight," he said, stumbling by them. The guards nearby laughed but said nothing, their smiles edged with something that nearly felt evil, like they knew something they didn't. Brant thought it strange that no one seemed to have seen the fireball. At least they were acting as if they hadn't.

Cat kept her head low. She had not been with the Legion long but she didn't want to take any chances that they might recognize her. Luckily, none did, paying them very little attention.

They walked past the raised portcullis and onto the main path. There were a few people about, but not many. It was getting late and most people were within the safe confines of their homes. The road led to a wide stone bridge that spanned the narrow river. After the bridge, the town spanned for miles to the left and right, most of the homes built along the meandering river.

"Go left," Brant ordered.

"How far?" Cat asked, still unsure who this stranger was that was helping them.

"Four blocks. It's Master Rand's estate."

Prince Jarak stopped. "You know Kulvar Rand?"

"I do. I've been staying with him for the last year. I'd be happy to tell you the story but let's get you to safety first. Besides, one of his servants knows a thing or two about healing and perhaps she can help you."

"Alright, let's go," the prince murmured, his voice strained from the pain of his burns. "But we need to stop at a house on the way."

"Whose? We need to get you to safety," Brant said, his irritation and concern evident.

"A friend. It is just ahead."

They found the house quickly, a small home tucked neatly between two larger homes on the other side of the river. The wooden door was locked but lantern light illuminated the window to the left of the entry. Brant knocked.

Several moments later a young man opened the door. He was wearing gray leggings and a heavy wool tunic over a long sleeved cotton shirt. It was Rath. When Jarak had returned from Lyone they had gotten together several times, but between Jarak's busy days and Rath's work as a scribe for the king, contact had been minimal. His eyes widened when he saw Jarak's condition, his chest blackened by burns, while being supported by two strangers.

"Rath, you need to come with us," Jarak moaned.

"What happened?"

"Listen. My mother and father are dead and there has been an attempt on my life. I think something even worse is going to happen tonight."

As if on cue, screams suddenly sounded in the distance. They listened, glancing apprehensively behind them in the darkness. There was very little light coming from the city. Most of the houses were dark and locked up for the evening, though some windows still shone faintly with the soft light of candles and lanterns within. Most of the light, however, came from the myriad of stars twinkling in the clear fall sky, like thousands of shining eyes witnessing what was about to happen. More sharp screams pierced the calm of night, some of them sounding closer.

"What is happening?" Cat asked.

"I don't know," Brant replied. "But we need to get to Master Rand's house. Now!"

Jarak looked back at Rath. "Quickly, grab your things. We have to go."

The screams increased, filling the night with the sound of fear and death. Rath needed no further urging. "Give me a moment."

***

Kulvar Rand made his way to the palace entrance where he had left Kade. His second in command was talking to two Sentinels who were standing guard at the entrance. Kade approached when he saw him.

"How many Dygon Guards do we have in the city?" Kulvar asked, keeping his voice low so the Sentinels couldn't hear.

"We have near thirty. The rest are at Tanwen and Kreb securing the Kul-brite stores there. What is it?"

Kulvar looked around, unsure of who to trust or who might be listening. "Something is not right. Do you know these guards?" he asked, subtly indicating the men at the entrance.

"I do not. But I do not know many of the Sentinels," Kade responded, wondering where Kulvar was going with these questions.

"I don't recognize them, but as you said that could mean nothing. I'm not sure, but something seems amiss. I do not think the chef was involved in the murder of the king and queen."

"Then who?"

"That's what I'm going to try and find out. How soon can you get ten Dygon Guards here?"

"At the palace?"

"Yes."

"Not long. They are at the barracks now." The Dygon Guard had places to stay in all the cities in Dy'ain, private chambers outside the normal barracks. Being lords, and respected warriors, they were given better accommodations than the typical soldier.

"I want ten brought here as quickly as possible, and another twenty stationed at the main gate. Make sure they are outfitted for battle, and tell the men at the gate to be vigilant and watch for anything out of the ordinary."

"It will be done. Where should I meet you?"

"The conference room."

Kade nodded and ran from the palace. The two Sentinels, sensing something was amiss, looked about with uncertainty. But then again they were on high alert. Maybe he was just imagining things now. The fact was he did not know who to trust, so he said nothing to the guards.

He turned around and headed for the late king's conference room.

***

Daricon slammed his fist on the conference table. "I want him found! How can you lose the prince!?"

Captain Tul'gon stepped back, bowing his head. "My Lord, I have men searching the city as we speak. If he is alive we will find him."

They had found the bodies of the assassins but the prince's body was not among them. Mylena handed Daricon a glass of wine, hoping to calm him. "Husband, do not fret. Surely he is alive."

Suddenly the door burst open and two Sentinels crashed across the stone floor, their lifeless bodies spilling blood on the polished stone. At least fifty black clad men wearing black leather armor and wielding swords burst in and spread out, forming a perimeter around them.

Tul'gon, drawing his weapon, turned to face them. "What is this!? He stormed, looking angrily upon his dead men. "You will…"

He was cut short by a sword thrust through his chest. Daricon withdrew his Kul-brite blade and the captain fell to the ground, his lifeless body joining those of his comrades on the cold stone floor. "It's about time. Where have you been? I'm tired of this charade." Mylena stood next to him, her arm gently stroking his sword arm.

One of the dark clad figures stepped forward, pulling back the hood that had covered her head and revealing her identity. It was Lyra, and she did not look very happy. "I've been busy," she spat.

"Did you secure the gate and send up the signal?" It had been easy for Lyra to slowly infiltrate the city with fighters. The warriors that Kahn Taruk had recruited and trained were all from Kael or Argos, men whose physical appearance blended in well with the Dy'ainians. These men had been hand-picked and trained for two years by the finest Saricon fighters, and had also been taught the secrets of subterfuge and murder by some of the best assassins and thieves in Corvell. Two hundred highly trained men had been easy to hide within the city, disguised as common men they blended in with its inhabitants. Then, when everything had fallen into place and the two Saricon armies had arrived, they had been called upon, their plan set in motion by a lone spy who had warned them that the Saricons were in position.

And they had reacted quickly. Lyra had spent a week building a network of spies, each one having a specific duty to perform as part of the overall plan. Once the king and queen were dead, word had reached the men and they had quickly converged on the palace and main gate. Stealthily, they had killed the main guards in the palace, donning their uniforms and armor. The ruse would not last long. But it didn't need to. It provided just enough time to allow the Saricons entrance into the city. Lyra had joined them as they killed the gate guards, the men putting on their armor and uniforms. Then she had sent her fireball into the air signaling Kahn Taruk that the gate was under their control. As she spoke with Daricon, thousands of Saricons who had stealthily hidden themselves around the city were already attacking the outskirts of the city, as well as the gate, paving a way for the Saricon army to enter Cythera. Everything had gone perfectly, except for the fact that her entire crew was dead and the prince was still alive.

"Yes," Lyra replied testily, "but we have not yet secured the palace or the city. We dispatched the guards that saw us, but there are still others and they will be calling the alarm soon. There was no way they could hide all the bodies and the blood. It won't be long before the surviving Sentinels figure something is wrong."

"Not long at all," came a voice from behind them. Instantly the dark clad men ran to the center of the room as ten Dygon Guards burst in, led by Kulvar Rand. The men, their silver armor polished, their Kulbrite blades held low, flanked their leader. Each man was grim faced, poised, eyes narrowed, ready for action. "I had a feeling there was a rat behind all this."

Daricon stepped forward. "Master Rand, I must be honest and tell you it most certainly is not a pleasure to see you."

"Why did you do it?" Kulvar asked, stepping closer.

Daricon shrugged. "I have spent most of my entire life at the garrison, and for what? So my brother could live here in luxury? My wife here," Daricon said as Mylena stepped next to him, "showed me a better way."

"You mean Heln?"

"Yes. Join us. Heln rewards strong warriors. There is no need for further violence. Join us and help us bring Heln's word to everyone in Dy'ain."

Kulvar spit on the ground. "I would rather die in this room, with the memory of Dy'ainian kings around me."

"We have fifty skilled men. You are but ten."

"We are Dygon Guards." Kulvar Rand said nothing more, the energy of his aura coiling inside him like a snake. Suddenly he bolted forward, his men beside him. Despite the lightning speed of the Dygon attack, the superior numbers of the black clad warriors enabled them to close in on them as Daricon and Mylena retreated to the back of the room. Lyra, self-preservation always her first thought, joined them.

"We need to leave, and now!" Daricon shouted over the fighting. Mylena had suddenly changed, from the quiet submissive wife, to a warrior, fiercely gripping her short sword, her eyes wild with the prospect of danger.

"Why?" Lyra asked, but it took her only a few glances towards the fighting to answer her own question. The ten Dygon Guards were a whirlwind of silver steel as the black clad warriors were slowly, but inexorably, being slaughtered, cut down by the relentless barrage of Kulbrite blades. The floor became a slippery surface of crimson as the bodies piled up.

"We cannot defeat them!" Daricon shouted, the specter of fear in his voice.

"I have an idea, but it will be dangerous," Lyra suggested. Glancing back at the fighting she realized they would not have much time before the Dygon Guard were upon them. "Follow me."

She ran to the rear entry of the conference room which emptied onto a balcony overlooking the palace gardens. They seemed trapped. "What is your plan!?" Mylena asked impatiently.

"Come close to me," Lyra said. When they did she wrapped her arm around each of their waists. "I have a fly spell. But I've never enacted it with three people. And even if it is successful the landing may be rough."

Daricon looked back at the handful of his men that remained. He wasn't sure, but it appeared as if most of the Dygon Guard had survived. It would only be moments before they were upon them. "Do it," he said.

Bannerfall

Mylena and Daricon held on tightly as Lyra performed the spell. She had tasked some energy from them both when she had originally entered the room, from force of habit, and she was glad for it now. If she had waited, she would be tasking auras filled with negative energies. Within moments a howling wind spun beneath them lifting them off the stone balcony. "Hold on!" she yelled. Straining with all her skill and strength, she lifted the trio into the air and over the edge, heading for a dark side street beyond the palace walls.

Mylena screamed in fear as they hurtled down, descending so quickly they nearly hit the top of the palace wall. Surging the last of her energy into the spell, Lyra tried to slow their descent by creating a powerful updraft. But they were just too heavy. The alley street was rising to meet them at an alarming rate.

"Brace yourself!" Daricon shouted as he let go of Lyra at the last moment, jumping free from the whirling wind platform and hitting the stone pavers of the road with great force. Daricon was a skilled warrior, and agile, so it came natural for him to tuck and roll, lessening the impact. Sprawled across the road, bruised and scraped but not seriously hurt, Daricon watched Lyra and Mylena tumble across the stone pavers, arms and legs tangled in what looked like a painful landing. He scrambled to his feet and ran over to them, relieved to find that neither had any broken bones. Mylena had struck her head hard and blood poured from a long gash above her right eyebrow. They had suffered a number of cuts and bruises but they were able to stand.

Suddenly a horn sounded in the distance. It was a Saricon horn. It was the signal to converge on the gate house. Once Lyra had launched her fire signal, the Saricons, led by Karnack, had snuck into the outer city, indiscriminately slaughtering everyone they encountered, the sounds of their screams filling the night. At the same time, a thousand of the invaders ran directly to the gate house to help secure the gate with the men who were already there. Once at the gate, they would again use their horn to signal for Kahn Taruk's forces to swarm into the city, their combined forces killing any who stood in their way.

"Let's get to the gate," Daricon ordered.

***

Karnack stood in the inner courtyard just beyond the gate, a thousand of his men fanning out behind him. He was smiling, relishing the chaos before him, his axe held low and dripping blood. The civilians

Bannerfall

were frantically attempting to flee the murderous invaders, while the Legionnaires were trying to assess the chaotic situation and set up a proper defense. Officers shouted out orders but it was clear that no one was prepared for the fierceness of the attackers they now faced, their swords and axes dripping with the blood of their fellow Dy'ainians.

They had already killed several hundred Legionnaires who had tried to retake the gate. They had been caught totally by surprise, the suddenness and ferocity of the attack making it nearly impossible to raise any type of resistance. No one inside the city had suspected the Saricons would, or could, mount such a massive invasion with such stealth and surprise. Where had they come from? They had assumed the enemy was a half-day's ride away. Then, in the next instant, the city was suddenly overrun by them. The Legionnaires had no time to ponder the question as Saricon steel cut into them.

Continuous waves of Saricons rushed from the outer city to fill the inner courtyard. Hundreds ran up the stairs to the top of the wall to reinforce their brethren on the barbican. From there they moved along the wall in both directions trying to clear it of Legionnaires. The fighting was fierce along the wall and the sounds of steel on steel could be heard even above the screams of the officers and the frightened townsfolk near the gate. Nearly five hundred of the toughest, most battle tested Saricons remained near the barbican. They had to protect the gate mechanism at all cost. The gate must stay open until they could get Kahn Taruk's forces into the city.

Just as Karnack lifted his axe to give the signal to move forward, twenty silver armored warriors ran from the darkness to stand before them. The remaining Legionnaires, seeing the Dygon Guard plant their feet before the overwhelming enemy, found their courage and hastened to gather around them. Within moments the chaotic scene had turned from a rout to a defensive stand of several hundred defenders flanking the twenty Dygon Guard.

"I honor your courage!" Karnack shouted in Newain so all could hear. "But you cannot win this fight!"

There was a sudden commotion behind the Dygon Guard as Kulvar Rand and the seven surviving fighters rushed to the front to join their brethren. They were dripping with sweat and splashes of crimson had dulled the shine of their silver armor, but their eyes were hard with determination. After Daricon had escaped they had run with all haste to the main gate knowing that the fight would be there. They were correct.

Bannerfall

Master Rand stepped to the front, his sword held low. "Maybe we can't. But have no doubt that you will die by my blade. We will honor our late king and queen by drenching these pavers with Saricon blood!"

Karnack laughed, though the bravado of these thirty men had slightly unnerved him. But there was nothing else to say, so Karnack lifted his axe and screamed, "Heln!" Then he charged, several thousand massive Saricons behind him, and more were pouring through the gate every moment.

"Hold!" Kulvar shouted over the pounding feet of the Saricon horde. Legionnaires, knowing the Guard's capabilities, spread out, their shields held before them and their feet planted firmly. "Fuse now!" Eight of the men, including Kade and Kulvar Rand could Fuse, and they had already moved to the front. They knew their role and needed no orders. Eight blades burst with fire, as the Saricons were nearly upon them. "Now!" Instantly, thirty fighters, their bodies bursting with aura energy surged forward.

The Saricons at the front saw nothing but flashes of silver and aura flames before they died, their throats cut and their bodies pierced. Within moments the twenty seven warriors had killed a hundred men. Anyone watching from the rooftops would scarcely have believed what they were witnessing. Flaming Kul-brite blades created dancing arcs of energy as they cut through steel weapons and armor with ease.

Kulvar Rand went straight for Karnack, who, knowing that he must if he wanted to live, had brought forth his Fury. His eyes burst with red fire as he let the wild energy take over. Their bodies, enhanced by their respective powers, came together with tremendous force, sword and axe clashing in a burst of sparks. Two swings later and Karnack's axe had been sliced in half, each piece held in opposite hands. Desperately he threw the bladed portion at Master Rand and reached to his hip to draw his long knife. But he never made it. Kulvar Rand, surging more energy into legs, ducked beneath the blow, pushing forward and spinning on his toes, his flaming sword leading the attack. His blade struck Karnack's arm as it reached for his dagger, dropping it to the ground in a spray of blood. One stroke later and Karnack's head jerked back, his throat cut all the way to his spine. The Saricon war leader fell to the ground only to be trampled by the rush of the enemy as they pushed further forward.

Bannerfall

The thirty killed on a scale that no one had ever seen. But even as they cut through the center of the charging enemy, waves of Saricons surged around them, only to be met by the Legionnaires who had done their best to stay with the advancing Dygon Guard. And though more and more defenders were arriving as reinforcements for their comrades, trying to halt the advance of the invaders was like fighting off a charging kulg with a twig. Saricon axes and swords pounded relentlessly on the shields, their sheer numbers forcing them backwards. And their short spears, thrown with great power and accuracy, burst through their defenses, creating holes in the shield wall, and allowing the crazed enemy to break through. As the Dygon Guard cut through the center of the Saricon wave, the enemy slowly poured around them like cockroaches, cutting them off from the rest of the Legion. It wasn't long before they were trapped, surrounded by nearly a thousand Saricon fighters screaming for their blood.

Kade fought next to Kulvar Rand, both working in unison as they danced and sliced their way through the enemy, their fiery blades unstoppable. But they knew, as did the others, that they could not keep it up much longer. Soon, very soon, they would exhaust their auras, and no matter how skilled or tough they were, they would not be able to continue fighting.

"For honor!" Kade screamed over the din of battle. The fifteen remaining Dygon Guards kept close, protecting each other's flanks. They responded to Kade's battle cry in kind, shouting, "Honor!" in unison.

Kade had barely finished his battle cry when he was suddenly struck in the chest by a Saricon spear, catapulting him into the back of another Guard. He was dead before he hit the ground. The heavy weapon had pierced his armor, as well as his heart. The wave of Saricons continued to push in on them. But the dead were piling up so thickly that movement was difficult.

Kulvar growled, raw anger surging through him and giving him more energy. Decapitating the nearest enemy, he reached down and snatched up Kade's sword, spinning to take another Saricon in the chest.

Two more Guards fell. "For King and Queen!" Kulvar screamed. Each Dygon Guard had taken an oath to protect the King and Queen of House Dormath at all cost. Even though they were both dead, they would still protect their memory, honoring what they stood for in blood and deed.

Bannerfall

"Dormath!" the remaining men yelled in unison.

Kulvar fought with a skill unmatched and never before witnessed by anyone in Corvell or Belorth, his two fire blades killing twenty more men before he found himself alone, the only one remaining of his brave and loyal men. The thirty had killed over three hundred men, their bodies piled awkwardly across the inner courtyard. His silver blades, forged to kill, had performed their task with deadly efficiency. Ten more Saricons fell as their weapons sought Kulvar's flesh. But his energy was waning, his body slowing, and that's when his blood was finally spilt. A spear took him in the hip, spinning him around like a top. As he spun an axe angled towards his head. Ducking beneath it, he pierced the axe wielder's heart, killing him instantly. Kulvar roared in defiance, trying desperately to find more energy. But there was none. His swords were now extinguished, their fire receding in a flash, his energy all but depleted. He urged his body to react against the attacks coming from all sides. But he was beyond exhausted and there was no more energy to draw upon. A sword thrust forward at him, deflecting off his armor before an axe then struck his shoulder, nearly taking his arm off. Falling to the ground, he looked up into the night sky, taking his last breath as Saricon steel cut into him. There was no pain as he glanced up at the stars sparkling above him. They drew the last of his consciousness upward, away from the gruesome reality in which he lay.

***

Kivalla was alive because of blind luck. During the king's dinner, just prior to the council meeting scheduled for later that evening, Kivalla had gone to his favorite bar to eat and think. His mind was often a constant whirlwind of thoughts. As the king's head advisor he was under a lot of pressure to be informed about events and issues within and without the kingdom. Sometimes he needed some wine and distraction to clear his head and help him put things in perspective. That's what he had hoped to accomplish this evening. He was on his way back to the palace when five men, clad in dark cloaks, ran by him, moving with purpose in the same direction. He thought it odd, and if something seemed odd or unusual to Kivalla, it would occupy his mind until he had figured it out, as if the problem were a sliver which needed to be patiently scraped and dug at until it was finally removed. He slowed his pace and moved more cautiously as he thought.

Bannerfall

It was a good thing too, for as he came to the last corner before the open courtyard to the palace gate, he saw at least six men in black, like dark wraiths converge on the Sentinels, quickly killing the two at the gate. Simultaneously, the Sentinels he could see on the wall lurched, as if struck by something, their bodies dropping away behind the battlements. Within moments the gate opened and ten more men moved out to help them, pulling the bodies inside quickly to shut the gate once again. Kivalla continued to watch, dumbstruck, as different men, wearing the Sentinels' armor, replaced the guards at the gate and on the wall. How had they gotten inside? What was happening? He couldn't believe it but it looked as if the palace were being taken over. Yet there were two hundred Sentinels inside; there was no way they could take them all without being noticed. Soon there would be a fight. Thinking quickly, he remembered seeing Captain Hagen at the bar, so he ran back with all haste and found him.

The captain was dining with two other Legionnaires that he did not know. Their conversation halted as the king's adviser ran to them from across the room, his face sweaty and his eyes wide with fright. "Captain Hagen!" he blurted, his voice revealing his panic.

"What is it Kivalla?" the captain asked, lowering his fork and leaning back in his chair. He was clearly concerned.

This time Kivalla lowered his voice so only they could hear. "Captain, the palace is under attack."

"What?!" the Captain exclaimed, fighting to keep his voice low. He jumped to his feet as his hand moved automatically to his sword. The two other Legionnaires stood up with him. "How do you know this?"

"While I was walking back to the palace, five men, cloaked in dark hooded capes ran by me, as if on some sort of mission. When I reached the front gate I saw more men in black converge on the Sentinels, taking them out quietly as well as the men on the wall. They seemed quite skilled, as they were able to accomplish this with incredible speed and almost total silence. Somehow they infiltrated the walls, taking out the guards on the wall as well. Then they put on the Sentinels' uniforms and armor and took their place. I don't know what is happening but it can't be good."

"There are more Sentinel's inside. They will be needing our help."

"How will we get in?"

"I don't know. Let's get to the barracks and get a force up there right away. Don't we have some Dygon Guard in the city right now?"

"We do," Kivalla answered. "Kulvar Rand will be at the council meeting scheduled this evening."

"I don't think there will be a meeting tonight. Come on, let's get more men," the captain said as he ran from the bar, the three others hurrying after him.

The sudden sounds of battle assaulted them as they ran from the building. The clash of weapons and the screams of men, women, and children filled the night air. Fifty men wearing black leather armor and carrying long swords moved relentlessly through the streets. They killed indiscriminately and methodically, without remorse, creating havoc and hysteria in their wake. Off in the distance a bright ball of fire shot into the air.

"That was a signal!" Kivalla yelled. "We are under attack!"

As they ran toward the palace, ten Legionnaires who had been stationed along the main street, joined them with swords drawn. The dark clad men were methodically making their way toward them, their weapons glistening crimson.

"Captain, what is happening?" one of the Legionnaires asked wild eyed.

"The palace has been taken. I'm sure the gate is under attack as we speak. But right now all I can see are those men massacring our people." Captain Hagen looked at the men, his eyes hard and his jaw clenched. He drew his sword. "Form up with me and prepare to defend your city." Then he looked at Kivalla. "Can you fight?"

"I have not been trained in the art of combat. But I will try. Do you have a weapon?"

One of the Legionnaires carried both an axe and a short sword. He gave the sword to Kivalla. "Use this." Kivalla took it with trembling hands.

Captain Hagen moved out into the street with his men, forming a line of Dy'ainian steel. Then he turned to Kivalla. "Listen, you should not be here," he said. "Stay behind us and if we fall you need to go to the docks and take a boat."

"I will not leave you," Kivalla said bravely, though his eyes betrayed his fear.

"You must. If the king survives this, he will need you. If the prince lives, he will need you as well. We each have our role, Kivalla."

Bannerfall

Captain Hagen swung his sword arm. "Mine is clear to me, just as yours should be clear to you. Now get behind us."

By this time five more Legionnaires had come running from the various roads that intersected the palace street to join them. Captain Hagen looked closer and noticed that the dark warriors had stopped. What were they doing? Then it came to him in a flash. They were opening a path to the palace, killing anyone who stood between them and the home of the royal family. Just as he came to this realization the sounds of battle moved closer, echoes of metal on metal coming from the palace and from the main entrance into the city.

He lifted his sword in the air. "Men of Dy'ain, your king needs you! It is time to uphold your oath! It is time to show these invaders that honor and courage runs strong in our blood!" Then he started forward, his fifteen men behind him.

The black clad warriors saw them coming, and one man ordered forty from the procession to meet the advancing threat. The Legionnaires, led by their captain, picked up speed, while the invaders crouched, their swords held before them, readying themselves for the attack.

Kivalla stood back with his pitiful sword, watching as they came together in a clash of steel, sword upon sword, adding to the cacophony of battle that was steadily drawing nearer from the gate. Bodies fell, cut and bleeding, and men screamed as they fought for their lives. A handful of Dy'ainian civilians, holding their own miscellaneous weapons, joined the fray, emboldened by the courage of the Legionnaires. Ten of the enemy were quickly killed, the heavily armored Legionnaires, aided by Captain Hagen's superior swordsmanship, were cutting into them with deadly effect. But the invaders greatly outnumbered them and within moments, reinforced by their comrades, the enemy began to push them back and the Dy'ainians soon began to fall, their blood mixing with that of their enemies on the cobblestone road.

Hundreds of civilians were frantically running towards the docks, hoping to escape, as Kivalla stood frozen, watching as the soldiers were cut down. He knew he should run. But he felt that somehow someone needed to document the courage and bravery he was witnessing. He wanted to run, but could not, his eyes recording everything so that he may tell others the story of this night.

Captain Hagen growled and moved like a cornered she bear protecting her cubs, lunging forward and back, his sword a blur as it deflected attacks that should have killed him, while simultaneously darting in, slashing sideways and dispatching countless invaders. Their bodies were piling up around him and still he deflected, spun, and attacked, until the cobblestones were slick with blood.

    Captain Hagen's heart was pounding so loudly in his ears that it was all he heard over the noise of battle. His lungs strained for air, and his sword felt increasingly heavy as he somehow managed to continue dispatching enemy soldiers. Finally he noticed he was alone among the invaders. His comrades had all been killed. Swords were now coming at him from all angles, yet still his well-trained body moved instinctively, and more of the enemy fell to his sword. For a brief moment his weary mind wondered how many he had killed. That was when he felt the searing pain of a sword slashing across his left bicep. Stumbling, he managed to run his sword through the man's chest, only to feel another blade slice the back of his leg. Screaming, he dropped to his knees, and with great effort he slowly swung his sword in an arc, hoping to catch another enemy. Time slowed as his mind drifted to his daughter. Had she escaped? His last thoughts were of her as enemy steel pierced his flesh from all angles.

    As Captain Hagen's body dropped to the ground Kivalla blinked for the first time. Awakening from his trance, he ran toward the eastern gate, toward the docks, joining the others fleeing the city. He ran in a daze, images of the carnage he had witnessed flashing in his mind. He made a vow…that somehow he would avenge the men whose courage and honor he had just witnessed. Their bravery demanded it, and he would make it happen.

    The scene at the docks was no better. Kivalla could see lantern lights out at sea as the few Dy'ainian ships that could muster their crews sailed out to meet the enemy navy. People shouted and screamed as they frantically hurried to find boats, while great explosions all around them sent flames into the air. Projectiles, presumably fired from the enemy vessels, landed amongst their own ships and some even made it the distance to the docks. Where they hit fiery explosions rocked the air, bright flashes of orange light illuminating the dark night. He had never before seen anything like it although he had read about the explosive devices used by the Saricons. The docks and the eastern wall were being bombarded with missiles from the Saricon ships, the invisible devices launched into the dark sky to land with devastating force. Sections of the docks were aflame and nearly half of the fishing and navy vessels were already burning, the light from the conflagration casting an eerie glow on the destruction.

Kivalla looked about frantically as he neared a section of the dock that was miraculously not aflame. Several smaller boats were already moving out into the harbor loaded with men, women, and children desperately trying to escape the destruction and death that had overtaken their homes. A shrill scream directed his attention to his right where he saw a small rowboat and a handful of people scrambling to climb aboard. A man lay on the wood planks nursing a bloody nose while a woman, held firmly in the grip of three men, was screaming at the top of her lungs. Standing near the injured man was his attacker, a stout club in his right hand. Kivalla looked down at his sword, took a deep breath, and ran to the boat.

"What's going on?" he asked, his short sword held low and non-threatening.

The man with the club turned and glared at him, his face a visage of rage. "Stay out of it! We are taking their boat!"

So that was it. Kivalla could see a young boy and girl already in the boat. It was the family's boat and they were trying to get away, but the three ruffians were attempting to steal the vessel. "It is not yours to take. Find another." Kivalla tried to sound as if he could back up his request, but he knew he sounded pathetic, and the men, like the predators they were, could sense it.

The injured man tried to stand when the club wielder kicked him in the stomach. Then he turned again to look at Kivalla. The scene around them was utter chaos as countless men, women, and families fled from the eastern gate to the docks, while Saricon missiles exploded around them, killing and maiming indiscriminately. Nearly a hundred refugees perished as they fled, while twice that number had been seriously wounded. The increasing sounds of battle from inside the city added to the chaos and sense of impending doom, emboldening the men to take action and secure the boat.

Without another word the man with the club lunged at Kivalla, the heavy weapon descending towards his head. Kivalla was not a trained fighter, but he instinctively lifted his sword arm to block the blow. The strength of the strike nearly knocked the sword into his face. But, despite the pain in his arm as the power of the strike reverberated through the sword, he was able to keep the club from crushing his skull.

Bannerfall

Then suddenly Kivalla's attacker was gone, flying through the air and off the dock to land with a splash in the cold harbor. Kivalla blinked in surprise, staring at the large man who had suddenly appeared before him, dressed in black clothing, black leather armor, and carrying a long sword. One of the men holding the woman drew a long knife and lunged towards the newcomer in black. Several sword swings later and the knife wielder was moaning in pain nursing a sliced arm and leg, his blood pooling around him on the wood planks. The other two men, wanting nothing to do with the swordsman, released the woman and ran off into the night.

The dark clad warrior helped the man with the bloody nose to his feet before he turned to Kivalla who, once he had gotten a good look at him, was taken aback by his stern visage. The man's large bald head displayed two prominent scars that ran from his eyebrows down both sides of his face to his chin. He looked more frightening than the thieves he had just run off. "Are you hurt?" he asked Kivalla.

"I'm fine. Thank you for coming to my aid."

"Thank you both for coming to *our* aid," the man with the broken nose said, clearly in pain. "I need to get my family out of here. It will be tight, but I'd like to repay you both by offering you passage."

Kivalla looked around. The situation at the docks was getting worse and he was afraid that it wouldn't be long before either the enemy navy docked and came ashore, or that the invaders from inside the city would make their way to the wharf. He didn't want to be around when either of those scenarios might happen. "I'll take you up on that," he said to the man.

"And I," the burly warrior said, scanning the darkness, his bloodied sword held at the ready.

"Good. I'm Banic and this is my wife, Loriel, my son, Tavi, and my daughter, Tayin."

"I'm Kivalla."

"I'm Banrigar," the warrior said as he looked around the chaos with uncertainty. "Get in and I'll push off."

Kivalla helped Banic into the boat and a few heartbeats later the heavily laden vessel, with Banrigar at the oars, silently disappeared into the night.

Elsewhere, Serix and Endler Ral fought valiantly just outside the palace grounds. Hundreds of Legionnaires had joined them when the thousands of Saricons had flooded into the city, which was now in total chaos. The invaders were slaughtering everyone they encountered, whether civilians or the Legionnaires who were trying to defend their city. They pillaged homes, businesses, and temples, filling the beleaguered city with the screams and futile pleas for mercy from those within, sounds that even the din of battle could not mask.

The wave of Saricon invaders seemed endless and the original three hundred defenders standing before the palace gates were now reduced to fifty, the bloody bodies of their comrades sprawled across the stone pavers, in testament to their last act of loyalty, protecting the memory of their king and queen. Word had reached them quickly that their beloved king and queen had been murdered, but soon after the city gate was secured by the Saricons and the city had been overrun by the enemy. They had had little time to prepare a defense.

Endler fought with sword and shield, pulling energy from the enemies before him and filtering it for Serix Rilonan. Serix, standing on his left, spun and dodged, his long sword delivering death as his left hand, crackling with blue energy, shot bolts of lightning into the howling conquerors. It was a hopeless scenario. The Legion shield wall was ready to collapse under the sheer number of the Saricon invaders.

"We cannot keep this up!" Serix yelled.

"What do you suggest?" Endler responded, taking a Saricon sword on his shield, sweeping low and cutting the man across his thigh.

"Plug the hole when I jump back!" Serix shouted to both Endler and the Legionnaire fighting on his left. At this point, only the luckiest and most able warriors remained…veteran fighters with years of experience. Without waiting for a response, Serix leaped back and the hole closed, both fighters sliding closer together.

It would be only moments before they would be overrun. Everyone would die. Serix, forced to make a difficult choice, pulled energy from Endler and focused on his last spell. It took him a moment, the intricacies of the spell more challenging. Pulling the energy from his tarnum, Serix spun and wove it, lacing it into a pattern of whirling wind. "Hold tight!" he yelled as he reached forward and gripped Endler around the waist, simultaneously pushing immense amounts of wind forward, knocking the enemy before them back three paces. Quickly, he redirected the wind under them, using the power of it to lift them off the ground.

Bannerfall

Endler screamed as they launched straight up into the air. One Saricon cocked his arm ready to throw a javelin, the close distance allowing for a sure hit as the two left the ground. But just as the weapon was about to be released, a soldier lunched forward and rammed his sword into his chest, just as two nearby Saricons cut the man down with brutal efficiency. The weapon dropped harmlessly to the ground as Endler looked down woefully at the young warrior's body as it lay still in the comfort of death.

Serix, perhaps the most skilled mage in Corvell, spun the wind under and around their legs, keeping them upright as they quickly moved away from the fighting and into the safety of darkness.

Filled with despair, they looked down and watched their men being cut down, the palace gate destroyed and now open. They could have died alongside their men, but Serix wasn't willing to give up just yet.

"What now?" Endler asked.

"We find Prince Jarak."

"Is he alive?"

Serix guided them over the city walls, looking for a safe place to land. "I hope so," he said wistfully.

Bannerfall

Epilogue

Brant scattered the table's contents onto the floor and helped Cat lay Jarak onto the flat surface. Ari stood beside him, his eyes wide with fright.

"Where is everyone?" Brant asked Ari, his voice tense.

"When the screams started, most left to find their families. I do not know what has become of them." Ari's eyes were now rimmed with tears. Like Ari, several of the servants lived at Master Rand's estate full time, but most had homes in town or the outer city and came to work every day.

"What of Rylene?"

"I sent her to Master Rand's study to collect a few things in case we need to leave in a hurry. What is happening out there?"

"Listen, Ari. The city is under attack. *We* are under attack. I need Rylene to see what she can do for Prince Jarak. Then we need to get out of here."

"That is Prince Jarak?" Ari asked incredulously.

"Yes. Now go get Rylene. You can gather what you think is important and send her down here! Hurry!"

Ari needed no further encouragement. He raced down the long hall and ran up the stairs to the study.

Brant turned to Cat. "How well can you fight?"

"I'm good. Who in Argon's name are you?"

"Now is not the time. Go and guard the door. If anyone breaks through the main gate make sure you call for help." Then he looked at Rath. "Can you fight?"

Shamefaced, Rath shook his head. "Not really. But I'm willing to help. Do you have a weapon?"

"Follow Ari to the study. There are weapons there. Find something you think will suit you and help Ari pack."

Rath nodded and ran after Ari.

Cat drew her sword. "What are you going to do?"

"Listen, we cannot stay here. They are going to ransack the city and kill everyone. We need to get the prince fit for travel. Then we need to leave."

"And go where?"

"I don't know."

A middle-aged woman in a brown muslin skirt and blouse, the servants' uniform at the Rand estate, ran from the hallway towards them. She was clearly frightened, but as soon as she saw Prince Jarak groaning on the table, his chest burnt, her fear seemed to vanish, replaced by a confident desire to help. "What happened to him?" she asked briskly as she moved to the table.

"He was hit by some sort of fiery spell, like a bolt of lightning."

She ran into the nearby kitchen, came back with a pair of shears, and went to work on his tunic, cutting along both sides until she could remove it without bringing it over his head. She frowned with concern at what she saw. Jarak's chest was badly burnt, with raw red blisters spreading from his chest to the underside of his chin.

He looked up at her, his face reflecting his severe pain. "How does it look?"

"We need to clean your wounds. It's going to hurt." Then she looked at Brant. "I will get the hot water. I need you to get me the roll of cotton that I keep in the pantry." Moving quickly, they both went about their tasks.

In a few moments they met back at the table, a bowl of hot water in her hand. She also held a clear bottle filled with brown liquid. "I need you to drink this," she said to Jarak.

"What is it?"

"It's made from the bark of a rare tree far to the north. It will numb your wits and ease the pain." Jarak was shaking his head but she cut him off. "Trust me, you will want it. I need to wash your burns to remove any dead tissue and skin. Then I will clean them further with alcohol before I bind them. It will be quite painful."

"We need to hurry," Brant said. Ari came running down the hallway with a large bag slung over his shoulder. Brant could not tell what was inside but it looked to be pretty full. Rath stood behind him. He too had a small bag and now carried a short sword at his belt. "Good, glad you are here. Now grab another bag and fill it with as much food and water as you can carry. As soon as we clean the prince's wounds we are leaving."

Ari ran into the kitchen to gather supplies while Rath went with him to help.

Bannerfall

"Here," Rylene said holding the bottle to Jarak's lips. He looked skeptically at it, wrinkled his nose, and took a deep drink. "Two more," she commanded. Following her orders, he took two more large gulps.

"Help!" Cat suddenly screamed from the entry.

Brant drew his sword. "Get him cleaned up! Hurry!" Then he raced towards the front door. Cat's sword was drawn but she was backing up from the door as something heavy repeatedly pounded on it. He slid quickly over to her on the smooth stone floor. "What is it?"

"I don't know! Probably Saricons!"

Brant growled, digging deep for his aura as the door was forced open by five hulking men who stormed in and spread out into the foyer. They smiled when they saw them. "Only two?" one of them said in Newain. "There is not much sport in that."

Brant looked at Cat and he could sense her anxiety. But he felt only anger. It wasn't a new feeling for him, but this time it was different. Before his anger had been wild and uncontrolled, but now it had a target, a focus, and he was able to draw upon it without losing his control. This was the second time he had seen a Saricon, once in the arena, and now here. But this time he faced five. "Take the one on the left."

"What about the others?"

Brant's hard eyes found hers. "Leave them for me."

The Saricon who had spoken sensed something wrong. Normally, their victims were terrified and begged for mercy. But not these two. In fact the man looked excited and eager to fight. He suffered a brief moment of doubt, but then he smiled, his hesitation vanishing, the plausibility of one man defeating four almost laughable. He was a war leader, trained to kill since birth, and his lineage had provided him trace amounts of the Fury. Sensing something different in the young man before him, he drew upon the Fury, urging the rising energy into his limbs.

That was when Brant charged, his aura energy pushing him forward like a charging bear, blue fire flaring from his Kul-brite sword. The leader's eyes suddenly flared blue, but before his smile could even turn to an expression of shock, Brant's sword had split his head in two, from ear to chin, the fire in his eyes extinguished like a candle in a gust of wind. As the axes and swords of the others sought his body they encountered only air.

Bannerfall

Cat quickly pushed away her initial fear and charged forward, her sword raised high. The warrior in front of her was large, even by Saricon standards, which was why she was baiting him with a high strike. He smiled smugly, lifting his axe to deflect her blow, as he raised his right foot and kicked out at her chest. Cat, having observed Brant's slide across the smooth stone, instinctively used that to her advantage. At the last moment she dropped her body to the smooth pavers and slid under and through his legs, her sword flashing out and slicing the ankle of the Saricon's support leg. He howled in pain and rage and dropped to his knee as Cat sprung up from the floor behind him.

Knowing the attack was coming, the Saricon whipped his heavy axe around with one hand hoping to catch her off guard. But before his blade made it around, she snapped her foot forward and struck the warrior in the back of his head. The strike jerked his head forward, thwarting his attack and forcing him to bring his left arm forward to catch himself from falling. The next thing he felt was a searing pain as Cat rammed her blade into his back. He fell face first onto the stone floor. Cat ripped her blade from his back and turned to help Brant. But it wasn't necessary. She turned just in time to see Brant's fiery blade cut through the sword of the one remaining Saricon, then quickly slicing through his shoulder and into his chest, cleaving his heart and lungs. Withdrawing the blade, its fire dissipated into the steel as the big warrior hit the floor. Brant was streaked with blood and the fire of battle still burned in his eyes.

Cat looked at him, and then to the four bodies lying on the floor, their blood pooling around them. "When this over I can't wait to hear your story."

"Let's survive first. Hurry, more may come. Let's get the prince and get out of here." They both ran into the kitchen to see Rylene wrapping clean bandages around Jarak's chest. He was barely conscious, like a drunk not quite asleep nor fully awake. Ari and Rath stood beside her, the two bags of supplies lying at their feet. "Are you finished?"

"Just about," Rylene said.

"Good. Rath and Ari will take the two bags. Rylene, fill a bag with as much of the healing supplies as you can carry. Cat, you help me with the prince."

"Where are we going?" she asked.

"The stables."

They made their way as quickly as they could to the stables, the distant screams and the sounds of battle spurring them forward. There were only three horses so they saddled them all. The largest, a bay stallion, would carry Brant and Jarak. The two sturdy mares would each carry Cat and Rath, and Rylene and Ari respectively. They strapped on their saddlebags and filled them with grain, tying down sleeping blankets and the two bags of provisions that Ari had collected. From the weapons rack in the barn Brant took two crossbows, giving one to Cat, along with a handful of bolts.

"How will we keep the prince on the horse?" Cat asked.

Brant frowned. He had been mulling over the problem the entire time they were preparing the horses.

"If we can position him behind you, Brant, then we can tie his wrists around your waist. It won't be comfortable for either one of you, but it should allow him to stay mounted," Rath suggested.

Having no better idea himself, they gave it a try. First, Brant lifted Jarak's prone body and draped him over the horse's back just behind the saddle. While Cat held his body in place, Brant mounted the animal. Then, with Rath's help, Cat was able to maneuver the prince's legs to straddle the horse. To help, Brant turned in the saddle and lifted his body upright by grabbing the neck of the new shirt and cloak they had dressed him in. While Cat held his lower body and Brant held him erect, Rath stood on a stool and used a length of rope to tie his arms around his waist. But that didn't work. As soon as they let go Jarak's body slumped down and he nearly fell off, taking Brant with him.

"Tie them around my neck." Brant ordered. "That way it will keep him upright and I can hold his arms with one hand while I use the reins with the other."

They did what he suggested and that seemed to work. "I hope we don't have to run for it," Brant said. A hard gallop would likely cause Jarak to slide off and they both would tumble to the ground.

Ari mounted his mare and Rylene jumped up behind him. She was not an experienced rider and her expression betrayed her trepidation. "Brant, there is an animal trail along the river's edge. It is hidden by brush and goes for many miles. I think that is our best chance of getting out of here without being spotted."

"Can the horses navigate it?"

"They can."

"Lead the way then. And be quiet."

Bannerfall

Without another word Ari rode into the darkness with Brant and Cat close behind him.

***

Tongra Taruk stood on the balcony looking out over the balustrade. The lingering sounds of battle could still be heard from the city below, the intermittent screams of women amidst the shouting and battle cries of the warriors. A few skirmishes were still being fought as the Saricon invaders found pockets of resistance. A massive battle axe leaned against the railing beside him, its blade caked with dried blood. He drank from a gold cup, the Kaelian wine washing away the taste of battle.

Standing beside him were Lord Daricon and his wife, Lady Mylena. They too sipped wine as they gazed down at the city below. Mylena, now dressed in armor and her face smeared with blood, no longer looked like the submissive wife. Long ago, when she was but fifteen, she had been planted where Daricon would find her. Her beauty was unparalleled, and Kahn Taruk knew that Lord Daricon would not be able to resist her charms. It wasn't fair really. He didn't have a chance. You see, Lady Mylena had a very unusual skill, more rare even than the Fury. She had been born with the Tinge, allowing her to manipulate the emotions of others to a slight degree. But Mylena was in fact a crossbreed, adding relevance to her cover story that she told long ago when Lord Daricon found her. The story she told long ago was that her mother was raped by a Saricon and that she was the product of that rape, raised by her father, a minor Kaelian lord, as if she was his own. Her Kaelian side did have traces of noble ancestry that could be traced along her mother's line. Her crossbreed heritage was not a lie, but she had never been raised by her Kaelian father. He had given her up when she was born, not able to look at her pale skin and blonde hair. Raised in an orphanage, she was later found by the Saricons, by Kahn Taruk. Unknown to Daricon, she had been placed before him long ago knowing that she would be able to infiltrate House Dormath. A blending of her Tinge ability, along with the Way, had molded her into something that had never been seen before. She could harness her own aura, like a Merger, using it to give her more speed or strength, or to increase her Tinge ability. This gave her even more power to manipulate the emotions of those around her. Consequently, her Tinge ability was far stronger than normal, but her Merger skills, since she was not of pure noble blood, were weaker, though they gave her a slight advantage in both strength and speed. And so it was, over the years, that she was able to slowly and subtly turn Daricon against his own brother. It had taken some time, close to eight years, but it had not been so difficult. He had long harbored some feelings of resentment and jealousy towards his older brother, feelings of insecurity born of being the younger son of the royal family. And then there was the frustration of being sent to Lyone to spend his life in relative solitude. For the most part he was able to bury or ignore those resentments, dutifully accepting his role in life. But Mylena was adept at digging them up, bringing them to the surface, and encouraging them to grow and fester until his mind became hers.

"What's it like betraying your own people?" Tongra Taruk asked him.

Daricon took another sip from his cup, pausing briefly before answering. "I thought it would be more difficult. But it's just progress. No kingdom lasts forever."

"And the murder of your own brother and the queen?"

"He lived in the light long enough. It's my turn now."

"Our turn," Lady Mylena said, her voice soft and sensual, as she leaned into Daricon's shoulder. Despite the treachery of her role in transforming Daricon into a usurper, she did in fact love him. They had developed a closer bond and a deeper love over the years, strengthened by their common purpose and connection with Heln. Once she had broken through his will, converting him had been easy, filling his mind with the benefits and power he could achieve by following the Saricon god.

"What's next?" Daricon asked.

"Once we destroy the last remnants of resistance, we will kill everyone who does not convert. Then we will have a coronation ceremony crowning the new king and queen of Dy'ain. You will be a figurehead, the symbol of leadership, someone the Dy'ainian people can look upon and not see a foreigner. But do not forget. I am the Tongra of Cythera."

"That was the deal," Daricon agreed. "What of Tanwen and Kreb?"

"Our armies will take those cities as well. Then I will place two new Tongras there to rule."

"What of the prince?"

Tongra Taruk shrugged. "We have not yet found him. But we will."

Despite the fact that Daricon had grown to like Jarak, he did not understand why he couldn't have killed him earlier when he had had the opportunity, and he voiced his concern. "I do not understand why you did not allow me to kill him earlier. I had many opportunities."

"By all accounts he was a just a spoiled boy with no real sense of duty. Our main target all along was the king and queen. The plan was to take the city first and then kill the prince. If you wanted him dead so much, why did you save him when you were ambushed on the road?"

Good question Daricon thought. The truth be told he had grown to like Jarak, and perhaps, if he were being totally honest, there was a part of him that hoped his death would not be necessary, that perhaps he would not become an impediment to their plans. But over time Jarak had grown into a strong young man of noble character, and that hope had soon succumbed to reality. "I reacted out of instinct, and I would be lying if I said I did not care about the boy."

"And now?"

Daricon shrugged. "His death is necessary. But I could have killed him many times after that ambush. Why did you not order me to do so?"

"At that point it was too much of a risk," Tongra Taruk said. "If you were suspected of foul play, then you would not have had the opportunity here, to kill your brother. The king and his wife were the target, not the prince. He is young and untried. He is of little consequence."

Daricon pursed his lips in thought. He wasn't so sure.

***

Ari had been correct. The dense brush that grew along the river's edge shielded them as they slowly rode west. It was slow going as the trail was narrow and often blocked by overhanging branches, forcing them to duck and twist in the saddle to avoid them. It was particularly difficult for Brant as Jarak's limp body shifted randomly, pulling him off balance, while the rope around his neck eventually rubbed his skin raw. In addition, the darkness of night forced them to move more slowly and carefully, hoping the horses would guide them to safety. The moon's

Bannerfall

glow provided pale intermittent light as voluminous gauzy clouds drifted lazily across the star filled sky. Finally, after several hours, they had passed the Saricon lines and emerged from the brush onto the rolling grasslands. The sun was beginning to rise and they needed to lengthen the distance between themselves and Cythera.

As they rode up a gentle hill, the sun's morning rays chasing away the cool night air, Brant stopped as Jarak stirred behind him. "The prince is awakening. Help me take him off."

Everyone dismounted and Rath and Cat moved quickly to Brant's horse, easing the prince's moaning body off as Brant lifted the rope from around his neck. Laying him gently on the grass Cat untied the rope around his wrists as Jarak's eyes fluttered open. Brant dismounted and joined them.

"How do you feel?" Cat asked.

Jarak sat up slowly and cringed in pain. "I've felt better. My chest feels as if it's still on fire."

Brant stood behind Cat, his silhouette framed by the rising sun. "Can you ride? We need to put more distance between us and the city."

"How long have we been riding?" Jarak asked.

"A few hours," Rath replied.

As Brant looked up the hill a sudden sparkle caught his eye. As he scanned the hill more carefully he saw it again, the sun's light reflecting off the tip of a javelin. Leaping forward, he drew his sword. "Get behind me!"

Four Saricons fanned out as they moved through the grass, weapons drawn. One carried the javelin, two carried swords and shields, and the fourth wielded a large two handed axe. They must be a scouting party.

Seeing the men everyone positioned themselves defensively behind Brant. Cat drew her sword and moved several paces to his right. Jarak stood on wobbly legs and drew his own sword, his stance pitiful as he hunched over in pain.

"What do we have here?" the Saricon carrying the axe said in Newain.

One of the swordsmen smiled. "Looks like we have some stragglers."

"Sorry," the man with the javelin said, "but we have our orders." He lifted the weapon and prepared to throw it at Brant, just as his comrades charged.

Bannerfall

Brant growled as he guided his aura into his legs, sprinting forward with incredible speed. In the arena he had had to use his powers sparingly so as not to draw attention to them. But now he had no such restraint. Merging his aura allowed him to not only move incredibly fast, but it also heightened his other senses, including his vision. He could have easily dodged the javelin hurtling towards him but he was worried it might strike someone behind him. So he flicked his sword down and away striking the javelin and redirecting it harmlessly to the grassy ground. The Saricon had barely enough time to draw his sword before Brant's Kul-brite blade sliced deeply across his chest, dropping him to the ground. Spinning on his right leg he then reversed direction and charged at the sword wielding Saricons who were nearly upon Cat and Jarak.

Jarak, knowing it was dangerous, tasked a small amount of energy from Rath, Rylene, and Ari. They stood behind him, frightened, their auras flashing in hues of red and orange. He knew he shouldn't have, but the three Saricons were nearly upon them and he would not be able to fight alongside Cat. He needed an edge. Besides, they were frightened, not angry; therefore their auras, though not clean, were not significantly tainted. He hoped that the small amount he needed would not cause him any lasting harm. But he also knew that the real danger in using any tainted energy was that in small amounts you did not notice it, but over time it could build up and lead to more serious physical and mental complications. Sometimes it was so subtle that the user didn't notice the changes, seeming as if they had always been there.

The axe man, screaming his battle cry, was just five paces away and had raised his weapon to strike. Thinking quickly Jarak spun a quick spell, weaving a short but powerful burst of energy with his free hand and shooting it forward at the last minute, concentrating it on one focal point, his face. It struck the warrior so forcefully it looked as if he had been punched by an invisible fist, his scream cut short as his neck snapped back, the power of it catapulting him backwards to the ground.

Meanwhile one of the swordsmen was nearly upon Cat, his shield held before him and his sword back and raised for a strike. The other swordsman charged at her flank. But before he could even begin to swing his sword down, Brant's blade had slashed him across the back, spinning him around as he screamed in pain. Quickly reversing direction Brant's sword then flashed up and across the man's chest, the Kul-brite steel cutting through his armor, killing him instantly.

Bannerfall

Cat dodged to the side, avoiding the man's shield and using her sword to block his attack. They traded several blows; the Saricon had the advantage since he carried a shield. But his shield failed to help him as Brant's sword darted in, stabbing him in the side as he raised his blade to strike. Cat, taking advantage, finished him off, her own sword finding his heart.

Meanwhile, Jarak had fought off his pain enough to run forward, stabbing the dazed Saricon in the chest as he moaned on the ground, his nose broken and bleeding from the impact of his spell. He died quickly, and Jarak, swooning in pain, dropped to his knees, his silver blade still buried in the man's body.

It was all over very quickly.

"Is anyone hurt?" Brant asked as he used the grass to wipe the blood from his blade.

Everyone mumbled that they were okay as Cat ran to Jarak. "Are you alright?"

Jarak, with Cat's help, slowly stood. "I'm fine. Just tired and hurting." His head throbbed from tasking the 'frightened' energy, but he didn't bother to tell them.

Cat looked down at the body of the Saricon. "Well done."

Jarak smiled weakly, looking over at the body of the swordsman. "You too."

Brant, seeing everyone was okay, turned around and gazed at the city far off in the distance, slowly releasing the tension of battle. His muscles still twitched with energy and the remnants of his aura, but after several deep breaths he was able to relax. Looking down at the city he wondered what was happening there. What horrors were being committed at the hands of the Saricons? He didn't know what was going to happen next, but he couldn't help thinking of Kulvar Rand. Was he alive? Was he fighting for his life? He couldn't face the thought that he might be dead. And it angered him knowing he was not fighting beside him. But for some reason he felt that his purpose was here, with the prince and this group of refugees who no longer had a home. Besides, Kulvar would expect him to protect the prince.

"Well done...again," Cat said as she moved next to him. Brant looked back and saw Ari, Rylene, and Rath attending to the prince.

"You as well."

They stood there for a while, gazing at the city below. It pained her to think of her people dying at the hands of the invaders while she and her new companions had managed to escape the carnage and were still alive. But she knew that her responsibility, *their* responsibility, was now to protect Jarak, their prince. They needed to get him to safety. What would happen next she had no idea. But if Jarak survived, House Dormath might survive. And then there would be hope.

"I can't believe the city has been taken," she whispered.

Brant said nothing. There was nothing he could say that could comfort her.

Thinking of her father, wondering if he was even still alive, Cat's eyes pooled with tears. She wiped them away as her expression became stolid. "We will get it back."

Crestfallen, her heart heavy with sorrow for her people, she turned and walked to her horse, ready to follow her prince into the unknown.

The End

Book two, The Banner Lord, coming in 2015!

Bannerfall

Join Jonas in the Cavalier Trilogy!

Praise for the Cavalier

"This intensely written novel of fantasy and magic, good and evil, draws you into a rich tapestry; the world that author Jason L. McWhirter has created."
   Fantasy book review (M.G. Russell)

"The writing is crisp and polished, and the narrative has a good level of description for a fantasy novel. Jonas is a sympathetic character who the reader immediately cares about…"
   Sift Book Review

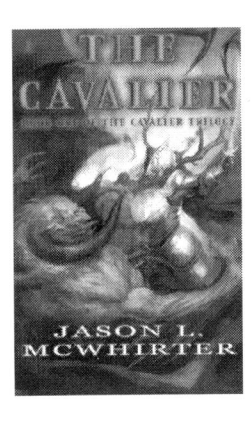

Bannerfall

Looking for something fantastic to read?

The Life of Ely is Jason L. McWhirter's first non-fantasy book. Eighteen years in the classroom as a teacher and coach has given him a unique perspective on the trials and tribulations that some students experience as they attempt to survive their adolescence. This story, although fiction, is inspired by these experiences.

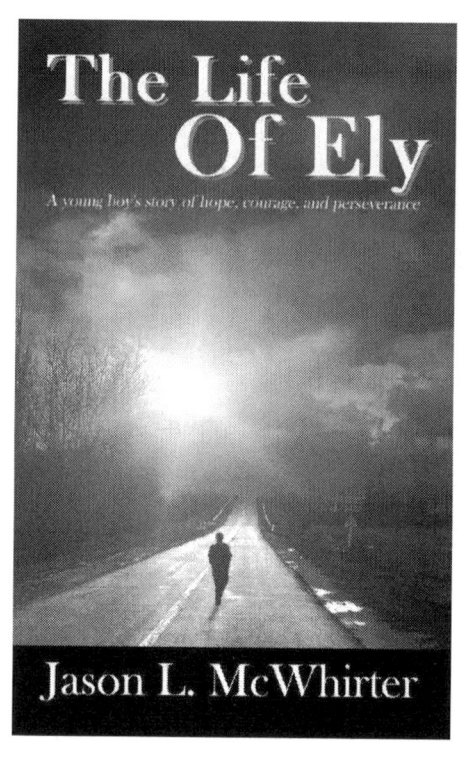

Look for it on Amazon and Barnes and Noble!

Made in the USA
San Bernardino, CA
07 July 2015